THE SILV [barcode: T0086008]

MORTAL MUSIC
The Seventh Silver Rush Mystery

2021—Will Rogers Medallion "Maverick" Award Finalist
2021—Macavity/Sue Feder Memorial Award
   for Best Historical Mystery Finalist
2020—*Foreword Reviews* Indie Bronze
   Award for Historical Fiction

"Meticulously researched and full of rich period details, *Mortal Music* is a gripping read. Nineteenth-century San Francisco springs to life in Ann Parker's capable hands, and her characters will stay with you long after you've finished the last page. Highly recommended."

> —Tasha Alexander, *New York Times* bestselling author of the Lady Emily mysteries

"It's late December 1881 in Parker's skillfully crafted seventh Silver Rush mystery. Richly nuanced period details and vivid characters enhance a plot that takes some surprising turns. The ambiguous ending will leave readers wondering what the future holds for astute, resourceful Inez."

> —*Publishers Weekly*

A DYING NOTE
The Sixth Silver Rush Mystery

2019—Macavity/Sue Feder Memorial Award
  for Best Historical Mystery Finalist
2019—Silver Falchion Award Finalist, Mystery
2019—"Lefty" Left Coast Crime Award
  Finalist, Best Historical Novel
2019—NCIBA Golden Poppy Award
  Finalist, Suspense/Mystery
2019—Best of the West—1st Place Winner in
  Mystery, Best Fiction by *True West Magazine*
2019—Will Rogers Medallion Award
  (Western Maverick) Finalist
2018—*Foreword Reviews* Indie Award Finalist, Mystery
2018—CIPA EVVY Winner, Mystery
2018—CIPA EVVY Awards 2nd Place
  Winner, Historical Fiction

"Set in 1881, Parker's exuberant sixth Silver Rush mystery brims with fascinating period details, flamboyant characters, and surprising plot twists."

—*Publishers Weekly*

"Parker, whose grandparents lived in Leadville, has a real knack for making us feel as though we have been transported to another time and place, and her characters breathe life into the vividly evoked landscape. A fine entry in a series that deserves more attention."

—*Booklist*

"By far the best of the mysteries featuring Parker's clever heroine. In addition to its historical interest, it provides a more complex problem to solve and leaves open a future in which her crime solver works with a mysterious new partner."

—*Kirkus Reviews*

"The San Francisco setting is richly described, giving the reader a fascinating glimpse of the period."

—Historical Novel Society

WHAT GOLD BUYS
The Fifth Silver Rush Mystery

2017—Bruce Alexander Historical Mystery Award Finalist
2017—Macavity/Sue Feder Memorial Award
    for Best Historical Novel Finalist
2017—Will Rogers Medallion Award
    (Western Romance) Finalist
2017—"Lefty" Left Coast Crime Award
    Finalist, Best Historical Novel
2015–2016—Sarton Women's Book Award
    (Historical Fiction) Finalist

"At last a new Silver Rush mystery from Ann Parker! And this one lives up to everything I've come to expect from one of the most authentic and evocative historical series around. Long live Inez!"

—Rhys Bowen, *New York Times* bestselling author

"If you haven't heard of Ms. Parker or her work, now's the time to ante up and go all in."

—*B&N Reads*

"Parker wraps up the mystery deftly but leaves Inez's future sufficiently unresolved so that readers will eagerly await the next installment."

—*Publishers Weekly*, Starred Review

"Once again, the fifth from Parker is much better history than mystery, drawing the reader into the stunning beauty and harsh realities of life in 1880s Colorado."

—*Kirkus Reviews*

"Parker expertly captures the roughness of a mining town where saloon owners and brothel madams seek to separate prospectors from their money."

—Historical Novel Society

MERCURY'S RISE
The Fourth Silver Rush Mystery

2012—Macavity/Sue Feder Historical Mystery Award Finalist
2012—Bruce Alexander Historical Mystery Award Winner
2012—Colorado Book Award Finalist
2012—WILLA Literary Award Finalist
2011—Agatha Best Historical Mystery Award Finalist
2011—"Recommended Read" of 2011:
  Colorado Country Life Magazine
2011—"Favorite Read" in Western
  Mysteries: *True West Magazine*

"A dazzling amount of historical detail is woven in yet never overpowers this story of deceit and greed. Laden with intrigue, this will also appeal to readers of historical Westerns. Parker's depth of knowledge coupled with an all-too-human cast leaves us eager to see what Inez will do next. Encore!"

—*Library Journal*

"Parker smoothly mixes the personal dramas and the detection in an installment that's an easy jumping-on point for newcomers. Fans of independent female sleuths like Rhys Bowen's Molly Murphy and Laurie King's Mary Russell will be satisfied."

—*Publishers Weekly*

"Featuring new characters and an intriguing variation in setting, this is an excellent addition to a steadily improving series."

—*Booklist*

"Parker remains worth reading for the historical detail and the descriptions of a stunning area of Colorado."

—*Kirkus Reviews*

LEADEN SKIES
The Third Silver Rush Mystery

2010—Colorado Book Award Finalist

"Parker's deft evocation of a lost era in Western American history—the life of the mining boom town—and her complex characterization make *Leaden Skies* an absorbing read. Her final, cliff-hanging sentence will make every reader desperate for the next installment in Inez Stannert's epic tale. A riveting historical mystery."

—Stephanie Barron, bestselling author

"Parker is proficient in showing the crossroads between civilization and the frontier, including emerging new roles for women. A cliffhanger ending sets a promising stage for the next installment."

—*Publishers Weekly*

"Parker has created a lively historical tale with a strong female protagonist. The intricate plot, lively characters, and vividly realized historical landscape will appeal to those interested in the Old West as well as to historical-mystery fans."

—*Booklist*

IRON TIES
The Second Silver Rush Mystery

2007—Winner of the Colorado Book
    Award for Best Genre Fiction
2007—Arizona Book Award Honorable Mention
    for Best Mystery/Suspense Novel

"Plenty of convincing action bodes well for a long and successful series."

—*Publishers Weekly*, Starred Review

"The characters have depth, their motivations are subtle, and their pain very human. Add carefully researched and fascinating period detail, and one has a well-crafted novel that will appeal to readers of mysteries, historical fiction, and genre westerns."

—*Booklist*

"Full of sharply etched characters set firmly in history and pulled along by a narrative engine as powerful as any of the locomotives getting ready in 1880 to connect Leadville to the outside world."

—*Chicago Tribune*

SILVER LIES
The First Silver Rush Mystery

2004—Winner of the WILLA Literary
   Award for Historical Fiction
2003—Best Mysteries of 2003—Pick by *Publishers*
   Weekly and the *Chicago Tribune*
2003—Spur Award Finalist
2003—Bruce Alexander Award Finalist
   for Best Historical Mystery
2002—Colorado Gold Award for Best Mystery

"*Silver Lies* is a tale of greed, lust, and deception set in Leadville in its heyday, when men—and not a few women—stopped at nothing, not even murder, to strike it rich. Ann Parker gets it just right, and the result is a terrific debut novel."

—Margaret Coel, *New York Times* bestselling author

"Drawing on historic facts and figures of 1870s Colorado, Parker tells a gripping tale of love, greed, and murder in the Old West, with a cast of convincing, larger-than-life characters, including a brief appearance from Bat Masterson himself."

—*Publishers Weekly*, Starred Review

"Like the wonderful black-and-white photograph of historic Leadville on its cover, her first novel, which won a regional writing contest last year, combines a kind of gritty grandeur with a knowing wisdom about the way the present shapes our perceptions of the past."

—*Chicago Tribune*

Also by Ann Parker

The Silver Rush Mysteries

Silver Lies
Iron Ties
Leaden Skies
Mercury's Rise
What Gold Buys
A Dying Note
Mortal Music

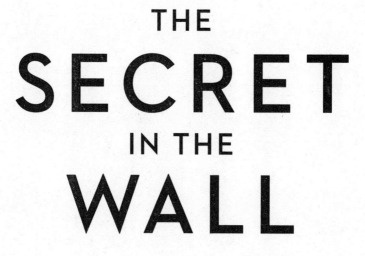

THE
SECRET
IN THE
WALL

THE
SECRET
IN THE
WALL

A SILVER RUSH MYSTERY

ANN PARKER

Poisoned Pen
PRESS

Copyright © 2022 by Ann Parker
Cover and internal design © 2022 by Sourcebooks
Cover design by Sandra Chiu
Cover images © Richard Jenkins Photography, Sakemomo/
Shutterstock, paseven/Shutterstock

Sourcebooks, Poisoned Pen Press, and the colophon
are registered trademarks of Sourcebooks.

All rights reserved. No part of this book may be reproduced in any form or by
any electronic or mechanical means including information storage and retrieval
systems—except in the case of brief quotations embodied in critical articles or
reviews—without permission in writing from its publisher, Sourcebooks.

The characters and events portrayed in this book are fictitious or are used
fictitiously. Apart from well-known historical figures, any similarity to real
persons, living or dead, is purely coincidental and not intended by the author.

Published by Poisoned Pen Press, an imprint of Sourcebooks
P.O. Box 4410, Naperville, Illinois 60567-4410
(630) 961-3900
sourcebooks.com

Library of Congress Cataloging-in-Publication Data

Names: Parker, Ann, author.
Title: The secret in the wall / Ann Parker.
Description: Naperville, Illinois : Poisoned Pen Press, [2022] | Series: A
    silver rush mystery | Includes bibliographical references.
Identifiers: LCCN 2021014770 (print) | LCCN 2021014771
    (ebook) | (trade paperback) | (epub)
Subjects: GSAFD: Mystery fiction.
Classification: LCC PS3616.A744 S43 2022 (print) | LCC PS3616.A744
    (ebook) | DDC 813/.6--dc23
LC record available at https://lccn.loc.gov/2021014770
LC ebook record available at https://lccn.loc.gov/2021014771

Printed and bound in the United States of America.
SB 10 9 8 7 6 5 4 3 2 1

Chapter One

Long vacant, the house smelled of dust and decay.

The light from an assembly of flickering lanterns sent shadows dancing over the peeling wallpaper in the kitchen, hiding and revealing the bulk of a neglected cast-iron stove, a rusted pie safe, and an oversized oak icebox. Still, for a house that had been sealed up for almost twenty years, it could have been worse.

Inez Stannert, standing apart from the handful of folks waiting in the kitchen with her, cast an appraising eye around the gloomy room. The clutch of souls gathered near the entry to the kitchen pantry seemed to shift about uneasily in the wavering illumination. The uncertain lighting only served to conceal the house's better qualities and increase the general atmosphere of abandonment. Inez knew from her earlier inspection that the building had "good bones." If it hadn't, she would never have agreed to buy it in concert with Moira Krause, the young widow who owned the adjoining boardinghouse.

But the dust. And that smell.

The place needed a good airing and a thorough cleaning, and soon. However, Moira had wanted to have a little ceremony first, to celebrate the purchase and commemorate the moment when her current boardinghouse and this, its common-wall twin, could be joined to form a single establishment.

Inez wondered what was taking Moira so long—after all, she only had to walk from the house next door. She had sent them all ahead, and now here they were, waiting. Impatience tightened like a hand around her throat. Or was it the dust that made it hard to breathe? She swore she could see her breath forming and disappearing in the dust motes hanging in the stagnant air.

"This place looks like a haunted house," came a whisper at her elbow. Inez glanced down at her thirteen-year-old ward, Antonia Gizzi, who shifted from foot to foot while eyeing the room. Inez noted that, although she had checked and approved Antonia's appearance earlier that evening, the girl's chin now sported a smudge of dust, her bonnet was askew, corkscrew strands of dark curly hair had somehow escaped her braid, and her coat was buttoned crookedly. It was as if all of Inez's efforts to impose order and harmony upon her ward succumbed to the forces of chaos as soon as Inez glanced away.

"Or maybe a pirate hideout," Antonia continued. "Didn't you say a sea captain lived here? Maybe he was captain of a pirate ship. Maybe he hid his treasure here." She looked down at the floor, scuffing the linoleum with her dusty boot. "Maybe under the floors."

Inez shushed her, then murmured, "The man who sold us this building is Bertram Taylor. His *father* was the captain. Mr. Taylor inherited this house when his father died recently. Mrs. Krause told me Mr. Taylor's father was a Navy captain for the Union during the war and that he later worked for a large steamship company. He was most definitely not a pirate, and there is no treasure here."

This was not the first time that pirates and treasure had popped up in their conversations. Inez knew that Antonia was avidly reading installments of *Treasure Island, or, the Mutiny of the Hispaniola* in the weekly penny magazine *Young Folks.* The girl was now obsessed with the wharves, ships, and brigands. After school, Antonia sometimes took the long way around to pass by the city's waterfront. On those occasions, upon arriving "home" at D & S House of Music and Oriental Curiosities, she would burst in through the door with the latest nautical news: "The *SS Australia* is at the wharf at Stewart and Folsom Streets!" she'd announce. "That's the Oceanic Steamship Company! Picking up mail for Honolulu, I'll bet." She could rattle off the kind of ship, how it was rigged, its tonnage, ad nauseam. Inez was alternately amused and exasperated. She disapproved of these forays but knew putting her foot down would only cause the girl to go behind her back.

Before Inez could say more, the scent of bay rum washed over her and a voice that sounded as if it had been made for shouting over the roar of the open ocean added, "Pirates, no, little Miss. Mrs. Stannert is right about that. However, many a good man has been shanghaied in this very city and forced into conscription on ships of a less-than-respectable nature."

Antonia's mismatched eyes—one brown, the other a blue-green hazel—widened. "D'you mean slavers, Captain Edward?"

"Of a sort," said Edward with a sideways wink at Inez, then added, "And it's not 'Captain,' little Miss. I was never a captain, only a master-at-arms."

Inez turned toward the speaker. "Well, Master Edward, surely it has been a long time since such doings occurred in the city."

Edward, a robust, craggy man, who Inez estimated was in his

late forties or early fifties, gave her a slight smile. During a meal shared at Mrs. Krause's boardinghouse table, he had explained to Inez how he had long since "retired" from plying the open waters to a job keeping order on San Francisco's docks. She had been struck at the time by his eyes—an unusual muddy blue-green, the color of the surf at San Francisco's Ocean Beach on a summer afternoon—his jovial spirit, and his impeccable manners.

Edward answered, "Not as long as you might think, ma'am. San Francisco may be more civilized away from the water, but it maintains much of its rougher history and nature near the wharves."

Inez frowned a little. She suspected that his remark, rather than serving as a warning to Antonia, would only fuel the girl's curiosity and boldness to explore the docks.

Apparently thinking she disbelieved his statement, Edward added, "I may not frequent the old Barbary Coast haunts anymore, having become overly fond of Mrs. Krause's cooking, but I can assure you 'tis true." He winked again. "These days, after dinner, I'm more inclined to nap or indulge in a game of cribbage than go out and about."

One of the other boarders muttered, "Where would Mrs. Krause be? I thought she was following us directly. My throat's gettin' dry, and I'm looking forward to wetting my whistle on some of that cider she promised."

A murmur of agreement circled the room. Moira had promised that all who elected to attend the ceremony would receive a slice of homemade apple pie and a dram of cider afterward. Inez thought the promise was the main reason why the few who had obediently gathered in the dank building remained, instead of disappearing to engage in other after-dinner activities.

The front door slammed, a faraway echo in the empty house.

A symphony of hurried footsteps followed—light tick-tock taps punctuated by heavier, slower thumps. As if summoned, Moira hastened into the kitchen, her glossy auburn hair in a neat braid coronet, her unbuttoned coat revealing a starched and embroidered apron. Her daughter, freckle-faced eight-year-old Charlotte, attired in a miniature version of her mother's apron, clutched her sleeve. The gloom of the kitchen seemed to flee in the face of Moira's single-minded determination.

Bustling in her wake was her friend, Mrs. Nolan, who ran the boardinghouse a few blocks distant, where Inez and Antonia took their meals. The gray-haired Mrs. Nolan puffed over to Inez and whispered, "Ooo, that took a little longer than I thought it would. Had to set out the pies, dessert plates, napkins, and silverware for the celebration afterward. She is a stickler for details, is our Moira. Likes everything proper and 'just so.'"

As Mrs. Nolan explained and excused, a man of short and rotund stature strutted into the kitchen as though he owned the place, travel writing desk under one arm.

Upton.

Inez wrinkled her nose in distaste. The lawyer was a necessary part of the evening, but that didn't mean she had to like the man. Mutton-chopped and top-hatted, Sherman Upton had acted on behalf of Bertram Taylor. Upton had made it clear he felt it was beneath him to negotiate with the two women, so Inez was all the more gratified that she and Moira had managed to wrangle a very reasonable price for the building, including all the goods and furnishings. It had helped immensely that Taylor was apparently more interested in having money in hand than in haggling. Neither woman had met nor seen hide nor hair of him.

Two familiar figures dressed in the caps and rough jackets of tradesmen, father and son locksmiths Joe and Paulie Harris, slid into the room behind Upton. Whereas Joe Harris had an arthritic one-sided hobble and was no taller than the lawyer he dogged, Paulie was tall, lanky, and quiet, a shadow to the more pugnacious paterfamilias. They had stationed themselves by the front door this evening, barring entry to any curious passersby who might wonder about the excitement in the long-vacant residence.

Now that all were assembled, Inez was certain the locksmiths had secured the door before joining the others in the kitchen. Upton set up his portable desk atop the sturdy kitchen table. As he pulled out legal papers, ink bottles, pens, ink blotter, and his barrister's seal from the desk's various compartments, Moira looked around at the congregation.

"We are now all accounted for," she announced and clasped her hands over her apron. "Thank for your patience. This is a momentous occasion for me. Five years ago, when my dearly departed husband bought the residence on the other side of these walls, he had his eye set on buying this one as well. It was ever our intention to expand our ability to provide room-and-board in a proper Christian environment for working people such as yourselves. I am sure he is now watching and approving from Heaven."

She stopped, and a shadow of sorrow flitted across her face. With a resolute lift of her chin, she continued, "And there are many to thank among the living. First, Mrs. Nolan, who introduced me to Mrs. Stannert."

"Oh now," murmured Mrs. Nolan. Inez thought she saw the grandmotherly boardinghouse owner blush. "Just helping where I can."

Moira continued, "And Mr. Upton, who negotiated the sale." Upton peered disdainfully down his nose, which could not have been easy to do given his lack of height. Moira turned to the Harrises, who were standing by the kitchen entrance. "And

Mr. Harris, who faithfully performed his duty as locksmith and caretaker of the property for many years, at the behest of the former owner, Captain Taylor."

Inez vividly recalled their first inspection of the property, with the faithful Joe Harris hovering at their heels as they examined the house, its fixtures, and its furnishings. Moira had explained that Bertram Taylor's father had originally charged Joe Harris with keeping watch over the locked and empty property. The elder locksmith had taken this task very seriously, even refusing entry to Inez and Moira when they had wanted to inspect the building. He had only relented when they had contacted Upton, who had told Harris to let them in.

Moira addressed Upton. "Shall we sign the papers now?"

Upton said briskly as if he wished to be done and on his way, "Please. Both of you, Mrs. Krause and Mrs. Stannert, since you are listed as co-owners. Mr. Taylor has already done his part, as you'll see." Inez and Moira moved to opposite ends of the desk. Upton, in the middle, handed them pens and pushed a bottle of ink toward each, saying, "Multiple copies, so sign all of them." He pointed, "Here, here, and here," and stepped back. Inez dipped her pen and scrawled her signature in a manner that would probably have earned her a frown from her expensive private tutor back when she was a child of privilege in New York City.

Moira was forming the letters of her name carefully, slowly, in proper Spencerian fashion. Inez wanted to tap her foot to hurry Moira along but forbore. Much like Upton, Inez itched for the formalities and Moira's little ceremony to be over and done with but for a different reason. Once she and Moira were legally the owners, the elder Harris would, perforce, have to give them the keys to the building's intricately fashioned door locks—which he had personally designed and manufactured—something he had resisted doing.

When the papers were signed, Upton laid them out on the table to blot and to stamp with his official seal. Moira turned to Edward and said, "Master Edward, did you bring everything?"

The former seaman had brought a heavy sledgehammer and a knapsack with him. He nodded, opened the sack, and pulled out a horseshoe, hammer, and nails.

"Excellent!" Moira gave an imperious nod. "Please, mount it above the pantry door before we go any further."

Inez stifled a sigh and an impulse to roll her eyes. Moira had many good qualities, including caution, determination, and an iron strength behind her soft voice, but Inez found her stubborn acceptance of supernatural causation annoying. Also, how Moira squared this belief with her equally strong faith in the tenents of Christianity was a mystery to Inez. Edward positioned a chair that looked as if it had not been sat on for decades underneath the entrance to the large pantry and climbed upon it. Horseshoe and nails in one hand, hammer in the other, he asked, "Points up or down, Mrs. Krause?" Inez had noticed how his tone changed, became gentler, when he spoke to Moira. That, combined with the way he glanced at her when she wasn't looking, had Inez suspecting Master Edward was sweet on his landlady.

"Why, points up, of course, to hold the luck!"

He set the metal crescent tight above the entry with two well-placed blows.

Moira nodded her approval. "And now, for the wall." She turned to the crowd. "How fortunate that the kitchen pantries of the two houses are opposite each other. Once we join them together, they shall provide a handy pass-through."

While she spoke, Edward climbed off the chair, removed his jacket, and laid it neatly over the ladderback before retrieving the sledgehammer and returning to the pantry.

Moira picked up a lamp and beckoned to Inez. "Mrs. Stannert, would you care to bring another light forward and hold it high so Master Edward and the rest can see?"

Inez picked up the lamp from the kitchen table that had helped to illuminate the documents they had signed. She moved past the boarders, holding the long skirts of her petticoat, dress, and coat away from their shuffling feet. The smallish group had squeezed shoulder to shoulder into the wide entry of the pantry to gain a better view. Or perhaps they were simply maneuvering to see who would be the first to stampede through the opening to the kitchen on the other side, where the promised pie and cider awaited.

Antonia had advanced to the front of the pack and was now whispering something to little Charlotte, who stood by her side. Inez wagered Antonia had told Charlotte to keep an eye out for any treasure that might have been secreted behind the wall. Inez thought the most that the space behind the plaster and wood might reveal was a tangle of webs and maybe a nest of spiders.

Or maybe rats.

She shuddered and sincerely hoped not. Murderers, con men, lunatics, and thieves—she could and had faced many such without blinking. But sharp-toothed rodents were a different matter.

She took a post by Antonia and Charlotte to one side of the doorframe opposite Moira. Nudging the girls, she warned, "Not too close. You could be hit by the debris."

Master Edward spat into his hands, rubbed them together, and picked up the sledgehammer. Inez turned the wick up to provide as much light to the bare interior as possible and held the lamp aloft. Moira did likewise. Edward took a couple practice swings. The thought flashed through Inez's mind that the heavy tool would make a handy weapon for those who could heft it and it would certainly be capable of smashing a rat flat, leaving no need for her to draw her pocket revolver, should one leap from behind the wall.

Edward planted a blow on a large faint gray stain on the ancient whitewash. Plaster exploded into dust and the lath strips beneath cracked, loud as a gunshot in the enclosure. He swung twice more. The dust in the pantry thickened into a fog and a long, jagged gap emerged in the wall. Inez retreated a step, hooking Antonia's coat collar and pulling her back when the girl crept forward for a better view. The retired master-at-arms stopped, set down the heavy tool, and wiped his face, whitened with powdered plaster, with a sleeve. He then picked up the hammer and swung again, widening the hole, which now stretched from floor to shoulder-height.

As he prepared to deliver another blow, he stopped. Inez saw his back stiffen. He lowered the sledgehammer to his side and muttered, "Son of a…"

Something, a pale shadow where they expected nothing but blackness, shifted in what should have been empty space between the walls.

Frowning, Inez lifted her lamp higher. Her light caught the glint of what looked like an eye. A chill skittered down her neck, cold as a breath of mountain winter.

Moira screamed. The light from her lamp dipped.

Edward backed out of the pantry, holding his sledgehammer up before him like a weapon. A skeleton, its single, impossible eye fixed upon the gaping observers, tilted out of the hole. Clothed in a mostly intact greatcoat, with color and details obscured by stains, time, and dust, it slumped out of the breech.

"Lord have mercy!" yelped Mrs. Nolan.

Inez sucked in a strangled lungful of plaster and damp.

The boarders' startled shouts and cries racketed around in the kitchen, intensified by the bare walls and tin ceiling.

The rest happened in a handful of seconds, although to Inez the actions seemed slow and deliberate, the sounds muffled but distinct, as if underwater. As the clothed bones hit the floor, a threadbare sack, apparently wedged high and behind the body, dislodged as well. The bag tumbled onto the shoulders of the coat with a *wump* and a symphony of metallic clinks. The tie holding it closed gave way, releasing a shower of gold coins. The impact jarred the skull, which, long freed from the confines of sinews and flesh, parted company from the spine with a jounce and rocked onto one cheekbone.

The eye Inez had seen in the lamplight popped out of the skull.

The white glass ball rolled across the pantry floor toward the retreating boarders, its painted blue iris and black pupil winking up at them, over and over, as it spun into and out of view. Charlotte had buried her face in her mother's apron, and Moira was backing away from the scene, clutching her daughter to her.

Belatedly, Inez turned to cover Antonia's gaze from the sight. Mouth agape, Antonia gawked at the scene in the pantry.

As Inez reached for her, Antonia whispered, "Pirates!"

Chapter Two

"You can't do this," Inez repeated, staring hard at Detective Lynch. Initially, she had been glad to see him walk into the kitchen, believing that with him in charge the bizarre situation might be handled quickly and relatively painlessly. After all, she had had dealings with the detective before and, for the most part, had found him agreeable and sensible. Additionally, he was father to Michael Lynch, Antonia's school friend, so there was that connection as well.

But now, they had come to an impasse.

The police detective smoothed his ginger-colored mustache and sighed. He glanced at his colleague, who just glared at Inez through heavy-lidded eyes.

It was two hours after the glass eye had rolled across the floor, shocking everyone, it seemed, except Antonia. While one of the boarders had dashed out to notify the police, Inez had taken charge when it had quickly become apparent that Moira was too shaken to do so. Inez had directed all the boarders to wait off to one side, leaving them to murmur amongst themselves, and, with Moira's blessing, had hustled the two young girls off with Mrs. Nolan for the night.

"But why?" Antonia had objected, even as Mrs. Nolan took each girl firmly by the hand and pulled them toward the front door.

"School tomorrow for you both," snapped Inez. "What happens next is grown-up affairs and none of yours."

Mrs. Nolan, stalwart that she was, said, "There's half a custard pie yet to be eaten at my place, and I have the perfect room for the two of you to bed down for the night. We'll have flapjacks in the morning. Afterward, you'll have plenty of time to scurry home and prepare for school."

Antonia's pleas and protests had faded down the hall, only to be cut off with the slamming of the door.

The scene was vastly different now. The dusty kitchen was brightly lit with several lanterns supplied by the police. The skeletal remains and the runaway glass eye had been carted off to the coroner. Two other policemen were questioning the other witnesses. The worn canvas bag, its contents resecured, rested on the floor between Inez and Moira.

"You can't take the money," Inez crossed her arms, defiant. "It came with the house. Mrs. Krause and I bought the house and all its contents." She nodded at the signed bill of sale on the kitchen table. "Ergo, the money belongs to us, just as much as that table does."

The other detective—Inez couldn't recall whether he had been introduced as Detective MacKay or MacCabe—rolled his eyes and stuck his thumbs into his belt. "Ah, so the corpse would be yours to deal with as well, then? You plan to give it an honest burial when all is said and done?"

That gave Inez pause. Before she could respond, Moira, who had been clutching the small cross at her throat, burst out, "Of course we will! Once we know the poor man's name, we shall be sure he is buried properly as befits his station, whatever it may be, and his final resting place marked."

Inez's mouth tightened. She recognized the stubbornness in Moira's tone. This would not be something she could talk the woman out of. When Moira had asked the detectives what would happen to the corpse after the coroner was done, Detective Whoever-he-was had said in an offhand manner, "The city'll find a spot for him in the pauper's cemetery." That had clearly horrified Moira. And here was the result.

Inez decided now was not the time to argue about the desiccated corpse. She was tired and getting more chilled by the moment. The cold, in no way lessened by the bright light of the lanterns, seeped up from the old linoleum through the soles of her Sunday-best boots and was creeping up her limbs. She glanced down. Her boots and the hem of her long dark cloak were powdered with white dust, reminding her of a grave. She gave herself a mental shake.

Best focus on the disposition of the money for now.

She returned her gaze to Detective Lynch, whom she deemed the senior of the two officers and more likely to listen to reason. "If a sack of walnuts had fallen out of the wall with the deceased, would you insist on taking it into your custody?"

"Mrs. Stannert, be reasonable," said Lynch. "Walnuts are not at all in the same category as..." he nodded at the bag. "This is evidence of a possible crime. Surely you can see that."

"So, you think he might have been murdered with a bag of gold coins?"

The second detective spoke up. "A blow to the head with something like that could certainly brain a man. Or the money could've been motive for murder."

"Then why would someone leave it here, walled up with the corpse?"

Moira interrupted, sounding distressed, "It is not Christian to speak so indifferently of the poor departed soul."

Lynch held up a hand. "Hold now. If the sack of money does indeed legally belong to you, it will be returned."

"Perhaps somewhat lighter than before?" asked Inez.

He frowned. "You think we're a bit light-fingered, now, do you?"

Inez decided to tread carefully. From what she knew of him, the detective was an honest man, as honest as anyone could be. But the character of Lynch's partner was unknown to her, and the siren song of treasure had drowned the scruples of many decent souls. "No, of course not. Not you, Detective."

"We will count it out together, then, right now, on that table," said Lynch. "And I'll give you a receipt."

Inez turned to Moira to gauge her reaction. Moira worried her lower lip between her teeth, looking close to tears. Clearly, the entire incident, culminating with the tiff over the corpse and the gold, disturbed her. "Mrs. Krause," Inez said gently, "do you want me to handle this matter?"

There was a commotion toward the front of the house. The small group turned just as an unfamiliar patrolman burst into the kitchen followed closely by the two locksmiths. "Pardon all," the officer whipped off his cap and wiped his perspiring forehead. "Detective Lynch, sir, there's trouble at the docks. You and Mac and t'others are needed there. Soon's you can manage."

The other two policemen appeared at the entryway to the kitchen. "We've talked to all the witnesses," announced one to Lynch. "Shall we let them go?"

Inez stepped forward. "So, you have seen what you need to see? We'd like to break through the far wall to complete the passageway to the connecting house. If not tonight, then tomorrow."

Lynch shot a sharp-eyed glance at her. "Not yet. I don't want anyone nosing around in the wall until we've decided what's what. 'Tis a sizeable amount of gold. And we've no idea how the corpse came to be there, or why."

"But when can we resume work on the passage?"

"When we're done with our investigation."

"And when will that be?"

"I will let you know," said Lynch shortly. "Until then, no one is to be poking about from either side."

"But—" Inez began.

"The far wall is to remain intact until I give the say-so. Do I make myself clear?" He stared at Inez, then at Moira. Moira nodded. Inez tightened her mouth and said nothing. Lynch turned to his partner. "Did you see anything in the wall space?"

Detective Mac-Something shrugged his massive shoulders. "I stepped in and flashed the lantern around. Saw curtains of dusty cobwebs. 'Tis like tryin' to pierce the fog with a light. Didn't fancy fightin' my way through the grime. Not much to see in the dark besides vermin droppings. No reason t' go any further."

Inez thought that the detective's reluctance to explore might have had to do with his size. Given his bulk, he probably would have had a hard time squeezing between the two walls.

"Well, we'll take a better look when we return. For now, we're going to move that—" Lynch pointed to the enormous icebox— "in front of the pantry to block that hole in the wall. I don't want any mischief on either side." He eyed his fellow detective and the three clustered patrolmen and said, "We'll need additional hands to move that monster. Bring the brawny fellow in here, along with any others who can put their backs into it."

Inez addressed Moira. "Do you want to go back home with the boarders? I daresay a spot of cider would do everyone good. I will stay here and finish the business with the police."

"Yes, thank you, Mrs. Stannert." Moira picked up her lantern, looked up at the pantry entry and turned back to Inez, despair in her eyes. "It's cursed. Cursed!"

Inez lifted her eyebrows in question. In reply, Moira pointed above the pantry door. The horseshoe Master Edward had nailed above the door had lost one of the securing nails and rotated. The points of the heel now pointed downward.

"All the luck has run out," she whispered. "No good will come of what we have found here. None at all."

Chapter Three

Antonia shifted in the unfamiliar bed she shared with Charlotte. Even the candle that Mrs. Nolan had left burning for the girls didn't make it easier to sleep. Antonia's mind was full of skeletons and glass eyeballs. Of bony hands gripping the floor and rattling bones crawling with a clatter toward her as she backed away into the dark.

"Antonia, are you asleep?"

Charlotte's whispered breath was warm on the nape of Antonia's neck. Antonia's eyes popped open. She felt the girl's wool-stockinged foot kick her in the knee.

"No," said Antonia and shifted onto her back, crossing her arms over the quilt that buried them both.

The long flannel nightshirts Mrs. Nolan had insisted they change into smelled of camphor. Antonia sneezed.

"D'you think he was in the wall the whole time?" Charlotte pulled herself to one elbow, looking at Antonia.

Antonia shrugged. "Probably."

She felt Charlotte shiver. "Ugh."

Dead bodies didn't spook Antonia much. She'd seen plenty in Leadville, Colorado, when she and her maman had lived in a shack in Stillborn Alley. But a *skeleton*…

Charlotte sighed and plopped on her back, copying Antonia's position. "I wish my pa was here. He was so brave. He wasn't scared of anything."

Antonia glanced at her. "He was, what, a seaman? Petty officer?"

"Nooooo. He was a lieutenant on a sloop-of-war during the War to preserve the Union." She sounded like she was reciting in school. Then her tone changed. "He got shot at and everything, but he never wavered, and he should've been made a captain. That's what Ma says."

Antonia turned her head to better see Charlotte's profile. "Is that where he is now? Off at sea?" Her mind wandered to the piers and ships she'd seen the other day.

"Nooooo. He's in Heaven, like Ma said. He set sail for China four years ago, and his ship went down in a storm with all souls on board."

"Oh, that's sad," said Antonia. "D'you remember him?"

"Not much. I was just barely four. A baby."

"So it's just you and your ma, now?"

"Yep. How about you? It's just you and Mrs. Stannert?"

"Yep."

"She's your ma?"

"No, she's my…" Antonia hesitated. She and Mrs. S, as she usually called her, had created a story when they came to San Francisco from Leadville. Mrs. S had said that if anyone asked, Antonia should say they were related. "She's my aunt."

"So, where're your parents? Is your da around? Or is he dead too, like mine?"

Antonia turned to face away from Charlotte. The question, asked in the dead of night, hurt like poking at a sore tooth.

She was used to hearing it at school. There, it was always, "Where's your ma? Who's your da? Are you an orphan? Why d'you live with your aunt, and why d'you have different last names? Your last name is Gizzi, your skin's all dark, and your eyes are strange. Are you a *Gypsy* orphan?" She was tired of the sneers and even more of the wide-eyed pity. Tired of not having friends. Well, Detective Lynch's son, Michael, was her friend. But "Copper Mick" was the only one who'd talk to her. Until now.

She opened her mouth, struggling to answer Charlotte.

Maybe it was the skeleton and the bag of gold. Maybe it was reading about Long John Silver and Captain Flint in *Treasure Island*. Maybe it was all that hanging around the waterfront, looking at those beautiful ships, and wishing she could be a boy, smuggle aboard, and sail off and have adventures. Maybe because of Charlotte's da being an almost-captain of a ship. Whatever the cause, what popped out was, "*My* papa was a pirate captain, from Spain. He sailed the Spanish Main and died in battle."

Charlotte's gasp caused Antonia to twist around and look at her. The younger girl's eyes were wide. She looked like Antonia had just said she was descended from royalty.

"Your da was a *pirate*?" Charlotte asked. "A *Spanish* pirate? And your ma, was she a pirate queen?"

Well, what could she say? She was sure stuck now.

"Of course," said Antonia matter-of-factly. "Maman came from French and Italian noble blood. She gave it all up, to go to sea with Papa." It was as if all the tales she'd invented, lying awake nights in her bed in the apartment above the music store, were suddenly forcing their way through her lips. In a desperate bid to insert a little truth into the ever-expanding lie, she added, "Maman was a fortune-teller, too, and could see the future."

At least the first part was true. As for the second, it was what Maman had always said.

"She's dead too?" Charlotte sounded sad but also kind of impressed. "Is that why you live with your aunt?"

"Maman died by Papa's side, fighting a rival pirate band on the high seas. Y'see, they'd made a blood oath that they would never forsake each other. So, yeah, I was mostly raised by Mrs. S."

"Was she a pirate too?"

"Naw, but she's a first-rate gambler and card sharp."

"No!" This time, Charlotte sounded alarmed.

Antonia bit her lip. Oh, she'd done it now, letting that little bit of truth slip out. "Not anymore," she said hastily. "But that's why she's so good with money, and business deals, and stuff. Your ma was smart to join up with my aunt. She'll take good care of you both."

"So, why are you and her here, in San Francisco? Ma told me your aunt runs a music store and helps people who need help. I don't understand."

"Well, we're kinda here in disguise. You see, we came to San Francisco to…to…" Antonia's brain skittered around, "to try and find the leader of the pirates who killed my parents. We heard he's here. Hiding out. And we came to start a new life, of course. But if the wrong people learn who we are and that we're here—" She drew a finger across her neck.

Antonia scrutinized Charlotte's expression in the flickering candlelight. The younger girl had pulled a strand of her straw-colored hair out of her braid and was sucking on it, looking troubled. Antonia grew alarmed. "I could get in real big trouble if you say anything about this to anyone. To your ma, or anyone at your school, or anything." One small comfort: she went to Lincoln School on Third, while Charlotte had told her she went to a Catholic school. It wasn't like they'd be seeing each other on the playground.

Then, she hit on an idea. "If you spit-promise that you won't tell anyone, I'll show you something special I haven't shown to anyone. It's a special pirate knife Maman left for me."

Charlotte brightened. Antonia sat up in bed, spit into her palm, and held out her hand. Charlotte did the same and they shook. Antonia jumped out of bed, padded over to her coat, and pulled out the most precious object she owned, her maman's little folding knife. She brought it back to the bed and sat on the edge. Charlotte crawled out of the bedclothes to sit beside her, wool-socked feet dangling over the side.

Antonia continued, "This is a *salvavirgo*. Maman called it a *carraca* because it makes these little clicking noises when you open it." She demonstrated with a swift roll of the wrist.

"Wow," breathed Charlotte. "Can I hold it?"

Antonia thumbed the knife closed. Charlotte took it carefully from Antonia's hand, held it up to the candlelight, and examined the handle. Delicate little flowers were carved into the ivory at the top of the handle where the blade folded. Below that, a small inlaid figure of a fox gazed over its shoulder. Seeing the knife in Charlotte's grip made Antonia feel uneasy. She held out her hand and said abruptly, "I need to put it away now." Charlotte gave it back. Antonia padded back to her clothes, and, suddenly afraid that Charlotte might be tempted to steal it, she pretended to put it in her boot but slid it up the cuff of her nightshirt instead.

Once back in bed, she closed her eyes, saying, "G'night. Remember, you promised. We made an oath. We're like blood sisters now."

A movement above her and the tickle of a strand of hair across her cheek caused her eyelids to open. Charlotte's serious face loomed above her as she peered closely at Antonia. "Your eyes are so magical and your hair so curly and pretty. I bet that's why."

Confused, Antonia said, "Why what?"

"It's all because you're a pirate princess." The awe in Charlotte's voice was clear. She smiled in the shadowy half-light and settled back down onto her pillow, whispering to herself, "I'm blood sisters with a *pirate princess.*"

"That's right," said Antonia. "Now, go to sleep. And remember, mum's the word." She turned her back to Charlotte. She felt the younger girl snuggle her back up against her own. A yawn and a murmured, "Mum's the word," drifted back to her.

Antonia closed her eyes, determined to block out the guilt and the sudden unease that enveloped her. She curled her hands against her cheek, the cool weight of her knife pillowed by the flannel sleeve, and drifted to sleep, hoping Charlotte would keep her promise.

Chapter Four

Clanging bells shattered Inez's dreams of the past.

Danger!

Mind fuzzy, Inez instinctively groped under her pillow, searching for her Remington pocket revolver.

Then, awareness crept in. It wasn't the ringing of the fire bells. It wasn't a call to danger. Merely the usual morning call of the multitude of places to worship that surrounded her neighborhood in San Francisco.

Her hand slid out from under the pillow, empty. Inez sat up slowly, heart still pounding, and pushed straggling strands of dark hair out of her face. In that gray time when waking stalks slumber, she'd dreamt she was back in Leadville, Colorado, the raw boomtown set in a high-mountain valley nestled between the ranges and peaks of the Colorado Rockies. Erected hastily by those more intent on making money from the silver rush than in creating sound structures, the town had been just one lit lucifer away from a major conflagration when she left it in autumn 1880, nearly a year and a half ago.

But she was not there now, she reminded herself. She was in San Francisco, California. The "Paris of the West," perched on the edge of the Pacific Ocean. Also built with wood, but with an ever-growing proportion of buildings constructed of stone and brick. San Francisco was not a brash youngster of a city like Leadville. It had a certain gravitas that only promised to increase as its role as a financial and industrial anchor in the Far West became more assured.

Inez closed her eyes, the discordant music of large metal bells washing over her. It had been a while since Leadville had claimed her dreams. Why now? Could it have been something about the previous night? Something about the debacle that had turned Moira's little party into a horror tale of walled-in, long-dead corpses? Or her consequent set-to with the local constabulary? Whatever prompted her uneasy dreams, she had to deal with the situation in the here and now. She could not wave it away like a troublesome dream, given that legal and financial agreements bound her to the young boardinghouse owner.

Inez opened her eyes, drew up her knees, and curled her toes in her wool nightsocks, thinking of what that meant. Along with running the D & S House of Music and Curiosities, Inez made loans to women who needed financial infusions to expand or otherwise enhance their small businesses. When Moira had approached Inez, she had explained that Bertram Taylor, the son of the deceased owner, had sent his lawyer to offer to sell the house "lock, stock, and barrel" at a reduced price. She'd added, "It is a golden opportunity. I just need to match the savings I already have to buy it outright."

Moira had come recommended by Mrs. Nolan, who ran her own boardinghouse where Inez and Antonia took their meals. What swayed Inez in the end was not hard facts and figures, but Mrs. Nolan's alternating expressions of praise and pity directed at the young boardinghouse owner. "Married young and well to Mr. Krause. He was a Navy lieutenant during the War to preserve the Union, signed onto various merchant steamships afterward, lots of responsibility, a true man of the sea. Many years her senior but truly a love match. No one could've been happier at the arrival of little Charlotte than her father! He called her his 'little princess.' Such a terrible thing when he died at sea."

"Terrible," agreed Inez.

"She has handled everything on her own, ever since," said Mrs. Nolan. "Running the house, raising a child, all of it, while mourning all the while."

Inez had thought of her time running the Silver Queen Saloon in Leadville, when she believed her own husband dead. How difficult it had been. And she had not been alone, but had employees and a business partner. Additionally, she had sent her young son East to be raised by her wealthy family, and she had eventually taken a lover, Reverend Justice B. Sands. Moira had apparently persevered alone, raising her daughter single-handedly. Inez's estimation of Moira had gone up several notches.

"I commend Mrs. Krause for her fortitude in the face of such sorrows and burdens," she had said. "In your opinion, does her business thrive? Does she seem to struggle financially? Has she ever turned to you or anyone else for a loan?" Inez was deliberately blunt. Sometimes a blunt question took the responder by surprise and resulted in a blunt answer, or an answer so embellished with verbal flourishes that it practically shouted it was a lie.

Mrs. Nolan had replied, "I've not seen nor heard a sign of trouble. Moira is careful with a penny. Although her Christian compassion sometimes means it's the church poor and needy mariner that benefit from her thrift, not her bank account."

Inez, having watched Mrs. Nolan closely as she answered, was convinced the woman told the truth. At least, as far as she knew it.

After satisfying herself with the help of the Dun & Company credit report that the widow Krause was indeed solvent, Inez had set up an inspection of the house with Moira. Arranging for such was not easy. Mr. Upton had to contact Bertram Taylor and then the elder locksmith Joe Harris, who seemed to be the only one who ever entered the building.

Inez had to admit now her suspicions had been lulled by the tour of the structure. Fully furnished, it looked as if its occupants had departed on a trip long ago, only to never return. Her normally clear-eyed examination was further softened by the discovery of a beautiful parlor grand piano, draped and silent in one of the two parlors. The piano was a match to the one Inez had labored over as a child, where music had been the one solace of that dark period of her life.

How could she say no?

So she said yes.

Thinking back on all this from her bed, Inez hoped she would not come to regret forging an agreement with Moira.

Inez heard a door slam—the downstairs entrance to the apartment. Staccato, rapid footfalls signaled that Antonia had returned from her night at Mrs. Nolan's house.

Inez rose and pulled on a flannel wrapper just as the main door to their second-floor apartment banged open. Seconds later, Antonia braked her impetuous advance at the threshold of Inez's bedroom. "D'the police know who the stiff was? Was he a pirate? How did he die? Was he murdered? How much gold was in the bag? Are we rich?"

"And good morning to you, Antonia," said Inez, with admonishment in her tone. "Let us begin our conversation anew."

Antonia sighed. "Good morning, Mrs. S."

"Much better. Now, did you sleep well? Did you breakfast at Mrs. Nolan's?"

The girl shrugged. "Charlotte kicks in her sleep, like she's running all night long. Mrs. Nolan made us oatmeal with brown sugar, butter, and cream. And she fixed lunch for Charlotte and me t' take to school. Bread, cheese, and pickles." Antonia brightened. "And we each got an orange!" She held up a battered tin bucket. "Mrs. Nolan let me borrow this for lunch today. Said I could bring it back tonight when we come for dinner."

Inez noticed that Antonia's clothes from the previous evening looked brushed and the pleats at the bottom of her calf-length skirt were freshly pressed. The girl's dark hair, usually so impervious to brush and comb, had been subdued into two tight braids. Even her boots looked freshly polished. Clearly, Mrs. Nolan had been busy making sure Antonia would be ready for school when she left the boardinghouse that morning.

"Did you thank her for everything she did for you and Charlotte?"

Antonia's gaze flickered to the side. "Uh."

Inez raised an eyebrow.

The girl grimaced. "I forgot."

"You will thank her tonight. In fact, after school you'll pen her a note thanking her for everything she did and bring it to her this evening."

"Yes'm." She bounced on the balls of her feet. "Please, ma'am. Would you please tell me what happened after the police got there last night?"

Inez relented. "To answer your questions: The identity of the deceased is still unknown. The manner of his death is still a mystery. As to the gold, it is not all *ours*. I am in partnership with Mrs. Krause. Thus, it belongs to both her and me."

Antonia took a step into the room. "Is the treasure here? Is it
Spanish doubloons?"

"The coins are with the police." A situation Inez hoped to
change as soon as possible. "Now. I have much to do today, and
you mustn't be late to school. Get your satchel and hurry along.
Come straight to the store after school. No lollygagging by the
waterfront."

"No, ma'am. I mean, yes, ma'am." Antonia disappeared from
the entryway. Her footsteps headed to her bedroom above
the storefront. A moment later, her voice drifted to Inez. "Oh.
Charlotte and I were talking, and we wondered… Could I go
over to Charlotte's tonight for dinner and help her with her
numbers? And maybe spend the night since tomorrow isn't a
school day?"

Inez, laying out her clothes for the day, paused. "Does Mrs.
Krause know about this?"

"Charlotte's gonna ask her today. But she's sure her ma will
say yes. We figured we could do our schoolwork together, and
I'd help her with her multiplication and fractions. She goes to a
Saint Something-or-other school."

Inez folded her arms, stared at the outfit she'd chosen—a
light-gray business-like walking suit, with touches of rose and
maroon—and pondered the girl's request. She was pleased that
Antonia and Charlotte had formed a bond. A young girl from
a Catholic school, Charlotte seemed, from Inez's observations,
to be quiet and obedient to her mother. Not the type to cause
trouble, she might be a good influence on her rambunctious,
impulsive ward. It sounded like an ideal situation.

So why did she feel a trifle suspicious?

It was true the girl had an innate grasp of mathematical
constructs. Her teacher, Miss Pierce, commended her work
in that subject, even as she condemned Antonia's "atrocious"

penmanship. Antonia could help the younger girl and at the same time complete her own lessons. Inez knew Moira ran a tight ship at the boardinghouse and would not tolerate any improprieties. When she met Moira later that day, she would verify Charlotte had asked permission and determine Moira's thoughts on the arrangement.

Antonia reappeared in the doorway, swinging her satchel by its strap. "So, can I? Please?"

"We shall see. I'll talk it over with Mrs. Krause later today, when I see her. If she has sanctioned this arrangement, then I suppose I will allow it."

Antonia grinned, white teeth flashing against her dark complexion. "Great!"

"Don't forget your school bonnet," Inez added. "It's hanging at the bottom of the stairs. And don't fling your satchel around like that. You'll break the strap."

"Yes, ma'am!" In a flash, the girl was gone. The apartment door slammed. The thumps as Antonia took the stairs down, two at a time, echoed through the flat. A final, distant slam from the street-level door and then…silence.

"After all, how much trouble could she possibly get into over there?" Inez said out loud to herself. "It's better than spending her afternoons by the East Street wharves."

Inez pushed her vague concerns aside and focused on the day ahead. No need to worry about opening up the music store. She had two reliable employees to handle that: store manager Thomas Welles, a rock-steady family man and accomplished pianist, and John Hee, who handled instrument repairs and was the expert on the store's Oriental wares. She would leave a note letting them know she would be in later, allowing herself time to identify a lawyer who could help her "liberate" the gold from the police.

And I know just the person who might know one.

Assured that her day was sufficiently mapped out, Inez shed her wrapper and turned her attention to her morning's ablutions.

Chapter Five

It was a brisk ten-minute walk from Inez's apartment above the store on the corner of Pine and Kearney to the magnificent Palace Hotel, which occupied an entire city block on San Francisco's main business thoroughfare, Market Street.

Inez paused at the hotel's entrance on New Montgomery, extracted a rosewater-scented handkerchief, and held it to her nose. The last few times she had ventured in on foot, the odor of horse piss and excrement had been particularly strong. She proceeded under the stone arch onto the marble-tiled promenade. Trying to keep her distance from the circular driveway with its stream of horse-drawn conveyances, she marched along, eyes fixed on the lobby entrance at the top of the circle. The jingle of harnesses, squeak of carriage springs, and chatter of visitors warred with the shouts of drivers as carriages pulled up to the lobby entrance and disgorged passengers and luggage before swallowing those waiting to board.

Seven floors of arcaded galleries soared above, forming continuous promenades for guests to observe the activity below.

Arcing over all, an opaque leaded-glass skylight peered down like the eye of God watching His creations move hither and thither throughout the hotel. With accommodations for more than a thousand guests and a staff of employees numbering well into the hundreds, the building was massive enough to form a small city.

Inez circumvented a couple and their travel trunks, waiting for the next available carriage, and passed through the tropical garden filled with exotic plants, marble statuary, and stone fountains that fronted the lobby. Once inside, Inez tucked her handkerchief into one sleeve, making sure that it was hidden under the gray-and-maroon-striped cuff. Now, a decision had to be made. She was there on a mission for information. What would yield the best results: Announce her presence and declare her desire for a meeting? Or simply show up, unannounced?

The decision was made for her when she spied a hotel clerk she knew, Mr. Miller, idle behind the main desk. When Inez and Antonia had first arrived in the city, they had spent some months in residence at the Palace Hotel. As a result, Inez had her "favorites" among the staff, including Miller. She approached the clerk, a man of indeterminate middle age, with smooth brown hair and a glossy mustache. He reminded her of nothing so much as one of those sleek brown seals that frequented the sand and rocks at Ocean Beach.

She summoned a smile. He smiled back. She said, "Good morning, Mr. Miller."

"And good day to you, Mrs. Stannert. A pleasure to see you, as always. What can we do for you today?"

"I am here to see Mr. de Bruijn. No appointment, I'm afraid. I am hoping he is available."

"One moment. I'll ring him, and we shall see." He disappeared into the office behind the desk. Inez knew that the hotel had a telephone system that could call from floor to floor, and even into some of the more upscale suites.

He reappeared. "Mr. de Bruijn would be happy to receive you. His office is on the third floor, number—"

"Thank you, I know the way." She softened her remark with another smile before heading to the bank of hydraulic "rising rooms."

Once on the third floor she began the journey down the long hall to the office of private investigator Wolter Roeland de Bruijn. She spied him waiting for her outside his door.

It had been some time since their paths had intersected, and she scrutinized him as she approached. Despite all that had transpired between them, he appeared much the same, at least on the outside. He was about her height, that is, five eleven or so. Well-groomed and well-favored. Circumspect, with a vaguely Continental air and a serious mien. Straight dark hair and a short Van Dyke beard, the mustache curling up a bit at the ends.

Today, he was dressed in a somber suit that fit him perfectly and was neither too expensive nor too cheap. He could have passed as one of the city's many anonymous businessmen. Not flash, as some of the stock operators were wont to be with their bright checked sack jackets and loud voices. Nor ostentatious, like the wealthy industrialists who wore their obviously bespoke suits, silk top hats, and diamond cuff links. Yet, she knew that in his line of work, he could—and did—assume the appearances of such, just as easily as he could assume the rough form of a lowly confidence man playing fast and loose with a deck of cards.

He greeted Inez with the habitual small bow that she found so charming and said in a pleasant but neutral tone, "Mrs. Stannert. Good to see you." His dark-brown eyes lingered on hers for a beat longer than necessary, his gaze warmer than the simple greeting warranted. Her pulse quickened in response. He added, "Please, come in."

"Thank you, Mr. de Bruijn." She mirrored his polite, impersonal voice.

He stepped aside to let her enter. Once inside, she swung around to face him, a noncommittal remark about the weather upon her lips, and nearly collided with him. Startled, not realizing he'd closed the door and was at her heels, she took a step back.

He did the same.

"Pardon!" they said simultaneously.

Inez felt a flush rise to her face. Subsequent to their previous "entanglements" while working together to resolve an incident of some criminality and concern, Inez had wrestled over the nature of their relationship. She had finally decided the best way forward was to keep her interactions with de Bruijn on a cordial but strictly professional footing. That being so, why was she now having trouble controlling the heat that radiated from her cheeks? She fanned herself with one maroon-suede-gloved hand. "The Palace should find a method to ventilate its central court. Far too warm, and far too aromatic. The horses, you understand."

He granted her a small smile. A neat, carefully controlled smile.

Neat. Careful. Controlled.

Those three words served to sum up the man she had met under less-than-ideal circumstances in the fall of the previous year.

He was an enigma.

And she could never resist an enigma.

Which was probably why, she thought wryly, she had ended

up eloping with the charismatic and charming Mark Stannert in the first place and then turning to the mysterious and alluringly dangerous Reverend Justice Sands in the second place. She had responded to Mark because she had been young and naive. As for Justice, well, she had been lonely and aching. There had been others who had passed through her life and, occasionally, her bed during her rocky marriage and before the reverend. With them, she had either been seeking revenge—for Mark's cheating ways by giving him a taste of his own medicine—or been just plain foolish and impulsive.

Now, she was no longer young, nor was she lonely. And, please God, she was no longer foolish and impulsive. She hoped. In any case, she was determined de Bruijn would not move into the vacuum caused by the absence of her ex-husband and her lover. All this raced through her mind as she regained her composure. Inez cleared her throat and said, "Thank you for seeing me on the spur of the moment. I will not take much of your time."

"It is always a pleasure to see you, Mrs. Stannert." Had he put a special emphasis on the word *always* she wondered. He continued, "Then this is not a social visit, I gather."

"I would like your advice."

His lips twitched. "You want my advice?" The hint of amusement in his tone set her more at ease.

"Indeed. Specifically, I am looking for a recommendation."

He gestured to his desk, at the other end of the room. Sunlight filtered in aslant from the southerly facing bay window. "May I take your coat? Shall I ring for coffee?"

"Oh, none of that will be necessary. This will be quick."

She pondered the choice of chairs for visitors as de Bruijn circled to the other side of the desk. Two leather club chairs on the right for the gentlemen and two floral-patterned, befringed chairs on the left for the ladies. Disdaining such an obvious ploy, Inez had often made it a point to sit in the leather chairs. But she hated to be too predictable. Adjusting the drape in her narrow overskirt, Inez lowered herself primly into the left-most embroidered seat and leaned her umbrella against the edge of his desk. De Bruijn, who had remained standing until she sat, lowered himself as well.

"So, have you been keeping busy, Mr. de Bruijn?" Inez eyed his desk, empty of papers, holding only the normal accoutrements and a standing business card holder of silver.

De Bruijn's cards were a study in simplicity, consisting of three lines of type stating:

W. R. DE BRUIJN.
PRIVATE DETECTIVE. INQUIRY AGENT.
FINDER OF THE LOST.

He laced his fingers on the top of the desk. "Busy enough. And you, Mrs. Stannert? The store is doing well, I hope."

"Tolerably well. Things have improved vastly over the last month or so."

"Due to your efforts and acumen, I am certain."

Inez bestowed a small smile upon him for the compliment. She knew he would not have said it if the words were empty or untrue. When he was simply being himself, de Bruijn did not lie, although he was quite adept at verbal sidestepping. She kept her smile minimal, because she was certain he knew that compliments on her business sense were much more appreciated than flattery regarding her physical attributes. And flattery in any form put her on her guard. "Thank you. However, as I said, I am not here to conduct idle chitchat but have something I must ask."

Concern crossed his face. "Does this regard Antonia?"

Inez knew de Bruijn had a special interest in Antonia, having been close to the girl's now-deceased mother. Just how close, Inez had her suspicions but never risked probing too deeply. There were many doors to his past that remained tightly locked against Inez's curiosity.

"No, no." She flipped her hand in dismissal. "Antonia is fine. Doing well at school, no recent scuffles. For a change. She even asked if she might tutor a young student who needs help with arithmetic. It will be a welcome change from her constant obsession on pirates, sailing ships, and the docks."

Inez leaned forward. "This involves a business matter. Given your specialty as 'finder of the lost,'" she flicked a finger at the calling card holder, "I hoped you might be able to recommend a lawyer. Someone who specializes in property law. Not real property as in buildings but personal property. Tangible items. Objects."

His brow furrowed the tiniest bit. "A personal property lawyer? May I ask why? Perhaps I can help."

"Oh, there is a small disagreement. A misunderstanding. A misinterpretation of the law, I suspect. I know a bit about the legal ins and outs regarding real property but not the other. I am thinking a legal expert can help me nip this particular dispute in the bud." She tipped her head to one side. "So, are you saying that you have the appellation 'attorney-at-law' attached to your name as well?"

"I am not a lawyer, but much as you, I have acquired a working knowledge of the basic laws pertaining to my field of inquiry." He raised his eyebrows, clearly inviting a confidence.

She raised hers in return and kept her silence. It seemed wisest to not involve him in her affairs, business or personal, especially until she felt she could control her reaction to him.

After a moment, de Bruijn gave a slight shrug. "As you wish. I have not worked with any attorneys since arriving in the city last year. However, a gentleman came to see me recently who might be able to assist you." He opened a side drawer of his desk, pulled out a handful of business cards, and began to shuffle through them. "Ah, yes. Here." He slid a card across the polished top of the dark walnut desk.

Inez picked it up and examined it. "L. A. Buckley, attorney-at-law," she said aloud. "Hmmm. Office nearby. And he has a telephone. Excellent. I will see if he is available today. May I keep this for now? I will return it for your records."

"Certainly."

She paused in the act of tucking it into her reticule. "Am I to understand that you have not worked with this gentleman?"

"No. I have not."

"So you cannot vouch for him? His conduct? His competence?"

De Bruijn shook his head. "All I can tell you is that he came to speak to me at the recommendation of the hotel manager."

"Well, then, I shall draw my own conclusions about Mr. Buckley when I meet him." She stood, gathered her umbrella, and slipped the braided silk loop over her wrist.

He stood as well and walked her to the door. As he opened it for her, he said, "If you decide against him and need another recommendation, I would be happy to—"

"Help. Yes, I know." She softened her tone, which she feared had been a little sharp. After all, she told herself, he was just being kind. "I will let you know what I think of Mr. Buckley." She touched his arm lightly, in unspoken apology and gratitude, and left.

Chapter Six

Wolter de Bruijn watched Mrs. Stannert walk down the hall toward the mechanical lifts—ramrod straight posture, determined stride, umbrella swinging with each step.

She didn't look back.

She was, he thought, an enigma.

Shaking his head, he returned to his desk and pulled out paperwork for a just-completed case for one of the hotel's residents. Or rather, *about* one of the residents. According to the hotel manager, Warren Leland, a female guest had claimed that her valuable bracelet had been stolen. She accused the help of taking it and demanded monetary recompense from the hotel. "I have my doubts about the lady in question," said Leland. "I do not believe she is on the up-and-up. But she is threatening to go to the police and the newspapers, so we must take her claim seriously."

As de Bruijn had discovered, the lady was indeed not on the up-and-up.

The bracelet had been seen by many during a dinner party

at the hotel. Various observers offered it had flashed brightly as the lady had gestured and maneuvered her fan in a way as to attract attention. Most described it as a dazzling array of gems set in intricately fashioned silver. However, it turned out to be not of silver and gems but composed of pewter and leaded glass. Additionally, it was not stolen but tucked into a secret drawer of the lady's travel box of toiletries. Once her scheme to extract a considerable sum from the hotel in exchange for her "loss" and her silence was revealed, the language she heaped upon de Bruijn made it very clear that she was also no lady.

Needless to say, she was no longer residing at the Palace.

De Bruijn intended to finish the report, give it to Leland that morning, and close the matter. But now that he was back at his desk and his papers, his attention wandered.

Perhaps it was Mrs. Stannert's unexpected visit and the "lady who was no lady" of this recent case that led him to ponder further on his morning visitor. Mrs. Stannert, too, could transform in the most unexpected ways. From no-nonsense business-woman, to coquette, to high-society matron...not to mention the time she had donned trousers and infiltrated one of the most desperate dives of the city. He thought he had her defined, only to have her shift again, like a wraith or wisp of smoke.

Having her surface at his office after a studied month-long absence had been a surprise. The feelings that had welled up at seeing her were no less perturbing. That she was extremely attractive was a given. That she had a force of will she could channel into charm and seduction was alarming. That she was, on top of it all, highly intelligent and an excellent dissembler was a warning that he could never take what she did or said as gospel. Knowing her as well as he did—that is, well enough to realize he didn't really know her at all—made him doubly suspicious and guarded in her presence. Yet, when she fixed her hazel-eyed gaze upon him and pinned him in his chair with an apologetic smile, which was all the more seductive for being unaffected and open, he could feel his guard slipping. When she unexpectedly asked for his help, he had been compelled to offer such. Then, having apparently gotten what she wanted, away she went.

For a while, after their first acquaintance in the fall, she had drawn him into her and Antonia's orbit. They had met for the occasional meal, attended the occasional theater event together, and even strolled Woodward's Gardens so Antonia could ride the rotary boat. But events at the turn of the year had put a strain on the previously easygoing nature of their interactions. And for the past month—nothing.

Yet, here she was again. Smiling, gracious, and proper, with none of the imperious "Queen of the Silver Queen Saloon" quality that he had heard about during his investigations in Leadville.

Leadville. Where he had first become curious about the enigma that was Inez Stannert.

Not just an enigma, but a dangerous woman as well. And, he reminded himself, a woman with a no-less-dangerous lover. De Bruijn suspected Mrs. Stannert and Reverend Sands, although separated by distance, remained in contact. De Bruijn made it a point not to delve into Mrs. Stannert's life any further than he had already, however. That she was guardian of Antonia, the girl who had brought him West and now held him here, was enough.

Or so he told himself.

Still, he found himself wondering when Mrs. Stannert would next sail into sight and under what circumstances.

A knock on the door broke his reverie. A glance at the mantel clock told him he had frittered away the time. His next appointment had arrived.

"A moment," he called out. He swept the papers into the

drawer, stood, tugged his waistcoat smooth, and donned his jacket before answering the door.

Standing in the hallway, a simple purse clutched protectively before her with both hands, was his prospective client. A plump young woman, surely less than thirty, dressed in a proper, few-frills, "Sunday best" costume of a hard-working middle-class woman. She said tentatively, "Mr. de Brown?"

Long resigned to having his surname mangled in many ways, de Bruijn simply bowed and said, "Good afternoon, Mrs. Krause. I am Mr. de Bruijn. It was good of Mrs. Nolan to recommend me to you. Please, come inside. I understand you run a boardinghouse and have encountered troubles of some sort. How may I help you?"

She stepped onto the threshold and stopped. He opened the door wider, wondering if entering a man's rooms alone was giving her pause. For not the first time, he thought of the liabilities of working solo.

Before he could offer that they talk in the public dining room, she burst out, "Mrs. Nolan said you specialize in locating things that are lost. I have an unusual, perhaps impossible, request. I will understand if you do not take my case."

So, she was afraid he would demur. That explained her "one foot out the door" pose. Striving to set her at ease, he said, "I assure you, I have dealt with many unusual requests in my line of work. Whatever you have lost, I will do everything in my power to make sure it is found."

She took a deep breath. "I am glad to hear that because the trail will be quite cold, and I don't quite know how you will uncover what I wish you to find. It involves a man—at least, I think it is a man—who died long ago. We do not know exactly when. His, ah, earthly remains were found inside a wall of my boardinghouse." She squeezed her eyes shut and swayed a little.

He moved toward her, just in case she might faint, and her eyes flew open. "His identity, how he got there, is a mystery." She squared her shoulders, then said with vehement resolve, "I want to bury him properly. To do so, I need to know who he is. I want you to find his name."

Chapter Seven

Inez was immediately impressed upon meeting attorney-at-law Leander Alderon Buckley. Truthfully, she was pleased even before entering his plush office. When she had telephoned from the music store and requested an appointment after offering the briefest of summaries as to her quandary, his clerk had said, "Someone just cancelled an appointment. If you can be here in half an hour, he could see you then."

"Excellent!" she exclaimed. "I shall be there."

Inez was glad that, on the previous evening while waiting for the police to arrive, she had convinced Moira to let her store the legal paperwork from the purchase in the music store safe. That made it easy for her to grab the deed and her copy of the bill of sale. Almost as an afterthought, she also extracted her copy of her business agreement with Moira. She secured the papers in a lockable carpetbag. Umbrella and carpetbag in hand, Inez made the short walk down Pine to the main thoroughfare of Montgomery. Buckley's office was on the third floor of the Montgomery Block building, a solid-looking edifice of stone that looked capable of withstanding the ages and the very forces of nature. It was only upon entering that she detected a little fraying about the edges, an air of genteel shabbiness as an elegant suit long out of style might possess.

All that vanished beyond the door with the gilt lettering L. A. BUCKLEY, ATTORNEY-AT-LAW. Inez entered the office and announced herself to the bespectacled young clerk in the anteroom. "Ah, yes," he said, half standing behind his desk. "We were expecting you, Mrs. Stannert."

No sooner had her name left his lips than the interior door burst open. "Mrs. Stannert, welcome!" boomed a man Inez could only conjecture was L. A. Buckley himself. He strode over to her, advancing with purpose and speed like a ship under sail in a gale. She instinctively raised her hand, as much to slow his progress as to greet him. He took her gloved fingers promptly, but gently, then released them at once. Inez craned her neck up to see his face. Standing well over six feet, Buckley had a physical presence that matched his verve.

"Leander Alderon Buckley, at your service, ma'am," he said in a voice with less volume but still of sonorous timbre. "Come into my office, and let's see what I can do for you."

The clerk had sunk back into his chair and managed to muster a "Will you need anything from me, sir? To take notes, or...?"

"No need," Buckley said. "This should be straightforward enough." He ushered Inez into the back room, saying, "This way, if you would."

She could appreciate that he would have quite an effect upon a judge or jury or opposing counsel. In addition to his prodigious height and a voice to match, he sported piercing blue eyes and an impressive beard of gray-streaked russet. In contrast, his cranium sported nary a hair and was as polished as the expansive oak table in his private office. He guided her to one end of the table, away from the partially open window. The sound of horse-drawn streetcars below mixed with the cooing of pigeons jostling on the outside windowsill. He apologized for the noise before closing the window. "I feed the birds regularly around this time of day, and they are as faithful to the clock as a watchman on his rounds."

He returned and took a seat not across from her but cattycorner. She noted the arrangement unobtrusively set him up as an ally, sending the message *I am on your side*. With a gaze simultaneously shrewd and kind, he took her measure in a manner restrained but thorough.

"I am pleased and honored you would contact me," he began, "and will endeavor to answer any questions you have. To whom do I owe the referral?"

Inez forbore to answer, taking a moment to survey his inner sanctum. A wall of glass-doored bookcases, shelves bending under heavy tomes. A couple of tall, free-standing, dark-wood cabinets. A sturdy table off to one side stacked with thick, massive ledgers, dwarfed by a massive rolltop desk. An ornate credenza, featuring a selection of brandy and sherries with attendant crystal ware. The wall above the credenza featured framed newspaper articles as well as framed declarations and certificates decorated with important-looking seals. She looked back at him. "Mr. de Bruijn, a private investigator in the Palace Hotel, gave me your business card." She placed the card on the table. "I was looking for a recommendation for a personal property lawyer, and he supplied this."

"Ah." Buckley settled back in his chair. "Yes, I recall. I made a courtesy call upon Mr. de Bruijn. It seemed our areas of expertise might intersect." He smiled.

She smiled in return. "So, you have been in practice in the city for some time, I gather?"

"Decades, Mrs. Stannert. I have seen men rise and fall and rise again. Quite the march of fortune and folly over the years." He leaned forward slightly. "There is little I have not dealt with. If you wish, I shall gladly relate some of the more interesting cases I've handled in the past. For instance, a fellow was on the trail of *ursus arctos horribilis*—a grizzly bear—only to have another fellow happen upon the beast and kill and claim it for himself. So, is the pelt the property of the man who pursued or the man who pulled the trigger and set hand upon the creature?" He spread his arms. "How would you rule, Mrs. Stannert?"

"Possession is nine-tenths of the law," Inez ventured.

"And the court agrees!" His hands descended to the table. "Most of the matters that come my way, however, are familial in nature. Mother against child. Brother against brother. Who owns the diamonds? Who gets the silver stock certificates? And so forth. The principles in such cases can best a grizzly when it comes to viciousness. Now, from what my clerk told me, your matter sounds like a simple one, compared to those."

"It should be a simple matter, except for the police involvement," Inez said dryly. She sketched out the situation. Her partnership with Moira. Their purchase of the residence conjoining Moira's boardinghouse. The discovery of the skeletal remains and the gold. The confiscation of the coins by the detectives.

"I cannot see any legal reason for them to hold what was found in the house, unless they think it pertains to the death of the unfortunate individual," he said.

"A remark was made that perhaps the sack of coins was used to kill him." She nodded in response to his skeptical expression. "A weak reason, at best."

"At best. This happened yesterday, you say? Were the remains taken to the coroner for determination of method of death?"

"That was what the detectives said."

"And the detectives' names are?"

"Lynch and," she hesitated, "I did not quite catch the name of the second one. MacCabe or MacKay, I believe."

"Detective Martin Lynch is as honest as any in the force. Erwin MacKay, recently promoted from foot patrol. Do you have a receipt?"

She nodded. "We counted the gold together, and they gave me this." She pulled the receipt from her carpetbag and set it on the table. "My signature and the signatures of the detectives are at the bottom."

He glanced at it. "Two thousand dollars in double eagles? That is a fair bit of coinage."

"Indeed. Which is why I am anxious to have it back in my," she corrected herself, "our—that is, my and Mrs. Krause's—possession."

"Straightforward enough. May I see the bill of sale for the building?"

She extracted the remaining papers from her bag, adding, "Here is the deed and the agreement between Mrs. Krause and me as well."

"I appreciate you being so thoroughly prepared." He retrieved reading spectacles from his desk and returned to the sale papers on the table. Inez watched him scan the lines of legalese, then stop. He glanced up. "This is Captain Taylor's estate?"

Surprised, she said, "Yes. You knew him?"

"I did. At least while he resided here. The captain and his family left years ago, as I recall." He shuffled to the last pages with the signatures. "The son, Bertram, inherited, I see. Ah. He hired Sherman Upton as his counsel." Buckley returned the papers to Inez. "I could settle this situation for you easily enough, Mrs. Stannert."

She put the documents back in her carpetbag. "How soon? And for how much?"

"I gather from the order of your questions that you would like to conclude this matter quickly." He pulled out a pocket watch and clicked open the cover. His watch fob, a gold nugget the size of his thumbnail, swung from the gold chain. "I'll have my clerk call the station. If the gentlemen I need to confer with are available, you shall have your property back in your possession within the hour."

Pleased at his confidence, she leaned back, then frowned a little and repeated, "How much?"

"Should things go as expected, five dollars should cover my time. Perhaps it will be even less." He hesitated, then said, "I do not wish to offend your, ah, moral sensibilities, however, there most likely will be, shall we say, ancillary expenses at the station."

Bribes. I should have known. Resigned, she asked, "How much?"

"No more than what you will pay me for this little adventure. And I shall make certain every penny, or I should say every double eagle, is accounted for, or there will be the Lord Harry to pay."

"Very well. You have a client. What do I need to sign?"

He nodded approvingly. "A woman who knows her mind. A refreshing diversion from my usual clientele. I will have my clerk set up a simple contract. But first, the telephone call." He excused himself and disappeared into the anteroom, pulling the door behind him. However, it didn't close completely and, as doors in old buildings are wont to do, it eased back open in a slow, lackadaisical fashion.

The conversation in the other room became clearer, and Inez heard Buckley say to his clerk, "...Find out if Tobin is available. If not, try Crowley. A minute with one or the other is all I need."

Crowley, the chief of police?

Inez inclined her ear toward the door, curious. There was the unmistakable two-buzz ring for the Central Station, a pause, then the clerk began shouting, clearly trying to make his voice heard down a cranky wire, "Hello? Ahoy! Central Office, can you hear me? This is telephone number sixty-two. Sixty-two wants fifteen. Yes, that's right. The Police Office."

Buckley reappeared in the inner-office doorway. He smiled apologetically at Inez, grasped the brass knob, and gave the recalcitrant door a resolute tug. It shut with a decisive snap, the voices cut off. Inez sighed, her eavesdropping efforts defeated.

About two minutes later by the mantel clock, Buckley bounded in and swept to the hat rack by his desk. "Success is ours, Mrs. Stannert." He gathered a top hat from several different styles hanging from the various arms of the rack and shrugged into a black coat. "I will have my clerk give you the contract for your inspection while I am about our business. I will return shortly." He grabbed a leather gladstone bag.

She stood and gathered her umbrella. "I shall accompany you. I can sign the contract when we return."

He looked at her curiously. "As you wish." Then he added, not unkindly, "It will be more efficacious for me to conduct this affair alone. I am certain you understand that the people I will be talking with will be more...compliant...in a private setting. No offense meant, Mrs. Stannert."

Of course. She now realized why he had suggested she wait here. If pressure was to be exerted, favors requested, lucre offered, it had to be done behind closed doors and without witnesses. "No offense taken," she replied. "I shall simply take the air around the plaza while you do what you must do." Inez hated to cool her heels, but if that was what was required, so be it.

The Central Police Station was conveniently located a mere block away, across from Portsmouth Plaza in the "old" city hall, with the "new" city hall still under construction after ten years. At the foot of the stairs leading to the entrance, Buckley turned to Inez and said, "This shouldn't take long."

"You know where to find me," she responded. As he hurried up the stairs, she opened her umbrella, which did double duty as a parasol, and crossed the street to Portsmouth Plaza. From there, she aimlessly strolled its paths, which radiated out from the center of the plaza like the spokes on a wheel.

She ignored the idlers lingering on the walkways and along the iron-rail fence enclosing the square. Instead, she focused on observing the patterns cast by the severely trimmed trees that lined the paths, listening to the screeches of the seagulls and the clatter of a horsecar going past on its iron track, and reveling in the mild warmth of the afternoon sun. She tried to avoid wondering how long it would really take for Buckley to conduct his "business" and retrieve the money that belonged to her.

And to Moira, of course.

Twenty minutes later, she spied Buckley leaving city hall and returned to meet him.

He tipped his hat and she asked, "Success?"

"Smooth sailing all the way, Mrs. Stannert. Shall we return to my office and complete the paperwork?"

They were at the corner of Clay when a voice behind them said, "Buckley. Hold up."

Not just any voice, but a familiar voice. MacKay. He of the rolling eyes and dismissive bearing. She had the feeling he was not stopping them just to say hello.

Buckley half turned. "Detective? What is it?" The words could have sounded belligerent, but instead they sounded vaguely benevolent.

MacKay circled around them to block their journey, widened his stance, and narrowed his eyes. "What's this I hear about ye removing evidence from the property room?"

"All taken care of, my good man. All copacetic. Speak to your chief. Or Tobin, if you're so inclined."

"Ah, you and your backroom poker playin' cronies, thick as thieves. Just wink and look the other way while we sweat and spill our blood tryin' to uphold law and order on the streets." His ire boiled over them. Inez gripped her open umbrella tighter, wondering if she could be accused of assault if she thrust its open canopy at him and demanded he move aside.

"You misunderstand, MacKay." Buckley's tone was as paternal as a pat on the head.

MacKay's hands balled into fists. His angry squint moved to Inez. She glared back at him. He rolled his eyes then refocused on Buckley. "So, *she* found you lyin' in wait somewhere, you snake in the grass, just waitin' for someone to come round complaining about injustice, looking for a loophole to thread words through. Like finds like."

The prick of fear inside her spiked into hot indignation. "How dare you!" The words were out before she could ponder the wisdom of saying them out loud.

Buckley took Inez's arm and said, "Stop right there, MacKay." The honey in his voice was gone, replaced with a steely edge. "You are speaking of my client, and your speech is verging on slander. I can well understand your disappointment that private property, which should never have been seized in the first place, is now being returned to its rightful owner. But that is no cause to impugn my client, Mrs. Stannert's, good character. Cease and desist. And *move out of our way.*"

Inez was tempted to yank her elbow from Buckley's protective grasp and continue giving MacKay a piece of her mind. However, common sense whispered that she let Buckley—whom she had hired to speak for her—deal with the furious detective.

From his posture, Inez suspected MacKay would not budge, and she wondered what Buckley's next move would be. Then, from the direction of City Hall, Inez heard a shout, "Mack!" and she glanced behind her. Detective Lynch was striding up the sidewalk toward them, face twisted in concern. Still some distance away, he yelled, "Mack, we're wanted at the station. Now."

MacKay leaned to see around Inez, and his tight-fisted focus shifted. Buckley sidestepped away from him, pulling Inez along. "Mind the gutter, Mrs. Stannert." Buckley's hand on her arm guided and supported her as he navigated them into and across the street.

Once on the sidewalk, Inez extracted herself from his grip and exhaled in relief. "Thank you, Mr. Buckley." She readjusted her hat, which had slipped loose from its pins. "Perhaps Detective MacKay was counting on the so-called evidence to pad his pockets or pay his bills?"

"Perhaps," said Buckley. He paused. "The amount impounded was more than a detective makes in a year and almost twice the salary of a patrolman. Few can afford to buy a residence in the city. MacKay wouldn't be the first to be tempted to lift a little from the property room. Although something like this is of such high value and visibility that if a portion went missing, it would be noticed. All of it is accounted for, by the way."

As they went up the stairs to his office, Inez said, "I am most grateful for your service. Clearly, I could not have waltzed in there myself and demanded they return the money to me."

"You could have," Buckley said, his voice shaded with amusement. "It would have been intriguing to observe you wresting the goods from the strong arms of the law. Be that as it may, we have your property restored."

He opened the office door for her and asked his clerk, who was busy filing papers, "Is the contract ready?"

"On your table, sir."

"Good man."

Once they were settled again, Buckley pushed aside the waiting contract and set the gladstone on the table between them. "Do you plan on taking the money directly to the bank? If you are undecided and cannot store it securely, I could hold it for you." He nodded at the massive safe tucked next to one of the bookcases.

Alarm bells rang and questions rose in Inez's mind: How much does a personal property lawyer make in a year? What is the cost of upkeep for this office and a clerk? "No need, but thank you." The safe in her music store, although not as massive as his, was up to the task of holding the gold until she and Moira could work out a plan. Inez smiled brightly. "I have taken up enough of your valuable time. Let us count the money together, and I shall sign your papers."

Once she had assured herself all the coins were accounted for, she stuffed the canvas sack of gold into her capacious carpetbag and fastened the lock. He slid the paperwork to her, along with a pen and ink bottle. "If you change your mind or need further assistance—"

"I will call on you," Inez said, reading through the single page form. She nodded her acceptance and signed. "I could have a bank draft delivered tomorrow morning. Is that satisfactory?"

The *whunk* of a heavy door smacking a wall sounded from the anteroom.

"Sir!" yelped the clerk.

"I want to speak to your boss right now!"

Upton.

Why, all of a sudden, were all the disagreeable men involved in her recent transaction with Moira showing up at once? Inez wanted to roll her eyes but refrained from emulating MacKay.

"He's with a client," said the clerk. "No, don't—"

Buckley rose as the inner office door banged open. In marched attorney Sherman Upton, waistcoated belly first, arrogance not far behind. "Buckley! I understand you and your client here have absconded with the rightful inheritance of my client, Mr. Taylor." He swiveled on the balls of his feet and gestured grandly behind him.

Bertram Taylor? Frowning, Inez got to her feet. A slight figure detached itself from the shadows behind the indignant lawyer and entered the room.

A young man, brown hair falling into the saddest set of blue eyes Inez had ever seen, gazed back at her and said hesitantly, "Excuse me, are you Mrs. Krause?"

Chapter Eight

Upton's apoplectic flush deepened. He turned to his client. "As I explained on our way here, this is Mrs. Stannert. She is Mrs. Krause's business partner. She handled most of the arrangements of the real estate transaction."

Inez stepped forward and offered her hand. "Your counsel is correct, sir. I am Mrs. Stannert. And you are Mr. Taylor?"

"Yes, ma'am." He took her hand, his touch light as a whisper. It was like shaking hands with a phantom.

Upton refocused on Buckley. "When my client signed this agreement, it was for the property—the building, the land—and the contents inside the dwelling. Inside the residence, Buckley. The currency was uncovered within the walls, not in the domicile."

"What nonsense!" snapped Buckley. "No judge in his right mind would entertain an argument like that. You take that position, you'll be thrown out on your ear."

Upton raised his voice. "Besides, Mr. Taylor had no idea there was anything in the walls. If he had, obviously, he would not have sold the building."

"Upton, if your client had sold the house and the walls instantly crumbled to dust because they held termites and rot within, you would be shouting *caveat emptor!*" Buckley stopped, and bowed in Inez and Taylor's direction. "Pardon us for engaging in this clash of legal nonsense." He ushered them into the anteroom, Upton hot on his heels. Buckley continued, "Mr. Taylor, Mrs. Stannert, please make yourselves comfortable out here while Mr. Upton and I resolve this matter in my office."

The clerk, hovering behind paper stacks, asked, "Would you like me to take notes, sir?"

"No need. Just make sure our clients are settled while we hash this out, if you will." With that, he gestured to the inner office, saying, "After you. Sir." He looked as though what he really wanted to do was toss Upton out the window to the pigeons.

Upton raised his many chins in the air and reentered the inner sanctum as if it were his own. Buckley followed, saying, "Now look here, Upton, I know what you're trying to do." He shut the door with more force than necessary. The heavy panel cut off all discernible words, only the rumble of raised voices seeping through.

The nameless clerk gestured at a clutch of chairs and an upholstered settee. "Have a seat, please."

Inez sat in the center of the settee, leaving Taylor to choose a chair. She thought of the high-grade liquor displayed on Buckley's credenza. Right then, she wouldn't have said no to a glass of whiskey, neat. But circumstances dictated that such an offer would not be forthcoming. She brought her attention back to Taylor, who looked from one chair to another, seeming uncertain whether he should choose one nearby or at a distance.

"We might as well become acquainted, Mr. Taylor," she said pleasantly. The voices of their lawyers, still unintelligible, raised in pitch beyond the door. "Our lawyers may be busy for a while yet." She nodded at the nearest chair, and he sank into it, removing his bowler at last. She noticed the black crape hatband. "My condolences on your loss," she said. He stared blankly. Inez gestured at the mourning band, adding, unnecessarily she thought, "Your father."

His face flooded with comprehension. "Oh. Yes. Thank you, Mrs. Stannert. It was some months ago now." He lapsed into silence. There was an offhandedness to his response that puzzled her, but she tried to be charitable, thinking that Upton's revelation probably disconcerted him.

Taylor shifted in his chair, glancing at her and then away. He ran his left hand over his hair, and Inez noticed his fingers were stained with ink. *An office worker, then. It seems he did not follow his father onto the sea.*

"So…" She tried to find another entry point for conversation. "Do you work in the city?"

He nodded and focused on her at last. "At the mint. On Fifth."

"The United States Mint?" She sat back, intrigued. It almost seemed like too much of a coincidence that a fortune in coins should be secreted in the walls of the building he had owned and relinquished, and here he was, a money man. Of sorts, anyway.

"What do you do there?" she asked.

"I'm a clerk. I track shipments mostly. I know Chinese, so I am also occasionally called upon to translate." There it was, a hint of pride. *A man wedded to his work, perhaps?* She nodded, a wordless encouragement for him to elaborate, but he did not.

"So…" She felt as if she were lifting conversational boulders, one by one, and attempting to hand them to him, only to have each one thud to the ground. "You live here, in the city?"

"Across the bay." He looked down at the hat in his hands.

"But…" She hesitated, wondering if discussion of the residence might be wiser to avoid, but she couldn't help it. "Your house. That is, the dwelling that was your house." She needed to be careful what she said. "Why didn't you just live there since your work is right downtown?"

"It wasn't mine."

Now *she* was disconcerted. "I was led to believe you inherited it from your father. Does this mean it was not yours to sell?" A tangle of legal horrors loomed in her imagination.

"Oh, no, sorry. That's not what I meant." He looked toward the inner office, as if hoping for rescue from their awkward exchange. Buckley and Upton's voices rose and fell in tempo and intensity from behind the door. "My uncle lived there. We— that is, Mother and I, and of course Father, when he was not at sea—lived next door."

"Ah. But your father owned it, correct?"

He nodded. "He inherited it from his brother."

She cocked her head. "Your uncle passed, then?"

"A casualty of the war."

Inez decided she didn't dare inquire as to which side, and to guess wrong would certainly bring the stuttering conversation to an abrupt halt. She opted for general sympathy saying, "Ah, so many died then. So many families lost loved ones."

Her words, or perhaps it was her tone, captured his attention at last, and she marked how his stiff posture eased. "Yes, that's true. I say he died in the war, but we don't really know what happened. He sent us letters at first. When they stopped coming, we hoped his correspondence had just gone astray. We hoped he would return at war's end, but he didn't. Father's efforts to track down his fate came up empty. We were forced to accept that he had died fighting for the Union on the battlefield or from some illness."

The pain and sorrow in his face took her by surprise. The war had been over for nearly twenty years. Deciding to respond to the grief, rather than the reality, she repeated, more heartfelt this time, "Again, my condolences."

He looked away. "I was very young when he left. And we left, too, and lived in Monterey while Father sailed with the Pacific squadron. At least I have my memories of Uncle Jack to keep me company and the knowledge that he died for country and honor. He had a ready smile and an abundance of patience and affection for me. Since we lived side by side, I was always running between the two houses. Uncle Jack was a father to me."

Not a "second father," but a father.

"I am surprised you sold the property, since it apparently holds fond memories for you," Inez remarked.

The reticence returned. "Once Father passed, there was no reason to keep it. I prefer living in Oakland. It has a small Chinatown. It's nice." He stopped talking again.

Inez cast about, striving to keep the tiny trickle of words from drying up. Her gaze fell upon the opposite wall, which held a handsome pair of Oriental scroll paintings bracketing a shelf with a collection of black-and-gold lacquer boxes and what looked like Chinese snuff bottles. "So..." she said, clutching at straws. "China. Fascinating culture. You mentioned Chinatown. Have you an interest in the Orient?"

He finally smiled. "After the war, Father took a position with the Pacific Mail Steamship Company. We left California and moved to China. Mother and I loved it there." Now he sounded a little wistful. "As you say, a fascinating place."

"Your father held onto the house, both houses, even after you moved abroad?"

He nodded. "Father sold our home to Mr. Krause a few years ago but held fast to Uncle Jack's home. He never said why. Mother and I thought perhaps he hoped his brother would eventually return."

"Did your father know Mr. Krause?"

He nodded. "Mr. Krause sailed with Father for a while."

"Did you know him as well?" Inez was trying to gauge the depth of Taylor's acquaintance with the Krauses. Since he had mistaken her for Moira on their meeting just a few minutes ago here in the office, he clearly had never met the boarding-house owner—Inez was many inches taller and her hair color, skin tone, and physique were entirely different. However, if Mr. Krause had been a family friend, that might ameliorate any inclination Taylor might have to pursue the found fortune.

He shook his head. "Not at all." His eyes narrowed, and she got the impression he was finally "seeing" her. "When Mr. Upton told me about the gold, I was astounded. One hundred twenty-dollar gold pieces? Truly? He told me they were in the wall space between the two kitchens but didn't go into any details. How did they come to be there? How were they found?"

Inez opened her mouth to explain, then hesitated. Did Taylor know that Moira intended to convert his beloved uncle's home into a boardinghouse? About her plans to subdivide rooms, add water closets and gas lighting, and replace the dated wallpaper? Inez sensed he might not view such changes in a positive light. He had sold quickly, true, but remarked on his fond memories.

Inez glanced at the clerk, hoping for a distraction, and found him staring at her and Taylor. Caught eavesdropping, he at least had the grace to blush. He cleared his throat and said, "Yes, Mrs. Stannert? May I help you?"

The rumble of voices in the inner office grew louder, angrier.

The door flew open. Upton marched out and pointed a finger at Taylor. "Not a word!" he said. Taylor rocked back in his chair, looking shocked.

Upton continued, "Don't say another word to her." The finger now stabbed at Inez. She bristled. "Not a word to any of them!" That finger now waved wildly, first toward the clerk behind his desk, then toward Buckley, striding out of the office, then around the room in general. "We are leaving. Now. I shall explain when we are away from here."

Taylor stood and looked at Inez. "It was a pleasure meeting you, Mrs. Stannert."

"No, indeed it was *not*," snapped Upton. "I told you the two women were taking advantage of your haste to sell and here's the proof! If you had held onto the property—"

"What we uncovered in the wall would have stayed in the wall," said Inez, unable to keep silent. "The gold and the body would have remained entombed, and no one would have been the wiser." She saw Taylor's expression and stopped.

"Body? What body?" He looked from Inez, to Buckley, to Upton. "*What* body?"

One mutton-chopped cheek twitched visibly. "Not here," Upton said through gritted teeth. "I'll explain later."

He yanked open the hallway door as Taylor said, voice rising, "What haven't you told me, Mr. Upton?"

Upton hustled him out of the office.

The door slammed shut. Inez turned to Buckley. "Should I be concerned?"

He shook his head. "Sound and fury, signifying nothing. Do not let it worry you."

"Since that is what Macbeth said as Birnam Wood marched and his world collapsed, I am not reassured."

Buckley smiled faintly, but the frown lines on his brow remained. "Upton is being a fool. Probably trying to impress his client." He stroked his beard and added, "Sherman Upton is out of his depth in trying to argue personal property law. And he knows it."

Inez sighed and gathered her locked carpetbag from the

table. "I should be on my way. I have no doubt that I have taken up much more than five dollars' worth of your time."

He smiled. "Between the mystery of the gold and the corpse in the walls and Upton's hysteria, this has been an interesting interlude. Quite out of the ordinary, which I appreciate. I feel fully compensated by the entertainment." He hesitated. "I should like to accompany you when you leave here. I feel honor-bound to ensure that you and the gold arrive safely at your destination. Upton's client had a certain lean and hungry look about him."

"And now you quote Julius Caesar. Do you think young Mr. Taylor is a Brutus in disguise and may attempt to stab me on the city streets? It's not the Ides of March yet. Besides, I did not see 'lean and hungry.' More hangdog, whipped puppy."

"I would disagree. In any case, please do me the favor of humoring your most humble attorney in this matter," said Buckley.

Inez balked at his avuncular attitude, but she reminded herself that back in Leadville she never took the saloon's weekly receipts to the bank without the company of a trusted male companion hauling a very visible rifle. Now, as then, caution was required when carrying large sums of money about. Besides, her pocket revolver was in the apartment, still under her pillow. It had never occurred to her to bring it with her to a conference with a lawyer.

She said, "Very well," and surrendered the heavy carpetbag to his waiting hand. Buckley nodded approvingly, went to his rolltop desk, and extracted an older model Smith and Wesson. He slid it into his pocket, and they set out.

"So what of this corpse in the wall?" Buckley asked as they headed to Kearney.

"Mrs. Krause volunteered us to make burial arrangements once the coroner has finished his examination. But she wants the poor soul's name." Inez shook her head. "Unearthing his identity at this point is probably impossible." She slowed as the intersection of Pine drew closer. "I should have asked Mr. Taylor about the glass eye," she said, half to herself.

"Glass eye?" Buckley sounded bemused.

Inez glanced up at him. She had to admit that hiring Buckley was proving a plus. He could prove handy if Upton made a pest of himself or if further legal issues with the agreement arose. "That's right," she said. "When the skeletal remains tumbled out, the eye went rolling across the linoleum." She caught herself. "I mean no disrespect to the dead. Still, it was quite a shock to us all."

"All?" Buckley frowned. "So others saw the body and…?" He hefted the carpetbag.

"Oh, yes. Most of Mrs. Krause's boarders were there. It was to be a little party, but that's not what happened, of course."

"Who else?"

She hesitated, wondering why he wanted to know. *Well, what's the harm in telling him.* "Let me see. Upton showed but not Mr. Taylor, although he'd been invited. I met him for the first time just now, in your office. Let's see, who else was present? Mrs. Nolan, a mutual friend of Mrs. Krause's and mine. The Harrises, father and son locksmiths. They kept an eye on the place while it was unoccupied. And of course, the police and the detectives shortly after."

"That is unfortunate."

They had reached the music store. Inez turned and asked, "What do you mean?"

"As I explained to you earlier, what you have here is not a minor fortune. Men have been killed for far less in this town. And, not to alarm you, women as well."

"I shall be careful," she said, relieving him of the carpetbag.

"When the time comes to take it to the bank, I shall be sure to have someone accompany me."

She refrained from saying that she also would be sure to pocket her own revolver and have it loaded and ready.

Chapter Nine

Buckley opened the door for her, and Inez realized he intended to enter the music store. He confirmed this when he said, "I have passed by your store many times without venturing in, a lapse I shall rectify now, since we are here."

There was no graceful way she could enter, turn around, and shut the door in his face. *After all, suppose he ends up buying something?* The lawyers who came to D & S House of Music and Oriental Curiosities often seemed to have the discretionary income to indulge in the more high-end goods. Too, the display of Oriental art in the anteroom of Buckley's office indicated an interest in collecting. She didn't peg him as the musical type, however. To check her hunch, she asked, "Do you play an instrument, Mr. Buckley?"

"Not a single solitary note," he said cheerfully. "Complete tin ear. The best I can do is whistle 'Sweet Betsy from Pike.'" He drifted to the side to inspect a Chinese bronze figurine of a woman holding an urn. "Very nice," he said.

Thomas Welles joined them. Mindful of the carpetbag she

clutched and its contents, she decided to hand Buckley off to her manager. She introduced the two men, then turned to Buckley. "Mr. Welles will take excellent care of you. If you have any questions Mr. Welles cannot answer, we have an expert on staff who can help you."

After shaking Buckley's hand, Welles said to Inez, "A quick word, Mrs. Stannert." They stepped to the side, and Welles lowered his voice. "You have a visitor. She arrived just a short while ago and is waiting in the back. Said she had to speak to you as soon as possible and asked when you'd be in. I told her I didn't know." There was a polite pointedness to his statement.

Inez winced, thinking that she really had to keep Welles better informed of her schedule. "Very well. Her name?"

"Mrs. Krause."

Inez raised her eyebrows. She had intended to swing by Moira's after securing the coins in the store safe and discuss the best place to deposit the money as well as the girls' proposal to study and spend the night together. It appeared that they would be having that conversation sooner rather than later.

Welles added, "She saw the lesson room and asked to wait in there. I checked that the door to your private office was locked."

Inez nodded, glad of Welles's thoroughness.

She bade her adieu to Buckley and hurried through the showroom to the rear of the store, a walled-off section that ran the width of the building. The space was large enough to house Inez's private office on one side, a middle "business" area holding a large round table for meeting with suppliers and associates, and the lesson room where Inez taught piano at the other end. Carpetbag in hand, she opened the door leading to the store's back rooms and stepped into the meeting area. Halting notes from Stephen Foster's "Beautiful Dreamer" filled the air. Behind the glass wall of the lesson room, Moira sat at one of the two uprights, head bent over the keyboard, picking out the melody and harmony. Inez set the carpetbag on the round table, walked up to the glass, and tapped on it with her gloved knuckles. Moira lifted her head, startled. Inez observed she was wearing a simple brown suit, complete with lace cuffs and a small brown felt hat with a tiny blue feather. Clearly, she had come from somewhere she felt required dressing in her Sunday best. And clearly from her expression she was not looking forward to telling Inez whatever it was she had to say. Inez wondered if Charlotte had already asked her mother if Antonia could come over. Perhaps Moira had said no and was here to explain.

Inez opened the door to the lesson room and said, "Let's sit out here, at the table. I am glad to see you, as I intended to seek you out later. I have good news to share." Inez figured that her recapture of the found money could only be construed as good news.

Moira closed the fallboard and rose, gathering up a small brown purse that matched her outfit and fawn-colored gloves. "I hope you don't mind that I waited in here. It's been a while since I had time to sit at a piano. 'Beautiful Dreamer' was one of my husband's favorite songs. I would play, and he would sing. He had a wonderful baritone." Her voice faltered, and she looked away.

Inez gave Moira a beat to compose herself, then said, "The new house has a very nice parlor grand piano, although it is older. I am certain I could find a buyer for it unless you'd prefer to keep it where it is."

Moira shook her head. "I have no need of a second piano. I have a serviceable upright that the boarders occasionally play. I don't have the time."

Inez recalled the upright piano in the cozy, informal parlor by the dining room. "No need to decide now," she said, leading

Moira to the round mahogany table. After they were both seated, she continued, "My news involves the coins. I retrieved them from the police and have them here." She indicated the carpet-bag on the table. "What did you want to speak to me about?"

Moira bit her lip, then seemed to gather her resolve. "I know you are not particularly interested in the identity of the poor soul who was boarded up in the wall."

"Now, Moira, I am not bereft of compassion." Inez had to admit, but only to herself, that what she felt was more curiosity than sympathy for the unknown deceased.

"I cannot let him go unnamed to a pauper's grave. It's not right." She lifted her chin slightly. "So, I hired an investigator to find out who he is."

Inez leaned forward, the carpetbag momentarily forgotten. "You *what*?"

"I explained the situation to him. He said it was a most unusual request. We negotiated a flat fee, very reasonable. After I signed his contract, I was answering his questions about who owned the house previously and details about the sale, and, of course, your name came up. At that point, he strongly suggested that I tell you about my hiring him. He said he knows you."

That sealed it. "Let me guess. You probably spoke to Mrs. Nolan, and she recommended Mr. de Bruijn at the Palace Hotel. That is who you hired."

The look on Moira's face told Inez she was right.

Inez closed her eyes, and tried to rein in her frustration and, yes, her anger at having control over the situation slip from her fingers. "You should have consulted with me first," Inez finally said. "If I knew this matter was of such import to you, I would have—"

Moira shook her head, which was just as well since Inez wasn't certain what she would have done, short of tried to talk her out of pursuing this particular course of action. "No, Mrs. Stannert. I am taking this on as my personal responsibility. I will pay the costs from my share of the money. Once Mr. de Bruijn delivers the man's name to me, I will pay for a proper burial and headstone. Speaking of such," she looked down at her hands, fingers tightly laced together on the table top. "Mr. de Bruijn would like to examine what was retrieved from the wall. Not just the…remains but the clothes and the gold. He thinks they might hold clues to the man's identity."

"He does, does he?" Inez's mind raced. If nothing else, maybe she could get ahead of de Bruijn, see what was to be seen, and draw her own conclusions before he had a chance to get too far into his investigation. She could perhaps direct the narrative with Moira before de Bruijn marched in with his "the whole truth and nothing but the truth" way of doing things. Not that Inez was averse to telling the truth, but she might nudge it one way or the other. Plus, once de Bruijn turned his attention to the case, who knew what Pandora's Box he would pry open and how it might affect the ownership of the coins. "I doubt there is anything that will shed any light on the topic. The corpse and its clothes are with the coroner, and the money is just money. The canvas bag hasn't any identifying marks. What could he possibly hope to learn from a pile of coins?"

Moira's face settled into the stubborn expression Inez had seen before. "Nevertheless. It will not do any harm to let him look. Would you prefer I take the money to him?"

"No!" An image of Moira carrying a minor fortune through the crowds on Market Street flashed through Inez's mind. Inez pulled herself together. "I will put the money in the store safe, and Mr. de Bruijn can come view it here. But we should decide what bank to deposit it all in—"

Moira was shaking her head again. "No banks."

"Whyever not?"

"I don't trust banks." Her hands balled into fists, then she opened them and set her palms flat on the table. "Why do you think I came to you when the opportunity to buy the house arose? I would never turn to a banker for a loan. All they do is ruin good people who are only looking for help. I'd rather take the coins and bury them back in the wall."

"Moira, this is ridiculous. I have several accounts with different banks in town. We could go to the Bank of California on Monday and talk to my banker there."

Moira glanced away, mouth set in a straight line, then back at Inez. "Mr. de Bruijn also said I should consider getting a lawyer."

"He *what*?"

She looked down at her little purse, then back at Inez. "It has to do with the two houses being joined like they are. He said that it is possible I legally have sole ownership of the gold."

Inez returned her gaze. "Surely, Mrs. Krause, you do not want to bring lawyers and their exorbitant fees into the mix." She allowed an ominous edge to creep into her tone. "After all, we are business partners. Let's not let a good arrangement dissolve into acrimony. We are on the same side."

Moira nodded emphatically. "I immediately told him I would do no such thing. It would be a grave disservice to our trust in each other after all you've done for me and all we've been through. I could not have bought the house without your help. I am forever grateful and in your debt. Oh, I should add he made the suggestion before he heard who my business partner is. Once I told him, he said he has nothing but the highest regard for you and your integrity."

Inez smiled tightly, wondering if, after all the deals she had struck over the years and all the countless hours she had spent at the poker table and behind the bar reading people, seeking their tells, their weaknesses, and their strengths, she wasn't about to be outdone by a young boardinghouse keeper of "meek and mild demeanor."

"I am glad you have such faith in me," said Inez, telling herself she must not underestimate Moira in the future. "I will store the gold here in the safe, for now."

Moira said, "Thank you," and stood. "So, you will speak with Mr. de Bruijn? Since you know each other."

"Oh, I will certainly speak with him," said Inez grimly.

"Excellent! And Charlotte told me that Antonia offered to help her with her numbers. Perhaps you both would join us for dinner tonight? And Antonia could spend the night?"

"Ah, yes. Antonia mentioned this to me. As long as Antonia gets her chores done this afternoon, I will allow it. And we would be glad to join you for dinner. Thank you."

"Good! Charlotte is so looking forward to spending time with Antonia. It's wonderful the girls have taken to each other. I cannot help but think the relationship will benefit them both."

"I agree." At least Inez fervently hoped that would be the case. At first, she had wondered if Antonia's wild ways might rub off on the well-behaved Charlotte. Now, she wondered if Charlotte, like her mother, might be less compliant than she appeared.

As soon as Moira left, Inez unlocked the carpetbag and pulled out the canvas sack. She weighed it in her hands. A clue in the coins? Could there be?

She spilled the currency out of the bag in a golden river of metallic music upon the table.

She turned over the sack. Both sides were completely unremarkable.

Next, she turned her attention to the coins themselves, in all their glittering glory. Viewing them now, she realized they all had the same uniform sheen. None showed the patina of age or the dull edges of wear. Inez picked up one coin, scrutinizing it closely, and then another and another.

Could it be?

With growing incredulity, Inez smoothed them out in a single layer and turned them over so all were heads up. She then surveyed the small army of Lady Liberty profiles, all gazing left.

"Damn," she said softly.

All of the coins, without exception, looked new. And all were stamped the same year: 1863.

Chapter Ten

Antonia wasn't sure what was going on, but one thing was for sure: Mrs. S had something on her mind.

After school, Antonia had come to the store without "dilly-dallying," just like she'd promised. Her only detour had been to deliver a hastily composed thank-you note to Mrs. Nolan. As soon as she got to the music store, Antonia started her chores without even being asked. She didn't want to give Mrs. S any reason to say she couldn't go to Charlotte's house that night. Her first chore was dusting all the store's glass cabinets and the big grand piano that sat in the middle of the room. She wasn't allowed to dust anything else, because Mrs. S was afraid she might smack one of the instruments hanging on the walls with the feather duster and knock it off its peg or maybe knock over a Chinese vase.

The Chinese things were expensive and valuable Mrs. S told her again and again. Breaking one was like taking a hundred-dollar bill and burning it up. Antonia found it hard to believe it cost that much to buy one of those vases, even though some of them were fancy, with birds and deer and flowers painted on them. Whenever she dusted, if Mrs. S wasn't nearby, then sour-faced Mr. Welles was right at her elbow, muttering don't touch this and don't touch that.

After the dusting, she swept the plank floor with a broom and ran the carpet sweeper over the rug where the big piano was. Mrs. S usually nagged her to be sure to get under the piano with the sweeper. But not today.

Instead, when Mrs. S came out from the back of the store, looking distracted, she just nodded to Antonia. Then she headed over to John Hee and Mr. Welles, who were talking by the sheet music shelves. Antonia pushed the carpet sweeper toward the back of the store, intending to dump the dust out the back door into the alley. She slowed as she passed the three grown-ups. Through the clackety-clack of the rollers, she heard John Hee say, "The attorney, he speak Chinese very well."

Mrs. S said, "Hmmm. Interesting. Unusual, but after all, he's had a practice in the city for decades. Perhaps he has had Chinese clients. And he collects Oriental art. So he bought the figurine?"

After Antonia flung the dirt into the alley, she tucked the carpet sweeper into its corner and moseyed back out in time to hear Mr. Welles say, "I didn't see any problem with him opening an account. You think he's a shyster who won't pay his bills?"

Mrs. S frowned. "He's probably fine. But do let me know if he returns." She stopped. Her head turned, and she pinned Antonia with a look that told Antonia she'd been caught listening.

Whoops.

Mrs. S said, "Antonia, we have been invited to dinner at Mrs. Krause's boardinghouse, and you can spend the night with Charlotte. Go along now to the apartment and pack your things in your valise. I'll be there presently."

"Yes, ma'am!" Antonia grabbed her book bag and slunk to the door, aware of the silence and weight of eyes behind her. She reached for the knob and Mrs. S added, "Good job on doing your chores without being asked." Antonia said again, "Yes, ma'am!" remembering to add, "Thank you. And after school I gave Mrs. Nolan a thank-you note too." She pulled the door open. The bell above the door uttered a grumpy *clunk* and croaked out the same strangled sound when it shut behind her. Out on the sidewalk, Antonia exhaled with a whoosh and wandered to the corner. She hooked a hand on the lamppost and spun around it a few times before stopping to look up Pine, which got steeper and steeper heading toward the ocean. She hung onto the post and watched a streetcar climb the hill.

How did the poor horses keep going up and down the hills all day, pulling carloads of people, without falling over in a heap on the street? Of course, sometimes they did, which was kind of exciting. Sometimes the horses even died right there, with the conductors trying to whip them to their feet, which was kind of sad. It was a tough life, being a horse in San Francisco, she decided. If she were one of them, she'd probably run away the first chance she got, as soon as they took the harness off her.

Her gaze landed on the store across the street that sold pet birds. A silly little almost-a-rhyme formed in her head: *Birds in cages, horses with traces, dusters on vases.*

Everyone had a job to do. That's what Mrs. S said.

According to Mrs. S, Antonia's job was to study hard, do well in school, and do her chores. But ever since they'd come to San Francisco, Antonia had felt restless. She wanted to be free, to escape the traces, break out of the cages, maybe even break the vases. Since she'd started reading *Treasure Island*, she couldn't stop thinking what it'd be like to find a secret treasure map, hop aboard a ship like the *Hispaniola*, and sail off to an island where she could fight the bad pirates, befriend the good pirates, and uncover a chest with doubloons or pieces of eight.

But that would never happen. She sighed into the cool, salt-laden city air. Girls didn't have adventures like that. Heck, boys didn't have adventures like that, except in books. Although they could grow up and become coppers, and detectives, and reporters. What would she be able to do? Mrs. S said she'd "find her way" as she got older, but Antonia didn't want to wait until then. She wanted more than school and chores and Mrs. Nolan's beef stew, and she wanted it *now*.

Well, at least she'd get to visit Charlotte tonight. And maybe after she'd helped Charlotte with her fractions, they could make up stories about pirates on the high seas and buried treasure and sword fights at sea.

Antonia spun around the post one more time and let go. She ran back down Kearney, past the music store with its big display window, to the door that led to the apartment above. Through the street door, up the staircase, two steps at a time, through the apartment door. Plenty of time to grab the valise and put in her nightgown, hairbrush, and stockings and underthings for tomorrow. And maybe she'd grab her copy of *Young Folks* magazine and read the latest installment of Jim Hawkins's adventures aloud to Charlotte before they went to sleep.

———

Antonia, who was sitting between Mrs. S and Charlotte at dinner, reckoned Mrs. Krause's fish stew was the best she'd ever tasted. Even better than Mrs. Nolan's, which was really saying something. She took a second helping and would've maybe taken a third, except Mrs. S shook her head and reminded her to save room for dessert.

When Mrs. S turned to talk to Master Edward—now there was a possible pirate, if ever there was one—Charlotte jabbed Antonia with one of her sharp elbows and whispered, "Ma had a big fight with Mr. Harris today, right before you got here."

"Who?"

"The old man who made the locks for the house next to us. He still has the only keys. Ma doesn't like that one bit." Charlotte wiggled a little. "Ma wants him to give her the keys and change the locks, but he said no."

"Why?" Antonia wasn't really all that interested, but it was better to talk to Charlotte than listen to Mrs. S talk to the captain about the weather.

Charlotte shrugged, then added, "And I think she had a fight with your aunt too."

Now that caught Antonia's attention. "With Mrs. S? What makes you think that?"

"Well, when I came home from school, Ma was watering her flowers on the front porch. She said she'd talked to your aunt, and you'd both come to dinner, and you'd get to spend the night! But her face was *mad*. Like this." Charlotte's almost invisible eyebrows drew together and her mouth turned down in a fierce frown.

"Maybe they argued about the gold," Antonia whispered back.

"Maybe. Maybe Ma wanted more. Two boarders are leaving. They told Ma they're moving out right away. They're afraid this place is full of bad luck because of the skeleton in the wall. That made Ma even madder. Even though she thinks it's bad luck too."

"Bad luck," Antonia breathed. She glanced at Mrs. Krause, sitting at the head of the table. She certainly wasn't doing a lot of smiling. And Mrs. S hadn't seemed too happy that afternoon either. Antonia wondered if they'd argued and if they had, whether it was about the gold or something else.

"And I've got a secret surprise to show you when everyone's asleep tonight," whispered Charlotte.

"A surprise? What is it?" Antonia's attention switched back to the younger girl.

Charlotte grinned a little. Since she still had a bit of a frown between her eyes, it gave her a strange look. "I can't tell you here, silly. It's a secret! What if someone else hears?"

"Charlotte, please pass the biscuits to Mrs. Stannert," said Charlotte's ma.

"Thank you, Mrs. Krause," said Mrs. S.

Well, thought Antonia, if they're still talking to each other and passing biscuits back and forth and saying please and thank you, whatever they argued about can't be *too* bad.

———

After dinner, Antonia said goodnight to Mrs. S, who gave her a hug and murmured, "Remember, best manners! Don't forget you have chores to do tomorrow," and left, leaving a lingering lemony-orange scent. Antonia and Charlotte went into Charlotte's room, which was just down the hall a bit from the kitchen.

Antonia tried to drill the younger girl on fractions. It was clear Charlotte was confused as to what a fraction was. For Antonia, who breathed numbers like they were air hardly without giving them much thought, it turned out to be harder to explain than she thought it would be. She finally swiped a copy of *The Morning Call* newspaper from the front parlor and cut its pages into pieces with Charlotte's little embroidery scissors. One sheet into two, another page into four, and another into sixteenths. After spreading out all the pieces, Antonia pulled three quarters together and said, "This is three-fourths." She placed the last quarter sheet with the rest and said, "Add one-fourth to three-fourths and you have…"

"One!" exulted Charlotte.

Antonia took away two quarters and said, "One-half plus…" She added three small sixteenth pieces.

"Plus three-sixteenths is…" Charlotte looked at the remaining sixteenth sheets, which Antonia had neatly arranged into quarters, and said tentatively, "That's eight little pieces plus three more. Uh, eleven-sixteenths?"

Antonia sat back on her heels. "That's right!" She added, "Teachers just want you to memorize the answers. They don't care how you get them. But if you get stuck trying to figure fractions out at home, you can always take another newspaper and cut it up like this. It works for multiplication too."

The bedroom door opened, and Mrs. Krause walked in with a water pitcher and two hand towels. "Time to get ready for bed, girls. I brought some warm water so you could clean up." She poured the water into the basin and gave each girl a towel. "I'll come back to say good night and turn down the lamp."

Antonia noticed that Mrs. Krause looked tired. *Really* tired. She wondered why there wasn't anyone to help Charlotte's ma. Even Mrs. Nolan hired a lady from Chinatown to help dust, sweep floors, and beat carpets.

"Cleaning up" ended with a lot of water splashed around the washstand and on the floor as Charlotte kept dipping her fingers in the bowl and flicking water at Antonia. "Stop it!" said Antonia, wiping a splatter off her face. She glanced down at her blue dress, which now had dark blue wet splotches. "I have to wear these clothes tomorrow!" She felt strange saying that, like she was a grown-up scolding Charlotte.

Charlotte stuck out her lower lip. "They'll dry."

"Yeah, but I don't want to go to bed with wet hair."

They had just pulled on nightclothes when Antonia heard floorboards creaking up the hallway. "Quick!" hissed Charlotte. They clambered into bed, the metal bedstead squeaking. Mrs. Krause entered, in wrapper and nightcap, her reddish-brown hair in a long braid over one shoulder. She said good night, kissed Charlotte on the forehead, turned down the lamp to the tiniest flicker, and left with the washbasin of used water. The door clicked shut behind her and the footsteps faded away. Antonia, who was facing the wall with its swirly-patterned wallpaper, felt Charlotte shift around next to her. The next thing she knew, she felt a tickly breath on her ear as Charlotte leaned over and whispered, "Don't go to sleep yet! I have to show you the surprise after Ma goes to bed."

Antonia wiggled around to face her. "How long is that?"

"Real soon."

"How will we know?"

"Listen!"

Antonia did and then realized what Charlotte meant. The girl's bed was up against the wall farthest from the kitchen, and apparently Mrs. Krause's bed was right on the other side. Antonia heard the gentle thump of a headboard against the wall and Mrs. Krause sigh. A few minutes later, soft, muffled snores leaked through the wall.

Charlotte heard it, too, because she bounced up out of bed and headed for the bedroom door, saying in a loud hiss, "Stay here!"

"Where are you going?" Antonia whispered, but Charlotte disappeared, leaving the door ajar.

Antonia heard the squeak of another door, saw the dark hallway lighten just a bit, and felt a cool breath of outside air, as Charlotte's voice drifted back into the room, "Puss, puss, puss!"

Hearing an overlapping chorus of faint meows, Antonia sat up. The distant door squeaked shut. And the gloom returned to the hallway, followed by the patter of approaching feet.

Charlotte reappeared in the bedroom with a cat under each arm. She nudged the door shut with her heel and came over to the bed. "Here!" She plunked the two cats on the quilt. "This is Lucky and Eclipse."

"Awww," Antonia held out a hand to the white cat with gray splotches. "Which one is this?"

"That's Lucky! Some hoodlum trapped him under a milk crate and left him in the alley behind our house when he was just a kitten. He's lucky we found him." Charlotte grabbed him up and gave him a fierce hug, which he didn't seem to mind a bit. She added, "We think his ma is a black cat that lives in the alley."

"And this one. What did you call him? He's pretty." Antonia tentatively stroked the second cat. Half his face was mostly black, and the other half was mostly orange.

"It's a she, and her name is Eclipse. My pa named her because she reminded him of an eclipse. That's when a shadow covers the moon. Or the sun. I forget which. Anyhow, she was born on Pa's ship, so she was a ship cat, but then he brought her home to Ma and me, and she became a land cat. Look! She has extra toes! That makes her even luckier than Lucky."

Antonia admired the multicolored cat and her extra toes. "Are they allowed inside?"

"Only at night. Ma usually lets them in before she goes to bed so they can hunt mice and spiders. But sometimes she forgets."

"I have a cat too," said Antonia. "Her name is Mia. She's gray with long fur. But she doesn't live with us right now. She's just a kitten. When she's older, maybe she can come live in the music store." *If I can talk Mrs. S into it.* Right then, Mia was staying with Carmella Donato, who owned the music store along with Mrs. S. Carmella was mostly at home, because her brother died and she was still in mourning. So, the deal was Mia lived with Carmella and Antonia visited. Part of Antonia's Saturday chores was to go to Carmella's and help with the baking. And play with Mia, of course. "Are Eclipse and Lucky the surprise you wanted to show me?" She scratched Eclipse between the ears and was rewarded with a purr and a head bump.

"Well, they *are* special, but I have something else to show you that's even better." Charlotte got out of bed, grabbed the oil lamp by the handle, and lowered her voice, "C'mon!"

Antonia cocked an ear toward the wall. Gentle snores wafted through, undisturbed. "Okay. I hope this is good."

"Oh, it is!" Charlotte stood by the door, dancing impatiently on tiptoes.

Antonia joined her, and Charlotte closed the door, saying, "Lucky and Eclipse have to stay in there. I don't want them following us."

"Following us where?"

Charlotte pattered up the hall and into the kitchen, with Antonia close behind. Antonia heard faint chicken noises from the backyard outside the kitchen as Charlotte grabbed a knife from the drainboard. Charlotte then crossed back to Antonia, opened a nearby door, and peered inside.

"Wait," said Antonia. "Where are we going?"

Charlotte turned and grinned. "On an adventure!" she said and stepped inside.

Antonia followed, curious. Charlotte had turned up the lamp, and Antonia could see they were in a large, walk-in pantry. The side walls had shelves all the way to the ceiling, with cans, jars, and sacks all lined up. The shelves were gone from the back wall, so it was just bare vertical boards with some sacks of flour on the floor. "What's so special about your pantry?"

Charlotte put the lamp on the floor and said, "Watch." She tugged a couple of the sacks aside. Antonia could now see that one of the boards close to the corner was uneven, with a slightly larger crack between it and the next board. It also had a split in it, with a chunk missing at the bottom, which left a little hole. Charlotte jammed her knife into the vertical space between the boards, wiggling it around. The edge of the broken board eased out, and she pulled on it. The board, which was about as tall as Antonia, nearly fell into her hands. She then pulled off the board next to it, which seemed just as loose.

Antonia breathed, "Wow!" The hole was now large enough to slide through, if you didn't mind squeezing sideways.

Charlotte grinned again. "Last night, when I let the cats in, Eclipse ran into the pantry and scratched around behind the bags. I think she was after a mouse—it probably went in that little hole at the bottom. I was looking at the board, because it was kind of busted, and I didn't want her to sneak through, and that's when I saw it was loose."

"So is this the surprise?"

"Yep! But there's more inside." Charlotte turned and wiggled through the opening. Once inside, in the dark, she looked like a small ghost in her white flannel nightdress. Her hand poked out the hole and waved impatiently. "Give me the light and come on."

Antonia did so. It was a tight squeeze, but she made it, with only a few wood splinters dusting the front of her nightclothes. When she got through, she peered around in the dim lamplight.

The space between the walls extended to her left and right, like a narrow hallway. Curtains of webs down nearly to her waist reflected the lamplight, blocking her view in either direction. In front of her was the rear of the big icebox blocking the hole to the other house. Antonia looked down. Bits of plaster covered the raw wood like snow. A darkish spot stained the part where she stood. The dead man's body had been right there, along with the gold. For years and years. It sent a shiver through the soles of her feet and her toes, a kind of delicious fear. Charlotte crouched, pointed to the right, and said, "Look."

Antonia bent down and looked. Beneath the thick webby mess, between the walls toward the back of the house, and only a few yards away, was a staircase—heading up.

She straightened up and looked at Charlotte in astonishment and admiration. "Stairs?"

"Yep! That's the surprise!"

"Where do they go?"

"I dunno. I decided I'd wait for you, 'cause we're blood sisters. Should we find out?"

Antonia shifted on her feet and thought. Abandoned house. Murdered pirate buried with a sack of gold. Hidden stairs. What waited at the top?

Maybe more hidden treasure?

She grinned at Charlotte. "Let's go, matey. But best we be quick about it. We wouldn't want the ship's captain—your ma—to catch us aboveboard before morning bells."

Chapter Eleven

Charlotte had the lamp. So, after they knocked away the cottony veils of web, getting the stuff all over their hair and nightgowns, she went first. Antonia followed, pretty much walking in the dark. She kept expecting her bare feet to step on a mouse or crunchy bug. A sneeze tickled the back of her nose. She clamped her nose shut with her fingers, trying to stop the sneeze from escaping.

Charlotte had moved away, and Antonia bumbled into one of the walls, stubbing a toe. She chanced taking her hand away, saying, "Wait up!" The sentence was punctuated with an explosive sneeze.

The lamplight jumped, and Charlotte yipped, "Sweet Jesus!"

Antonia blinked. When she and Maman had lived in a shack in Leadville's Stillborn Alley, Antonia had heard cussing that would've made even Jesus faint. And Mrs. S could really let loose when she thought no one was listening. But Charlotte, well, she was Catholic, and her ma was so prim and proper and all. Antonia figured Charlotte must've heard it from one of the boarders.

Lamplight blinded Antonia and brought her back to the passageway. "Hey!" She put up her arm to block the light.

Charlotte had returned and was shining the lamp into Antonia's eyes. "We gotta be quiet!" she said. "If anyone finds us, there'll be heck to pay."

"I know." Antonia pushed the lamp away from her face. "D'you think I sneezed on purpose?"

Charlotte looked down at Antonia's feet and said, "What's that?"

Something round glimmered by her left foot. A piece of glass? Or…"Gold," she breathed. She bent and picked up a coin.

Charlotte said, "Lemme see!" and grabbed it from her hand.

Antonia took that moment to seize the lamp. "Then gimme the light." She adjusted the flame a little higher and both girls bent their heads over the coin in Charlotte's palm.

"Piece of eight!" said Charlotte excitedly.

Antonia shushed her. "No it's not. Pieces of eight are silver. This is gold. Like those coins that were with the dead man."

"How d'you know it's like the other coins? Maybe this is a new one! Maybe there's a trail of gold, leading up the stairs to a treasure chest!" Charlotte's hand closed into a fist around the coin. "Let's go!"

"Okay, just keep it down. You're too loud."

"You're the one that sneezed!"

They returned to the stairs, Antonia holding the lamp low so they could see the floor and their feet. It sure looked like mice had been in the walls at some point. And spiders too. Antonia brushed aside a shriveled blob of web caught on the lamp chimney.

The two girls stopped at the bottom of the stairway and looked up. The steps were steep and narrow, with a handrail attached to one wall. They didn't look rickety, but under all that dust, who knew for sure? Antonia wondered if they would creak and how loud. Or if a board would crack and break. Well, someone had used them before, even if it was a long time ago. That set Antonia thinking. There had to be a secret door back toward the front of the house in one of the walls. After all, whoever used the secret staircase sure didn't break in through the back wall of the pantry.

Charlotte nudged her in the back. "What're you waiting for? Go on."

"Why me? You're smaller and lighter. Maybe you should go first."

"You go first. You've got the light, and you're older."

Antonia didn't see why age made much difference, but she reminded herself she'd faced all kinds of danger—crazy folks with guns, drunken bummers with knives—and there probably wasn't anything like that ahead. Except maybe another skeleton, stabbed to the wall with a sword through his ribcage. She gave the stairs another look. No footprints. Just faint trails and marks, probably made by mice or rats. No one had been up or down in a long time. So no one was waiting at the top, ready to pounce on two girls in nightdresses.

Antonia took a breath of damp, dusty air, set a foot on the first narrow tread, gripped the old wood rail with her free hand, and pulled up. From one step to the next, with Charlotte bumping her in the back with her head when she followed too closely.

"Stop it!" whispered Antonia.

"Go faster!" Charlotte whispered back.

Then Charlotte pointed. "What's that?" Something glimmered, a dim shimmering, above and ahead of them.

Antonia's first thought: *ghosts!* But she pushed it aside. She didn't hold with all the hooey of spirits wandering in the afterlife. When people died, they died, and they went into the ground, and the lucky ones got a headstone with their name. And that was that.

So, not a ghost. But what?

When they climbed closer, Antonia realized it was a window. A single, small pane, very grimy, about two hands wide. They reached a tiny landing at the top of the staircase and at the foot of another set of stairs, just as steep, heading up the opposite way. From the little platform, the window was just above eye level. Antonia used the sleeve of her nightdress to rub away some of the scum and peered out.

"What do you see?" whispered Charlotte, on tiptoes and leaning against Antonia's arm. "I want to see too!"

"It's too dark. I can't see anything." Antonia moved aside.

Charlotte put her nose against the pane. "Huh. I think I see the alley."

Antonia nodded. That made sense.

"C'mon, let's go up," said Charlotte.

The second set of stairs ended at another landing. In front of them was a wall with a metal ring in it.

"Huh," said Charlotte again.

Antonia shone the light around and spotted hinges. "It's a door." She handed the lamp to Charlotte and grabbed the ring. "This must be the doorknob." She tugged. Nothing happened, so she gave it a twist. The ring rotated stiffly, and she pulled. The door didn't budge.

She pulled harder. The door finally unstuck with a ripping noise and opened partway. Antonia thought the hinges were probably rusted and the door probably hadn't been opened in years and years. Charlotte inched around the door and said, "Look at this!" Antonia followed and gazed around.

They were in a long room, about twice as wide as Antonia was tall. Antonia guessed it ran along the back of the house.

Kind of like how the second-floor apartment she and Mrs. S lived in had a storage room that went the whole back length of the building. But this wasn't exactly a storage room, although there were some crates with their tops off stacked near the door they came in. They peeked inside a couple and only saw old straw packing, all matted and gritty.

The room had a rectangular table in the middle and six very dusty, uncomfortable-looking wooden chairs. A window, high above the table, let in only the darkness of night. A couple of framed pictures hung on the walls. The table had papers, two metal candlesticks with half-melted candles, and a wood case on it. The case was an odd shape, like a slice of pie but bigger. A big desk at the far end had an oil lamp on it and more papers and an old bottle of dried-up ink.

Charlotte turned in a circle. Shadows swirled and danced as the lamp spun. "D'you think there's any gold in here?" She sounded doubtful.

Antonia surveyed the room. It didn't look promising. "Maybe in the crates?"

Charlotte scrunched up her face. "I'm not gonna stick my hand in those."

Antonia agreed that it wasn't a pleasant prospect. "Let's look through the desk. Maybe we'll find something there." She still hoped to discover something that pointed to a pirate hideout.

They went over to the desk, which was set up such that a person sitting at it would be looking out at the room. It was huge, with a set of drawers on either end and a big space in the middle to scoot a chair in. Charlotte set the lamp on a corner of the desk, turned it up bright, and started opening the left set of drawers. Antonia stood in the spot where a chair would've been and shuffled through the papers on the desktop, growing increasingly frustrated. "The writing is all nonsense words," she grumbled. "Like this. *Ogzkeq.* What the heck is that?"

Charlotte kicked at the bottom drawer. "It's locked or stuck or something." She opened the one above it. "Empty." Then the next one up and said, "What's this?" She reached in and… "Gold!" she squeaked.

Antonia snatched the large gleaming disk from Charlotte's hand. Excitement gave way to disappointment. "This isn't gold. And it's not money or anything. It's too big."

"But it's round," Charlotte pointed out. "And heavy. And the right color. So, whatever it is, maybe it *is* made of gold."

"Maybe." Antonia weighed the object in her hand and examined it more closely as Charlotte circled around her to the righthand set of drawers. "It's like a big wheel with a smaller wheel inside it, joined in the middle," Antonia commented. "And it's got the alphabet around the edges of both wheels." She turned the small inner wheel experimentally, then held the object closer to the lamp. "There's some letters in the very middle, I think. But the paint's worn off." She turned it over and squinted. "There's a name on the back. F. Labarre?"

"It could be gold," Charlotte said again, stubbornly. "I found it. So it's mine." She grabbed it back.

"That's not fair," said Antonia. "You can't keep both the gold coin and this…thing."

Charlotte stuck out her lower lip, then looked away, her face hidden under a tangle of straw-colored hair.

Antonia pressed on. "After all, you wouldn't've come up here if I wasn't with you, right? And you asked me to go up the stairs first, and I did. And you couldn't've opened the door to this secret room all by yourself. It was stuck real tight. And we're mateys, right? Blood brothers, uh, sisters. Mateys always split the booty, fair and square."

"Oh, all right," grumbled Charlotte, "You can have this." She handed Antonia the disk and turned back to the desk drawers.

Antonia slipped it in the pocket of her nightdress, thinking she'd examine it more closely when she was home in her own room, and then wandered to the table. She bent over the large, scattered papers. Some were rolled up and fastened with string, some were flat. The one on top was held down by glass paper-weights on all four corners. The odd-shaped wood box sat in the middle of the sheet. "This looks like some kind of map," said Antonia. "It's got a compass on it. Tiny numbers all over the place." She moved the box to one side and read aloud, "Upper Part of San Francisco Bay, California." Excitement burbled up inside her. Could this be a map to treasure? There were some lines penciled on it, some circles, and arrows…

Charlotte came over with the lamp and said, "Look, out the window." And pointed.

Antonia looked up. The square wasn't black any more but a middling gray. Antonia wondered if it was moonlight. It couldn't be dawn already.

"Ma gets up sometimes afore the sun comes up and checks on me," said Charlotte. Her bottom teeth worried her top lip. "We'd better get back. Maybe you can stay an extra night? Think your aunt would let you stay another night? It's not a school night. Then we can come back and explore some more."

Antonia nodded. It was worth asking. And she'd really like to take a closer look at the map, see if she could figure it out. She wished she could take it with her, but it was way too big to fit in her valise, even if she rolled it up. "Okay. I just want to see what's in this." She pulled the wood box toward her. It was surprisingly heavy and scuffed and wrinkled the papers she dragged it over. Antonia unlatched a little silver latch and opened it.

Both girls gasped.

It was the most beautiful thing Antonia had ever seen—all shiny metal and glass, with big and tiny screws, little mirrors and lenses, all polished and free of dust. It had a graceful arc to the overall shape and the look of an instrument that did something very mysterious and precise.

"What is it?" breathed Charlotte. She leaned over the box and her breath misted one of the little glass pieces held in a special wooden holder along the side that also held a gold-colored cylinder.

"Dunno." Antonia cranked her head a bit to read the paper pasted on the inside of the case as Charlotte gingerly traced the metal arc that formed one edge of the instrument and the less burnished circles and part-circles of metal welded inside. Antonia read aloud, "Manufacturer of Nautical Instruments." Nautical instruments! A shiver of excitement ran across her shoulders. "Charlotte, it's a sextant! It's used on ships to help navigate on ocean voyages. It's used by sailors and…"

She and Charlotte looked at each other wide-eyed.

"Pirates!" whispered Charlotte.

Antonia closed the box reluctantly. Her fingers lingered, itching to pick it up and take the instrument with her. But it was safer here, hidden away, where no one knew it was except for the two of them. "I'll see if I can come back tonight. Maybe you can show your Ma how good you're getting at your fractions, and she'll say I can come back."

"Maybe I'll tell her there's a test on Monday I almost forgot about," said Charlotte, "and we need to do some more drills."

Antonia picked up the lamp, "Okay, let's go, but let's walk along that side." She headed to the wall opposite the window. She figured if there was a door that led from the secret room into the empty house, it'd have to be there.

She held the lamp up and trailed her other hand along the wall's vertical planks.

"What're you doing?" Charlotte asked.

"Looking for—" Her fingers snagged on an uneven edge, a panel that stuck out a little more than the rest. Her fingertips moved down the edge to the chair rail above the wainscoting, wandered along the top, and finally dipped into an unobtrusive handhold behind the wooden trim and the plank wall. Her fingers curled into the grip, and she grinned at Charlotte. "I was looking for...this." She pushed a lever at the bottom of the hold, and the nearly invisible door swung inward.

Chapter Twelve

"Wake up, sleepyheads."

Antonia opened bleary eyes, momentarily confused by the unfamiliar voice that interrupted her sleep. She couldn't remember where she was until she saw Mrs. Krause standing in the doorway to Charlotte's bedroom, holding a water pitcher and an empty washbowl.

It seemed to Antonia as though she and Charlotte had just squirmed back through the gap in the pantry, repositioned the planks and flour sacks, and tiptoed back to Charlotte's room. They'd fallen into bed, pushing aside Lucky and Eclipse, who were clearly sleeping on the job. Not that Antonia blamed them for curling up on Charlotte's quilt instead of chasing down mice.

"Girls, it's past time to rise," said Mrs. Krause.

Antonia twisted around to face the wall, wondering if she could pretend to be asleep a while longer. The mattress beneath her lurched as Charlotte sat up next to her with a bounce.

"Did we miss breakfast?" asked Charlotte, sounding as wide awake as if she'd gotten a full night's sleep. "I hope not."

She poked Antonia's shoulder. "Ma makes the best sourdough pancakes for breakfast. And we've got strawberry jam to put on them!" She turned back to her mother. "And bacon? Are we having bacon?"

Pancakes. Jam. Bacon.

Breakfast with Mrs. S was usually milk-and-sugar coffee and buttered toast. Sometimes it was just milk and bread and butter if they were in a hurry.

Pancakes! Jam! Bacon! Antonia's mouth watered. She sat up and rubbed her eyes.

Mrs. Krause was by the washstand, pouring water into the bowl. "There might be some bacon left if you dress quickly."

Charlotte hopped out of bed. Antonia followed.

Charlotte's ma turned to face them, continuing, "Now, after breakfast—" She stopped, and her eyebrows drew together. "What on earth happened to your nightclothes? And your feet!"

Antonia glanced down. Her feet looked if she'd run down a dirt path without shoes, kicking dust all along the way, and her bedgown was similarly filthy from their nighttime adventures. Wide-eyed, Antonia glanced at Charlotte, who was just as grimy.

Charlotte, eyes fixed on her ma, piped up, "You forgot to let Lucky and Eclipse in last night. They were meowing at the back door really loud, and you were already asleep." Her words came faster and faster. "So Antonia and me opened the back door for them and then I wanted to show Antonia the chickens and Cluck, the rooster, in the backyard and then I opened the door to the coop to show her the baby chicks and Henrietta got out and we had to catch her and—"

"In the middle of the night?" Mrs. Krause sounded like she couldn't decide whether to be mad or dismayed. "Charlotte! Whatever were you thinking? Or were you thinking at all?"

Charlotte hung her head. "I'm sorry, Ma."

Antonia decided she should bear some of the burden. After all, she and Charlotte had sworn an oath. If one of them was to get caned or keelhauled by the captain, it was only right that the other would too. "I'm sorry, Mrs. Krause, ma'am. It's my fault. I asked Charlotte if we could go look at them. Y'see, we don't have chickens where we live. I just wanted to take a peek. I didn't mean to make any trouble."

Mrs. Krause, pitcher dangling from one hand, surveyed the two girls. "Honestly. How you two got so dirty just going into the backyard is beyond me. You look as if you were rolling around in the dust." She shook her head. "Charlotte, wash day isn't until Monday. You'll need to wash your nightdress yourself and hope it's dry by tonight."

"Can Antonia stay over tonight too?" piped up Charlotte. "Please? I have a test on Monday, and Sister said I have to practice my arithmetic if I'm going to pass."

Mrs. Krause peered at Antonia dubiously. Antonia tried to look contrite, hopeful, and responsible, all at the same time. "Charlotte's fractions are improving. I think you'll be proud of her progress." The words slipped out sounding just like Persnickety Pierce, her teacher at Lincoln School.

Charlotte's ma hesitated, her mouth twisted into a slight frown. Antonia held her breath, thinking she looked more worried than mad.

Finally, Mrs. Krause sighed. "Well, if your aunt says it is all right with her, I suppose." She turned to her daughter. "But, Charlotte, you have your regular Saturday chores to do first."

Charlotte grinned at Antonia. "Today is chicken day. I pluck the chickens for dinner after Ma takes her hatchet and—" She chopped at the side of her neck with the edge of her hand, crossed her eyes, and stuck out her tongue. "Ma's real fast. The chickens don't even have time to screech and then their bodies run around for a while after their heads are off. But Henrietta's a good layer, so she won't get the axe, ever."

"That's enough!" Mrs. Krause snapped. "Honestly, Charlotte, no wonder the nuns say—" She stopped and looked at Antonia. "I imagine you have chores to do today as well."

Antonia nodded vigorously. "Oh, yes, ma'am, Mrs. Krause." Her Saturday chores were to help Carmella Donato with the baking and play with her own cat, Mia. She didn't mind those chores at all, which usually ended with her bringing back a bag of cannoli, sfogliatelle, or other Italian pastries for her and Mrs. S. But the rest of her Saturday chores were not much fun. At the apartment, she had to clean out the stove's ash box, trim all the lamp wicks and wipe down their glass chimneys, and finally dust and sweep the whole apartment and the stairs.

She thought she'd rather hack the heads off of chickens. At least that wouldn't be boring.

"Well, this all might work out for the best, then," said Mrs. Krause. She smoothed down her apron, went to the wardrobe, and began pulling out clothes for Charlotte. "It so happens I need to speak with Mrs. Stannert. Antonia, would you ask your aunt if she would come with you to dinner again tonight and if she would be able to stay afterward for a short while? I have an important matter I need to discuss with her."

Antonia's heart lifted. "Yes, ma'am. I'll be sure to tell her. Thank you, Mrs. Krause." She started plotting what she and Charlotte should do when they snuck back into the "Treasure House" that night and how they could escape detection the next morning.

Life was getting interesting, at last.

Chapter Thirteen

Inez's first thought on waking was to wonder how Antonia slept the previous night. Her second thought was there was much to do before she would have the opportunity to ask the girl herself. Inez had made sure Antonia understood that, after leaving the Krauses', she was to go directly to Carmella's to start her Saturday tasks. Inez trusted she would do so, since being with Carmella involved playing with her kitten and baking pastries.

Inez had her own Saturday routines, but she was setting them aside to deal with the issues she and Moira were facing.

First and foremost, she wanted to corner de Bruijn and find out what he was up to regarding the identity of the body in the wall. She couldn't imagine he'd had much time to begin his investigations. Hadn't he said he was fairly busy when they'd spoken earlier? And really, who cared about the corpse, besides Moira? It had probably been sealed off for a decade or two.

Inez thought it would be wisest to do a little investigating herself and present her findings to Moira before de Bruijn uncovered whatever he might uncover. In this way, she might be able to steer Moira to a conclusion that would benefit them both. Inez knew de Bruijn was honest to a fault. No doubt, he would simply hew to the line—provide his findings to Moira—and let the chips fall where they may without considering the ultimate result.

She could not allow that to happen.

These reflections propelled her out of bed and into hasty preparations for the morning. The store wouldn't open until noon, so she had several hours before then. She paused in front of the mirror, hairbrush suspended in midair, as a thought struck her. Rather than storm de Bruijn's office yet again, perhaps there was a more congenial way to go about extracting information from him that would yield better results. She could almost hear her mother's voice, which she had not heard in well over ten years, murmuring, *You catch more flies with honey than vinegar.*

In fact, she might be able to catch him off his guard, if she played her cards right. He was probably expecting her to be in high dudgeon, which was certainly her initial impulse.

Yes...a little honey might be called for in this case.

She finished brushing and pinning her hair, attached a lace collar and cuffs—which were, as it happened, the color of honey—gathered her cloak and hurried down and out of the apartment. She walked past the music store's large display window, let herself into the empty store, and headed to the telephone. She buzzed the Central Station, asked for the Palace Hotel, and tapped her foot as the operator made the connection. In response to the front office query, she asked to speak to Mr. de Bruijn, third floor, adding, "Please tell him it's Mrs. Stannert." A few clicks and hisses, and his voice, smooth and unruffled, with a hint of curiosity floated through the static. "Good morning, Mrs. Stannert. To what do I owe the pleasure?"

Sidestepping his question, she said pleasantly, "Would your

schedule permit you to join me for breakfast in the Palace Hotel dining room this morning?"

"At what time?"

"In fifteen minutes or so? Is that enough time?"

"Certainly. I look forward to seeing you."

"And I you, Mr. de Bruijn." She hung up and turned her attention to the safe thinking she would not bring all the gold but a handful of coins as a token of her goodwill. A drop of honey to snare the fly.

———

He was seated and waiting for her in the American Dining Room when she arrived. The spacious public room, located off the main lobby of the immense hotel, could accommodate six hundred, and on this particular morning, it seemed every chair was occupied. Waves of conversation washed over her as the maître d' escorted her skillfully through the vast array of tables. The incandescent lighting sparkled off crystal and silver tableware. The immaculate white tablecloths and white-and-gold finish of the walls appeared all the more blinding in the sharp, modern lighting, adding to the optical dazzle. To Inez, the result was the visual equivalent of a shout, and with the hundreds of voices murmuring and turning over each other as she wove past table after table of diners, she felt almost dizzy. De Bruijn had risen from a table toward the back, and she sank gratefully into the chair the maître d' held out for her.

Once she was seated and she and de Bruijn had exchanged greetings, she plunged in. "I do wish Mrs. Krause had consulted with me before contacting you. After all, she and I are financial partners as regards the acquired building, so I do believe I should have been part of the decision to pursue the matter of, well, the discovery in the wall."

She related all this with a smile and as pleasantly as possible to indicate that she was not angry, no not at all, but was simply, calmly, presenting the facts of the situation.

De Bruijn gave her a look that said he wasn't fooled by her demure behavior in the least.

So much for honey over vinegar. Inez abandoned that approach and decided to present her grievances head on. "To be blunt, I was taken by surprise, entirely, and expressed some displeasure that she took this step without discussing it with me beforehand. When she told me she had engaged you to identify the—" A slight shake of de Bruijn's head alerted her to the waiter, who had appeared to take her order. She cleared her throat and ordered coffee, toast, and a three-minute egg.

After the waiter had withdrawn, de Bruijn said, "Mrs. Krause informed me about your business arrangement after I had agreed to take up the investigation, and we had signed the contract." The chatter of hundreds of diners and the clinking of cutlery on fine china almost drowned out his voice, and she leaned forward the better to hear him.

He continued, "At that point I was bound by the agreement to keep whatever information passed between her and me as confidential. I advised her to tell you directly. Clearly, she did, because here we are."

"Indeed. Here we are." She narrowed her gaze at him. "So, tell me, have I any say in what transpires from this point forward?"

"Mrs. Krause is my client. I suggest you ask her if she would agree to allow me to brief you on my progress and the results."

"I see." It was more or less what she had expected him to say. The thought of going to Moira "hat in hand" smacked unpleasantly of begging to attend a party to which she had not been invited. To say it did not sit well was an understatement. "And if she demurs?"

He spread his hands. "As you know, Mrs. Stannert, I value your observational skills. I have seen firsthand how you are able to keep your wits about you under the most trying of circumstances. You saw what occurred when the wall was dismantled and afterward. I'd like to hear from you, as a witness, what happened that night. I'd also like to know any other information you have gleaned that might aid this investigation. After all, I assume you'd like this case resolved as much as Mrs. Krause does."

Hanging unspoken in the air was the caveat that if she did *not* agree with this eminently sensible assumption, she should tell him. Now. Instead, Inez fixed him with a bland stare.

He continued, "Mrs. Krause gave me her interpretation of what happened that evening, of course. She told me that after she left, you stayed behind to deal with the police and work out the details. I will be talking to them as well but would appreciate hearing your version of what transpired before I do so."

What could she say besides, "Of course"? She ran him through the people in attendance and the order of events— leaving out her rather sharp exchanges with Detective MacKay, Detective Lynch's obvious surprise at finding her, once again, at the scene of a grisly find, and her critical opinions of lawyer Sherman Upton.

"So the seller was not present?" de Bruijn asked.

"No. Mr. Upton was there as Bertram Taylor's representative. Upton brought the final paperwork already signed by Mr. Taylor. All was in order, and Mrs. Krause and I signed before the demolition of the pantry wall."

"Was there anything else in the wall besides the remains and the money?"

"Well, it wasn't as if I dodged the bones on the floor to take a peek. Oh! There was a glass eye. I suppose you heard about that. Needless to say, we were all in shock."

"Did anyone search inside the wallspace afterward? The police, for instance?"

She thought. "Detective MacKay stepped inside briefly. I remember he complained that it was full of cobwebs but otherwise looked empty. And I am not certain, but Mr. Edward might have ventured a quick look at some point."

"So, at the end of the evening, everyone left, and the hole in the wall remained open?"

"Well, yes and no. Detective Lynch decided the gap should be sealed up but not permanently in case they wanted to revisit it later. So, the law, a couple of the boarders, and the locksmith's son moved a large icebox in front of the pantry blocking the entry. The icebox was this monstrous iron affair. I was surprised they were able to maneuver it."

"I would like to look around the inside of the residence. Arrange to see the site where the body was found. Who has keys to the building?"

"After the detectives escorted us out, I saw Mr. Harris lock the front door. I believe he was going to deliver the keys to Mrs. Krause at some point."

The coffee appeared before her, as if by magic, as did the toast and egg.

"Do you know if anyone has been in the house since then?" asked de Bruijn.

Inez tapped sharply on the egg in the porcelain cup and peeled back the top of the shell. She was pleased to see the egg was done to perfection, with a custardy white and a soupy yolk. Her plate of toast sat nearby. De Bruijn declined her offer to share the toast. She mentally shrugged. If he wanted to sit over his cooling coffee and watch her eat, so be it.

"Well, it happened only the day before yesterday, hardly more than twenty-four hours ago. As far as I know, no one has been back. At least, Mrs. Krause did not comment on such when I saw her last evening."

His eyes shuttered. Inez recognized it as one of his "tells," indicating he wanted to keep what he was thinking to himself. "Who is the locksmith?" he asked.

Inez swallowed a mouthful of toast. "Harris. The business is Harris and Son. I believe the father's first name is Joseph. The son is Paulie. Didn't Mrs. Krause tell you all this?"

"And the deceased was taken by the police to the coroner."

"Yes." She decided right then and there to pay a visit to the coroner as soon as feasible. Perhaps that very morning. "Speaking of," Inez took a breath, "Mrs. Krause told me you wished to examine the coins." She pushed her now empty dishes aside and opened her purse. "This is a sample. I was not about to bring it all. That would be neither practical nor prudent. However, I looked them all over, and they are all the same." She pulled out a small velvet bag that had originally held a tin of violin rosin and handed it to him.

He poured the few gold coins onto the tablecloth and turned them over, one at a time, inspecting both sides. "I would still like to examine the entire collection. And the bag they came in. I understand you are holding everything in your store safe."

"The bag is just an old, ordinary canvas bag with a tie. I'm not certain what you hope to discover from it."

"I cannot say until I see it. All the coins are the same, you say?"

She nodded and picked up her cup of now lukewarm coffee. "Every one of the hundred is a double eagle struck in 1863."

"This sample you brought were all minted in San Francisco as well."

She clutched her cup convulsively, almost splashing the dark liquid on the spotless tablecloth. "What?"

He pushed one gold piece across the table toward her. "Here, on the reverse, directly above the *N* in TWENTY. The *S* shows that this coin was struck here in San Francisco."

Inez squinted at the coin, silently cursing her modest far-sightedness and her reading spectacles, which presently sat on her desk at the music store. She said, "I did not notice that, I will admit." She held out her hand for the velvet bag.

He obligingly poured the coins back in and gave it to her. "When would be a convenient time for me to call?"

"Not today," Inez said, calculating rapidly. If her meeting with de Bruijn concluded in short order, she could visit the coroner, see if he had yet examined the remains, and weasel any infor-mation from him. She should have enough time before having to stop at Carmella's to report on the music store's business for the past week and gather up Antonia, who would no doubt be covered in flour and kitten scratches.

"Perhaps Sunday afternoon, if you are free," she said. "Although I would understand if you wish to wait until next week. I imagine you are very busy these days and probably much in demand by the hotel and its clientele?" She smiled, hoping the answer was yes and that identifying anonymous, long-deceased mortal remains was not his top priority.

He gave her one of his rare smiles, which always threatened to warm her heart to an unhealthy degree. "I stay busy."

"Well then. If I find out anything more about this mysterious business, I shall be certain to pass it along to you." *In due course,* she added to herself. The bill arrived for her breakfast. "It was a pleasure to see you this morning, Mr. de Bruijn."

"The pleasure is mine, Mrs. Stannert. I appreciate your will-ingness to help me in this matter."

Intending to pay for her meal, she reached for the check on the silver salver just as de Bruijn did the same, saying, "Allow me."

Their fingers brushed briefly above the small tray. The touch sent an electrifying buzz through her that caused her over-warm heart to pound a little harder. She hastily withdrew her hand. "Well, thank you, Mr. de Bruijn. I am not certain how much help I was."

A little stab of guilt accompanied her words—or did that feeling arise from a different quarter?—and she quickly added, "I shall look forward to seeing you tomorrow, if tomorrow suits. Say about three in the afternoon?"

Inez rose. De Bruijn did as well.

She added, "If something more important arises, I quite understand. Our little hidden wall mystery is but a small matter, I am certain, compared to the more urgent cases you no doubt have."

He smiled again. "Until tomorrow, Mrs. Stannert."

Chapter Fourteen

SATURDAY, MARCH 11

On her way out of the Palace Hotel, Inez stopped at the front desk and asked to see a current city directory. She knew from past experience the position of city coroner changed from year to year. Furthermore, post-mortem exams were sometimes conducted by the police surgeon or city physician before the deceased's remains eventually made their way to one of the city's undertakers. Inez had no idea where, in this process, the fellow whose bones fell out of the wall might be.

In any case, there was so little to examine, going directly to the coroner for information seemed best. Too, she had to admit that she was searching for reasons to go to the coroner rather than the police station. She had no desire to see Detective MacKay again and re-engage in verbal fisticuffs. Or bump into Detective Lynch, with whom she wanted to stay on good terms.

Inez paged through the directory to the section on city and county officers. Dr. Weeks was listed as the city and county coroner; the "Key to Public Offices" section provided his address. She was pleased to see the coroner's office was located on the corner of Sacramento and Webb—not far from the music store. That meant she could easily stop at her office on the way to his, put the coins back in the store's safe, and retrieve the papers showing she was part owner of the dwelling where the corpse was found, just in case anyone questioned her interest. Inez returned the directory, with her thanks, and glanced up at the large clock over the reception desk. It was hard to believe that consuming an egg and toast combined with the "short" discussion with de Bruijn had taken as long as it did. *Time's a-wasting.* She headed out, weaving past travelers and guests surging in and out of the hotel's entrance.

It was a fine March day for walking. The promise of spring was delivered in the warm sunshine that washed over her and brightened the stone, brick, and wood buildings of downtown. The slow passage of winter lingered on in the counterpoint coolness of the air. She strode briskly along, pondering what de Bruijn had discovered about the coins. Could all the coins have come from the San Francisco Mint? She had not closely studied the obverse of the gold pieces, a slipup on her part. Determined to be more mindful in the future, she decided to take a closer look at the canvas bag and its contents before he conducted his examination on the morrow.

She turned into the music store, breezed through to the office area, and stopped short on seeing Thomas Welles sorting through papers covering the surface of the round table. He glanced up, looking harassed, with bits of straw stuck to the sleeves of his jacket. "Say, Mrs. Stannert, have you seen the receipt for that shipment of figurines that arrived earlier this week? Several of them were broken when I opened the crate." He nodded to a wood box off to one side, its top boards removed and packing straw scattered about the floor. "Did you sign for them?"

Inez frowned, then remembered. "Oh, yes. I did." She had

been in a hurry to meet with Moira to discuss some of the final details of the property transfer when the delivery wagon had pulled up to the front of the store. John Hee—the store's expert on all objects pertaining to the Orient—was not about, so she had accepted the shipment, sight unseen, and directed the two delivery men to bring the crate to the back. She had tossed the receipt onto a stack of papers intending to tell John later. And then, she had promptly forgotten.

"I put it on the table," she added.

They both surveyed the welter of receipts, invoices, and what-all. Welles ventured, "Mrs. Stannert, would you like me to…do something with all this? Organize or file it for you?"

"I'll take care of it tomorrow," she assured him. "I have been occupied with other matters, which should resolve soon."

His expression implied he doubted her last statement, but all he said was, "I'll let John know what I found when he returns. He heard a pair of scroll paintings were available for a song in Oakland's Chinese quarter." He shrugged. "Not how he put it, but that's the gist."

"Excellent! And, yes, please tell him about the broken figurines. He'll know what to do. I should be back before closing." With that, she hurried into her private office to deposit the coins with the others in the safe and withdraw the deed for the house. With a nod to Welles, who was extracting bits of broken porcelain from the crate, she left. As she walked up Kearney Street to Sacramento, she sighed. It was probably time to turn more of the handling of the store's finances over to Welles. She had resisted, wanting to keep a finger on the pulse of the business since she was seldom available to greet and help customers and clients. But her attention was being increasingly consumed by her personal ventures, in which she endeavored to support women bettering their own small businesses.

She turned on Sacramento and proceeded past a wide stone two-story building, which occupied a large swath of property extending to tiny Webb Street. She stopped at the corner and examined a large sign mounted above the first story proclaiming "NATHANIEL GRAY'S COFFIN WAREROOMS." A smaller sign above the entrance read "N. GRAY & CO., UNDERTAKERS." The address matched the city coroner's. She assumed this meant the coroner worked hand in glove with the resident undertakers. Inez squared her shoulders and pushed through the door.

A gentleman dressed in the usual black with a fashionably tall collar hurried forward and asked if he could help. He seemed fractionally disappointed when she asked for the coroner's office. He led her past a display of "Barstow Metallic Caskets" to an inconspicuous side door in the rear of the building. Glad she didn't have to wander clueless through the "warerooms," Inez knocked and entered when invited by a male voice on the other side of the panel. A young man stood from behind a messy desk as she approached. She noted his drawn face, the jacket slung over the back of his chair, and his wilted collar. He introduced himself as Mr. McConachie, adding, "I work for the coroner." It was clearly a gentle prompt in case she had mistakenly wandered in while shopping for a casket for a recently departed loved one.

She gave her name, explained her business, and added, "I had hoped to find out if there was any information about the remains that were found entombed in the wall."

"Oh, yes." McConachie scrubbed his unruly blond hair, which could have used a decent pomade, and surveyed the chaotic mess of papers on the desk before him. Inez was uncomfortably reminded of the sorry state of the office table in her music store. "Excuse me, Mrs. Stannert. It's been a long night for us. A bit of a riot down by the docks last night, and we were

called in. The coroner and I have been here since midnight dealing with the, ah, aftermath. He and the city physician just left a
while ago for a spot of a meal. But I do recall this case, since it
came in just a couple of days ago and was so odd." He looked at
her, tired eyes hesitant. "Er, are you a relative of the deceased?"

"What? Oh, no. I am part owner of the building where the
poor fellow was found." She wondered if McConachie would
demand proof of ownership, but he only nodded.

She continued, "We, that is, Mrs. Krause and I, recently
bought the house. And, well, as good Christian women, we are
taking on the responsibility for proper burial of this unfortunate soul." She decided that, much as she'd tried to dissuade
Moira from assuming that particular mantel of responsibility,
it wouldn't hurt to offer it up in the current context. "Assuming
no one steps forward to claim him," she added. "Can you tell
me if there is any information on the identity or the means of
death?"

The young man looked down at the flood of papers before
him. "The official report is here somewhere. We still need to
deliver it to the detectives in charge, not that they have been
clamoring for it, and sign off on the death certificate. But I can
tell you in general what the findings were, if you'd like." He
looked up at her sheepishly. "I don't read all the reports, but this
was an unusual case and caught my attention."

"Yes, please."

"Do you want me to sum it up? I gather you are not a physician." He was polite but obviously thought this was a reasonable
assumption. "The details might be a little much for...feminine
sensibilities."

Inez thought of grisly scenes she'd witnessed in the past, of
the dead and the dying, the maimed in agony, and said, "Details,
please. I am not a physician but assure you I am quite able to

handle whatever you have to say." She gave him a small, matter-of-fact smile.

They locked eyes. Inez's gaze didn't waver as she waited for him to respond. He finally nodded and looked away, as if retrieving the facts from his memory. "Very well, then. To begin, since the skeleton fell out of the wall and onto the floor, we have no idea what its condition was while it was in place. A glass eye, so clearly some past trauma there, although no old injury was apparent in the orbit, that is, the eye socket. What interested us most was the damage to the hyoid bone. That's a horseshoe-shaped bone in the front of the neck, between the chin and the thyroid cartilage. In the living, it is attached with ligaments, but once the flesh falls away, so does the hyoid. In life, it isn't easily damaged, given its position, so a broken hyoid is often indicative of strangulation or throttling. Although I do recall a case where a hyoid was broken from a kick in the neck by a horse, so we cannot say for certain how the damage occurred. We also cannot say whether the damage occurred antemortem or postmortem. Although we can assume, I think, that he was dead when interred."

"If he had been living and breathing, I doubt he would have allowed himself to be walled up," Inez observed. "You said 'he.' So, conclusively a man?"

McConachie nodded.

"His age?"

He shrugged. "Not young, not advanced in years. Bones fully formed. Teeth worn, two missing on the left in the back, top and bottom. Probably late thirties or so when he died."

"How long had he been in there, any idea?"

He sighed and finally lowered himself into a worn office chair, which gave a weary creak. He gestured for her to sit as well. "There was some uncertainty about that. Probably at least ten years. Perhaps longer. Fifteen? The most interesting thing was the clothes, or what remained of them. They at least gave us a lower boundary on the date in question."

Inez tried to dredge up her recollection of what she saw that night in terms of attire. All she could say for certain was he'd been wrapped in a dark coat. But then her attention had been diverted by the glass eye and the gold. "And what is that?"

The assistant stood up. "The personal effects are in the back. Since you have taken responsibility for laying him to rest, I suppose I could show them to you."

He disappeared through a door, reappearing with a dark bundle before Inez had much of a chance to ponder what might be "interesting" about the cloth wrapped around the unidentified skeletal vestiges. He went to a large side table where she joined him. He unrolled the musty cloth, which turned out to be a moth-and-or-possibly-mouse-eaten greatcoat. She marveled that it was as intact as it was after all the years and credited the material, which appeared to be heavy wool. A pair of worn brogans rested on top of the laid-out coat. He moved the shoes aside, remarking, "Shoes, overcoat, nothing remarkable there. It's what he wore beneath that gave us pause."

He opened the coat, revealing what she surmised to be the tattered remnants of a jacket, moldy and discolored in places. The only way she guessed at the item was that someone had tried to piece bits like an incomplete puzzle—a scrap here, a scrap there. One strip of gray fabric held a double row of gold buttons. Another piece, a very tattered sleeve, had a single stained stripe of gold fabric circling the cuff.

Inez frowned, cold certainty creeping over her. "Is, or rather, was that a military jacket?"

McConachie, eyes fixed on the jacket, said, "That was what the coroner and the city physician were debating. The buttons have 'CSN' on them. So they are fairly certain this is the remnants of a Confederate Navy frock coat. There's little enough left of the rest of the clothes, but from what they saw, they believe the corpse was dressed in the uniform of a Confederate Navy officer."

Shocked, Inez stepped away from the table as if the remnants held some contagion.

He looked at her. "The question on all our minds is 'Why?'"

She stared back thinking that to his question she would add another: *And what is he doing walled up in a San Francisco house, far from the scenes of the war's naval battles?*

Chapter Fifteen

Deep down, Inez felt the coroner was right in his conclusion, but she still had to ask. "Are you certain about this? About the buttons and so on being Confederate-issue?"

"The coroner and city physician agreed. As for me, I was only five or so when the war ended, so I couldn't say. I never saw a rebel uniform." McConachie touched the faded stripe on the sleeve. "I was raised in Massachusetts. My family was blue. It was 'The War for the Union' all the way. At least, from what I recall." He shook his head. "I didn't think the war came this far west. I didn't think it touched San Francisco."

Inez refrained from saying that the war had touched everyone, everywhere, asking instead, "Could I take these clothes with me?"

He thought about it. "You'll need to sign a receipt and leave us your address in case the coroner wants them back for some reason. I'll get you something to carry them in." He hesitated. "We discarded the fragments that were probably underlayers. And what was left of the stockings. No information to be gained from them."

She nodded, glad she was spared from examining the bits of fabric that had been in close contact with the decomposing body.

He retrieved a paper for her to sign. She looked down through the list, which was very short: *dark wool overcoat; remnants of a possibly gray frock coat possibly lined with black silk serge, gold buttons inscribed "CSN"; heavy shoes; one glass eye.*

"No personal property?" she asked. "No pipe, pocket watch, knife, snuffbox, papers?"

"None. But papers probably would not have survived, in any case." He dipped a pen in a bottle of ink and handed it to her. "I'm guessing whoever took care to seal him up also took care to remove any identifying or personal items."

Why not remove the uniform as well, she wondered. Why not toss the body in the bay? Why, of all things, entomb it in the wall of a house?

There were no answers.

And, after all this time, no one to ask. The people she would have wanted to question, Captain Taylor and his brother, Jack Taylor, were deceased. At least according to the captain's son, Bertram.

She signed.

McConachie carefully rolled the fragile bits of cloth inside the coat and put the bundle into a burlap sack. He reached into one of the waiting shoes and pulled out the peripatetic glass eye. "We didn't want this to get misplaced," he explained, showing the orb to her. He added, "It's on the list you signed for, so you should take it along with the rest of the items."

She eyed the eye. "Very well. I suppose we will just bury it with him, when the time comes."

McConachie put the staring sphere back into the shoe and placed the shoes into the sack. "You could have him buried in the greatcoat, if you have nothing else. Have you chosen an undertaker yet?"

"Does he need to be moved soon?"

"The morgue is, ah, unusually short of space. And we do have other pressing cases. Distraught families demanding autopsies and answers regarding last night's rout and loss of their loved ones." He hesitated. "I am certain Mr. Gray would handle matters for you. Not that I'm advocating one business over another. The city has many fine undertakers."

Inez squinted in thought. "Where is the morgue?"

"Right here, in this building."

Coroner, morgue, undertaker, all under one roof. Very convenient.

"I should discuss it with the house's other owner, Mrs. Krause," Inez said. "She was most desirous of giving him a decent resting place. Could I let you know tomorrow or Monday?"

"Of course." He held out the sack to her. "I'll let the coroner know."

Inez took the bag from him and left the office. She hurried through the building, chased by visions of caskets and haunted by the faint chemical smells of turpentine and formaldehyde.

The black-clad gentleman who had greeted her when she entered was standing in the foyer. He stopped her before she could bolt out the front door and said kindly, "Should you need to return to the coroner's office, there is a more direct entrance on Webb."

Holding the bag off to the side so it wouldn't touch her cloak, she said, "I'll remember that." He opened the door for her, and she escaped the displays of wares for the dearly departed.

Back out on Sacramento, Inez exhaled with a quick sigh and began walking toward Kearney. She was glad she did not have to go far carrying the dead man's clothes. She could swear the smell of decay still clung to them and seeped into the burlap and, thence, onto her glove. Nonetheless, she was determined to take a closer look at the clothing as well as the bag that held the coins once she returned to the store. She decided when she was done that she would give her kidskin gloves a thorough washing and dowse them with lemon-verbena perfume.

She would also have to talk with Moira about the undertaker and about…Inez glanced down at the sack. She wondered how Moira would react to hearing that the body had probably been clothed in Confederate gray. Then she wondered if she needed to tell Moira at all. If she didn't, it would probably never come up. Moira would be focused on choosing a casket and a gravestone and fussing over the wording on the stone. If the subject of clothing arose, Inez could offer up the greatcoat and note, quite truthfully, that the rest had fairly rotted away.

A thought, a mental murmur, which had been pulling gently at her consciousness, became more insistent, louder. What, exactly, had Taylor said about his uncle? He'd indicated "Uncle Jack" had ostensibly fought in the War for the Union and that the family had received letters from the battlefield, or wherever Jack Taylor had been stationed, but eventually communication had ceased. When Jack did not return home after the war, the captain had tried to track down his whereabouts and what had happened, without success. Eventually, the family presumed Jack Taylor had died either in battle or from illness. *But suppose,* murmured that little voice, which now had her full attention, *unbeknownst to young Taylor, his Uncle Jack returned to the city after all. And suppose Captain Taylor discovered Jack was actually a wolf in sheep's clothing, or rather, a Johnny Reb in a nondescript overcoat?*

Or…

Perhaps Jack Taylor was a Union firebrand who killed someone who favored the Confederacy, maybe even someone prominent in the city during that time. Perhaps his brother helped him, and they walled in the body to prevent its discovery. Afterward, Jack skedaddled to the warfront where he met a sorry end, and Captain Taylor removed his family from the city.

Two possible stories, and Inez easily conjured up a handful more. With so little evidence to go on, anything was possible. She needed more details, and a close examination of the coins and clothes was the easiest place to start.

Not wanting to get sidetracked by conversation in the music store, Inez elected to turn into the alley that ran behind the building and enter by the back door. Once inside, she moved the papers on the round table to the sideboard and pulled out the old clothing. Using the greatcoat as a "tablecloth," she gingerly picked through what was left of the frock coat, examining the buttons with their CSN markings. She wondered if there had been any shoulder epaulettes. If so, they had probably gone the way of the other bits of rotted material. The pockets, or at least the remnants, were shredded and held only emptiness. The greatcoat, in better shape, was also bereft of names or clues. Resigned, Inez prepared to tackle the shoes, which were on the floor by her chair.

At that moment, Welles walked in. "Ah! I didn't know you were back. I talked to John Hee just now." He stopped and wrinkled his nose. "What's that moldy smell?" He took in the table—bereft of papers and now covered with a bewildering array of stained and ruined fabric. "Did I interrupt something?" The tone of voice, polite, because he was, after all, her employee, still managed to include a dollop of disbelief.

"It's nothing," she said briskly, furling the greatcoat around the rags as if they were a bedroll. "Something that turned up in an old building I have an interest in. As you were saying?"

Welles launched into a quick summary of John Hee's

acquisition of two fine scroll paintings, whose owner apparently didn't know their worth. "We thought we'd put them in the display window," he finished. "I'll bet they'll be gone within the week."

"Excellent." She glanced at the papers, now stacked on the sideboard. "I shall take care of those this evening."

"Good, because John's going to need the receipt to straighten out the problem with the shipment of figurines." Welles scratched the nape of his neck. "Since he speaks the lingo, it seemed better that he handle that problem, unless you think I should."

"Ask John what would work best for him," said Inez, thinking that perhaps having Welles glowering over the top of John's head at whoever was responsible might speed up the resolution.

After Welles left, Inez pushed the rolled-up fabric to one side and put the shoes on the table. She figured that before she turned to updating the music store's accounts, she might as well finish her examinations.

The shoes themselves were still fairly sturdy and had once been black. To Inez, they looked like ordinary men's brogans. She extracted the glass eye first, rolled it in her hand, and finally tucked it into an exposed pocket of the greatcoat for safekeeping. She then turned the shoes over. The soles and heels were intact. Inez turned the shoes right side up and noted there were no laces. Wiggling her gloved fingers, she debated, then slid her hand inside one of the shoes and dabbled around. She reached toward the toe box trying to ascertain if there might be anything of interest. At the very tip of the toe, the inner sole seemed loose. Or, if it wasn't an inner sole that was bunched up at the end, it was some kind of liner.

She picked at it with a finger and slowly worked around the edges, pulling it away from the floor of the shoe. She finally pulled it out. It looked to be a wool liner. The fabric was now much compressed and soiled but still bore the faint indent and stain of a foot. She grimaced and turned it over.

Stuck to the bottom was a thick piece of paper, apparently folded many times. Although it was hard to tell, it appeared to have writing or printing within the folds. With a growing sense of excitement, she carefully began to pry it off the bottom of the liner. She pulled at the wad of paper slowly, only to have the last-most layer, apparently well affixed to the bottom of the liner, rip and part ways with the rest. Her excitement turned to frustration and she muttered, "Oh, hell!"

Trying to keep her movements slow and steady, she gingerly started to pry the accordion-folded paper open, pleat by pleat. The first fold revealed the upper part of the paper, which, in elegant looping text of very faint ink, read:

> JEFFERSON DAVIS, *President of the Confederate States of America, to all Who shall see these Presents Greeting:*
>   *Know ye, That by virtue of the power vested in me by law, I have commissioned and do hereby commission, have authorized, and do hereby authorize—*

"Authorize what? Who?" muttered Inez. The next two pleats were firmly stuck together and resisted all her attempts to separate them. She gave up and moved on to the next fold, prying it open to find:

> *—to act as a private armed vessel in the service of the* CONFEDERATE STATES *on the high seas, against the United States of America, their Ships, Vessels, Goods and Effects, and those of their citizens, during the pendency of the war now existing between the said* CONFEDERATE STATES *and the said United States.*

> *This Commission to continue in force until revoked by the President of the CONFEDERATE STATES for the time being.*

The rest of the document was torn off, firmly welded to the liner by time and decay. But Inez had seen enough to know. She had found a Confederate naval commission for a "private armed vessel."

She eased back in the chair, stunned. The sudden upwelling of questions threatened to muddy her thinking. Who was this for? Was the commission for the eastern seaboard? Or for a vessel out here in the West? *Is this why he was killed?*

The jacket hidden under a nondescript greatcoat. The hidden commission. Were there any other mysteries to find?

She turned to the other shoe and, without preamble, thrust a gloved hand inside. Another insole. No paper attached to it, but as she pulled it out of the shoe, something rattled around inside. She stuck her hand back in and pulled out a key.

A small brass key with a tiny checkerboard pattern etched on the head.

A key not to a door but to a much smaller lock.

A lock for what? Holding what?

Another knock on the door and Welles was back, looking frazzled. A loud, belligerent voice wafted in from the front of the music store, saying, "Are you accusing me of smashing those there little statues?"

She heard John Hee say in a loud, insistent voice, "Not broken when packed. Not broken when packed."

"And why should anyone take the word of a heathen Chinaman?"

"We need your presence, as owner of the store," said Welles abruptly. "This threatens to get out of hand. I had two customers walk in during the argument, turn around, and walk right back out."

Inez rose, pocketing the key. "Very well. I'll take care of this." Cursing herself for not having examined the wares before taking possession, Inez thought that handling a disagreement over broken goods would be child's play compared to breaking up fights between obstreperous drunks, an activity she had excelled at in her Leadville saloon.

Of course, back then she'd always kept a shotgun behind the bar.

Out in the main room, the two brawny men who had delivered the crate were standing before the diminutive John Hee, glowering menacingly at him. Inez walked up, stood by John Hee, and said pleasantly, "Gentlemen, what is the trouble here?"

One of them pointed at John. "He's accusin' us of breaking the goods. If they were broke when you opened the box, it weren't us that done it."

John's lips were compressed into a tight line; his eyes glittered with anger. He had clearly just returned from conducting business, as he still held his derby hat in one hand and his long queue was tucked out of sight down the back of his jacket. "Not broken when packed," he repeated.

Inez looked at John and nodded. She sensed him relax a little.

"Mr. Hee, perhaps you could show us the damage," she said calmly, "and I will take it from there."

He brought the deliverymen and Inez over to the open crate, which was now behind one of the display cases. After showing them the shattered porcelain figurines, the ones with minor chips, and the ones still intact, he withdrew behind the curtain to his alcove. Inez had no doubt that, whatever he might be doing back there, he had an ear on their conversation.

It took a little gentling and a ladylike confession of inattentiveness at the time of delivery, but the transport men finally calmed down. The one who had talked the loudest and who also turned out to be the owner of the delivery service finally admitted, "Well, we mighta been a bit hasty ourselves when loading in Chinatown. We didn't want to linger late in the day, ya know."

Privately, Inez thought that no one in Chinatown would have bothered two such intimidating-looking men, but she let it pass with an understanding nod.

In the end, they agreed to knock off half of the delivery fee for that shipment and discount the next two. It would, Inez thought, not entirely cover the cost of the damage, but at least it allowed both parties to save face.

They had just left when Antonia swung in through the front door, a strangely excited expression on her face. Without preamble, the girl said, "Can I spend one more night at Charlotte's? And we're invited to dinner, again! It's roast chicken and potatoes tonight!"

Inez put a hand to her forehead. Recalling where that glove had been, she quickly lowered it. "What's this all about?"

"Charlotte's makin' good progress on her fractions, but she's got a test on Monday, and we just need to practice a little more so's she can pass, and her ma said it was okay if I stayed one more night if you said it was okay."

Inez held up a hand to stop the flow of excited gabble. "Let me think a moment."

Antonia waited, swinging her little valise of clothes and looking expectant and hopeful. Feeling irritated with Moira for the short notice, Inez glanced at the store's grandfather clock. If they were to accept the dinner invitation, they would have to leave soon. *So much for Antonia's chores and for my dealing with the music store's accounts today.* It then occurred to her that if Antonia were to spend the night away, she could work on the accounts late into the night and even into the early morning hours, if she wished.

And she did need to speak with Moira, sooner rather than later.

"Very well," said Inez. "You'll need to do your Saturday chores tomorrow because there's no time now. And when you go to bed, just wear what you wore last night." An expression flitted across the girl's face so fast she couldn't identify the emotion. "What?" she said sharply.

"Nothing." Her ward then bit her lip and said, "Well, actually, Charlotte and I went out to see her chickens, and my nightgown got kinda dusty."

"You went outside in your nightdress?" said Inez incredulously. "Whose idea was that?"

"Both of us." Now she looked abashed. "It's not so dirty. I'll just brush it off. And my nightcap's still clean."

Weary, Inez shut her eyes and wondered if she had been such a trial to her own mother. *Of course I was. Only we also had a nanny and a maid who bore the brunt of my misbehavior.*

She opened her eyes. "We'll get it laundered with the rest of the week's clothes. You can take your second nightgown for tonight. Keep it clean as you'll need to wear it next week."

"Yes, ma'am!" yipped Antonia dancing on her toes. "Yippee! I'll go get ready." She whirled out of the door, a little tornado of energy.

If I could only borrow some of that enthusiasm.

Inez passed by Welles, who had a customer. "The issue is taken care of," she murmured to him.

He nodded to show he'd heard and continued to extol the virtues of the banjo to the young gentleman. "All the young ladies are playing them these days," said Welles.

"It's all the rage," the gentleman agreed. "So you think the missus'd like one?"

Inez missed Welles's reply, but, given the enthusiastic tone of his response, she was certain he was agreeing.

Inez paused at the curtained alcove and knocked on the wood frame. John Hee appeared, eyebrows raised. "All taken care of," she said. "And next time, I'll be certain to examine the contents of any of your shipments before the deliverymen leave."

He nodded. "Thank you, Mrs. Stannert." And he disappeared back inside.

Inez hurried to the office in back, thinking she'd put the clothing items back in the bag and deposit the key from her pocket, the glass eye, and the commission in the safe. She paused, frowning a little. Had the paper been placed so, right by the insole? She thought she'd put it more to one side.

She surveyed the room. All was as she left it. At least, she thought so. She shook her head. She tore out of there so fast with Welles on hearing the growing fracas that it was entirely possible she'd pushed the paper to one side when rising from the chair.

In any case, it was still there, and that was what counted.

Inez secured the document, glass eye, and key before bundling the clothes and shoes and nudging them into the open space beneath the sideboard. She didn't want them in the safe but thought it best to keep them until Moira decided if she wanted them for the burial. Remembering she hadn't locked the back door when she'd entered earlier that afternoon, she did so now. No harm had been done. And, anyway, who would come sneaking in while the building was occupied?

Still, with the safe—which had been locked, thank goodness—and all the paperwork lying about, it made her uncomfortable to think she'd left it all unattended for even that short while. She leaned against the locked back door and assessed the room again. All seemed well. Satisfied for the most part, she walked through the music store, stopping to ask Welles to close up at day's end. "I'll do the paperwork tonight," she promised and then headed out the store to the apartment entrance to get ready for dinner and a heart-to-heart with Moira about the burial arrangements for the still-anonymous bones.

Chapter Sixteen

SATURDAY, MARCH 11

The first thing Inez did upon entering the apartment was to remove her gloves and toss them in the utilitarian kitchen sink, then scrub her hands thoroughly. Next, she went to her room to change for dinner. She finally shut the door on Antonia, who kept peeking in and asking if she was ready yet. There was certainly no need to wear Sunday best for a boardinghouse meal, but since Inez figured she would discuss business matters with Moira afterward, she wanted to strike a somber and professional note. A rust-brown outfit of a V-shaped cashmere casaque over a box-pleated underskirt with turned-back linen cuffs and a simple bar-pin at the throat seemed appropriate.

She lingered at the bedstand and finally took her small Remington pocket revolver from the drawer and slid it into her wool cloak, which hung on the back of her bedroom door. She would be returning after dark and then spending late hours in the store alone going over neglected paperwork. It just seemed prudent.

Inez had let down her shoulder-length hair and was giving it a quick brush when Antonia piped up on the other side of the door, "Are you almost ready, Mrs. S?"

"Are you packed?" Inez twisted her hair into a tight knot and stabbed it with pins.

"Yes, ma'am!"

Inez retrieved the small brown hat on the dresser and secured it with a hatpin.

"Are you ready *now*, Mrs. S?"

"Hold your horses, Antonia." Inez selected a pair of suede gloves from her glovebox, took her cloak off the hook, and opened the door. The girl practically tumbled into the room.

Inez wondered if she'd had an eye pressed to the keyhole. That thought was confirmed when Antonia said, "Why are you taking your gun? D'you think there's going to be trouble?"

"Prying eyes," Inez admonished. Antonia blushed. Inez relented enough to say, "A precaution is all. It will be dark when I return."

"Oh! I almost forgot! Charlotte's ma wants to talk to you after dinner."

"That will be convenient because I want to talk to her."

"What about?"

"Mrs. Krause and I have a few business items to discuss."

"Like the boarders all leaving because of the dead body?"

Inez raised her eyebrows. "Where did you hear that?"

"Charlotte told me. Oops. I guess I wasn't supposed to say that. And it's not *all* of them. Just a couple." She brightened. "Master Edward is still there. I saw him at breakfast."

Inez nodded, thinking. If boarders were leaving, that was unsettling, to say the least. But housing was not abundant in the city, so Moira probably wouldn't have trouble finding new boarders. In any case, now that Antonia had spilled the beans, she would be prepared. "Well, you are in a hurry for us to go, are you not? Let's get moving."

Antonia grinned and bolted away.

Following, Inez heard the girl clatter down the stairs to the entryway. "Careful!" she called. "One misstep and you'll tumble head over heels and break your neck."

Privately, Inez reflected that would probably never happen as Antonia was surefooted as a mountain goat. She then thought of her upcoming conversation with Moira and her plans to meet de Bruijn tomorrow. How much should she reveal to each about what she had uncovered? Whatever she decided, she'd have to take care to keep her stories straight.

A single misstep and who knows what will happen.

———

As Inez and Antonia turned up the block to the boardinghouse on O'Farrell, loud voices carried down the street. As they drew closer, Inez saw two men on the boardinghouse porch facing Moira at the open door. There was an argumentative tone to the raised voices, but Inez couldn't distinguish the words until Moira burst out, "I will not pay you a dime until you hand them over!"

"And you'll not get them until we're paid!" The gravelly tone alerted her to the identity of the speaker, as did the general stature of the two men: the speaker short, slightly stooped, and listing to the right. The second one taller, lankier, standing behind the shorter man. The locksmith, Joe Harris, and his son, Paulie.

Inez picked up her pace just as the elder locksmith said in a shout that carried to the road, "Curse you and yours to Hades and back! You'll be hearing from that lawyer, Upton, about this!"

Closer now, Inez could see splotches of color high on Moira's cheeks. Her arms were akimbo and her face ablaze with rage. "How dare you!" she shouted as he turned away.

He pulled his cap over his brow before storming in his tuck-and-tilt fashion down the porch stairs and onto the front walk. The son followed, tight-lipped.

Inez pulled Antonia behind her. Once the elder Harris reached the sidewalk, she stepped into his path halting his advance. "Mr. Harris, what is going on?" She kept her voice pitched even and low, reinforcing it with a wall of determination.

He glared at her. "Hysterical female. She has no respect. No respect for workin' men like us." He jabbed his thumb toward his son behind him. "No respect for the honor of those that lived here before. We'll talk to Mr. Upton. That's what we'll do. And the young Mr. Taylor. She owes us. She owes *them*! She will not get away with this."

Paulie gripped his father's shoulder. "Pa," he said, almost in a whisper. "Don't say anything more. Let's go." He glanced at Inez, a twist of apology in his smooth face, before he pulled his father away from Inez and the house.

Inez stared at their retreating backs, then looked at Moira, who avoided her gaze. The high color drained from Moira's face, and her hands unclenched. She smoothed the front of her apron again and again, as if the words thrown back and forth had soiled its white expanse.

Charlotte wiggled past her mother at the door and rocketed down the front path. "Anton-eee-yah!" she screeched. She almost knocked Antonia over with a fierce hug. "Hooray! You're here!" Antonia gave the smaller girl a hug back, and Charlotte grabbed her valise. "Come on! Dinner is almost ready."

Moira looked up, composure restored. "Girls, wash your hands, and you can help bring out the serving platters."

Antonia looked at Inez, who said, "Go along, then."

They ran up the steps and inside. Inez followed. Once the

door closed behind her, she asked Moira, "So, what was that fracas all about?"

Moira just shook her head and glanced toward the back of the house, where Inez could hear a lively chatter of ongoing conversation. "That was very regrettable. I hope the boarders did not hear. I'll explain everything after supper when we can talk privately. Just one question and I must get back to the kitchen and dining room." She took a deep breath. "Do you have keys to the other house?"

"Keys? No." Inez frowned. "Don't you have them?"

Moira's mouth compressed into a tight line. "No. Let's talk about this later." She gestured to a door to the side of the entry. "If you wish to wash up, please do so and join us when you are ready. We are preparing to sit." She hurried down the passageway that led to the dining room.

Inez lingered inside the dark-paneled entryway removing her gloves. The savory aroma of roasted chicken seasoned with rosemary wafted down the hallway accompanied by the voices of the boarders gathered in the dining room. She jumped as a figure detached itself from a turn in the staircase above.

Master Edward came down the stairs leading to the second floor, saying without preamble, "It was wrong, how he spoke to her."

Pulse still pounding from his unexpected appearance, Inez laid a hand on one of the newel posts decorating the staircase. "Good evening, Master Edward. So you heard it all?"

"Not all, but enough to know Harris had no right to talk to Mrs. Krause as he did." His face, usually creased in a smile, was now shadowed with a frown. "Joseph Harris is a stubborn mule of a man. Always has been."

"You know Mr. Harris? That is, aside from our interactions with him the other day?"

He bobbed his head. "We were shipmates before the war. Harris is loyal to a fault. To a *fault*, I say. And he should not have treated Mrs. Krause as he did. He'll have to answer for that and more to man or God, I know not which, but he surely will."

His tone sent a prickle of alarm up her neck. The former seaman, who had been so genial before, appeared an entirely different sort of man at that moment. Getting on the wrong side of Master Edward suddenly seemed a most unwise thing to do.

A shudder in the post under her hand and footsteps thumping above alerted her to the descent of another roomer. She released her hold on the post as an unfamiliar man came down the stairs.

Edward switched to a jolly tone. "You joining us again for supper, Mrs. Stannert?"

"It seems so, Master Edward."

"And your firecracker of a young lady too?"

A small smile. "Yes, indeed. Antonia is helping Mrs. Krause with the serving."

Edward rubbed his hands together. "Roast chicken tonight. We're in for a treat." He turned to the newcomer now standing beside him and said, "Mrs. Krause prepares the best victuals in any boardinghouse in the city. You'll not be sorry to have signed onto this ship."

Inez cast an eye over Edward's companion. The two men looked to be related. They both sported weathered, clean-shaven faces; similarly slicked-back, graying hair with a widow's peak; sturdy builds; and large hands. Or, in the case of Edward's companion, that would be "hand," as his left sleeve was empty and neatly pinned closed.

Edward said, "My manners! Allow me to perform introductions." He nodded to his colleague. "This fellow is my brother,

Mr. J. T. Edward, or Edward the Second. And this good lady is Mrs. Stannert, a confederate of Mrs. Krause's."

Inez blinked at the word "confederate"—the commission she had found still in the back of her mind—then manufactured a polite smile. "Pleased to meet you."

J.T. bobbed his head. "Charmed, madam. And tickled that you are 'pleased' to meet yet another old salt, taking after my older brother as I do." He gave his brother a nudge with his remaining arm. "However, I will say age and many years removed from the mast have reformed my former wicked ways, so you've nothing to fear."

"Are you visiting, then?" Inez inquired as they made their way to the dining room.

Master Edward spoke for his brother. "When rooms came up at loose ends, I convinced him 'twas time to move out of the hotel he'd been lolling in and take a berth here. Mrs. Krause makes sure we all toe the line, and there's no place that serves a better square meal for the price."

In the dining room, everyone was seated and the food was on the table. The two girls sat side by side. An empty chair waited by Antonia. Moira addressed Inez with forced cheeriness. "Mrs. Stannert, your chair is between Antonia and Miss Ashby. Miss Ashby is new to the house." A young woman with spectacles smiled at Inez and returned to unfolding her napkin.

Moira tapped her knife on her glass and chatter ceased. "Before we begin, I must ask: Who forgot to put the extra front door key back under the flowerpot?"

Master Edward, who had taken the chair across from Antonia, stood. "Eh. That would be me." He fished a key out of his trouser pocket. "I'll take care of it now."

"No need to interrupt dinner. Afterward is soon enough."

He repocketed the key and sat, looking like a schoolboy who

had received a reprieve from writing "I will remember to put the key back" a hundred times on the chalkboard.

Moira continued, "Mrs. Stannert, I see you've met our other new boarder, the second Mr. Edward. We are so glad the master's brother has joined us."

"Master, is it," said J.T. admiringly. "Ye've retained your rank on land, I see."

Master Edward turned to J.T., who was sitting next to him. "If Mrs. Krause wishes to call me such, who am I to say otherwise?"

J.T. leaned forward and directed his comments to Inez, across the table. "He's too modest by half. Edward the First should've been a captain. He went in through the hawsepipe and came out through the cabin window, for all that."

Antonia, who had been staring with unabashed curiosity at J.T.'s empty sleeve, wrinkled her nose in apparent confusion. Charlotte said, "In through the what?"

J.T. grinned. "Ye be the daughter of a sea-going officer, and ye don't ken what a hawsepipe is?" He winked at Inez.

Charlotte's face fell a little, and she shook her head.

"Ah, don't tease the lass, now," said Master Edward to his brother.

Moira cleared her throat loudly, bowed her head, and clasped her hands. Everyone around the table assumed the same posture, and Moira began, "Bless us, O Lord, and these, Thy gifts…"

Once grace was said and done, chatter picked up again as the dishes were passed around, and Master Edward turned to the girls. "On a ship, the hawsepipe is a hole in the bow that the anchor chain runs through. To say a fellow went in through the hawsepipe and came out through the cabin window means he started on the bottom rung of the lowest ladder and worked his way up through the ranks."

His brother nodded. "Such a man knows his way around a

ship, as does Edward the First here. Too, he's not just a master, but a master-at-arms. D'ye know what that is?"

The two girls shook their heads. J.T. leaned forward. "The master-at-arms is the man you want standin' by you in a fight. He's an expert at hand-to-hand combat and fighting under arms in close quarters, and he enforces the law at sea."

"All that's in the past now," said Master Edward.

His brother continued, "He would've gotten his due, too, if not for the one who lived here before." He glanced around the room. "Captain Taylor, now there was a hard man."

Inez looked up sharply from spearing a piece of chicken. "You knew Captain Taylor?"

J.T. seemed to puff up a little under the gaze of the three females across the table from him. "As did my brother here. We were both under Captain Taylor's command. As I said, he was a hard man. Harder than hardtack baked for ten years under a southern sun." He turned to his brother, who was nudging a bowl of baked potatoes at him. "How you suffered the man, brother, I'll never know. Surprised he didn't have mutiny on his vessel, blood on his hands."

"Enough of your windy tales," said Master Edward. "Or you'll call up the vengeance of ghosts."

The two girls' eyes widened.

J.T. set the bowl down and forked out a baked potato. "If any uneasy soul remains within these walls, it probably belongs to that poor boy of his. Whipped and beaten. Probably had the spirit driven right out of him."

"My ma sometimes thrashes me," admitted Charlotte.

Master Edward tsked-tsked and said, "An angel such as yourself, Miss Charlotte? That I cannot believe."

She nodded solemnly. "When I do something bad."

But Inez had something else on her mind. "By son, do you mean Bertram Taylor?"

J.T. raised gray eyebrows. "The very one."

Inez thought of Bertram and his quiet, constrained manner. Pity prodded her, along with curiosity. "So, you knew the Taylor family well?"

"Me and Edward the First here were on the ship that carried the captain and his family to China," said J.T. "We weren't intimates of the family, but we had eyes and ears, isn't that right, brother?" He nudged Master Edward.

Master Edward looked uncomfortable. "Ah. Best leave the past in the past, brother. It has no place in the here and now."

J.T. turned to Inez. "Pardon. My brother knows I have a tendency to prattle and hauls me up regularly on that account. You know Bertram Taylor?"

"Mrs. Krause and I bought the house next door from him," said Inez.

J.T. brightened. "Ah, yes. I heard of the bag of gold and the—" Master Edward cleared his throat loudly. His brother stopped and seemed at a loss for words before saying, "As said, I'd not be surprised if ghosts are a-wandering the halls."

Inez glanced at the girls, who seemed mesmerized by the talk of ghosts and whippings. Determined to change the subject, Inez asked, "So, you also sailed the Pacific?"

"A bit." J.T. applied a lump of butter to his potato. "However, I discovered 'twas not to my taste. Not like this one," he pointed his fork at his brother, "who did his seafaring out here, to the Orient and back. I sailed 'round the Horn and ended up around the Leewards and the Windwards. Antigua, Barbuda, St. Kitts, Jamaica, Barbados, Tobago."

"Barbados," breathed Antonia.

"How did you lose your arm?" piped up Charlotte, sawing away at her drumstick.

With a gleam in his eye, J.T. leaned over his dish of chicken, gravy, and potatoes. "'Twas a fight to the death an' there I was, cutlass drawn, standin' back to back with the famous pirate and privateer Jean Lafitte on his ship *The Pride*."

Antonia's mouth dropped open, and she leaned forward in turn, the ribbons at her collar dangling perilously close to the puddle of gravy on her plate.

Alarmed, Inez interrupted, trying to redirect her ward's attention and the conversation. "Antonia, please pass the salt."

Master Edward looked at his brother and snorted. "If you were standin' with Lafitte," he said, picking up the story thread, "you were a-holdin' up his skeleton by its collar. He died ere either of us were born. Stop with your stories. You'll give the lassies night frights."

He then addressed the girls, with an apologetic glance at Inez. "My younger brother here lost a tussle with a windlass, which claimed one of his limbs as its prize, and that's the truth of it. You can't believe two words out of ten that he gabbles about."

J.T. shrugged. The two brothers, who sounded as though they had been long separated, seemed very easy with each other. Beneath their banter and jibes, Inez sensed real respect and affection. Neither of which was ever guaranteed, even within the bonds of family. As she knew quite well from her own upbringing under the thumb of a harsh father, common blood did not confer love or even like, much less respect.

From there, Inez's thoughts slid to what J.T. had said about Captain Taylor and his son, Bertram. If it was true that the captain had been cruel to Bertram, past the usual punishments a stern father might mete out to a son, she understood a bit better why Bertram, in their brief conversation, had spoken of his father only in passing. So, as a child, had Bertram turned to his uncle, Jack Taylor, for paternal affection? How awful it must have been, then, for the beloved uncle to depart and never return.

Shaking her head, she brought herself back to the present. She leaned to the side and murmured to Antonia to put her drumstick down and use fork and knife to pare the meat off. Antonia, fingers and chin greasy from chicken fat, made a little face but complied. Inez hoped that all the talk of pirates and adventures on the high seas would not lead to more flights of imagination and secretive detours to the less savory parts of the San Francisco waterfront.

After dinner, which ended with two excellent raisin pies, Moira asked Antonia and Charlotte to clear the table. Some of the boarders drifted back to their rooms. The Edward brothers and a couple of other male boarders repaired to the back parlor, where Inez soon heard the piano come into play. The tune sounded like "Hard Times, Come Again No More," but the lyrics, which she couldn't hear clearly, involved hardtack. From the ensuing guffaws, Inez reasoned the words were probably not fit for "feminine sensibilities."

Moira, after instructing the girls, returned to Inez. "I do hope you can stay a while longer. This seems a good time for us to talk. And I do owe you an explanation for that unfortunate scene before dinner." She glanced toward the back parlor. "I don't usually allow that sort of music, but after all that's happened, well, I suppose it cannot hurt. Besides, Miss Ashby and the other women are not about. Otherwise, I should have to put an end to it."

Inez noted the tired lines around Moira's eyes and thought of all she did to keep the house running and in order, essentially by herself. The piles of paperwork in the music store suddenly appeared much smaller and more manageable.

"Where shall we go?" Inez asked.

"Someplace away from little ears. I think the front parlor."

They moved to the more formal sitting room in the front of

the house. The sky was graying, the shadows on the streets softening and blurring around the edges. Once the lamps were lit, they would jump again into sharp relief, but for now, it lent an air of undefined vagueness to the world outside.

Moira indicated a small sofa and took the nearby rocking chair. "I apologize for the abruptness of my question before dinner. I thought you had the keys to the house next door."

Inez shook her head. "I thought *you* had them by now."

"Surely there is more than the one set."

"I've only ever seen the ones Mr. Harris carries with him, and only twice. The first time was when we went through the house before placing an offer. The second time was the other night. The detectives and I were the last ones out with the Harrises, and I remember Mr. Harris turning and locking the door."

Moira sighed and leaned her head on one hand. "So, he may be the only one with keys."

"I could speak to Mr. Upton about this," said Inez, although she was loath to deal with the lawyer again. "Or we could hire a workhand to break the locks, the doors, whatever is needed, and replace the doors with our own locks and keys."

Even as Inez offered up what seemed an eminently sensible solution, Moira was shaking her head, that obstinate expression back. "No. It would invite bad luck. We have too much of that already. And the locks themselves are unbreakable. The place seems cursed. Oh, if I'd known the trouble this would cause, I would have never started down this path."

"But we have," said Inez, reminding her that they were in it together. "Now, what did Mr. Harris want? It sounded like he was demanding payment. For what?"

"He wanted payment for their time Thursday evening, for unlocking the house and assuring only invited guests entered." Her eyes narrowed. "I said not until we got the keys. I believe you heard the rest. He was extremely rude! And completely unreasonable!"

Inez thought that, given what she'd heard, the unreasonableness went both ways. "No matter what, the keys should certainly be in our possession. I shall pursue that."

"Thank you." Moira rocked a little. "Now, to the boarders. It's only right to tell you. Two left yesterday, two more this morning, giving essentially no notice."

Inez was horrified. "Four! That's nearly half your income!"

"I replaced the first two right away. Master Edward's brother had been waiting for a room to open, and Miss Ashby is a schoolteacher I know from church." She shifted in the rocker. The runners squeaked. "Did you have a chance to speak with Mr. de Bruijn?"

"Oh, yes. He wants to view the spot where we found everything." Inez paused and added, just in case it wasn't clear, "He wants entrance to the house."

Moira leaned her head back against the rocker and closed her eyes. "What does he hope to find? And besides, he can't go in until the police give us leave to complete the passageway or we can unlock the door. It all comes back to that. Oh, there must be another way, another avenue he can pursue."

Inez thought of all she had planned to discuss with Moira, including burial arrangements for the remains, her visit to the coroner. And there were the items she had found in the shoes. A naval commission. No name attached. A small key. No idea what it opened. She kept her peace.

Moira opened her eyes. "I know you think I am being silly about all this. But until we can name the soul who has waited so long to be found and lay him to rest, there will be no resolution. No moving forward."

Inez thought a brick through a window would be one way to

move things forward. Break a pane, climb through, and take the bloody doors off their hinges. None of which had been expressly forbidden by Detective Lynch.

Moira stirred. "I should let you go. I have after-dinner chores, and Charlotte should practice her fractions again to prepare for her test." A brief smile brightened Moira's face. "Antonia has worked miracles. Thank you for letting her stay another night with us."

Inez nodded. "I am glad the girls have become such good friends." The two women stood. Inez said, "I shall pursue this matter of the key. Perhaps I will visit Mr. Harris myself." She had an overwhelming desire to face him down and wrest the keys from him, physically, verbally, legally, or all three. Suddenly, it felt as if the locksmith was the fulcrum, the pivot to the problem before her. If he would just relent and hand them over! Inez decided that before visiting Upton, she'd try to deal directly with the Harrises. If all it took was token payment for their help that ill-fated evening, well then, she'd pay them herself. Whatever they were owed.

Anything to get the keys.

Anything to get that damn house unlocked.

Chapter Seventeen

SATURDAY, MARCH 11

"...and it said he was commissioned to be commander of a *private armed vessel*," Antonia whispered to Charlotte.

The two girls lay almost nose to nose, heads on pillows in Charlotte's bed, talking low. They expected Charlotte's ma to come in any minute to say good night and turn down the lamp.

Antonia added, "D'you know what that means?"

Charlotte shook her head. Her nightcap slid off her head, covering one of her eyes like a pirate's eyepatch.

Antonia was tempted to imitate Edward the Second and say, "Ye be the daughter of a sea-going officer, and ye don't ken the meaning?" But she was too excited to tease. "It means the dead man was in charge of a *privateer*!"

Her feet wiggled in excitement under the quilt. She still couldn't believe her luck. Mrs. S had left the dead pirate's coat and stuff right there on the table in the back of the music store. Antonia'd walked in the back door at first, ready to tell Mrs. S she'd start her chores right away and beg to stay overnight at Charlotte's again, and...there it was! The old paper with fancy curly writing in brown ink that almost looked like dried blood, and…maybe it was!

"What's a privateer?" asked Charlotte. Her breath, smelling of onions and roast chicken, hit Antonia in the face. Antonia ignored it.

"A privateer is a ship that is owned by a person. It doesn't belong to a company or a navy or anything like that. And it's armed with cannons and guns and everything. The paper said the Confederate States gave the commander permission to attack ships of the United States. So he could take the ships as prizes, take the crews hostage, and if there was treasure, he'd take that too!"

"So he was a *pirate*!" whispered Charlotte gleefully. "You were right, Antonia!" She pumped her legs under the covers as if she were jumping while lying down, and her sharp little knee-caps jabbed Antonia.

"Ow! Stop!" The kicks distracted Antonia, who was about to explain that a privateer wasn't *exactly* a pirate but just kind of sort of one.

"Sorry!" said Charlotte.

The girls discussed their plans for exploring the house in whispers. Antonia suggested they finish exploring the secret room and then look through the rest of the house, starting at the top and working down to the kitchen.

The door swung open. "Girls, are you still awake?" Mrs. Krause asked.

They rolled away from each other, and Charlotte answered in a sleepy voice, "Noooooo."

Antonia, staring at the wall about six inches away, heard the soft swish of Mrs. Krause's long skirts as she came into the room. "Time to rest. And Charlotte, remember we have early Mass tomorrow. When I wake you up, you'll come into my bed-room to dress. Antonia can sleep until we return."

"Okay, Mama. I'll be quiet as a mouse. Promise!"

Antonia watched the shadows deepen and the pattern of the wallpaper fade into darkness as Mrs. Krause dimmed the lamp. "G'night, Mrs. Krause," she said.

"Good night, Antonia. And thank you for helping Charlotte. I heard her reciting her times tables today. She has improved greatly thanks to you."

Antonia felt proud and guilty all at once. So what if they were also planning on a little secret "treasure hunt" after dark? That didn't mean she hadn't done some good as well.

"You're welcome," she said, trying to sound sleepy. She listened as Mrs. Krause's soft footsteps were followed by the creak and click of the door. Antonia exhaled at the same time as Charlotte, and Antonia realized they'd both been holding their breath.

Charlotte whispered, "Now, we gotta wait until we hear Ma snoring." She poked Antonia in the spine.

Antonia flinched. "Stop it!"

"Don't fall asleep!"

"I won't!"

But she did. The bed was so cozy, and the quilt was a heavy one that felt like being wrapped in a big warm ball of softness...

The bed jiggled. Antonia jerked awake to hear Charlotte say, "Let's go!"

Antonia turned over, the quilt tangling with her night-dress, and raised herself on one elbow. The lamp was still low. Charlotte was down on the rug on her knees, digging around under her bed. Antonia sat up. "What're you doing?"

"Getting ready!" Charlotte popped up and threw a pair of stockings at Antonia. They landed on her lap. "Here. Put these on your feet."

Antonia picked one up. It was grimy and smelled like sour milk. "What's this?"

"Dirty socks that are going out Monday to the laundry in Chineetown."

Antonia frowned. "You mean Chinatown?"

"That's what I said. Chineetown!"

"Whose socks are they?" She eyed them, dubiously. "Yours?"

"No, silly! I think they're Master Edward's."

Antonia wrinkled her nose but pulled them on. At least they were nice and thick and already dirty, so it wouldn't matter if they got even dirtier. She glanced up at Charlotte, who looked like a ghost with her head and most of her body hidden under what looked like a big white shirt. The sleeves wiggled around in an impressively ghoulish fashion as she struggled underneath. "What're you doing?" Antonia asked again.

Charlotte's head popped out the open neck of the shirt. "I got this from the laundry bags too! I figured it'll keep my night-clothes clean so Ma won't ask how I got my second nightdress dirty."

Sure enough, the shirt almost covered Charlotte's nightgown completely. She also had big wool socks on, just like the ones she'd given Antonia.

"Did you get a shirt for me?" Antonia asked.

Charlotte shook her head. "Noooooo."

Antonia thought. Then smiled. "That's okay. I'll just do this." She wiggled out of her nightdress, turned it inside out, and put it back on. "And when we come back to bed, I'll just put it on right-side out."

"That's right smart!" said Charlotte approvingly. "Are you ready?"

"Ready!" Antonia took up the lamp, and the two girls tiptoed out of the room.

The girls found the two cats, Eclipse and Lucky, sniffing around the boarded-up entry in the pantry. "Shoo, pussycats.

You can't come with us!" hissed Charlotte. She picked up Lucky. He struggled as she carried him out of the pantry; Eclipse chased after them. Charlotte gently dropped Lucky onto the kitchen floor. He landed gracefully on all fours, and she scurried back to the pantry. Lucky attempted to dash in after her. Charlotte shut the door quickly but quietly in his face. One little white paw, claws extended, snuck in through the crack under the door. "No, Lucky! Back!" She pushed his paw out.

"You'd better shut the door tight," warned Antonia. "And we'd better block the opening after we go through. What if they somehow get in and get stuck inside the wall?"

"That won't happen," scoffed Charlotte.

Antonia wasn't so sure. It seemed a worrisome possibility. If the cats did sneak into the wall somehow, they'd for sure make a ruckus, and someone might hear.

The girls pulled down the boards and wiggled through. Antonia tried to block the opening after they were in the space between the walls. It wasn't as easy as she thought it would be. She could hear indignant mews and little claws scratching at the door. The cats were making a fuss, and Antonia didn't want the boards she was juggling to fall down and make a clatter on top of that. "Damn!" she muttered. "I don't think this'll work."

"Ooooooo, you said a bad word! The devil'll come get you and tear out your tongue!" Charlotte danced around on her toes. "C'mon. They won't get in. They can't open the door."

The noise stopped. Antonia sighed in relief, figuring they'd probably gotten bored and gone off to hunt mice.

As they went up the hidden staircase to the room at the top, the chickens outside set up a clucking and the rooster squawked. "What's bothering them?" Antonia asked.

"Oh, they just get all excited over nothing. They're really stupid," said Charlotte, adding, "You'd think when they see Ma coming with her little axe, they'd know that's when they should get all excited and start running around saying *chook chook chook*, but they don't."

Once inside the secret room, Antonia put the lamp on the table, turned the wick up, and spent a minute looking around. Everything was as they'd left it the previous night. Her gaze swept the walls, stopping at the sight of a flag nailed above the door they'd just entered. She pointed. "Look, Charlotte! Up there, above the door. It's a Confederate flag!" She wondered how she'd missed it the previous night but then remembered they'd kept the light low and had been mostly exploring the table and desk, not high on the walls.

Antonia continued, "So this must've been a secret hideout for a band of Confederate privateers. Maybe they mutinied, killed the commander, and stuffed him in the wall with the booty! Maybe they meant to come back for it and didn't!" Her mind raced. "Maybe there's *more* treasure in this house. I'll bet there is."

"Huh," said Charlotte, who was back at the desk, pulling out the drawers again. "Maybe."

"I'm gonna call this place 'Treasure House.' Like the story *Treasure Island*," continued Antonia. "So, what're you looking for in there?"

"I dunno," Charlotte said, rustling through papers. "More treasure? A pirate map?"

"They must've left in a hurry and planned to come back. Why would they leave all this otherwise?" said Antonia, inspecting the map and papers on the table. She lifted one end of the map to see if there was anything interesting underneath and frowned. "What's this?"

The map had been hanging over the table edge. Now, with it flopped back, she could see a keyhole in the table apron. She experimentally hooked her fingers under the panel and explored the length. Sure enough, the center section held a drawer cleverly "disguised" by the fancy carving in the wood.

She gave the drawer a tug. Locked.

Antonia bent down and looked closer at the keyhole. "I bet I could open this if I had a couple of hairpins," she muttered. "I'll bring some next time."

Next time. She felt a little flurry of excitement in her chest at the thought that she and Charlotte would no doubt be back, making more midnight visits to the Treasure House.

"What's that?" Charlotte was suddenly there, hovering by her side.

"A drawer in the table." Antonia said. "It's locked."

Charlotte peered at it. "Huh. I wonder if this will work." She held up a key with a fancy pattern on its head that matched the carving on the drawer.

Before Antonia could snatch the key, Charlotte inserted it in the lock and squeaked with delight. "It works!" She added, "I found it in the desk all mixed up with the papers." She pointed to the giant desk facing the room. Antonia could just see a drift of papers to the side, where Charlotte had tossed them on the floor in her search.

As Charlotte pulled out the drawer, something rattled within its depths. Charlotte reached in, but Antonia was quicker and pulled out a small wood inlaid box. "Hey," said Charlotte petulantly. "I saw it first. And I found the key."

Antonia decided not to argue that the box was too far inside the drawer for either of them to see. Instead, she said, "Well, I found the drawer. And I could've opened it even without a key."

She turned the box around in her hands, admiring the tiny checkered wood trim—little squares of dark, light, dark, light— all the way around the edges and along the top. "Besides, it's locked." She showed Charlotte the front, with its brass latch and keyhole, and continued, "Did you find a key to *this*?"

Charlotte pouted.

"I know I can open it at home," Antonia said. "And I promise I'll share whatever's inside, okay? We're mateys. We split the treasure, fifty-fifty."

"Ooookay." Charlotte glanced around. "How about we explore the rest of the house? I want to see what else there is. Maybe there's more booty! Maybe some jewels, silver, and more gold."

Maybe another dead body. Antonia shook the thought off. If there'd been anything like that, Mrs. S and Charlotte's ma would've known. Mrs. S had mentioned that they'd taken a look at the inside of the house before they bought it. A dead body out in the open, that might've put the kibosh on their dealings for sure. But like Charlotte said, there could be other interesting things. After all, they'd found the hidden room with what looked like an expensive sextant sitting on top of what might be a pirate map and now this little fancy box hidden in a locked drawer.

Antonia debated what to do with the box. She didn't want to leave it in the room. She pulled an arm out of one sleeve and into her nightdress, maneuvered the box under the hem into her waiting hand, and tried to stuff it into the pocket of her inside-out flannel nightgown.

It fit.

Sort of.

If she didn't jounce around too much.

The top of the box jutted out of the pocket, its sharp corners poking her skin while she put her arm back through the sleeve.

Charlotte watched the whole operation, nose scrunched. "What're you doing?"

Antonia shrugged. The box bumped against her hip. "Taking it with us."

Charlotte marched to the wall that held the hidden door to the rest of the house. "Let's go. I want to explore some more!"

"Not so loud." Antonia picked up the lamp and followed. "All we need is for one of the boarders to hear our voices. They'll come searching, and if they find us, we'll be in big trouble!"

"They can't come find us, 'cause they don't have the keys," Charlotte pointed out. "They'll probably just think they're hearing ghosts. If we hear them talking, we'll do this." And she made a spooky *ooooooooo* sound.

"Stop it," grumbled Antonia, feeling for the hidden catch on the chair rail. "We need to be quiet. Let's pretend an evil pirate captain is in the house. He's looking for us because we're mutineers from his ship. If he finds us, he'll slit our throats!"

"Yikes!" Charlotte grinned then whispered loudly, "We have to find the captain's treasure so we can bribe the rest of the crew to mutiny with us!"

Antonia nodded, satisfied that Charlotte would keep the fantasy in mind. She handed the lamp to Charlotte, grasped the handhold, and pulled. The panel eased inward, and they stepped through.

Charlotte held up the lamp and sneezed. "Dusty."

"Hold your nose next time it tickles," said Antonia. "I don't think anyone hearing you sneeze will think you're a ghost."

"There's nothing here anyway," grumbled Charlotte.

She was right. The small room looked ordinary and was disappointingly bare. "Let's check the other rooms up here. This must be the third floor. After we're done, we can go down to the second floor, see what's there, and do the main floor last," Antonia said. "We gotta be careful with the rooms that have windows. If anyone sees a light shining—"

"They'll think it's a ghost!" said Charlotte.

Antonia sighed. "Gimme the lamp."

They did a quick tour of the rest of the floor. There was another small room along the back and a large front room facing the street, both empty.

"It doesn't look like anyone lived here at all," said Charlotte.

"Well, maybe they cleared out this part of the house when whoever lived here left."

"You mean whoever killed the one-eyed pirate and put him in the wall?"

Antonia shrugged. "Maybe. Or maybe whoever lived here came home after a long trip at sea, maybe a year later, said 'Phew! It stinks in here!' and moved out."

The second floor was more interesting. After sneaking down creaky house stairs, the girls found another big bedroom facing the street, with two smaller rooms in the back. They all had windows with worn-out drapes full of holes and rips, so Antonia turned the lamp as low as she could without extinguishing it. These rooms had furniture covered with dustcloths. The white shapes hunched around, looking like misshapen ghosts, giving Antonia the willies, although she'd never say so to Charlotte.

After checking the rooms, they decided to start their search in the big bedroom. Pulling back the dustcovers on the biggest object revealed a bed with a towering headboard of dark, carved wood that reminded Antonia of the table in the secret room upstairs. The other sheets concealed a couple of boring chairs, a washstand with a marble top, and a dresser. The girls opened all the drawers and peered under the bed. All they found was a thick layer of dust. Antonia swallowed her disappointment. Charlotte was more vocal. "Where's all the treasure?" she asked, stomping on the braided rug at the foot of the bed. A puff of dust rose up around her outsized woolen sock.

"We haven't explored the back rooms or downstairs yet," Antonia reminded her.

The two small rooms in the back of the house were equally disappointing.

Charlotte sighed. "Let's go downstairs."

Antonia said, "We oughta put the sheets back on the furniture in case your ma or Mrs. S gets the house keys. You don't want them to suspect someone's been in here snooping around."

They had just finished pulling up the last dustcover and were in one of the little rear rooms when Antonia picked up the lamp and heard…something…outside.

A cut-off yell? A dog yip?

Whatever it was, it was immediately drowned out by a jumble of clucks, squawks, and bird-like screeches and hollers.

Antonia froze, clutching the lamp, hardly breathing. "What's *that*?"

Charlotte stood by the door, standing on one leg and rubbing her ankle with one wool-socked foot. "Oh, just the chickens. They make all kinds of funny noises."

"At *night*?"

Charlotte scratched her nose, leaving a smudge behind. "Sometimes. If a stray cat or dog gets in and bothers them. Lucky and Eclipse know better, 'cause Cluck, the rooster, chases them away." She shrugged. "Could even be someone all tipsy in the back alley. Once a man who was half-seas over decided to sleep in the chicken coop. The chickens fussed so loud they woke me up. I got Ma, and she got Master Edward, and he rousted the drunk out of the coop and chased him away."

"Huh." Somewhat mollified, Antonia joined Charlotte, and they started down the creaky, squeaky staircase to the main floor. Antonia couldn't help thinking that they were now a long way from the hidden room, now two staircases away at the other end of the house. What if someone broke in and came after them? A real person, not some make-believe evil pirate captain-king.

What would they do?

She hadn't considered that before. But she did now, after the chickens and the weird noise from the backyard. And she didn't even have her knife with her to protect them. *Some pirate princess I am.*

"You're walking too slow," Charlotte said in a loud not-quite-a-whisper. Antonia hurried down the rest of the stairs. They were now in the entryway by the front door. Charlotte headed into what looked like a front parlor, while Antonia stood so the lamp cast light into the parlor as well as around the hallway. She stared at the front door, recalling how Mrs. S had mentioned the locks on the front and back doors were special, one-of-a-kind, specially made locks that were unbreakable.

So no escaping through the front or back doors, even if she and Charlotte wanted to. Antonia spotted a walking cane with a burly wooden knob in the hall stand. Setting the nightlamp down, she went over, pulled it out, and swung it a little. It would make a good weapon, she decided. And maybe useful for tapping on walls and floors looking for hidden compartments or doors. After all, whoever had used the secret staircase originally must've had a way to enter from the first floor that didn't require knocking down a wall. She was about to tell Charlotte they should search for a secret door that would get them inside the wall when she heard a sound she *did* recognize. A sound that sent chills shooting up her neck.

The distant metallic scrape of a key turning in a lock.

Chapter Eighteen

The sound wasn't coming from the front door, right in front of her, but from deep inside the house. From the back.

With a gasp, she doused the light. What should she grab as a possible weapon? The lamp? The cane? The lamp was useless, unless she intended to throw it. She set it on the hall stand, hoping it would look like it belonged there, snatched the cane, and dashed into the front parlor. Enough light leaked through the worn drapes to show Charlotte, crouched by the front window, lifting the lid of a window seat.

Antonia grabbed her arm. "Someone's coming in the back," she hissed. "With a key."

Charlotte's grip on the lid slipped, and it banged shut.

"Jesus!" Antonia at least had wits enough not to yell. "Come on. We have to hide!"

They ran to the parlor door. Antonia, eyes trained on the dark entryway, hearing sharpened by fear, heard a door screech open and shut. Then, the tread of someone not bothering to disguise his advance. And why would he bother to? He'd think he was alone in the house. Antonia was determined it would stay that way.

She pulled Charlotte back into the parlor as a dim light in the hallway grew brighter. Whoever it was, he was coming their way. With a light.

She tugged Charlotte behind the open parlor door, and they flattened against the wall. Antonia peered through the crack in the hinges into the hallway. She gripped the cane tight in one sweat-slippery hand, put her mouth close to Charlotte's ear, and whispered, "Stay quiet as a mouse." Charlotte gave a little nod, her breathing trembly and shallow. Antonia's heart beat so hard she was sure the pounding echoed throughout the room. A bright pool of light swept past the crack at the door, followed by a shadow figure and footsteps going up the creaky stairs.

Relief turned to horror as Antonia tried to recall: Had she left the upstairs door to the secret room wide open? She couldn't remember.

If she did, and he found it, he would also find the secret room and the staircase in the wall. And he would go down and see the hole in the pantry. And he might go through it, into the other house, while everyone was asleep. Antonia didn't want to think about what might happen after that.

And it would be all her and Charlotte's fault.

Antonia heard footsteps in the big bedroom above them on the second floor. She mashed her lips against Charlotte's ear again, said, "We gotta get out of here," and grabbed Charlotte's hand. The two girls ran, silent in their wool socks, toward the rear of the house. They passed a dim opening that Antonia was pretty sure led to the kitchen. The door had to be near. She handed the cane to Charlotte and, arm outstretched, scooted forward in quick steps. The dull glimmer of the doorknob formed out of the dark, just before her fingers touched the wood panel of the door.

Antonia turned to Charlotte. The whites of the young girl's eyes and the blur of loose hair around her shoulders were barely visible. She whispered, "When I open the door, we run, fast as we can." She gripped the cold metal doorknob and twisted. It didn't move.

Footfalls sounded in the small room overhead. Antonia put both hands on the knob and twisted harder. Nothing. She turned to Charlotte. "It's locked!"

The footsteps above faded, moving toward the front of the house. *Maybe he's heading for the stairs.* If so, they were trapped, with no time to retreat to the parlor. Antonia dragged Charlotte away from the door, whispering, "We have to hide!"

"Where?" Her question came out as a tiny squeak.

"In here!" They bumbled into the kitchen. A weak light from the direction of the alley bled through the dirty window over the sink. The tenor of footsteps changed, and Antonia heard the creak of the staircase. He was coming downstairs. After that, who knows? He might head to the front parlor. He might head out the back door.

Or he might come to the kitchen.

For a moment, Antonia considered breaking the window. But he'd probably come running fast, and they'd have to somehow clamber up onto the sink and out over broken glass to escape. No, it'd be better to hole up until he left.

Charlotte clung to her arm, shivering. "Where do we hide?" she whimpered.

Antonia looked around wildly. She'd been in tight spots before but not with a younger kid she had to protect. Behind the kitchen door? But no. If he came in and walked toward the sink, the minute he turned around he'd see them, their white clothes bright as day. Her gaze slid over the table, chairs, sink, and cast iron stove and locked onto the towering icebox blocking the pantry door. One side had three stacked square doors. The other side had one smallish door up high, probably for ice. Most of that side was covered by a large rectangular door for the main compartment.

Would the space inside be big enough to hold them both?

It had to be.

She dragged Charlotte toward the icebox, levered up the handle of the largest door to release the latch, and breathed a sigh of relief when it swung open as silently as if its hinges had been oiled the previous day.

Charlotte tried to pull away. "We'll suffocate and die in there!"

"No we won't," panted Antonia. "Go!" She grabbed the cane from Charlotte and shoved the younger girl inside. She twisted the lever handle so it pointed down again, just like all the others on the face of the icebox. Bringing the cane with her, she climbed into the metal-lined interior, pressing her back against Charlotte's bent legs.

The cold of the metal penetrated Antonia's flannel nightclothes, settling on her skin. Holding the cane between her knees, she hooked her fingers around the thick door's inner edge and pulled the panel toward them. With the latch sticking out, the door couldn't close completely. She eased the door open a little, then gathered a bit of her nightdress hem and mashed it between the inner edge of the door and the icebox frame. Gripping the inside edge of the door with her fingertips, she pulled it toward her, hard as she could. Jammed in place by the cloth against the doorframe, the door stayed "stuck," nearly closed but not quite.

She hoped that, if he came into the kitchen and happened to glance at the icebox, the door would *look* shut. She also hoped the door didn't come unstuck, swing open, and tumble her and Charlotte onto the floor. Cramped into a crouch, Antonia pressed back against Charlotte trying to straighten her legs a little. She wiggled a bit as one of the girl's knees dug into her spine.

They were a tangle of nightclothes, loose hair, limbs, and the cane. Charlotte's chin dug into the top of Antonia's shoulder. Her rapid breathing whooshed past Antonia's ear. One of her shins was wedged tight against Antonia's side. A corner of the little wooden box jabbed Antonia's hip. Antonia was sure it'd leave a bruise. But if a bruise was the worst that happened—

The linoleum popped as the intruder stepped into the kitchen. Both girls sucked in their breath. There was a soft whisper of sound, and Antonia realized the trespasser was talking to himself. Or herself. She couldn't tell if it was a man or woman who'd entered and now stood inside, muttering in a low voice.

The whispers slithered into the metal box, unencumbered. Antonia screwed up her face as a soft flood of foreign but oddly familiar words wound around her. Although she couldn't interpret what was being said, she could tell the intruder was not happy, but angry. Desperate. A frantic feverishness surged through the mutterings. She recognized not words but phrasing. The tumble of syllables reminded her of when John Hee from the music store spoke in his native tongue. It also brought to mind the times she had been in Chinatown and heard the rise and fall of conversations in a language from a faraway land, the sound of voices trickling like rain off a roof.

Then, Antonia caught it: syllables she'd heard before. *Shenmah.* Charlotte's whisper, hot against her cheek, confirmed her suspicion: "Chinee!"

Antonia nodded to let Charlotte know she'd heard and understood.

Whoever was out there was muttering in Chinese.

Chapter Nineteen

SATURDAY, MARCH 11

Antonia wished she could see who was muttering and walking aimlessly around the kitchen. Each time the footsteps and whispering voice brushed past the icebox where she and Charlotte were hiding, Charlotte's trembling intensified. Antonia was afraid the tremors would set her to shaking and the cane to knocking on the compartment's metal lining.

It felt like the intruder was in the kitchen forever. But eventually the faint slap of steps on linoleum gave way to the creak of wood floorboards. Antonia held her breath, listening. The metallic scrape of a key was followed by the louder squeal of the back door opening and closing. After a pause, she heard another, fainter scrape as the intruder locked the door behind him. Antonia thought she could even hear the shudder of feet on the backyard porch and stairs. A bit of chicken-fuss erupted, convincing her that she was right: the intruder had left.

She sighed with relief, and her tense muscles eased. The pressure of Charlotte's knee increased against Antonia's spine. "Can we get out now?" Charlotte whispered and pushed harder.

Antonia's back twinged in response. "I can't breathe, and I've got cricks in my legs."

Antonia shoved the door open and, using the cane, managed to uncurl and stagger out onto her feet. She felt like she'd never run again from all the muscle cramps.

Charlotte inched out and sank to all fours. "Yeow! My feet don't work. They're all pins and needles."

"We weren't in there that long," scoffed Antonia, then regretted her words. It had seemed like a long time to her, too, but it was probably only a few minutes. Maybe five. She held out the cane. "Use this. Stand up and stomp your feet. But do it quiet."

"There's no one awake to hear us," grumbled Charlotte, pulling herself upright with the stick.

Antonia glanced at the open icebox. "The hole Master Edward made in the wall is just on the other side." Another thought occurred to her. "Suppose your ma heard the chickens, got up to see what the ruckus was, and then decided to check on us?"

Never mind that the skulker might come back. Having Mrs. Krause poke her head into Charlotte's bedroom and find the bed empty, start looking for them, and find the hole in the pantry or—even worse!—catch them sneaking out of it... Now *that* was scary!

"It takes more'n a little cluckety to wake Ma," said Charlotte. "She sleeps like a log."

Antonia shut and latched the icebox door. "Come on. Let's go."

They scurried to the entryway, where Antonia replaced the cane and grabbed the extinguished night lamp, saying to Charlotte, "If this isn't on your bedstand in the morning, your ma's gonna ask about it." In the dark, they climbed the two flights of stairs to the third story. Antonia promised herself she would bring matches, just in case, next time.

If there is a next time. This time had been a little too close. And who knows when the intruder might return? He had a key and could come back and explore any time he wanted.

Antonia didn't want to admit it, but she was spooked. She sure hoped the hidden door on the third floor was not closed. It'd be hard to locate, especially without a light. She was pretty sure the intruder hadn't found it. He hadn't been in the house very long—even though it had seemed like forever!—and she hadn't heard him go up the squeaky stairs to the third floor.

Relief surged through Antonia when she spotted the faint shadow that told her the hidden door was ajar and their escape route open. "We're lucky he didn't come up here and find this door," she said, pushing the wall panel wider so they could slip through.

"Who do you think it was?" asked Charlotte. "Mr. Harris?"

"Who else could it be?" Antonia countered. "Unless maybe his son. But do they speak Chinese?" Now that they were back in the secret room with the door to the rest of the "Treasure House" closed, Antonia felt better. But that didn't mean she wanted to hang around and debate who it could've been. She added, "Come on. Let's get back to your room and talk there."

They managed to get down the narrow staircase in the wall without falling down the steep stairs thanks to the railing and the little bit of light coming in the tiny window on the landing. After blocking the hole in the pantry, the girls snuck back into Charlotte's bedroom. Antonia, relieved to hear Mrs. Krause's peaceful snores beyond the wallpaper, whispered to Charlotte, "Maybe we should tell your ma about someone being inside that house."

"No!" Charlotte sounded alarmed. "We can't let her know we heard or saw anything! She'll think it's an evil spirit, and that will make things worse!"

"But if Mr. Harris is sneaking around…"

Charlotte grabbed her arm. "Maybe he just wanted to say good-bye to the house. He just walked around. He didn't take anything."

"We don't know that," countered Antonia, thinking of the treasures she and Charlotte had made off with.

Charlotte shook Antonia's arm. "Promise me. We're blood sisters, and you have to promise me that you won't say anything. If Ma finds out we've been sneaking around, we'll be in sooooo much trouble! She'll beat the living tar out of me! And she might say I can't see you anymore."

Antonia's stomach dropped. "Really? She wouldn't let us be friends?"

The younger girl squeezed Antonia's arm tighter, making it hard for her to move. "Promise me! Promise me!"

The little wood box in Antonia's pocket pressed up against her hip, the sharp corners poking her like a guilty conscience. "Okay. I promise," she said, thinking that, well, whoever it was, was gone anyway. And they didn't really know who it was. It might've been the locksmith, but maybe it wasn't, and if it wasn't, then they'd be tattling on the wrong person.

Charlotte let go, leaving Antonia's arm burning where her little fingers had dug in.

Antonia rubbed her arm in the dark. "You know, it might not've been Mr. Harris at all. Maybe someone else has the keys. Maybe that lawyer with the face like he'd sucked on a lemon. He had all the papers that your ma and Mrs. S had to sign before Master Edward could break down the wall."

"Maybe," said Charlotte, lighting the lamp. "Does he speak Chinee?"

"*Chinese*, Charlotte. It's pronounced *Chinese*. And I don't know if *any* of them speak Chinese." Antonia had to admit, that stumped her.

"Okay, okay. *Chinese*. Eeesh. I'm tired. I wanna go to bed." Charlotte yanked off the borrowed shirt and socks and shook dust from the hem of her nightdress. Meanwhile, Antonia pulled off her flannel gown, reversed it to right-side out, and stuffed the little inlaid box with its unknown contents into her valise. She had tugged off the stinky socks and was balling them up to toss under the bed when she heard Charlotte mutter something.

"What?" asked Antonia, keeping her voice low.

"Your nightshirt. You had it on inside out. That's good luck. Maybe that's why we didn't get caught. But switching it around to right-side out on the same day brings bad luck."

Antonia wanted to roll her eyes but just said, "It's not the same day. It's gotta be after midnight now."

They climbed into bed, Antonia first so she lay next to the wall. The sheets were cold. She shivered and pulled her feet up under the gown, rubbing them together.

"I wish we could've stayed longer," said Charlotte wistfully from her side of the bed. "It was a good adventure. We found that box. And got to explore more of the Treasure House." The terror of the past hour seemed to have drifted away.

"We can go back another time," said Antonia, thinking that they really hadn't explored the main floor rooms much. "Maybe your ma would let me come over again next weekend."

Charlotte yawned. "You and your aunt should come live here next time someone leaves."

Antonia smiled in spite of her concern. To live in the same house, to have a friend she could see every day after school and chickens in the backyard, and to get to listen to the Edwards' stories of sailing around Barbados and the Orient over dinner each night—

The Orient!

She rolled over to face Charlotte. The girl was lying on her back chewing on a strand of her straw-colored hair, eyes all droopy-sleepy. "Charlotte, how did you know that person was speaking Chinese?"

"Ohhh—" It was a sleepy exhalation. "Master Edward taught me some words. He sailed to all those Orient places long ago. He sometimes buys fish for Ma to cook for dinner in Chineetown. He says they have the best fish, and he knows how to haggle with them in their heathen language. That's what Ma calls it, a heathen language. So I don't tell her he taught me how to say good morning and good evening and even count to ten. I like it. It doesn't sound like a heathen language to me. Listen: *Yī, èr, sān, sì, wǔ, liù...*" She drifted off.

Master Edward?

Antonia stared at the dim lamp flame flickering on the bedside table. She thought of his creased face and twinkly eyes. His smile and his funny eyebrows. His kindly way of speaking to her and Charlotte. Then she thought of some other "kindly" people from her past who'd turned out to be badder than bad. People with all kinds of secrets they didn't want known.

Could it have been Master Edward in the house? Maybe he knew the locksmith. Maybe Master Edward got a key from old Mr. Harris. Maybe they were in cahoots.

But why would he go inside that old house?

Maybe he's looking for hidden treasure, like us.

She thought of what she and Charlotte had found in the hidden room—the objects, the maps, the papers. Maybe Master Edward knew the one-eyed dead man from his seafaring days. Maybe Master Edward was a privateer too! Then she remembered what Edward the Second had said about his brother at dinner. That he was an expert at fighting hand-to-hand in close quarters. But Edward the Second also said his brother was a good guy, who enforced the law at sea. And what had Master Edward replied? "All that's in the past now."

Suddenly, the quilt and her flannel nightgown weren't near enough to warm her up.

Chapter Twenty

"Antonia! Wake up!" Charlotte's perky voice sliced through Antonia's dream about chasing a kitten through the back alleys of Leadville in a bitter cold winter.

Eyes shut, Antonia said, "Aren't you supposed to go to Mass?"

"We're back! You didn't even move when Ma woke me, and we tiptoed out of the room. You were asleep like a *log*!"

"Logs don't sleep," muttered Antonia and opened one eye. "Is that your church clothes?"

Charlotte pranced around in a frilly dress that had more ruffles and ribbons than fabric. "Yep. But I have to change, and you need to get dressed so we can help Ma with breakfast."

On cue, Mrs. Krause appeared in the bedroom doorway tying on a clean apron. "Good morning, Antonia. Both of you, dress for the day quickly, please. I need you to gather eggs for breakfast." With that, Mrs. Krause left, closing the door behind her.

Antonia staggered out of bed. She wished she could wash the dust from the previous night off her arms and legs, but that'd have to wait until she got home. She shucked off her itchy night-dress and looked up to see Charlotte was down to her chemise and petticoat. The chemise had a little lace along the neck and sleeves and the petticoat was the same. Antonia twisted her mouth. All the frilly stuff was so silly. Who was going to see it anyway? Despite having to change out of one outfit and into another, Charlotte was ready first. Antonia was struggling with the laces on one of her boots, which had inexplicably become knotted. "Dang it," she muttered.

"I'll race you to the coop!" Charlotte said cheerfully. She dashed out the door, and Antonia heard her say, "Where's the egg basket, Ma?"

"Where it always is, Charlotte. By the back door."

Lucky, the black-and-white cat, raced into the bedroom. Antonia finished tying her shoe and scratched behind his ears. "Maybe this'll be a lucky day after all," she said to the cat, then stood and stretched. He purred and wove around her feet. The smell of bacon and biscuits floated in through the open door, and Antonia headed out to the kitchen.

"Good morning, young lady."

She jumped as Master Edward and his brother appeared in the hallway. "Morning," she said, eyeing the master-at-arms warily. He didn't look like he'd been sneaking around half the night in an old, dusty house.

His brother smacked his lips gleefully. "Bacon and biscuits? A breakfast feast."

Master Edward said, "Ah, wait until you have Mrs. Krause's scrambled eggs. Light and fluffy as a cloud."

Eggs! She was supposed to help gather them! Antonia hurried to the kitchen, where Mrs. Krause was busy over the stove turning bacon with a long-handled fork. "Charlotte just went out," she said, not looking up from the two cast iron frying pans.

Right then, Charlotte's voice floated in through the screen back door. "Mama?" There was something peculiar in how she said the word. Something shaky. "Mama, come here quick."

Mrs. Krause sighed irritably. "Antonia, could you go help Charlotte? Perhaps Cluck is being particularly ornery today or Henrietta won't move off her eggs."

Mrs. Krause hadn't even finished talking before Antonia banged through the back door. Charlotte stood by the coop, the basket on the ground. A feathered lump lay nearby. Antonia headed over, thinking it was a sleeping chicken. As she got closer, her throat tightened. No sleeping chicken ever looked like *that*.

It was Cluck, the rooster.

His head was nearly hacked off, hanging onto the neck by a glistening skein of skin. His red comb was painted with dried blood. A similar brown stain, sucked into the thirsty dirt-packed dust, spread beneath and around the feathered body. Antonia looked at Charlotte, questions ready to tumble out.

But Charlotte wasn't looking at Antonia or at Cluck.

Her face, even paler than usual, was directed at the back of the Treasure House. She whispered, "Look," and pointed. Antonia followed her gaze and finger to the small back porch.

Something was there.

Something big, lying on the boards. Only instead of feathers flapping in the bright morning breeze, it was the corner of a worn black jacket. Hands clenched into fists, Antonia headed toward the back porch of the Treasure House as Charlotte screamed, "Mama! Mama! Come quick!"

The black-coated shape took human form. A man, Antonia thought, because there were pants and the hand flopped onto the top step was hairy and didn't look like a woman's. She put one foot on the bottom stair and steeled herself to climb the other four to the porch. The blood here wasn't entirely dry, although the old wood planks had soaked up a lot.

Who is it?

That was the overriding question in Antonia's mind as she stepped up the first stair, then the second. She couldn't force herself to move any faster. It was as if the man was asleep, lying there in a mess of bloody clothes, and she was charged with not waking him.

Not that he'd be waking up on this side of the living.

The head was turned away. The hair was all bloody, so she had no idea what color it might be. She stepped up the third stair.

A sharp clickety-click followed by a rattle-y caw-caw sent her reeling back down the steps. A rush of feathered wings brushed the top of her head. Antonia spun around to see a crow soar away from her, coming to perch on the coop. It shifted side to side restlessly, making sharp caws and clickety noises. Almost as if it were warning Antonia to not continue forward.

"Holy Mother of—!" Mrs. Krause hurried to Charlotte, hand over her mouth as if she hadn't meant to say that, to almost take the Lord's name in vain, but couldn't help herself. She clasped Charlotte to her side. Charlotte buried her face in her mother's apron. Boarders were now coming out the back door. One of them said, "Mrs. Krause! What is going on? The bacon is burning on the stove!"

Antonia knew this was her only chance. If she wanted to see who was lying on the porch, she'd have to do it now. She forced herself up the stairs. The feet were closest to her, the trousers rucked up revealing one hairy white calf and… She blinked, not sure if she was really seeing what she thought she was seeing. The other was wood. A peg leg? She moved up to the ruined head, only partially aware of the fact that the skull was split open, with the brains partly poking out. She stepped around to see the face, or what could be seen of it through the bloody scrim. Still, she could see enough to finally identify who lay there as dead as dead could be.

Old Mr. Harris. The locksmith.

"Antonia!"

Numb, Antonia turned at Mrs. Krause's voice. The woman stood there, a commanding hand outstretched in her direction, a hard-edged expression on her face as if she had gathered all the pieces of her emotions, glued them together, and hidden them away. Mrs. Krause said, "Come here, this instant." Without taking her eyes from Antonia she called out, "Someone get the police."

Antonia felt strangely light, as if her feet weren't really on the ground and her mind was floating away on the currents. She turned, went down the steps, and started slowly toward Charlotte and her mother. The crow on the coop took off again, its shadow passing over Antonia.

The boarders crowded behind Mrs. Krause, looking everything from horrified to curious. Master Edward and his brother, both of whom had their linen napkins tucked into their collars, stood apart from the others. Edward the Second ripped off his napkin and said, "Police you say? Straightaway, ma'am. There's a call box on the corner of the block. Right, brother?"

Master Edward nodded, and his brother raced back into the boardinghouse. The door slammed shut.

Eyes fixed on the old house, Mrs. Krause whispered, "Six crows. Death walks among us now."

Antonia turned and followed her gaze. A bunch of crows preened and muttered on the roof above the porch and the body, their black feathers glistening in the morning sun.

Master Edward lifted anchor from his spot and drifted over

to the mother and daughter. "Now, Mrs. Krause," he said sooth-ingly, "the birds have naught to do with this. Set the old tales out of your mind. Naught we can do for the poor soul there. Let's care for the living now, eh?" He patted Charlotte on the head.

Antonia halted by the coop of anxious chickens. She didn't want to come any closer to the master-at-arms, with his big hands, his piercing eyes, his slightly hunched posture. He reminded her of a vulture. He didn't seem so friendly anymore.

Master Edward was regarding her in a similarly wary fashion, with a slight frown. She could see his scrutiny shift from her, to the body on the porch, then back to her. His eyes narrowed slightly, speculative, cold.

All of a sudden, Antonia felt very much alone.

Chapter Twenty-One

A persistent *tap-tap-tap* pulled Inez out of a too-short sleep. She awakened with an unladylike snort to find she'd fallen asleep on her back. The hairpins at the back of her head poked her further awake, and she sat up, looking blearily around.

Somehow, she had managed to sleep through the cacophony of church and cathedral bells that beckoned parishioners to services early Sunday mornings. That, and her apparently open-mouthed slumbering position, could be directly attributed, she thought, to her almost-all-night vigil in the music store's office and the downing of copious cups of coffee dosed with whiskey. As the hours had ticked by, the ratio of J. H. Cutter Old Bourbon Whisky to the Hills Brothers "Finest Arabian Roast" had increased until the final cup was bereft of all caffeine.

The tapping outside the door was beginning to mirror the pounding of her head. "A moment," she called, rubbing her eyes. At least she had managed to shed her day clothes for nightwear, even if she hadn't brushed out her hair.

It had to be Antonia. No one else could have breached the

downstairs door. But now Inez realized she had thrown the bolt on the upstairs door that led to the apartment proper. She sighed and glanced at the pocket watch on the bedstand. She had not expected the girl until quite a bit later in the morning and had hoped to catch up on some much-needed sleep.

The hours of dealing with the drifts of paper by lamplight had been unpleasant but absolutely necessary. She had sifted, sorted, and organized. She reviewed and recorded. She compared the amounts of the accounts receivable and payable to be sure there were sufficient funds coming in from receivables to pay what she owed. She calculated employee wages, wrote paychecks, and updated employee financial records. The store's business ledgers were finally up to date, their columns of numbers checked and double-checked. Her final task had been to create a list of the names of customers in arrears on their accounts. She was appalled at herself for letting the business paperwork slide into the mess it had become.

In the end, as far as she could tell in the wee, predawn hours, the business was doing well. In fact, it seemed to run quite well without her.

She pulled her cashmere and silk dressing gown off the peg by the bedroom door and wrapped it around, tying the cord loosely around her waist. "Yes, yes, coming. Patience, patience," she said irritably.

This early in the morning, the San Francisco damp seemed to intrude everywhere, rising up through the soles of her bare feet. The tapping continued until she threw back the bolt and opened the door, saying, "You're early—" and stopped in shock.

De Bruijn, looking neat and proper for a Sunday with his standard black jacket and bowler hat, lowered the silver-handled cane he'd been using to knock on the door and stared back with an equally confounded expression.

The flush that enveloped her banished the chill from her limbs. Her first impulse was to slam the door in his face and shout at him through the wood panel. Instead, she crossed her arms defensively over her breasts, took a step backward, and demanded, "How did you get in here?"

His gaze flickered to her chest, which was probably inevitable given her stance only called attention to that part of her anatomy, then quickly rose to her face. "The street door was ajar."

"I didn't—" She stopped again. It was entirely possible she hadn't closed the door tightly. As for locking it… "I thought you were Antonia. She spent the night with the Krauses. What are you doing here? We're not scheduled to meet until later today. Much later. Mid-afternoon. Is there some sort of emergency?"

He didn't retreat as she expected him to but stood his ground. At that close distance, she caught a shadowed concern darken his visage at her mention of Antonia and the Krauses. "I received a message from Detective Lynch. Something has happened at Mrs. Krause's boardinghouse. Or rather, in the next-door property."

Her heart clutched. "Antonia!"

He shook his head. "It has nothing to do with her, or he would have said so. At the very least, he would have sent a runner here for you." He added gently, "He knows where she lives."

She set one hand against the doorframe, knees weak from the sudden release of dread.

Now he looked away, as if observing her fear dissolve into relief was too intimate for him. "Detective Lynch requested my presence as soon as possible. I suspect the request comes from Mrs. Krause, since she engaged me for the matter we plan to discuss later today."

His gaze returned to her. "Since you and Mrs. Krause are

joint owners of the property in question, I thought you would wish to be there as well." His dark eyes took in her state of dishabille, and she felt the flush return to her skin. He continued, obviously striving for a neutral yet tactful tone, "I shall let them know you have been notified and will be there presently."

"No!" she said. "Wait here. I'll go with you. I won't be long."

Ever the gentleman, he only raised his eyebrows. But she knew right away what he was thinking, what that expression of polite doubt implied. "Mr. de Bruijn, I can, when necessary, complete my toilette in far less time than the average woman." She added pointedly, "I am not, and have never been, the average woman. As you must surely know by now."

He pulled out his pocket watch. "How long do you need?"

"Ten minutes. Not a minute more." And she shut the door.

It had been quite a while since she had been called upon to don her clothing in such a rapid fashion, but she found her fingers still knew what to do and where shortcuts could be taken. Too, there was no need to pull out fresh attire. Yesterday's outfit was near at hand. True, it was in a bit of a crumpled state, given that she had simply tossed it on a nearby chair and not bothered to hang it up overnight, but that was of little consequence under the circumstances.

In a flash, the clothes on the chair were replaced by the nightdress and robe. Inez flung on yesterday's stockings and garters, cotton drawers, chemise, and corset. For the latter, she was glad that all she had to do was fasten the front and not fuss with the laces, which were still tied. Then came the camisole, the petticoat, and finally the skirt and casaque. She was thankful the top had large buttons down the front, not a hundred tiny ones.

The shoes took longer than expected, since she fumbled her boot hook, and it rolled under the bed. She grabbed her brown hat, stabbed it with hatpins, and prayed that the state of her hair, not undone but not smooth either, would escape notice.

As Inez raced through her preparations, she envisioned de Bruijn on the second-floor landing, pocket watch in hand. This imagined posture only served to vex her and increase the speed with which she dressed. When she threw open the door for the second time within half an hour, gloves in hand, she was ready to lob a snappish response to the expected pointed reflection on the time. Instead, she saw him at the bottom of the stairs standing by the half-open door to the street. He had taken her cloak off the peg by the entryway and was holding it out for her.

"I hailed a hack for us," he said as she hurried down the stairs.

"Good thinking." She turned so he could settle the cloak on her shoulders. "You didn't actually say what the trouble is," she added as she stepped out onto the sidewalk.

Once she was in the carriage and had arranged her skirts, de Bruijn stepped in, sat across from her, and folded his hands over the top of his cane. "Someone has been murdered."

She gaped at him, arms half-raised to straighten her hat, which had been knocked askew as she entered the carriage. "In the boardinghouse?"

"The victim was found behind the building next door. The one that you and Mrs. Krause now own."

Inez squeezed her eyes shut. "Well. This certainly adds credence to Moira's claim the place is cursed," she muttered. "Oh, why did I ever agree to this venture?" Then realizing how callous that sounded, she opened her eyes. De Bruijn was looking at her, not with disgust or horror, thank goodness. Rather, he seemed curious, as if waiting for her to explain further.

For a moment she was tempted to blurt it all out, right there and then in the privacy of the carriage enclosure. Her finding the commission and the key in the entombed man's shoes. Her misgivings about Moira's streak of stubbornness. Her vague uneasiness about the sudden blossoming of intense friendship between Antonia and Charlotte. Her neglect of the store.

She swallowed it all and said instead, "Forgive me. That was unbelievably cold of me to say. Is the identity of the deceased known?"

"The message to me was very brief," de Bruijn said in his quaint formal way.

It was at anxiety-inducing times like this that his undeniable European upbringing—whatever it was, for Inez had not been able to ferret out much about his background—seemed to rise to the fore, cloaking him in utter urbanity. It was sometimes hard for her to remember that he was a chameleon, who could and did change his appearance, his attitude, his apparent social status as easily as he exchanged a working-man's cap for a bigwig's top hat or a simple sack suit for bespoke eveningwear.

Their carriage clipped a curb, jostling them about and giving rise to an unintelligible growl from the driver above. Inez realized they were traveling fast for city streets. De Bruijn must have paid for speed. As the carriage swayed around a corner, they locked eyes across the narrow carriage floor, and despite her growing anxiety, she felt an unspoken rapport.

There he sat, cool as a continental cucumber. That was one of the things she admired about him, albeit grudgingly because it was also annoying at times. Murder, mayhem, even madness— she had seen him face it all without flinching, without losing his head or his ability to reason.

Suddenly, she was glad he had stopped at her apartment, had acquiesced to her desire to accompany him, and had dashed out to capture a hack while she wrestled with her boot hook. Inez fought an impulse to reach across the small gulf between them, take his hand, and say "thank you." Better, she thought, to focus on what lay ahead and not get distracted.

She looked out the window, breaking eye contact. "I hope the girls did not view the scene. In any case, I imagine Mrs. Krause will be in pieces, considering how the corpse in the wall rattled her so."

"Detective Lynch is there. From what I've observed, he is one of the best on the force. If anyone knows how to handle such complex circumstances, he does."

The carriage slowed and squeaked to a stop. He gave Inez a small nod and smile of encouragement as the driver opened the door. De Bruijn exited first and offered his hand to help her alight. While he paid the driver, Inez gazed at the two houses. Alike in style but with one well groomed, the other needing a good coat of paint and much care. She thought of them as siblings: one cossetted, the other neglected. Conjoined by walls and secrets.

They approached the boardinghouse, and de Bruijn gave the doorbell ringer a twist. The bell rang deep inside, and they waited. Inez hoped against hope that whoever had the misfortune to be murdered in the backyard was a vagrant, who had had the bad luck to be set upon by local hoodlums. It would not be the first time Inez had witnessed such. Both California's San Francisco and Colorado's Leadville had a bad element that thrived under cover of night's darkness. And although she hated to think so, it would be more "tolerable" if it were a random occurrence involving a random stranger.

But what if it were one of Moira's boarders? If that were the case, Inez could envision a general exodus, as Moira's home took on the reputation of being a house of ill omen. *Oh, that would be the worst.*

A heavy tread alerted them that someone was approaching

from inside. The door opened, and Detective Lynch stood there, surveying them both. "Ah, good. I'm glad you are here, Mr. de Bruijn. And I see you've brought Mrs. Stannert with you. Just as well."

Inez stepped forward. "How is Antonia? Where is she?"

Lynch stood back to let her and de Bruijn enter. "Miss Antonia is with the younger girl, Miss Charlotte, in the dining room. They are both doing as well as can be expected under the circumstances. We have finished talking with them as well as most of the boarders. Mrs. Stannert, you are free to take Miss Antonia home as soon as we are done here."

"Let me see her for myself," said Inez, "then I will answer any questions you have."

Lynch stopped her from brushing past him. "A few words with you first." He added, more kindly, "Mrs. Stannert, I understand. I have children too. Please, trust me when I say she is all right. This will take just a few minutes."

Inez glanced at de Bruijn, who gave her a reassuring nod. She tried to rein in her anxiety and impatience. "Very well."

De Bruijn spoke up. "Detective, do you know who the victim is?"

Lynch removed his hat and brushed his sleeve across his forehead a trifle wearily.

"Ah, that. Might as well tell you. If I don't, you'll find out soon enough, as all who are here are a-twitter about it."

Inez gave voice to her silent fear. "One of the boarders?"

The detective settled his cap back on his hair, which was a distinctive ginger-red that marked all the Lynches. "'Tis a locksmith. Harris, by name. I gather he is known by most all here."

Shocked, Inez asked, "The elder or younger Harris? Joe or Paulie?"

Lynch said, "Ah, yes. I recall mention they are in the same line of work. Like father like son. 'Tis the elder, Joseph Harris."

"Are you sure?" she asked.

"A boarder, Mr. Edward, made a positive identification, as did your young Antonia."

"Antonia?" Inez couldn't fathom why Lynch would have let her view the corpse of a murdered man.

"She and Miss Charlotte found the victim. According to the girls, they were in the yard gathering eggs and found someone had killed the rooster. Then they spotted a figure lying on the porch. Antonia went up to see who it was. This was before the girls knew he was dead, I gather. Thought he was a bummer, sleeping it off."

Inez shuddered. Unfortunately, Antonia was no stranger to death in its various forms. When Inez had first met the girl, she had been living in and roaming the back alleys of Leadville under the direst circumstances in the worst part of town. But still.

Lynch continued, "The victim's son is on the way here. Of course, I did not ask Mrs. Krause or any of the boarders to view and put a name to the deceased. Mr. Edward volunteered, and that was enough. 'Twas a gruesome death, although I'd guess it was quick enough."

"Which Edward identified him? Edward the First or Edward the Second?" she asked, remembering Master Edward's ominous denunciation of Harris's treatment of Moira. At Lynch's puzzled expression, she waved a hand. "Never mind." She'd figure it out later. The pounding in her head, which had vanished on the carriage ride, had returned.

"Was a weapon found?" de Bruijn inquired. "Any clues as to the perpetrator?"

Lynch hesitated. His blue-eyed gaze flicked to Inez. "Perhaps it's best we talk of that apart, Mr. de Bruijn. 'Tis not a fit subject for mixed company."

Inez said, "Are you afraid of disturbing my feminine sensibilities, Detective Lynch? If so, please put that thought aside and continue."

His lips compressed beneath his waxed mustache. He looked at de Bruijn, who said, "If what you wish to say is more broadly known by those inside, there is no reason to demur. Besides, Mrs. Stannert is quite capable of remaining silent, if required."

Lynch seemed to weigh de Bruijn's words, then sighed. "Let's speak outside." The three stepped out onto the front porch, Lynch shutting the door behind them. "There's no keeping information close on this one, I suppose. As you say, they were all gabbing away amongst themselves when we arrived."

It rankled Inez that it apparently required de Bruijn weighing in to change the detective's mind, but she set that aside to attend to his words.

"We did not find anything that could have produced the fatal wound. Of course, the coroner will perform his examination, but it was clearly a sharp-edged weapon, wielded inexpertly. One blow didn't quite do it, so there was a rush to finish the job. That's just my opinion, you understand. And there is this—" He glanced again at Inez but addressed his remarks to de Bruijn. "Mrs. Krause has an axe she uses to slaughter the chickens. Her boarders have verified that she keeps it in the backyard, in a chopping block by the chicken coop, and that she keeps it very well sharpened. The axe is nowhere to be found."

Chapter Twenty-Two

SUNDAY, MARCH 12

Inez thought of the shouting match between the older Harris and Moira the previous evening. How many besides her, Antonia, and Master Edward had heard them throw invectives at each other? Inez did not believe Moira capable of murder, but might others think differently?

"And the murderer?" she asked.

"We are still in the early stages of investigation," said Lynch slowly.

"It could have been a hoodlum, could it not?" she pressed. "Someone looking for an easy mark. Falling upon the man, surprising him in the dark."

"Well, now," said Lynch sharply, "we don't know what happened. No one seems to have heard any disturbance, aside from the chickens making some noise."

De Bruijn frowned. "And what was Mr. Harris doing here in the first place?"

"Now *that* we would like to know," said Lynch.

Did he enter the house? Is it unlocked? Where are the keys? Inez was trying to formulate one or all of those questions without sounding coldhearted when Lynch said, "And before you ask, Mrs. Stannert—and I assume this is on your mind, for it was Mrs. Krause's first query herself—he had no keys on his person."

The rattle of horse and carriage interrupted their conversation. A hack pulled up to the house, and the door flew open before the wheels had stopped turning. The young Mr. Harris jumped out, raced up the walkway, then stopped on the lower porch step. He looked up at the three of them gathered outside the door. "Detective Lynch? I am Paulie Harris. I got your message. I would have been here sooner, but Mother, when she heard about Father..." Harris stopped. Inez thought she saw his eyes water. He whipped off his cap and swiped a quick hand across his face before climbing the remaining stairs.

"Thank you for coming, Mr. Harris," said Lynch. He put a hand on the younger man's shoulder as if to steady him. "We need you to view the deceased and see if you can identify him. Normally we'd wait until he'd been to the coroner and undertaker, but in this case, since several have suggested it may be your father, we thought best to have you come see for yourself."

"Of course, no, of course. Father went out last night and did not return, which is unlike him. This morning Mother was nearly beside herself. It is better that we know sooner rather than later." Harris's soft voice broke as he struggled to regain his composure. He took a deep breath. "I am ready, then."

Lynch nodded. "Detective Rose will meet you and me at the back door and accompany us to the spot." He looked at Inez and de Bruijn. "If you would follow and wait in the dining room. I'd like a word with each of you, separately, once Mr. Harris and I are done."

He opened the door and gestured for them all to enter.

The dining room was a tense, confined rumble of voices.

From the hallway, Inez could see all the residents of the house assembled about the table as if for a meal, even though no food, no plates, sat before them. They were all in deep conversation. Although conversation was perhaps not the right word, for everyone was talking and no one listening.

When Lynch and Paulie Harris entered the dining room, conversation snapped to silence. All eyes were on the young locksmith as he made his way through to the kitchen. As soon as the two were out of sight, the buzz picked up again at an increased volume. Inez paused under the archway leading to the dining room, de Bruijn at her side, trying to get the sense of the scene before entering. Antonia and Charlotte, sitting in the same chairs as the previous night, spotted them first. A flicker of relief brightened Antonia's drawn face, but then she bit her lip and looked down, fiddling with the catch of the valise on her lap. Charlotte glanced at Antonia as if to take her cue from the older girl. Inez caught more than a little guilt in the glance.

What have those two been up to?

Inez immediately chided herself for the thought. After all, if Antonia had been the one to see the dead locksmith close up, close enough to identify him, of course she would be shaken. And if Charlotte had been nearby...

Moira sat at the head of the table, a handkerchief clutched tight in one hand, listening to the elderly couple who occupied the third floor, whose names Inez had forgotten. De Bruijn took Inez's elbow, a touch of encouragement to nudge her forward. Moira saw them and half-rose from her chair with a tremulous smile. Inez suspected that smile was meant for de Bruijn, who was instead observing Antonia's bent head with a worried frown. He leaned close to Inez and said in a low voice, "You should take Antonia home and away from here as soon as you have spoken with Detective Lynch."

Inez hesitated. "I should talk to Moira."

"Let me do that."

Inez nodded and went over to Antonia, laying a gentle hand on the girl's tousled head. Antonia's shoulders moved a little, but that was all the sign she gave that she knew Inez was near. Inez sighed and looked up to find Moira staring at her, smile replaced with stony scrutiny. Moira's narrow gaze seemed to pick Inez's appearance apart from hat to hem before moving to de Bruijn, who stood slightly to one side—close, if needed; somewhat removed, if not.

The light dawned as Inez realized what Moira was seeing: her business partner arriving in the company of the urbane and admittedly pleasing-to-the-eye private investigator *she* had hired. What's more, Inez felt and probably looked disheveled, and, most damning, she was wearing the same clothes she had worn the previous night. The conclusion Moira had drawn from this scenario was obvious.

And so, *so* wrong.

The elderly woman from the third floor lifted a querulous voice. "When can we return to our rooms? I have missed church and breakfast and am about to miss my morning nap!"

Inez sat in the empty chair by Antonia. "Antonia, Detective Lynch wants to speak to me. After that, we will leave." Seeking to comfort her ward, she covered Antonia's hand, which was still toying with the clasp on the valise, with her own. Antonia's fingers bunched up beneath her palm.

The snap of the back door closing sent everyone into high alert. Lynch and the young locksmith appeared. The two were accompanied by another man, who Inez thought was probably the aforementioned Detective Rose. Harris, looking shaken, slumped against the wall, obviously trying to compose himself.

Lynch stepped forward and raised his voice, even though the

room was completely silent. "Ladies, gentlemen, thank you for your help. You may repair to your rooms or go on about your business. If any of you recall hearing or seeing anything beyond what you've already told us—"

"Just the chickens making a ruckus," said J. T. Edward.

"And the kittens making such a noise with their running and rumpusing up and down the hallway and stairs," said the wife of the elderly couple. "And don't forget the ghosts in the walls!"

Antonia's fingers twitched, and she pulled her hand away from Inez's.

"Ghosts, chickens, cats, yes, we've taken note," said Lynch, sounding very serious. "If anything else comes to mind—"

"We'll be sure to tell you!" said the other half of the elderly couple.

Lynch turned to Paulie Harris. "So sorry for your loss," he said gruffly. "We'll do what we can to find the one responsible."

Harris nodded.

"I or Detective Rose will come speak with you later," he continued. "We'd like to know more about your father's whereabouts yesterday. It could help in our investigation." Lynch turned to Inez. "Now, Mrs. Stannert, a few minutes, please. Then you, Mr. de Bruijn."

Charlotte grabbed Antonia's arm. "Can Antonia and I be excused?" She seemed to be addressing the room at large. Moira broke away from the elderly couple and came over.

"Why don't the two of you go back to your room, Charlotte, until Mrs. Stannert is ready to take Antonia home." Her tone was studied and polite, despite the strain on her face.

Inez stood. "We will talk later, Mrs. Krause."

"Yes. Tomorrow, perhaps?" Her eyes bored into Inez. "There were no keys. He had no keys upon him. My axe is gone. The police think it was used to commit this awful crime. That house brings nothing but ill fortune and death. And those awful crows…"

Inez frowned, trying to follow the logic of this. "Crows?"

Antonia seemed to finally come around. She stood and said, "Come on, Charlotte. Let's go to your room like your ma said." She looked at Inez for permission. Some of the color had returned to her face, and she looked more like herself. Inez nodded. "Go."

At that point the teacher, Miss Ashby, approached Moira and said in an undertone, all in a rush, "Mrs. Krause, I'm sorry, but I am giving notice as of today. I cannot stay." She glanced at Inez as if looking for an ally, then back at Moira. "I am sure you understand. I will pack my things and call for them later this week if you could just store them here for a few days for me."

"Miss Ashby," Moira sounded bewildered, "where will you go on such short notice?"

"I have cousins in the city. They are expecting me today for dinner. They will be happy to have me stay with them until I find another place."

With that, Miss Ashby joined the other boarders leaving the dining area. Moira wouldn't meet Inez's eyes, instead turning toward the kitchen. "The bacon and toast burned to cinders this morning. I have a mess to clean up."

Inez suspected "the mess" referred to more than just the morning's destroyed victuals. Inez wondered how many other boarders would give notice before the day was done.

Lynch had moved out into the hallway. "Mrs. Stannert, meet me in the front parlor, if you will." It was a polite command.

Inez was gathering herself together when Paulie Harris cleared his throat at her elbow. She turned, surprised. She had forgotten he was still in the room. "Ma'am, Mrs. Stannert, I would like a word with you as well. Not now but perhaps tomorrow?

Briefly?" He fumbled in his jacket pocket and handed her a business card: Harris & Son, Locksmiths, with an address south of Market. "I'd appreciate it. Mother and I will need to...make arrangements but not tomorrow."

He looked at Inez with such misery that she said against her better judgment, "Very well. It will have to be early." With a pang of guilt for not saying it sooner, she added, "And my sincere condolences to you and your mother on the tragic death of your father."

"Thank you." He looked away. "Early is fine. Any time after daybreak."

After he left the room, Inez turned to de Bruijn, who still stood patiently nearby. "Perhaps he has a set of keys in the shop to give us," she said. "Odd that the locksmith was here without keys. Perhaps the murderer took them. And what was he doing here in the first place?"

"I could see a case being made that he was out for a late walk, came to this area, which was familiar to him, and was set upon by a stranger," said de Bruijn. "A crime of opportunity. I am not saying that is what happened, simply that it presents a sensible scenario. One that does not require much investigation. Given that the force is stretched thin throughout the city, particularly the detective unit, I suspect the detectives will want to close the case quickly."

He glanced over Inez's shoulder. "Detective Lynch is expecting you in the front parlor. Best not to keep him waiting. I will go speak with Mrs. Krause while you answer his questions."

A lot of clanking and clanging of iron kitchenware emanated from the kitchen as if in response.

"If you would, ask her what she meant by the crows," Inez said and headed to the parlor.

The detective stood by the large front window, gazing out

at the street, hands clasped behind his back. He turned when Inez entered and indicated one of the many chairs. She said, "I would prefer to stand, since you indicated this would be brief."

"As you wish." He pulled out a small leather notebook but did not open it. Simply tapped it on the edge of a curio table full of nautical-themed knickknacks, including a miniature ship in a glass bottle. "Strange how we first have a body tumble out of the wall of the house next door to this fine boarding establishment, and now, another is found on the back porch of the same dwelling. All within the space of a handful of days. And with the same people—more or less—in attendance. What do you make of that, Mrs. Stannert?"

She spread her hands. "I was not here when Mr. Harris was discovered. However, I agree with you. It is strange. Do you think there is a connection?"

"If there is, it is separated by decades." He switched subjects abruptly. "I understand you were witness to an argument between Mrs. Krause and the two Harrises last evening."

She blinked. "Well, yes. How did you hear of that?"

He smiled wryly. "Most all inside the house heard it, at least the parts that were shouted. And Miss Antonia heard as well, since she was with you. I'd like your take on it."

Without knowing what was heard and reported, there was no sense in prevaricating. She decided she had no choice but to relate what she could recall. So she did.

He took no notes. Simply nodded from time to time, which reinforced her suspicion that she was verifying what he already knew. When she finished, he said, "Did the Harrises say anything directly to you as they left?"

"Well, the elder Mr. Harris was quite hot under the collar. He said he would go speak to Sherman Upton, the lawyer who was acting on behalf of the seller, Bertram Taylor. Paulie Harris tried to calm his father, and eventually, they took off."

"Did Joe Harris threaten you in any way?"

"Of course not!"

"Did he threaten Mrs. Krause?"

"No, but there was much flinging of words back and forth, and he did—" she stopped.

"He did what?"

"He did accuse her of being…hysterical," she said the word slowly, hating the very sound of it. In her experience, it was a term often slapped upon women who took a stand and an appellation that tended to stick.

"Did she seem overwrought or hysterical to you?"

"No more than anyone might be under the circumstances."

"Did Joe Harris say anything else?"

"He did say, 'She will not get away with this.'"

"And what was the argument about, do you know?"

Inez bristled. "Of course I know. And I suspect you do, too, since you've talked to Mrs. Krause and everyone else here. The entire brouhaha concerned the blasted keys to the house next door!"

His eyebrows rose at the expletive, but she barreled on. "Either through neglect or for some obscure reason that I cannot fathom, Joe Harris did not turn them over to Mrs. Krause or me once the sale was complete. The locks on the doors appear to be one-of-a-kind, so, as a result, the building remains sealed up tight as a drum and just as inaccessible."

The tapping on the table eased. He tucked the notebook back into an inner pocket. "Why not break the door or a window?"

"You'll have to talk to Moira about that. I have tried to reason—" Inez stopped. She didn't want to go into Moira's superstitious nature, which would only serve to reinforce the notion of her being a "hysterical" woman. Inez finished stiffly, "I suppose Mrs. Krause and I will have to do something of the sort now, unless Paulie Harris has a set of keys at the shop."

"After the Harrises left, did Mrs. Krause or the boarders say anything to you about the quarrel?"

Inez found her attention wandering to the bottled ship on the nearby table. That such an object, symbolizing life on the free and open seas, should be confined in glass. Trapped.

She tore her gaze away and considered. "Mrs. Krause and I discussed the keys later, after dinner. I offered to go visit Mr. Harris the next day, that would be today, and see if I could resolve the situation. I also said I would go to Mr. Upton, if necessary."

Then, she remembered. "Oh! Master Edward. He was inside and apparently listening while Mrs. Krause and Mr. Harris were going at it. He told me he thought the older Mr. Harris was quite rude to her. He said—" She stopped again, wondering if she might be unfairly focusing the eye of the law on the former seaman.

"He said...?" prodded Lynch.

She cleared her throat. "He said it was wrong for Mr. Harris to treat Mrs. Krause so and that Mr. Harris would have to answer for his behavior and...more."

"More?"

She gave a small shrug. "I don't know what he was referring to. However, Master Edward indicated he knew Joe Harris in the past."

Lynch nodded. "Thank you. If you think of anything else that might help our investigation, please contact me. Would you let Mr. de Bruijn know I'd like to speak with him?"

"Of course. We are done?"

"We are."

Inez stopped at the door and, trying for a light and friendly tone, said, "So, where is your shadow today?"

He was leafing through his notebook and looked up, puzzled. "Shadow?"

"Detective MacKay."

"Ah." He returned to his notebook. Inez saw a muscle jump in his jaw. "MacKay's been reassigned."

Surprised, Inez wanted to inquire about this development, but it was clear from his posture that Lynch had said all he was going to say on the matter.

She went to the kitchen to tell de Bruijn his presence was required in the parlor. The private investigator sat at the scarred kitchen table with Moira. She had her elbows on the table, her head in her hands. Inez heard her say, "I do not know what I am going to do. I just—"

Spotting Inez, de Bruijn cleared his throat, cutting off Moira mid-sentence. "We can talk more tomorrow, Mrs. Krause. I see Detective Lynch has sent Mrs. Stannert to summon me. Let me think on what you've said."

Moira straightened, touched her hair. "Certainly, Mr. de Bruijn. Mrs. Stannert, I imagine you are eager to take Antonia home. Now would be a good time."

She stood, returned to the sink, picked up a washrag, and set to scrubbing. The smell of charred bacon and burnt toast lingered, not yet vanquished by the biting scent of lye soap.

Inez followed de Bruijn into the hall and asked in a low voice, "What was that about?"

He stopped and faced her. "I'll explain when we meet later today."

"So, you still intend to come by?"

"Of course." He smoothed his short beard, which was already immaculately groomed. "And there is a new development that should please you. Mrs. Krause has agreed that I can bring you into the investigation."

"Good!" It should have been that way from the start, but she was not about to quibble. "In that case, I have some things to discuss with you as well."

He managed to look a trifle amused even while remaining serious. "'In that case?' So, you were not going to mention these 'things' if circumstances had remained as they were?"

Inez looked at him blandly. "The detective is expecting you in the front parlor. Best not to keep him waiting." She went to find Charlotte's room, which she recalled as being between Moira's private chamber and the kitchen. The door was cracked. She pushed it open to find the two girls sitting cross-legged on the floor, heads almost touching over a piece of paper. Antonia was sketching with a pencil, saying, "And the little window is sixteen stairs up, right about here."

"Antonia, it's time for us to leave."

Both girls startled. Charlotte whipped the paper out from under Antonia's pencil and folded it up. "I guess you gotta go now, Antonia. I'm sorry about...well. You know."

Antonia nodded, shoved her pencil into her open valise, and stood. "Just remember your fractions. Recite them today, three times. I bet you'll do real good on the test tomorrow."

"Test? Oh, the test! Yes, I'll practice." Charlotte trailed Antonia and Inez down the hall. "Maybe I can get Miss Ashby to listen to me recite. I don't think Ma will have time today." She sounded wistful. "I hope you come back soon, Antonia."

"Maybe." Antonia glanced at Inez and added, "Maybe when it's not a school night."

At the door, Charlotte gave Antonia a fierce hug. "I wish you could stay. I wish you could stay forever! Oh, and you too, Mrs. Stannert."

Inez smiled down at Charlotte. Wisps of her straw-colored hair had fallen over her ears and her collar was crooked. Inez wanted to reach out and straighten her collar, smooth her hair, clean the faint smudge of dirt from her nose. "I am certain we'll be back again sometime soon. Perhaps you might want to come by and see where Antonia lives sometime."

"Oh! That would be fun. But Antonia has to come here for overnights."

"Because we can concentrate better here," said Antonia quickly. "And Mrs. Krause is a great cook."

"There is that," said Inez, thinking about her own nonexistent culinary skills.

"And Antonia isn't afraid of anything. Not ghosts, not dead bodies, not *pirates*."

"Hmmm," said Inez noncommittally.

Antonia glared at Charlotte and said, "*Make-believe* ghosts and pirates."

"Right. But real dead bodies."

Inez suppressed a shudder and said, "Best you go see if you can help your mother, Charlotte." The girl nodded and headed to the kitchen, humming to herself. Inez glanced at the closed parlor door. The murmur of male voices told her de Bruijn was still in there with Lynch. She wondered how that conversation was going. She bet the police detective was not peppering de Bruijn with question after question as he had done with her.

She led Antonia down to the sidewalk, said, "This way," and began walking up O'Farrell to Jones Street. "Aren't we going home?" Antonia asked, clutching her valise in front of her. "That's the other way."

Inez stopped at the corner of Jones and began looking for an available hire. "Unfortunately, I have things to do, and I don't want you rattling around by yourself after what you've been through. So, I am taking you to Mrs. Nolan's for now. I'll return in a few hours, we'll have Sunday dinner, and then we'll go home together."

"I don't want to go to Mrs. Nolan's." She sounded sullen.

"It's just for a bit." A buggy halted for them, and Inez gave the driver Mrs. Nolan's address.

As they entered the carriage, Antonia burst out, "If you weren't going to take me home, why couldn't I have just stayed there with Charlotte?"

Inez looked at her coolly. "Mrs. Krause made it plain that it was time for us to go. It has been a difficult day for everyone. She needs time for herself and Charlotte."

"Bah! She doesn't pay any attention to Charlotte. Treats her like an orphan."

"That's ridiculous!" Inez said sharply, then shook her head, tamping down her irritation. She continued in a gentle tone, "I understand you identified Mr. Harris's body on the porch. Why did you go up there? Surely you could tell something was wrong. Why didn't you call for Mrs. Krause? Or get one of the gentlemen boarders to look?"

Antonia sneered, and Inez saw a flash of the girl she had first met in Leadville during the terrible autumn of 1880: distrustful, dodgy, closed unto herself, with an exterior as hard as a little river stone. "Why ask any of them when I could see for myself? Besides, if I'd done that, they would've told me to stay back and then said, 'You're a kid. A girl. Don't look, you'll faint.'" She glared at Inez. "I bet someone bashed Mr. Harris and cut him up with Mrs. Krause's axe. His brains were all over the porch. And I didn't faint when I looked. And I told the coppers what I saw and didn't even throw up."

A lump rose in Inez's throat. She didn't know if she felt sorrow for Antonia's lost innocence or a touch of perverse pride in the girl's strength in the face of situations that would have had most people reaching for smelling salts or a bucket to retch in.

The carriage arrived at their destination. Inez paid the driver, and she and Antonia went up to Mrs. Nolan's boardinghouse, where they normally took their suppers. Mrs. Nolan opened the door, and Inez started to explain the situation, trying to be vague.

She'd hardly started when Mrs. Nolan clapped a hand to her breast. "And Antonia was at Mrs. Krause's when it happened? Oh, heavens above! Come in, come in. Antonia, did you have breakfast?" At Antonia's head shake, Mrs. Nolan continued, "We'll take care of that right now!"

Inez said, "I'll be as quick as I can." Antonia started to turn toward the kitchen. Inez said, "Antonia, I'll take your valise home for you," and reached for the handle.

"No!" Antonia clutched her valise close. "I'll keep it with me. It's got my books."

Mystified, Inez watched Antonia walk away without saying goodbye. Mrs. Nolan sighed and shook her head. "Poor little thing. Don't you worry, Mrs. Stannert. I'll cosset her and make sure she gets plenty to eat. She's probably peckish and out of sorts from what happened. Oh, yes, I've already heard the story. You say you have errands to run today? On a Sunday?"

"Actually, I have tasks at the store and must then speak with Mr. de Bruijn. You remember him, of course."

Her eyes brightened. "Of course! You're meeting with him? Bring him to dinner! There is always room at the table for such a polite gentleman. Elevates the table conversation. The boarders and I so enjoyed his presence last time you brought him around for a meal."

Inez smiled a tight smile, recollecting the avid interest her bringing a gentleman to dinner had engendered. "Oh, yes. I remember."

"I recommended him to Moira, you know, when she was looking for help with that, ah, well, I'd rather not speak of it, but you know *the problem in the wall*. Heavens, that place is cursed! Two murders at the same place. How could that even be?"

Inez shook her head. "I have no idea."

But I intend to find out.

Chapter Twenty-Three

Back in her apartment, Inez did all that she'd neglected to do before her hurried departure that morning with de Bruijn. She hung her outfit to air, washed, and changed into fresh underclothes and a comfortable plaid everyday dress with a high collar. Finally, she gave her dark hair a thorough brushing, scenting it with rosewater before pinning it into a neat knot.

Telling herself she needed to eat something before dinner, she rummaged through the minimally stocked kitchen, uncovering the *cornetti* Antonia had brought from Carmella's the previous day. Inez devoured one, leaving two for Monday morning's breakfast. The citrus fragrance, faint but noticeable, filled her senses as she stood at the kitchen window, contemplated the busy street below, and pondered her upcoming meeting with de Bruijn.

Now that Moira had agreed to her being informed on de Bruijn's investigation, did that mean he had to impart all he had learned so far to her? And would he be compelled to answer all her questions as well? She found the idea rather titillating.

Sunday being ostensibly a day of rest, she expected she would have the store to herself, so she and de Bruijn could meet uninterrupted.

Once in the office, she took a few minutes to look through her unopened private mail. There were a couple of letters from people in Leadville, which she set aside for later. Instead, she opened the letter from her sister, Harmony, in New York. Harmony's letter, as usual, was full of details on Inez's son, three-and-a-half-year-old William, and his accomplishments:

Willie loves to run and does not cry when he falls and skins his knees. He finds the stairs vastly entertaining and marches up and down them for hours. "No" is still his favorite word. I talk about his "Tante Inez" and how much you love him and say someday we shall all take a train and visit you in San Francisco...

With a lump in her throat, Inez set the letter aside. Giving Harmony and her husband legal guardianship of William had been one of the hardest things she had ever done, but she never regretted it. Her son was where he needed to be. Back East he was well cared for by family and physicians who kept him robust and healthy despite his physical frailties, which had compelled Inez to place him in her sister's arms and send him East from Leadville almost three years ago. Inevitably, thoughts of William turned to thoughts of Antonia. Antonia had had no one to turn to, so Inez had taken the girl into her life and her heart. Again, Inez never regretted this decision, but sometimes she doubted her qualifications for raising the strong-willed girl. She fervently hoped she was half as good a guardian to Antonia as Harmony was to William.

One letter she had been expecting was not in the slim pile

before her. Although correspondence between her and Reverend Sands sometimes lagged, his latest reply was taking longer than usual. Frowning, she drummed her fingers on the desk. She reminded herself she would not take on the distasteful role of forsaken woman pining for her long-absent lover, and he was not the kind who would simply vanish without a word. She was hardly pining. There was plenty on her plate, and de Bruijn was due at any moment. She swept the letters into a desk drawer and shut them away, along with her thoughts and her complicated past.

When de Bruijn tapped on the back door of the office with his silver-headed walking stick, she had readied a pot of coffee, a small covered sugar bowl, which, amazingly enough, still had some sugar in it, and two clean cups. The cups had necessitated some scrambling about once she realized all the available crockery in the office area was in a state of disgrace.

He rested the cane by the back door, placed his bowler on the table, and accepted her offer of coffee but turned down the offer of "a little something extra" from a proffered bottle of brandy. Inez went into her private office and opened the safe. She gathered up the bag of gold coins and paused over the Confederate commission and the small key. Before offering those up, she wanted to see whether this would truly be a two-way conversation or not.

She shut the safe, returned to the round table, and slid into the chair next to him. Setting the bag on the table, she remarked, "It is hard to believe this all began just a few days ago."

He nodded. "Mrs. Krause came to see me Friday morning, and here it is Sunday." He reached for the bag, but she set her hand upon it, pulling it fractionally in her direction.

"Just so I am clear, Mr. de Bruijn," she said pleasantly, "what did Mrs. Krause agree to in your discussion in the kitchen?"

He sat back and laced his fingers over his waistcoat, looking at her steadily.

"Are you permitted to brief me? Are we working together?"

He exhaled loudly. To her it sounded like a sigh of acknow-ledgment.

"What," Inez pressed, "did she say exactly?"

His gaze shifted to the left as if recalling the conversation. He said slowly, "Her precise words were 'Tell her anything she wants to know. Do whatever you think is best.'"

Inez sat back, triumphant. "Well, then. It seems clear enough. She is allowing you to do as you see fit and for me to be part of the investigation, so it seems we are now partners in this ven-ture." She pushed the coin bag toward him. "In that case, once you have looked this over, I have something more to show you." *A little honey to sweeten the pot.*

"I am, of course, always grateful to have your assistance, Mrs. Stannert."

She marveled at how smoothly he moved from reluctance to acceptance. A clever move if he hoped to lull her into compla-cency and then gently set her to one side.

He tipped the bag, spilling the coins in a slow yellow river onto the polished mahogany. Turning over a random number, he said, "If this is a representative sample, they are probably all from the San Francisco Mint."

He picked up the bag and inspected both sides.

"As I told you," said Inez, "no markings on the material."

He shook it a little, turned it inside out, and, without a word, set it before her.

Astonished, Inez read the stamped ink inscription on the bag: U.S. MINT CENTS. She looked at the double eagles on the table and sputtered, "Those certainly aren't pennies!" then grudgingly added, "I never thought to turn the bag inside out. What made you do so?"

"Look at the seams," said de Bruijn.

Inez picked up the empty bag and reversed it so the stamp was on the inside. Sure enough, small, ragged seams lined the edges. "Well, I never claimed to be a seamstress." She dropped it onto the table. "Why a bag for pennies, do you think?"

"I expect cent bags were much more plentiful than those for double eagle coins. Less noticeable if missing. Less memorable if seen."

She began to scoop the coins back into the bag, stopping once in a while to examine them. All displayed the tiny "*S*" mintmark under the eagle's tail. "So, do you think these were taken from the mint illegally?"

"It is possible."

"Might someone at the mint know more?"

"That is also possible. But finding someone knowledgeable and willing to talk about it could prove difficult."

Inez frowned. *Didn't Bertram Taylor say he worked at the mint?* She had paid little heed to their awkward conversation in the anterior room of Buckley's law office, being far more concerned with what the two lawyers were saying behind the closed door.

He leaned toward her. "What are you frowning about?"

"The coins seem little enough to go on if the objective is to uncover the dead man's name," she replied. "But now, since we are partners, I have something else I'd like to show you. Call it a goodwill gesture and proof of my commitment to cooperate."

She rose and pulled out the bundle of cloth as well as the shoes. Taking care not to cover the bag of coins, she dumped them on the table. "I retrieved these from the coroner's office yesterday."

"So I heard," said de Bruijn dryly. He stood, unrolled the remains of the double-breasted overcoat, and scrutinized the rags within.

"I understand you have been busy, so you can thank me for handling this task for you," said Inez.

Ignoring her comment, he picked up the shred with buttons and said, "This looks military in nature."

"My thought exactly. Now, let me show you what I found in his shoes." She went to the safe and brought back the naval commission and the small brass key, setting them before de Bruijn.

He gingerly picked up the fragile paper by the edges and read aloud, "Confederate States." He set it back down on the table. "It seems the nameless man was involved in your war."

Your war.

Those two words told her: No matter how many years had passed since his arrival in the states, he was still not of this country. Did he even have a homeland? She studied him anew. Perhaps that explained why he had taken up being "finder of the lost" as his mission and profession. Perhaps he, himself, was lost. A man without roots.

He picked up the key. "What does this open?"

"I don't know." She took back the commission and re-folded it carefully. "My guess? Something that is either still in the house or long gone. It is too small to open the front or back doors. Unfortunately." She looked up at him. "I'd gladly heave a brick through a window, but Mrs. Krause refuses to consider us entering the house except by an unlocked door. Perhaps you can convince her otherwise. You have certain powers of persuasion."

"Perhaps." He set the key down. "It seems there is little more to be gained from what we have here. And there is a complication. Of sorts."

"Which is?"

He smoothed his beard. *That gesture again.* She was discovering more of his "tells" as time went on. This one seemed to arise when he was pondering a new bit of information he was preparing to impart. Particularly, she thought, when he was not certain how that information would be received.

"As I mentioned, the city's detective force is shorthanded. Recent trouble on the piers has consumed much of their attention, so solving Harris's murder is not their highest priority. Detective Lynch knows of my investigation for Mrs. Krause and asked that I look into Harris's death as well." His eyes shifted again. "It is not my usual practice to work with police. However—"

"However, there is always a first time." Inez smiled, seeing a way forward. "In that case, perhaps we can work in tandem. Since you will be busy looking into Harris's death, I presume, why don't I see what I can uncover regarding the identity of the poor fellow in the wall? I may know someone at the mint, and I can look into doings in the city during the war."

"Very well. Provided you keep me abreast of developments," said de Bruijn. He slid the key across the surface to her. "If you believe the situation is becoming dangerous, best to retreat and let me know."

"Oh, I shall be careful." She picked up the small key and shook her head. "I thought San Francisco too far west, too caught up in gold discoveries, railroads, and industrialization and growth to be much involved in the war. I was being naive. The war touched everyone, whether they fought in it or not, whether it touched their families or not. Why should it be any different in California than it was in New York or Colorado?"

"I agree. The horrors of war are far reaching. If I may change the subject, how is Antonia after this morning?"

Inez tipped her hand this way and that. "I took her to Mrs. Nolan's for the afternoon. I did not want her rattling around by herself upstairs. Or eavesdropping on our conversation, which she is quite capable of. When I asked her why she approached the body, she said someone had to. Hardly a justification. She claims she is fine, that what she saw was no worse than what she's seen before. But something has shifted in her. She is more like she was in Leadville. You know."

"I don't know."

"Oh! Of course. I sometimes forget you two didn't meet until San Francisco, given that you knew her mother in Denver—" She stopped short. His expression warned her she was about to step into forbidden territory. She did not delve into certain topics with de Bruijn. His relationship with Antonia's now-deceased mother was one such.

To bridge the awkward pause, Inez picked up the key and tapped it on the table. "She has retreated into herself. Presents the same hard-edged, suspicious aspect as when I first met her. Furthermore, I am certain she is hiding something. She is back to lying and prevaricating. Which she is very good at, by the way." She stood. "But why not draw your own conclusions? Come with me to Mrs. Nolan's for Sunday dinner, and see Antonia for yourself."

He rose as well. "An intriguing invitation. I accept, provided I am not intruding."

"Intruding? Hardly." She smiled. "Mrs. Nolan specifically asked if you would grace the dinner table and help 'elevate' the conversation. And if we walk, we will have time to share our plans for tomorrow. With two unsolved murders to unravel, there is much to discuss."

Chapter Twenty-Four

SUNDAY, MARCH 12

When de Bruijn joined Inez at Mrs. Nolan's table for Sunday dinner, Inez marked the spike of interest and approval from all in attendance. From all, that is, except Antonia, who glowered at him, then focused on her plate, responding in monosyllables to his questions. Inez bristled at her rudeness. De Bruijn took it in stride, remarking to Inez when no one else could hear, "Given what she's been through, her behavior is understandable."

With overeager conversationalists and Antonia's attitude notwithstanding, Inez found it a perfectly unremarkable evening and a pleasant hiatus from current events.

———

MONDAY, MARCH 13

Monday morning was the usual race to get Antonia off to school on time. Inez was glad Mrs. Nolan had prepared Antonia's lunch and sent it home with them as the girl was moving slower than usual and acting glum and snappish. Inez tried to be patient and understanding given Sunday's horrific events. But patience, she'd be the first to admit, was not her strong suit.

Finally, Inez slammed a plate with a *cornetti* and a mug of warm milk and coffee in front of her ward at the small kitchen table and asked in exasperation, "What is *wrong* with you?"

Instead of mentioning the dead locksmith, Antonia demanded, "Is he going to come to Mrs. Nolan's all the time now?"

Still thinking of Joe Harris, Inez said, "He who?"

"He. Mr. Worthless Rotten Brown!"

Inez reared back, surprised. "You mean Mr. de Bruijn? You haven't called him that since… What brought this up?"

"Well, he went with you to Mrs. Nolan's at Christmas when I wasn't even here. And last night, everyone seemed to know him. They were talking and…"

"And what?"

"Nothing," she muttered. "Is he going to be hanging around from now on? Around here?"

Inez crossed her arms. *Ah-ha. I think I see where this is going.* "Mrs. Krause hired Mr. de Bruijn to uncover the identity of the man in the wall, and Detective Lynch has asked for his aid in solving Mr. Harris's murder. I will be helping Mr. de Bruijn in his investigations. So, yes, he may be 'hanging around,' as you put it, since he and I will need to coordinate and converse."

Antonia sneered and grabbed her lunch pail and the breakfast pastry, ignoring the coffee-milk. "Huh. I never heard it called *that* before."

"What called what?"

"Coordinate and converse." The way she said the words made Inez drop her jaw. Antonia continued, "Bread and butter. Put four quarters on the spit. Pirooting."

Inez was no stranger to coarse slang. And she knew Antonia had seen and heard much while living with her mother amongst the cribs, brothels, and bordellos in Leadville's red-light district. But she was still stunned to hear such vulgarities roll out of the girl's mouth. She suspected Antonia was trying for maximum shock, angling to get the last word and validate her accusations while leaving Inez speechless. Inez decided to deal with the issue head-on, along with giving the girl a taste of her own medicine.

Antonia turned to leave. Inez, moving swiftly, reached the door first and blocked it, forcing Antonia to halt before her. "You misunderstand," she said calmly. "Mr. de Bruijn and I are not and have not been canoodling, fadoodling, or engaging in horizontal refreshment."

Antonia's eyes widened.

Inez continued, "As I just told you, he and I are collaborating to uncover the truth in both cases. I am taking you into our confidence by telling you this. I expect you to treat what I've told you with discretion." She paused, thinking of all the time Antonia had spent with the Krauses so close to the locus of trouble. "If you know anything which might shed light on these events, I expect you to tell me. And to tell me everything. Understood?"

Antonia's gaze flickered away.

Inez said, "Well?"

Antonia shifted on her feet. "Charlotte and me were talking afterward. Yesterday. In her room. The bloke in the wall had a glass eye. Mr. Harris had a wooden leg. They must've been pirates. That's what we think. We think there's more treasure in the house."

Inez weighed Antonia's words and reactions. Something in her behavior and tone put Inez in mind of a painted fireplace screen, which provided a filtered version of the heat and light while hiding the true nature of the flames. "Anything else?"

Antonia shook her head. "Are you gonna be here when I get home?" It sounded almost like an accusation.

"Of course." Inez pressed her lips together, considering. Perhaps she was being too hard on the girl, who might be suffering under the unpredictability of Inez's actions and absences the last few days. "This morning I have tasks to do for the investigation. I'll be talking to the young Mr. Harris, for one. This afternoon I will be in the lesson room teaching students. After school, let me know you're home, then you can come up to the apartment or read in the back room until I'm done. At five o'clock, you and I shall walk to Mrs. Nolan's for dinner as usual."

Antonia nodded and shifted her book bag onto her shoulder. "I gotta go, or I'm gonna be late for school."

"Well, we can't have that, can we?" She wanted to give the girl a hug, tell her that all would soon return to normal. That she would protect and care for Antonia with every fiber of her being. That she would always be there for her. Instead, she smoothed and straightened Antonia's collar with a gentle hand before moving aside and opening the door. "I'll see you after school," she repeated and watched Antonia clatter down the stairs and out the street-level door.

When she was certain Antonia was gone, Inez went to the girl's room and surveyed her domain. Antonia had done a cursory job of making her bed, the quilt rumpled and crooked. Her nightdress lay in a heap on a chair. Inez picked up the gown and hung it on its peg. Spying a dust-gray film on the hem, she lifted the material to examine it more closely and exclaimed in disgust. The inside of the nightgown was streaked with grime.

What has she been up to?

The simplest explanation would be that her ward had ignored the directive to pack clean nightwear for Saturday night and had simply repacked the same dirty gown from the night before. It would not be the first time Antonia had donned clothes destined for the wash.

But why was it filthy on the inside and not the outside? The girl's two nightgowns were identical. And Inez hadn't recalled seeing the other gown in the laundry, which was to be picked up that day.

It was enough to send Inez on a hunt.

She was averse to prying, but given recent events, she felt compelled to search for the other nightgown. And, if she was being honest with herself, she hoped to allay her sense that Antonia was hiding something more insidious than dusty nightwear.

If she was, Inez thought, it wouldn't necessarily have to do with the current goings-on. Antonia tended to be light-fingered. She might have stolen something. It could be as innocent as a pastry spirited from Carmella's kitchen without asking, a special treat intended for a surreptitious late-night snack. Or a book, a magazine, penny candy. Those were the most innocuous items that rose to mind. Or, she could have squirreled away a stern note from school she was supposed to deliver to Inez. Such missives had been known to go "astray" before.

Inez peered under the bed, opened the dresser drawers, examined the slight wardrobe, feeling increasingly guilty as each hiding spot revealed nothing but what one would expect. Dust underneath the bed, haphazardly folded items in the drawers, a near-empty ink bottle and several broken nibs in the drawer of the small table where Antonia practiced cursive or read books and magazines. The only "contraband" was a crumpled, much-thumbed copy of *Young Folks* mashed under the pillow. Reading after dark was not an unforgivable crime. Inez riffled the pages, pausing at one turned-down corner to read:

...Ever since they had found the skeleton and got upon this train of thought, they had spoken lower and lower, and they had almost got to whispering by now, so that the sound of their talk hardly interrupted the silence of the wood. All of a sudden, out of the middle of the trees in front of us, a thin, high, trembling voice struck up the well-known air and words:

"Fifteen men on the dead man's chest—
Yo-ho-ho, and a bottle of rum!"

Inez half-groaned, thinking she'd be driven to rum herself if Antonia's obsession continued much longer. She flipped the magazine closed, slid it back under the pillow, and tugged the bedding straight. A small lump under the covers near the foot of the bed stayed stubbornly in place. It had been invisible amongst the rumpled blankets, but with the bed now neatened, the bump was obvious. Inez peeled back the covers. There, squashed against the footboard, was the second nightgown.

She yanked it out, gave it a good shake, and uttered an oath. The gown in her hand was just as filthy outside as its twin on the peg was on the inside. Vexed, Inez said aloud, "What have you been up to, Antonia?" Whatever it was, it apparently involved gallivanting outside in nightclothes on the very night and perhaps in the same area where a man had been murdered. When Inez considered what could have happened, her blood ran cold. *I must put an end to this!*

With a final glance around, she repaired to her own room and put the found nightgown in her own wardrobe, determined to have a serious talk with Antonia that afternoon. Thus resolved, she prepared for the day.

———

Before heading to the locksmith shop, Inez detoured into the empty music store and placed a call to her lawyer, Leander Alderon Buckley. The telephone exchange's Central Office was clearly busy. It took some shouting and toe-tapping before she was connected with telephone number sixty-two. Buckley's clerk answered, and Inez asked to speak to the lawyer. Shortly thereafter, Buckley's jovial tone came onto the line. Inez said, "Good morning," and added a summary reminder of who she was, and Buckley responded, "Mrs. Stannert! Of course I remember you. It's only been a few days."

Thus reassured, Inez asked the question uppermost in her mind. "The keys to the house—you know which house I am referring to—are they considered part and parcel of the personal property I and Mrs. Krause now own?"

"An interesting question. House fixtures are generally considered part of the property when they are attached to the property. If personal property is affixed or fastened to the real estate, then it becomes a house fixture. As I recall, the bill of sale included all the property left in the house. Were the keys in the house?"

"Unfortunately not."

"Are they called out specifically in the bill of sale?"

"I am almost certain they aren't. I haven't the paperwork in front of me. I just assumed when we bought the house it included the door keys!" Inez then grumbled, "What a pickle."

"A pickle?"

Inez chose her words carefully. "The keys were not handed over to me or to Mrs. Krause. There was some initial confusion over who had them, and once we realized it was the locksmith, he refused to part with them. And now he's been murdered behind that accursed house."

"Oh, yes. I heard about his demise." His tone had turned from jovial to somber. "I didn't realize lost keys were involved."

"You heard?" Inez was surprised at how quickly news had spread.

"Well, certain personages in the central police station know I have an interest in these goings-on."

"You do?"

"Of course. To start with, there's the issue you brought to me, the disposition of the gold. And then MacKay's unseemly and quite unprofessional conduct when he confronted you in the street. By the way, he will not be inflicting his brand of harassment upon you again." His tone became expansive, self-congratulatory. "I had a word with his higher-ups after that set-to, and he's been reduced to the ranks of street patrol."

Inez winced. "Ah." That explained Detective Lynch's curtness when she had asked about MacKay's whereabouts. She wondered if he blamed her for his partner's demotion. Or worse, whether MacKay himself blamed her for his ignominious return to the streets.

"Furthermore," Buckley continued, "I'll admit to a certain knowledge of the Taylor homes, having plied my trade here on the golden city's shores for quite some time. I've been pondering this the past few days. Captain Taylor and his brother, Jack, left to serve in the war, as many did. After the war, when many returned but the Taylors did not, the stories emerged."

Inez pressed the telephone receiver harder to her ear. "What stories?"

"Whispers that the two houses remained empty because neither brother could bring himself to cross the thresholds given certain dark secrets hidden within. Tales of ghosts and curses passed around the local saloons, growing with each telling. Eventually, the two places were adjudged jinxed by the common man, who would hold his breath if he had to walk past them. Some talked of a falling-out between the brothers before their parting and of 'a fortune in the houses,' which one could interpret as the buildings being valuable as they are well-built and managed to survive the city's earthquakes and fires. The first quakes I experienced were in the early '60s, and the two residences stood then. I remember the ones in '65 and '68 clearly. In both cases, we thought Judgment Day had arrived."

Inez wondered if she might be paying by the minute for his musings. But he wasn't on retainer, so she decided he just enjoyed the sound of his own voice and the captive audience at the other end of the line.

He continued, "I counted the Taylor house tales as nothing more than yarns told by boys and those who had been in their cups. However, all that talk faded away. Several years ago when Captain Taylor sold one of the houses to the Krauses and no ghosts, treasures, or curses emerged, even those who loved retelling old tales gave a shrug. I wonder how many remember those stories now."

Inez's scalp tingled. "Why didn't you tell me this earlier!"

"Well, by the time we met, you had already purchased the property."

"Mr. Upton should have said something," muttered Inez.

"Since he represented the seller, it wasn't his place to warn you. I imagine young Mr. Taylor was glad to be shut of the place. He no doubt viewed it as an albatross. He's probably not heard the old stories, being young when they left and having returned to the area only recently, so I heard. Although perhaps he now regrets selling, what with the discovery of the gold." He cleared his throat. "So, back to your concern. Were the keys taken by the police? If so, it will be a simple matter for me to retrieve them, should you so wish."

"The keys are… Well, I'm not certain where they are. Detective Lynch told us they were not found on the corpse, and he has no reason to lie. I plan to speak with the locksmith's son. I'm hoping he found the originals or duplicates in the shop and is willing to hand them over. But if not…"

"I see." He was quiet a moment. "It is logical that, when you bought the building, you bought the locks mounted on the doors. The locks would be considered fixtures and the keys are an essential part of the locks. I would be happy to accompany you to your meeting with the locksmith's son and make that point."

"No need," Inez assured him quickly.

"Perhaps, then, you'd like me to speak with Mr. Upton, and he could speak with his client, the young Mr. Taylor. Upton left town on Friday and won't return until the end of the week, but I could chase him down when he returns to straighten this matter out for you."

Buckley seemed intent on inserting himself into the process, so she decided to defer then delay. "How kind of you, thank you. And thank you, too, for your clarifications. But let me speak with the locksmith's son first. There may be no need to bring anyone else into this."

"As you wish. Just out of curiosity," his tone became sharply inquisitive, as only a lawyer's tone can, "why don't you and Mrs. Krause simply engage a handyman to take one of the doors off the hinges? Or remove a window? I thought the walls between the two residences had been broken through at one point. I don't quite understand—"

So much for defer and delay. Inez covered her mouth with one hand and leaned close to the microphone box, the better to distort her own voice. "Mr. Buckley? Mr. Buckley? Oh, dear. I cannot hear a word you are saying. You sound like you are at the bottom of a well, lots of echo. The line has gone bad. Thank you again for your help. I will let you know if your services are needed."

She disconnected, grabbed her reticule with the locksmith's business card, and dashed out the back door as the phone began to buzz.

Chapter Twenty-Five

MONDAY, MARCH 13

Inez located the "Harris & Son, Locksmiths" shop on Third Street, just past Verona Place. A dusty window fronting the street showcased bundles of keys, large and small, as well as a random collection of locks of various sizes and complexity. A few ornately designed boxes, perhaps meant for jewelry or cigars, also were on display, delicate keys protruding from their locks. To one side was an array of knives and other sharp cutlery, reminding Inez uncomfortably of the elder Harris's method of demise.

She was further assured that she had arrived at the proper address by a large trade sign in the shape of a skeleton key swinging from a pair of iron chains above the entrance. The "CLOSED" placard was displayed in the window, not surprising given the recent death. The door handle was wrapped with black crepe and tied with a black ribbon. Inez spotted the doorbell and gave it a couple twists. A bell clattered somewhere inside. She peered through the windowpane. The shop area was small, composed mostly of a glassed-in case acting as a counter.

It wasn't long before Paulie's tall stooped figure pushed through a curtain behind it. He circled the glass case, approached the entrance, and opened the door.

"Thank you for coming, Mrs. Stannert." He looked tired, with lines about his youthful eyes, and was dressed somberly. A faded black waistcoat was buttoned tight over nondescript work trousers and a collarless workman's shirt of blue. Without a cap, his unfashionably long dark-brown hair flopped forward nearly to his eyes.

Inez entered, saying, "Morning, Mr. Harris. Again, I am sorry for your loss."

"Thank you," Paulie said, nearly inaudibly. He continued, "And thank you for making the trip here. I need to be close to Mother today." He glanced briefly overhead. Inez surmised from his glance the Harrises lived above the store. Paulie circled back around the counter, indicating she should do the same, and said, "If you don't mind, we'll be able to speak more comfortably in the back of the store." He pushed the curtain aside so she could enter.

The area behind the drape was primarily set up as a workshop. However, a nearby corner was done up as a cozy sitting area with four chairs, a table, and a parlor stove, now cold and unlit. A lamp on a wrought-iron stand provided light. In the rear of the building, light leaked around an ill-fitting back door and through a large but dusty window, doing its best to illuminate the rest of the large space. Paulie gestured to the chairs and said, "Please, make yourself comfortable. Pardon me for not having anything to offer in the way of refreshment."

She was struck by his extreme politeness and even more so by the complete absence of any company. She had assumed the brotherhood of locksmiths would gather quickly in support when one of their own had died. Or that there would at least be neighbors. Perhaps they were upstairs with the bereaved Mrs. Harris.

Sitting in the nearest chair, Inez searched for a way into the conversation. She did not want to seem cold, by jumping right into the business of the missing keys, or nosy, by inquiring whether the Harrises had family or neighbors to support them in their time of travail.

Paulie Harris solved Inez's dilemma by settling himself in the chair opposite hers, resting his elbows on his knees, and saying, "I apologize if what I say sounds cold and unfeeling, but the reason I asked to meet with you has everything to do with my father's death. I understand you sometimes make personal loans at fair rates to small businesses. I am hoping you will consider making such to me at this time."

Inez hesitated. Here was an opening to ask questions, get answers, and gain cooperation before explaining she only engaged in such business deals with women.

Paulie waited for her answer. The lines of strain and worry in his face made him look more like his father than ever. Inez glanced around the workshop. A shroud of sadness seemed to linger over the machinery and tools. She wanted to help this grieving young man. However...

Inez said gently, "Mr. Harris, I will tell you what I tell the other men who seek help from me. I limit my clientele to women who operate their own businesses." She hesitated. She wanted to find some way to bend this, her overarching principle. "Does your mother, by chance, have a hand in running the shop? Perhaps she does the books?"

He was shaking his head. "Mother is blind. The business has always been in my father's hands, but now, it is in mine alone, and much sooner than expected. I had hoped to turn things around myself, given time. However, God has willed it otherwise. I find myself in the position of not even having enough in our accounts to give Father a decent burial."

"Have you tried one of the smaller, local banks? Other lenders? I could suggest a few."

He took a deep breath. "I'd previously explored other avenues without success. And now, I have a confession. Back when terms were being negotiated for the house, Mr. Upton mentioned you and your role in the sale. So I had time to find out a bit about what you do, aside from owning the music store. And of course, I was there when Mrs. Krause gave the pretty speech about how you made it possible for her to expand her boardinghouse business. So I knew, even before I asked you for this meeting, that you only dealt with women. If I had other choices, I would not take this step. But I have seen you are an honest woman. And discreet. Used to keeping secrets. I hope you will keep mine."

To Inez's astonishment, Paulie undid the top buttons of his waistcoat and workshirt, revealing a turn of tight linen over unmistakable cleavage. Meeting Inez's eyes, the young locksmith said, "My given name was Pauline."

Inez held up a hand. "You have made your point. No need to disrobe further."

Paulie fastened up the shirt and waistcoat, buttoning them all the way to the top. "I hope I have not shocked you, Mrs. Stannert."

Inez thought of her own times venturing out in trousers, disguised as a man, and said wryly, "It would take much more than this to shock me, Miss Harris."

"Please call me 'Paulie' or 'Mr. Harris.' It is the name I've used most of my life. And a slip of the tongue could mean the loss of what meager business I have and bring shame upon our family name. Not that there are many who would care. Father didn't make many friends. So, shall we talk?"

Inez's mind churned furiously. *Miss Harris—no, that is Mr. Harris—must be in desperate straits to share such a secret with me.* She appraised the quiet locksmith anew. Faced with Paulie's plea for discretion, Inez decided it would be wisest to simply continue to think of Paulie as a man, lessening any chances of a verbal slip up. Given Paulie's visible ease with his clothing and name of choice, his secret would not be a difficult one to keep. *Perhaps we can come to an agreement that works to both of our advantages.*

"If I may be blunt, Mr. Harris, what sum are you hoping to borrow?" Inez asked.

Paulie focused on his tightly clasped hands, which Inez now noticed were long-fingered and slender. "I'd like enough to bury Father as Mother would wish and to revive the business. If one hundred dollars is not out of line, it is what I would ask for."

He glanced at Inez, who kept her expression neutral. *A modest amount. Worth it, if I can get what I want in return.*

Apparently encouraged by Inez's silence, Paulie continued, "I did all the books for the business. I can show them to you. Explain my plans for the future. Father was never interested in what I had to say. Although the sign reads 'Harris and Son,' this was, first and foremost, his business. As only men can enter the locksmithing trade and I am an only child, Father raised me as a son. I was happy to go along and content to follow in his footsteps and learn a skill that would support us all when he could no longer do so. I owe him everything for encouraging me to be the person I am and for teaching me the basics of the trade."

Paulie looked around the work area, and Inez followed his gaze. A blacksmithing setup occupied some of the space in the back, along with a large grinding wheel. A couple of workbenches sat on opposite sides of the room. Mysterious implements hung on wall pegs along with other trappings Inez could not identify.

Paulie sighed. "We did not, of course, expect his death so soon. Or in such a fashion."

"I am inclined to lend you the money," said Inez. "However, there are conditions. I must know the relationship between your father and Captain Taylor. What is it about that house? There is some dark history in it, clearly, some dark history. And I *must* have the keys to the doors of that"—she almost said *damned*—"house. Your father refused to give us the keys right up to the end."

Paulie's shoulders slumped. At first Inez thought despair bowed them low and the locksmith was going to turn down her offer. But when Paulie looked up, Inez realized the easing was relief at having a burden lifted.

"I'll tell you what I know. My father was beholden to Captain Taylor. They sailed together as young men. Father lost his leg, and his life at sea ended before I was born. But his bond and loyalty to Captain Taylor remained."

"What about Captain Taylor's brother?"

Paulie frowned. "Father never spoke of him much, except as he related to the captain. Captain Taylor was the younger of the two. His brother worked here in the city and had the houses built as you saw them. From what Father said, the two brothers were close. I believe it was a comfort to Bertram Taylor and his mother to have the brother next door, given that the captain was at sea for long stretches of time."

Inez recalled her brief conversation with the captain's son in the lawyer's office. "I believe you're right. The one time I met with Bertram Taylor, he spoke fondly of his uncle."

"When the captain and his brother departed to fight in the war, the captain charged Father with keeping watch over the two homes and to make special locks for both. Father's expertise was the design and manufacture of ingenious locks: unbreakable, unpickable. He handled all such requests. It was a specialty he intended to teach me, but..." Paulie shrugged.

"So your father has always had access to the house? Did he simply check the perimeter and the locks, or did he go inside?"

"He went inside from time to time to be sure things were undisturbed." Paulie looked down at his hands. "He never took me into his confidence regarding the particulars of his arrangements with the captain. What I can tell you with certainty is Captain Taylor supported us for years, when he and his family moved first to the southern part of the state during the war, and then after, when they went to China. I have been keeping the business and household books since I was fourteen, so I was aware of his payments and what it meant to us. When the Krauses bought the first house, he continued to pay Father handsomely. But I saw the writing on the wall. So, once I had the necessary skills, I started to build the cutlery side of the business."

"I understood that Captain Taylor and Bertram returned to California, where the captain passed. Do you know if Mrs. Taylor is still living?"

"According to Father, she went the way of all the earth and was laid to rest in the Orient. When the Taylors returned, I knew the captain was old and probably failing. I wondered what would happen when he passed. My father, however, had complete faith in the captain and his son and said repeatedly, 'As long as the house of Taylor stands, all will be well.'"

Inez raised her eyebrows. "He was partly right. The house still stands, building and bloodline."

Paulie sighed. "But all is *not* well. When Captain Taylor died, my father was confident Bertram Taylor would hold onto the remaining property as the captain had. It was always, 'He will not sell the house, upon his soul.' But he did." Paulie leaned back. "He sold it to you and Mrs. Krause."

Inez shifted in the chair, feeling the shadows close in around her. "Had I known all that would transpire, I would not have financed the venture. It's brought nothing but grief."

"And now, grief upon Mother and me as well." Paulie's sorrow settled on the empty chairs.

Inez waited for the locksmith to compose himself, then said, "When your father refused to give Mrs. Krause and me the keys, he was trying to do what he thought the captain would want."

"That's possible. I had no idea anything was amiss before Saturday evening when Father and I went to the boardinghouse and met you on the sidewalk. Although he had been in a foul mood ever since the sale, his humor darkened further when the corpse fell out of the wall."

"Did he say anything about it afterward? Who it might be? What it was doing there?"

Paulie shook his head. "If he had suspicions, he didn't share them with me. My father's lips were sealed as tightly as the locks he designed and installed on the doors."

Inez weighed whether to tell Paulie about the items in the dead man's shoes to see if it might shake a memory loose. *Not now. Not yet. Let's see where this goes.* "Do you have the keys? They were not found on his person. I hoped the originals or duplicates might be here."

"He always took the keys with him when he went to check the house. I have no reason to believe he did anything different the night he died. But you are right about duplicates. He kept them in the safe."

Inez's heart lifted. "Well, then. It sounds as if this will be a simple matter."

"Not so simple. I do not have the combination."

Her heart plummeted. "May I see the safe?"

Paulie led Inez to one of the workbenches and lit a lamp to

illuminate the heavy metal box underneath. Inez crouched a little, the better to see. It was a standard commercial combination safe. At least it wasn't a one-of-a-kind item like the house locks. But still, safe-cracking was not her specialty.

She glanced at Paulie. "You're a locksmith. Can't you open it?"

"If it were a standard lock, I could. But not a combination lock."

"Well, you'll have to open it sooner or later."

"One of Father's old friends has the proper, ah, 'touch.' Many of the men he knew in the trade have fallen away, but I know a few, still. I should notify them of his passing, in any case."

They returned to the sitting area, and Inez decided to try another tack. "During the war, which side did your father favor?"

"Oh, he was for the Union. Absolutely. He and Captain Taylor both were. Even though I was very young, I remember Father talking about the war, cursing the Copperheads, the Confederate sympathizers, the secessionists—he called them the *secesh*. Father was a man of few words, but not when it came to the war. I think he longed to enlist, but as a one-legged man with a family, and so far removed from the action, he stayed at home."

"I am wondering if your father's death is connected to the findings in the wall," Inez spoke carefully, feeling her way. "You say the Taylors vacated both houses during the war years and did not return. You recall the coins that fell out with the corpse? They were minted in the city in 1863. All of them."

Preparing to sit, Paulie froze, then slowly stood. "The San Francisco Mint?"

Inez took her chair. "That's right. Since your father was a locksmith in the city during the war, I'm wondering if he had any connection with the mint during that time." Inez was certain Paulie got her drift: Could the elder Mr. Harris have stolen the coins? And what about the murdered man? Inez debated whether to reveal more, then decided to show another card in her hand. "The man in the wall had a Confederate naval commission hidden in his shoe."

Paulie stared in disbelief. "You think Father…? That he…? No. He would not. Not ever."

"Feelings ran deep during the war. You said yourself your father was a staunch Union man. And he was caretaker for the house all those years. Isn't it possible he knew its secrets? Think on it."

Still standing, Paulie looked away, fingers drumming on the antimacassar draped over the top of the chair. Inez let the silence stretch. Finally, the locksmith spoke. "I'm certain he never worked for the mint. I was young during the war but old enough to be aware of his work. But, there is something else."

"Yes?" Inez held her breath.

"It connects to the war and Captain Taylor." He spoke slowly as if imparting the information would be betraying a trust.

Seeking to allay Paulie's reluctance, Inez said, "I promise whatever you say will remain between us. I do not want to impugn your father or family in any way. I just want to get to the truth of his death and clear up the secrets that seem to poison the property I now own. Like an infection, secrets can fester and kill. It's best to flush them out."

"As long as I have your promise."

"You do."

Paulie sat and took a deep and troubled breath. "In addition to Captain Taylor, Father has—had—one other steady client. Alcatraz."

Inez blinked. "The island fortress in the bay?"

Paulie nodded. "It is also a military prison. Toward war's end, more cells were needed for all the prisoners. Father installed all the locks. I think Captain Taylor might have had a hand in getting him the job. Since then, Father has visited the island once a month, maintaining and installing as needed. Once I was old enough, he would take me along to help him." He smiled sadly. "Father was an old-school locksmith and could work iron, tin, brass, steel, metals of all kinds."

"It sounds like your father is—was—a much accomplished man in his field. But how does this relate to the war and Captain Taylor? Aside from the captain possibly arranging for your father's employment on the island."

"There is a prisoner there. Father made it a point to visit him and pass this man a packet every time. I think it contained money. Father kept me at a distance from their interactions, so I never heard what few words they might have exchanged. I asked Father about it once, and he said, 'It is a duty I perform for Captain Taylor. It is his business, not ours.' I found that very curious."

"Curious, indeed. Do you know the man's name? His crime?"

Paulie's hands, clasped between his knees, tightened, and the knuckles showed white. "The guards call him The Spider. His crime is treason. He was a Confederate sympathizer."

Inez sat back and stared. Finally, she said, "Are you returning to Alcatraz soon?"

"I would go tomorrow, but I must make arrangements. Father's remains could be released for burial within a few days. The detective said as much." Paulie cleared his throat. "Would you be willing to advance me a portion of the loan early tomorrow? I would like to secure a plot and a stone. It would break Mother's heart to have him buried in Potter's Field."

"Of course. I'll bring two copies of my standard agreement tomorrow morning for you to sign and the entire amount. No need to parcel it out."

Paulie shut his eyes. Inez sensed he was holding back tears.

"Thank you. This means the world to Mother and me." He opened his eyes. "In that case, I'll plan to go to Alcatraz day after tomorrow. I must tell them about Father, and I suppose I must talk to The Spider as well. I should let him know that, with the deaths of Captain Taylor and my father, whatever arrangement they had is ended."

"I want to hear what he has to say," said Inez. "I'm coming with you."

Paulie's brow furrowed. "Alcatraz is still a military installation. If I were to show up with a stranger, a woman, what possible explanation could I provide for your presence?"

"Tell them you have brought another locksmith who is available to assist you in the future with the tasks at hand." Inez noted Paulie's consternation. "I promise you, it will only be this once. You can say I changed my mind should they inquire in the future."

"But, as I explained, women are not allowed in the trade. I don't understand."

Inez smiled. "You are not the only one who is acquainted with the advantages inherent in donning trousers. When we meet the day after tomorrow, please address me as Mr. Stannert."

Chapter Twenty-Six

Inez and Paulie hammered out the timing for their next meetings. Tomorrow, Inez would come to the locksmith shop with a written agreement for Paulie to sign and the hundred-dollar loan. As for their trip to Alcatraz on Wednesday, Paulie said, "The steamer *General McPherson* leaves from the Washington Street Wharf at five minutes past six every morning."

Inez winced. Antonia would have to get herself off to school. Not that the girl wasn't capable, but given her recent change in attitude, Inez imagined playing hooky would be a great temptation. "There isn't a later departure?"

Paulie shook his head. "There is one at a quarter past four in the afternoon, but that is only good for those who are staying on the island overnight."

"Very well. I'll meet you at the wharf by six."

By the time Inez left the shop, she felt it was possible she was moving closer to clearing up some of the confusion and secrets swirling about the property she now partly owned. It was like being surrounded by the fog that sometimes rolled into the city and obscured all but what was closest. Walk forward, and the fog faded, revealing what was once hidden, little by little.

She just had to keep marching forward until all was clear.

Her next stop was the San Francisco Mint, where she hoped to get a word with Bertram Taylor. Inez had had occasion to stroll past the building but no reason to enter. It was hard to miss, taking up a large plot of land on the corner of Mission and Fifth streets. The building of blue-gray stone had the aspect of a Greek temple, with a wide set of stairs sweeping up from the sidewalk to a giant portico supported by six fluted columns. As a monument to the weighty power of money, one could find nothing finer on the West Coast.

Inez ascended the stone stairway to the entrance. The closer she got, the taller and wider the columns loomed. A stream of men in business-black flowed past her in each direction. She finally gained the entrance a little breathless. Whether from the climb or the pressure of commerce and wealth as symbolized by the building, which transformed tons of silver and gold into millions of dollars in coinage, she didn't stop to ponder.

Once inside, she paused, bewildered. The interior foyer was vast, with men and even a few women hurrying hither and thither. The drone of mostly male voices and the clatter of footsteps seemed to bounce off the brick walls and tall ceiling, magnifying as they did so. Looking up past the brass lighting fixtures, Inez spotted guards patrolling along a stately catwalk encircling the public space, eyes on the activity below. Spying a fellow in similar garb standing to one side of the doors she had just entered, Inez decided to ask him for assistance in finding Bertram Taylor.

The guard, whose face was well-seamed with years and graced with a handsome gray mustache, seemed to be aware she was heading his way. Yet, he stayed his post and awaited her arrival with a sharp-eyed gaze under bushy eyebrows. When she was close enough to be heard, she said, "I would like to speak to an employee of the mint, if it is possible."

"Oh, it's quite possible, madam," said the guard genially. "In fact, you already are. But you probably have a different person in mind. Give me the name; I shall see if I can help. The employee would need to be available, and your business must be completed by noon, when this public area closes to visitors."

Inez glanced at a large, prominently mounted clock at one end of the public room and realized it was nearly twelve. "I'm looking for Mr. Bertram Taylor."

A spark seemed to flash in those black eyes. "Ah. Whom shall I say is calling?"

"Mrs. Stannert. You can tell him it is an urgent matter about the house."

"The house," he repeated dubiously.

"Yes, he'll know what I'm referring to."

The guard beckoned to a younger colleague nearby, delivered both names, and added, "Mr. Taylor is a junior clerk in the General Department. Tell him Mrs. Stannert says the matter is urgent and about the house."

The younger guard didn't even blink at the strange message but merely nodded and strode across the room to one of the many doors leading into the interior of the building.

"And now, we wait," said the guard. "I hope he is available and that your business can be conducted in a few minutes. Otherwise, you shall have to try again tomorrow."

She hoped that wouldn't be the case. After her meeting with Paulie to complete the contract tomorrow, she would have a full day of giving piano lessons. Who knew what else would transpire as the day wore on?

"Ah!" said the friendly guard. "You are in luck. Here is young Taylor now."

Sure enough, Bertram Taylor, hatless, was hurrying toward her. He looked puzzled, she thought, and a little apprehensive. She held out her hand and tried to project reassurance and calm. "Mr. Taylor, I am sorry for the intrusion."

"Yes, well, we only have a few minutes before public hours are over," he said. He glanced at the older guard, who was watching people come and go, most of them going. Bertram nodded toward one of the mullioned windows overlooking the street. "Let's talk over there."

They went to the window, and Inez decided not to mince words. "There have been unfortunate happenings at the place you sold us. The locksmith, Joe Harris, has been murdered."

Bertram shuddered. "A horrific thing."

"You know about it?"

"Upton told me." Distracted, he raked a hand through his hair. "Mr. Harris could be volatile. Had a temper. Perhaps he got into a fight. But an axe. Terrible."

"It *was* terrible. Mrs. Krause's daughter and my niece, who was spending the night at the boardinghouse, discovered the body." She wasn't sure why she said that. It just rolled out.

He shivered. "I'm sorry to hear," he said almost inaudibly. "That shouldn't've happened."

"No, it shouldn't've. And now, Mrs. Krause is losing boarders as well."

"I…I'm sorry. But what do you expect from me?"

First things first. "Do you have the keys to the house?"

He looked at her with something close to horror. "No! Why would I?"

"I thought perhaps Mr. Harris gave them to you."

He was looking at her strangely, so she added quickly, "You

see, the evening before he died, he and Mrs. Krause had a tiff over the keys and, well, other things. He indicated he was going to talk to Mr. Upton and possibly you. It is…was…extremely peculiar. The locksmith's son has duplicates of the keys, but we won't be able to obtain them for a couple of days yet."

"And Mrs. Krause is losing boarders as a result of this… murder?"

"As I said. One gave notice yesterday shortly after Mr. Harris was found."

The clock began to strike noon. Inez hurried her words. "Regarding the person and the gold coins found in the wall, I feel certain there is a connection with the mint."

"Forgive me, Mrs. Stannert." Bertram stepped away from the window. "We will have to continue this conversation another time. I must return to work, and you must leave."

"Wait." She reached out for his jacket sleeve. He jerked away as if her touch was fire. "All the coins in the wall were minted in 1863."

He began walking toward the door he'd come from. "Long before my time."

She chased after him. "But not your uncle's! Didn't you say he worked at the mint until he joined the war effort?"

"I suppose I did." He continued walking as if an invisible string was pulling him back into the depths of the building.

"I know this sounds extraordinary, but could the man in the wall be him? Be your uncle?"

He whirled around, eyes wide with shock. "Why would you think that?"

"Well, after all, you never saw him actually leave, never had a chance to say goodbye. And you said yourself you two were very close, so why no farewell? Don't you think that strange? There were only letters that arrived later, ostensibly from him."

Bertram walked on, voice tight. "I saw the letters. My father showed them to me."

"Your father was a loyal Unionist." She hastened after him. He lengthened his stride. "And the man in the wall, I'm sorry to say, appeared to have Confederate leanings. And the coins, the bag, from the mint. Too much of a coincidence." She was babbling now.

Bertram, at the office door, spun around to face her. She halted. His blue eyes, which had seemed so sad when she'd first met him and then so lost and bewildered a few minutes ago, now blazed with anger. "This is my uncle you are speaking of. He was a good man, loyal and kind, at a time when few enough like him were around. You know nothing of him. I won't hear another word on this." He yanked the door open and Inez glimpsed a brick-lined corridor beyond, studded with other doors. "Goodbye, Mrs. Stannert."

"Did your uncle have a glass eye?" Inez called out, ignoring the startled glance of a businessman brushing past.

Bertram froze, his back to her. Without turning around, he said, "No," and disappeared inside the fortress, shutting the door behind him.

A chuckle at her elbow caused her to jump. The older guard stood there shaking his head. "Young Mr. Taylor couldn't have known his uncle well to have said that. Jack Taylor was chief clerk at the old mint right before he left. Everyone knew about his glass eye. It was no secret. It were only an eye."

Inez grasped the guard's words as if they were a lifeline in a stormy sea. "You worked at the mint when Jack Taylor was here?"

"Oh, yes. That were in the old mint on Commercial. Before they built the Granite Lady here."

He jingled a heavy ring of keys in one hand. "Time to leave, if you please, madam."

She glanced around to find she was the last visitor lingering in the open space.

The guard continued, "You may return tomorrow. Our public hours are nine to noon." He began escorting her toward the exit. He was very polite. However, Inez couldn't help feeling like an errant ewe being herded by a sheep dog toward the flock.

"I doubt Mr. Taylor will want to talk with me," she said. "I seem to have set fire to any bridges I might have built with him."

"The young ones are quick to judge." He said this in a consoling tone.

Inez slowed her pace. "How well did you know Jack Taylor?"

"Everyone knew everyone at the old mint. 'Twas a small operation compared to today."

"So you were there during the war?"

"Started in the late fifties. Back when she was a branch office. Been with her ever since."

They had reached the entrance. As he opened the door for her, she said quickly, "Would you be willing to meet with me later? I have some questions about the old mint. I would be eternally grateful."

"Eternally grateful? To listen to stories of times long past?" He smiled, but his eyes were leery. "Are you a lady reporter looking to write a little piece to entertain the masses?"

"I am looking for the truth. And I believe, although the young Mr. Taylor refuses to consider it, that Jack Taylor may have come to a sorry end."

"And why would you care about the Taylor family, madam?"

She hesitated. "I now own the old Taylor house. It appears that I bought more than I bargained for. It seems positively haunted by its previous owner. I should like to put those ghosts to rest."

Somehow, without realizing how it happened, she was

standing outside the building. She could see him thinking, turning over what she had said. Finally, he replied, "My workday ends at four. Tomorrow, if you should happen to be taking an afternoon constitutional at that time and stroll past the Granite Lady, it just might happen that we meet. Perhaps your constitutional would take us in the same direction."

She brightened. "Tomorrow. I imagine that is entirely a reasonable possibility, Mr. . . .?"

"Russo. At your service."

"And I am Mrs. Stannert, as you know."

"Perhaps tomorrow, when you return between the hours of nine and noon, Mr. Taylor will be more receptive to your questions. If afterward you would still like to hear a tale or two about the old mint during her war years, I leave work the same time every day."

With that, he shut the door.

Chapter Twenty-Seven

MONDAY, MARCH 13

Mondays, thought Antonia, were the worst days of the week.

And this was one of the worst school Mondays *ever*. Which was saying something, because she'd had some bad ones since she'd started school in San Francisco almost a year ago.

She sat on the steps in the back of Lincoln School, finishing up her cheese and pickle sandwich. Usually Mrs. Nolan, who made the sandwiches, put cheese on both sides of the pickle slices to keep the sourdough bread dry, but she'd forgotten or been in a hurry, so there was just one layer of cheese, and the pickle juice had soaked through the other slice of the bread, making it a sticky, stinky mess.

A stinky mess, just like her life.

It wasn't enough, she thought gloomily, that she'd seen real brains and broken bits of skull of someone she'd met before. The old locksmith, Mr. Harris, hadn't been exactly friendly, so it wasn't like she cared that he was dead. But he had been *some*one, even though someone unpleasant, and now he was *nothing*. Dead. It made Antonia think of all the people she had known who had been *some*one and then died. Mostly, of course, she thought of her maman. But she didn't want to remember that. Didn't want to remember the awful moment of finding her maman dead, but still warm, in their little back-alley shack in Leadville.

Antonia shook her head fiercely, trying to dislodge the memory.

Then, there was yesterday afternoon after she'd seen Mr. Harris, and the coppers had come, and she'd told Detective Lynch what she'd seen. Of course, she didn't say anything about the Chinese-speaking intruder who'd been wandering the house at the same time as she and Charlotte. Blood sisters didn't spill their secrets.

Once they'd been dismissed to Charlotte's room, they'd started drawing a map of Treasure House, so they'd know where all the rooms and staircases were and where they'd already looked for booty. Mrs. S had swooped in, plucked her up, and carried her off to Mrs. Nolan's. She'd promised to be back in time for dinner, but when she'd showed up, she'd had Mr. de Bruijn in tow. Antonia still wasn't sure about him. He was nice to her, but she didn't completely trust him.

He had been a part of Maman's life that she'd kept locked away from Antonia. Maman had refused to even let Antonia meet him. Then, he'd sent them to Leadville to wait for him, and he said that he did come for them, but by then it was too late. Antonia would never forgive him and blamed him for everything that had happened up there. Maman had died, and Antonia had left Leadville with Mrs. S. She wasn't sure why he'd suddenly popped up in San Francisco and weaseled his way into her and Mrs. S's lives. And she sure wasn't going to ask Mr. W. R. de Bruijn, or as she had privately named him in Leadville, Worthless Rotten Brown.

Anyhow, last night, there he was at Mrs. Nolan's Sunday dinner. Antonia'd been sitting next to Mrs. Nolan, who kept her
tied to her apron strings all afternoon and had fussed and kept
offering pie, pickles, and slices of homemade bread so Antonia
had been stuffed and not particularly hungry at dinner. That had
given Antonia plenty of time to watch Mrs. S and Mr. Worthless
Rotten Brown on the sly when they weren't watching her.

She couldn't be sure, but it seemed like they'd been making eyes at each other. Well, not *at* each other, because "that
look" had only been there when the other one was looking
elsewhere. Still, the way they sat side by side made Antonia feel
they'd shared something between them. Some secret that didn't
include her. Just like when her maman had had a secret life with
Worthless Rotten Brown that didn't include Antonia.

But the way Mrs. S and Worthless Rotten traded glances
hadn't exactly been a secret. Mrs. Nolan had nodded in their
direction and said in an undertone to Antonia, "Your aunt has
found such a *nice* gentleman caller. Such a welcome development, don't you think, Antonia?"

Antonia did *not* think. She didn't *want* to think.

But here she was at school thinking about it during lunch.
Antonia wiped her vinegar-damp fingers on the paper Mrs.
Nolan had wrapped the sandwich in. "I cannot fathom it, matey,"
she muttered to herself. "Besotted, the pair of them. The scuttle-
butt be flying about the dinner table that night."

Besides the comment from Mrs. Nolan, there had been
nudges and winks that passed like a whisper among the various
boarders. They had all seemed to know Mr. Worthless Rotten
and welcomed his presence. It surprised and alarmed her to hear
one of the doddering boarders mention that Worthless Rotten
had been there with Mrs. S for Christmas dinner. Christmas!
While she, Antonia, had been forced to tag along with Carmella

Donato down to southern California for the holiday. Never mind that she'd had a fun Christmas herself. She just didn't like that Mr. de Bruijn and Mrs. S might be...might have...might...

She mashed the wet sandwich wrapping into a ball and threw it viciously at the wall, where it left a wet splat-spot on the stone.

And now, her teacher, Miss Persnickety Pierce, had accused her of backsliding in penmanship and not paying attention in class. *Backsliding* sounded like a word for something particularly awful. Like something the whores in Leadville's back alley cribs might do.

She shuddered and pulled the apple out of her lunch bucket. Cradling it in the lap of her ink-stained pinafore, she reached back into the lunch bucket and pulled out her special treasure. The brass wheel-within-a-wheel lay on the palm of her hand, locked in its mystery. Both wheels had a complete alphabet engraved around their edges. She had just rotated them so the *A* on the big wheel lined up with the *A* on the little wheel when a shadow fell across her.

"Hi, Antonia." Her friend Michael Lynch folded his gangly length onto the stair beside her, reminding her of a stork coming to rest on the mudflats. "Haven't seen you in a while."

"Probably because you haven't been looking," she muttered.

Copper Mick removed his blue cap. He scrubbed at his hair, which was the color of a new penny, until it stood straight up. He claimed it was his hair color that led to the schoolyard nickname, although Antonia thought it was because his da was a police detective and most of his uncles and older brothers were on the force.

He said, "I *have* been looking. Is this where you've been hiding? Back here on the steps by yourself?"

She shrugged. She hated to admit to her lack of friends. But the girls in her class only invited her scorn. They were all ninnies, shrieking when the boys pulled their bonnet ribbons or made silly faces at them. And the boys would have nothing to do with her.

Instead of answering, she said, "So, did your da tell you to check on me and make sure I was okay?"

"Naw, 'course not." But the flush rising up his neck told her different.

"You're a lousy liar, Mick." Antonia nudged his elbow with her own to show she didn't mean to be mean. "Tell your da I'm fine."

Mick grinned, then looked serious. "Well, from what he said last night, sounded like you were smack dab in the middle of a nasty scene."

"Not really." She started twisting the wheels again. "The nasty part would've been when Mr. Harris was being chopped up with Mrs. Krause's axe. At least, I guess it was her axe. By the time I saw him on the back porch, he was *dead-dead-dead*, and the blood was mostly dry."

"At least you didn't go all swoony and yell for smelling salts like one of those prissy missies would've." He jerked his chin toward the clutch of girls talking in a corner of the playground. With their fluttery ribbons and still-white pinafores, they reminded Antonia of Mrs. Krause's hens, cackling away and clustered together.

Mick continued, "My da says you've got real grit and fortitude." He leaned over, peering at the disk in her hands. "Say, what's that you got there?"

She shrugged again. "I'm not sure."

"Where'd you get it?"

She almost said, "From a pirate hideout," but stopped herself, saying instead, "Found it."

"Can I see?"

She passed the disk to him and picked up her apple, rolling it between her hands.

He said, "Huh. It's got the initials CSA stamped on it. Hey, I think I know what this is! My grand-da has one he brought back from the war. He calls it one of his prized possessions." He looked over at her and repeated, "Where'd you get this?"

She ignored the question. "So, what is it?" She bit into her apple and sucked the juice out of the open wound.

"Tell you what. I'll trade you. I'll tell you if you share that apple with me."

She tossed the apple to him. He caught it, took a bite, and handed it back to her. Still chewing, he pointed to the center of the disk. "The CSA in the center stands for Confederate States of America. What you've got here is a Confederate code disk."

"What's that?" Antonia took another bite of the apple, trying to make it a big one because otherwise Mick would end up getting it all in three bites.

"It's for writing and decoding secret messages," he said. "The little *S.S.* under the CSA stands for Secret Service. I think."

"Secret messages?" Antonia felt a thrill run from her fingertips to her toes. "So spies and privateers for the Confederate States could use it to send messages to headquarters, talk about the next attack, what they'd gotten on their raids, and all that?"

"Well, sure. I suppose." He looked at her, his nose wrinkled up. "Did you say privateers?"

She handed him the apple. "You can eat the rest. Do you know how the code works?"

"I think so. Let me try to remember what Grand-da said." He chomped on the apple, chewed thoughtfully, and swallowed. "Usually there's a secret keyword or phrase that the person sending the message and the one receiving it both know. So, the person reading the dispatch would know *A* is actually, say, *E*, which would mean *B* is really *F* and *C* is—"

"*G!*" said Antonia excitedly. She thought of the papers with scrambled nonsense "words" she and Charlotte had found in the desk in the Treasure House. Maybe they were actually coded messages. "How d'you figure out what the key is, then?"

"Well, my grand-da said the Johnny Rebs had a few key phrases they liked to use. I don't remember what they were, though." He paused. "I could ask him, if you want."

"That'd be grand!" enthused Antonia. "Maybe you could ask him tonight and tell me tomorrow." Then, realizing he was looking at her strangely, she tried to tamp down her excitement. "If we knew the phrases, maybe you could borrow your grand-da's code disk, and you and I could write secret coded messages back and forth." Then, realizing how *that* sounded, she blushed about the same time he did. "Just for fun," she added quickly.

"Okay." He stood up, the long length of him unfolding up and up and up. Antonia stood, too, thinking that Copper Mick must've grown six inches since she'd met him almost six months ago. He gave the disk back to her and said, "I'll see if I can get Grand-da to explain it to me. But you gotta promise me something."

Antonia groaned and rolled her eyes. "What?"

"You gotta promise to stop avoiding me."

"I'm not avoiding you!" She slipped the disk into her pocket.

"Yes you are. You haven't talked to me in weeks. Well, a couple of weeks, at least. We used to walk around the city every day after school. Downtown. The waterfront. Exploring."

She squirmed. She knew he didn't much like going down to the waterfront, so she'd been giving him the slip after school. Too, Mrs. S didn't like her hanging around there either. That hadn't exactly stopped Antonia, but she had to be sneakier about it.

"I have more chores after school," she said. "I don't have as much time as I used to."

She could see he was disappointed, but he just nodded and said, "I'll let you know what Grand-da says."

One of the upper-grade teachers came out the back door ringing a bell. Mick tossed the apple core onto the dirt and said, "See you later, then?"

"Sure!" said Antonia, thinking she and Charlotte had to get back into the house. Sooner, rather than later. Never mind the ghosts and the dead locksmith. There were secret messages in there that they had to retrieve.

It wasn't buried treasure but just as good as.

———

The afternoon got a little better, particularly when Antonia got her mathematics test back. The perfect score cheered her up, but only until Persnickety Pierce said, after praising her, "Now, why can't you do the same on your history exams and penmanship assignments? I know you are smart and capable, Antonia. You need to apply yourself."

Apply yourself. What did that even mean? Apply as in use school paste to glue herself to the books and papers and pen and ink bottle until all the historical dates and events poured out onto paper in words formed from perfectly spaced letters that had perfect loops and ascenders and descenders?

At the end of the school day, she scampered down the stairs to Fifth Street. There was a ship that had come in the day before, the *Leonora.* Antonia had read about it in the newspaper and wanted to see it before it sailed away on some high-seas adventure to Honolulu or Sydney.

"Hello, Antonia!" piped up a familiar voice.

Antonia blinked. "Charlotte! What're you doing here?"

Charlotte beamed up at her. She looked younger and more girly than ever with her frilly bonnet, neatly plaited braids, clean, pressed outfit, and polished boots.

"Our school gets out before yours does. So, I thought I'd try to find you, and we could walk home partway together." She shuffled her feet a little. "Maybe you could show me where you live and your aunt's music store."

"Doesn't your ma expect you home?" Antonia asked.

Charlotte looked down, inspecting the toes of her shiny boots. "She won't mind if I'm a little late."

Antonia wondered if Charlotte was looking for an excuse not to go straight home. Given what had happened there yesterday, Antonia bet so.

"You're lucky you found me," said Antonia. "There's hundreds at this school. Come on."

They started walking, turning up Market Street toward the bay. As casually as she could, Antonia said, "Say, you wouldn't mind walking down to the waterfront, would you? The *Leonora* just got in. It took her seventy-five days to get to here from Hong Kong. I'd like to see her, and I don't know when she'll ship out again."

"Sure!" Charlotte lowered her voice. "Is it a privateer?"

"What? No! Just a regular ship." Antonia, who regularly studied the "Marine Intelligence" column in the *San Francisco Chronicle* and "Along the Wharves" in the *Daily Alta California* for the nautical comings and goings, launched into a lecture about the different kinds of ships. Barks were sailing vessels with three or more masts, with their fore- and mainmasts rigged square and the aftermost mast, or mizzen, rigged fore and aft. Schooners were fore- and aft-rigged with two or more masts, while brigs were two-masted and square-rigged. And schooners...

Antonia registered that Charlotte's eyes had glazed over, and she was just nodding mechanically. "Well," Antonia said, "doesn't matter. We can just walk and look at what's here."

They had reached the waterfront, with all its wonderful smells and sounds. A briny breeze, flavored by the stink of tar and things half-rotted and spoiled, mixed with a tinge of effluent. Waves slapped against pilings and hulls, lines hummed in the breeze, seagulls squawked and flapped out of the way of hurrying feet, only to land again as soon as danger had passed. The crash and boom of cargo being loaded and unloaded mixed with voices near and distant—all male, of course—which rose and fell like sea swells.

Antonia drank it all in, feeling happy for the first time that day, and then remembered. "Oh! I have something important to tell you."

"Something more about ships, er, vessels?" said Charlotte uncertainly.

"No, it's about that metal disk we found in the secret room of the Treasure House. I found out what it is." Antonia stopped and fished the disk out from her pocket. "This is a cipher disk for reading secret coded messages!"

Charlotte's mouth dropped open. "Secret messages?"

Antonia grinned. "You remember those papers we saw in the desk that were filled with scribbled nonsense words? The ones that didn't make sense?"

Charlotte nodded her head so hard Antonia thought it might just fall off her neck. "Well," she continued, "I think those were secret coded messages."

"Maybe messages about where more treasure is hidden?"

"Maybe!"

Charlotte clapped her hands. "That would be a blessing," she said, sounding like her mother. "Ma's real worried about the boardinghouse. About people leaving, and where she'll find the money to pay your aunt back. If we found more treasure, Ma won't have to worry so much!"

Antonia frowned. "But there's all the money that was with the dead privateer. I thought Mrs. S and your ma were going to split it up."

"Ma says it's tainted," whispered Charlotte. "She says it'd be bad luck to touch it or use it for anything other than burying that pirate or whatever he is. She says that's the only way his soul will be at peace. The money will give him a really nice place to lie for all eternity. Oh, and she needs to find out his name, too, so's they can bury him right. But if we found more money, more coins or treasure, she could use it to pay your aunt! And maybe we can buy another rooster and then she'd be happy again!"

"Get your ma to invite me over again for another night," said Antonia. "We need to get those messages out of the desk so we can break the code and search the rest of the house, before my aunt decides to break down the doors. I think she's losing patience with your ma and the whole thing about locks and keys and all. Especially now that Mr. Harris got the axe."

"Hey, Antonia!"

Antonia whirled around at Copper Mick's voice, right behind her. *What's he doing here?*

No sooner had she thought this than Mick said, "What're you doing here? I thought you had chores right after school. And anyway, you're not supposed to be down on the waterfront."

Caught out, Antonia bristled. She stepped toward him. "Who are you, my aunt? Are you spying on me? Did you follow me here?"

He retreated, looking as if her questions hit him like slaps on his face. She advanced, fists clenched. "If I'd wanted to walk with you, I'd've said so! Now, I'm busy. Go away!"

Having hurled those words at him, she turned and stomped away from the wharves, saying to Charlotte, "Come on. Let's go."

"But—" Charlotte scurried to keep up with her. "I thought you wanted to see that boat."

Antonia didn't answer. Just walked faster.

After another block, Charlotte said, "Who was that boy?"

"Just someone from school," Antonia muttered. "He's a pest. A real nosy busybody. Won't leave me alone." She knew she was being unfair to Mick lying about him like that. But right then she was so angry at being caught where she shouldn't've been she didn't care.

"Where are we going?" Charlotte clutched her bonnet and looked around. "Is this Washington Street? Are we going to Chineetown? I'm not allowed to go to Chineetown."

"Bah!" muttered Antonia. "We're not going to Chinatown. This is just the fastest way to the music store." She altered course at the next corner, taking Front Street to angle toward Market and catch Pine. "Besides, real pirate princesses would not be afeared to go to Chinatown, day or night. Real pirate princesses would brave the dark and dangerous streets of the Barbary Coast and slay any who dared cross swords with them."

"But we *are* pirate princesses. And blood sisters of the sea," said Charlotte stubbornly. "We found a secret room in a Treasure House. And messages from pirate spies. And we're looking for a fortune in gold. And we escaped from a scary Chineeman, who would've slit our throats if—"

"Don't say stuff like that," said Antonia. "A Chinaman, Mr. Hee, works at our music store. He's the nicest person you'd ever want to know. He fixes broken music instruments, knows a lot about Chinese art, and you better not say anything more like that about Chinese people, because it isn't true. Besides, other people speak Chinese too." *Like Mr. Worthless Rotten Brown.*

She thought about that. She'd heard him speak in Chinese to John Hee. And Mrs. S had said Charlotte's ma had hired him to figure out the dead man's name. So, could it have been Mr. Worthless Rotten muttering in Chinese and sneaking around the house? But she just couldn't see him taking an axe to anyone.

Her mind circled back to Master Edward. He'd seen the money and the body. He'd taught Charlotte to count to ten in Chinese. He'd sailed the Orient as a master-at-arms and knew all about weapons and fighting. *And killing, too, I'll bet.* At first she'd thought Master Edward was in cahoots with old Mr. Harris, but maybe they had a falling-out, and the two Edwards had ganged up and killed him. After all, Edward the Second even admitted to casting anchor in Barbados, and everyone knew Barbados had pirates! Antonia's throat tightened.

They'd reached the front of the music store. She turned to Charlotte and gripped her shoulders. "Listen. Don't get too chummy with the two Edwards."

Charlotte squinted. "Why? They're really nice. Master Edward sometimes brings me peppermint drops when he gets Ma fish for Friday dinners."

Antonia shook Charlotte's shoulders gently. "They just might not be as nice as they seem." Charlotte looked puzzled. Antonia added, "Master Edward broke down the wall and saw the body and all the gold. Maybe he and his brother are looking for more. And you told me Master Edward speaks Chinese. Remember?"

Charlotte's eyes widened. "Do you think…?"

"I don't know." Antonia let go. "But we can't let anyone suspect we know anything. Keep your ears open and your mouth shut. We'll get the letters, search the house, and figure it out."

"What'll we do if they have the keys and catch us snooping around?" She looked scared.

Antonia injected a brave tone into her reply. "We'll hear them coming, and we can hide. If they do see us, we'll run. Throw stuff at them. Break a window and escape. And if they catch us," she looked Charlotte in the eye, "I have my knife. And I know how to use it."

Chapter Twenty-Eight

MONDAY, MARCH 13

Inez usually enjoyed the music lessons she gave in the back of the store. Those students came from working-class families and, for the most part, were driven and determined to excel. She gleaned that, at some level, they saw mastery of the instrument as being a possible key to freedom from the hard, physical limitations of their parents' circumscribed lives. Recently, there had been an increase in requests for lessons from a wealthier level of San Francisco society. Those in this upper echelon, who engaged her to teach their daughters (for it was entirely "daughters") at their homes clearly viewed piano lessons as another way to chain their female offspring to the domestic sphere.

Whereas Inez charged what the market would bear to those who could easily afford it, she reduced her rates for those whose families struggled to cover the rent and groceries. Among the latter were several students who showed great promise. Inez sometimes felt she should be paying them for the pleasure of listening to them work a piece over and over until it was truly a thing of beauty. Patrick, her last student of the day and the son of her laundress, was one such.

Inez's attention normally would have been focused upon Patrick's rendition of Beethoven's Sonatina in F Major but not today. As the notes danced spritely along, her thoughts kept spinning back to Antonia's two nightdresses—both looking as if she'd used them as dust rags—and to her conversations with Bertram Taylor and the mint guard, Mr. Russo.

She felt, deep in her bones now, that the corpse was most likely Bertram's uncle, Jack Taylor. If that were the case, why did Bertram's father invent the fiction that Jack had joined the war on the side of the Union? *Perhaps covering his trail if he murdered Jack or had a hand in his death,* murmured a little voice. And why, when she asked, did Bertram deny his uncle had only one functioning eye? Is it possible he didn't know? He had been young when Jack Taylor disappeared, but still. Had Upton withheld details about the entombed body from Bertram, preferring to dwell on the gold instead? In that case, her question about the glass eye would have been a bolt out of the blue.

And did any of this have anything to do with the death of the elderly locksmith?

She remembered Master Edward saying the locksmith "would pay" for his ill-tempered exchange with Mrs. Krause. Were his mutterings a real threat or just a gallant defense of his landlady? Could Joe Harris and Master Edward have had a late-night confrontation that got out of hand and with the axe nearby...

With a start, she realized Patrick had finished and was awaiting her critique. "Very good, Patrick." She turned the pages of the sheet music and pointed. "Don't be tempted to start the crescendo, here, too soon. Watch the tempo, particularly the streams of sixteenth notes."

He nodded. "And?" He looked at her, obviously expecting more.

She smiled ruefully. "I confess my mind wandered while you played. I apologize, but you could also take it as a compliment. Clearly, there were no serious gaffes, or I would have been pulled out of my wool-gathering. In other words, I was transported by your performance."

That seemed to satisfy him. He smiled, then glanced at the black marble mantel clock perched on a nearby table. "I should be going. D'you have laundry for me to take home?"

"Ah, yes!" Inez rose and exited the lesson room. "Right here." The dirty linens and clothes were bundled into bags and sitting nearby. As he hefted the bags, she said, "Please give my best to your mother and your aunt."

"Yes'm. I will." He left through the back door into the alley.

Inez closed the door behind him and leaned against it. She'd told Antonia to let her know when she'd come home from school. But here it was, late afternoon, and there had been no tapping at the glass window that separated the lesson room from the rest of the area, no sudden slamming open of the back door. *Where is she?*

Inez decided to see if Antonia might be in the showroom, but the only people there were Welles and a customer, who was paging through a collection of sheet music. Welles came over to Inez. "A Mrs. Krause dropped off this note for you."

"Thank you," she took the folded paper. "Have you seen Antonia?"

"She hasn't come through."

Inez nodded. "I'm going to the apartment. If you see her, please send her up."

"Certainly." He searched her face. "You'll be back at the usual time?"

"Of course." Every Monday night, she gathered with Welles and a handful of local musicians to play penny-ante poker around the mahogany table in the back room. It was far from the high-stakes games Inez had been party to in Leadville and elsewhere in her past life, but she enjoyed the evening for the camaraderie as well as the gossip and updates on the local music world. In addition, their circle included Roger Haskell, publisher of the pro-labor newspaper *The Workingman's Voice* and an enthusiast of the music scene and its artists.

Haskell.

Ready to exit onto the street, she paused, wondering why she hadn't thought of the newsman earlier as a possible source of information. Haskell was a little south of fifty in age, a longtime city resident, and knew a great deal about the city's arts, politics, and business doings—past and present. Might he know about the Taylor family? And hadn't Haskell once mentioned he had a relative working at the mint? It wouldn't hurt to inquire. Inez decided she'd ask Haskell to linger after the poker game, ply him with her best brandy, and ask a few questions. De Bruijn would be dropping by as well to talk about their investigations. He could hear for himself what Haskell had to say, if anything.

Outside, Inez walked the few steps to the door leading to her upstairs apartment. Before entering, she unfolded the note and read:

Dear Mrs. Stannert, Good news—I already have a boarder for Miss Ashby's room! He came knocking not two hours after I hung the vacancy sign out this morning. Mr. Morton is a very serious, industrious gentleman and paid for two weeks in advance. Also, another man inquired about an hour later, as I had not gotten around to taking the sign down. He is interested should another vacancy arise. Respectfully, M.K.

Inez refolded the note and slid it into her pocket. She was pleased Moira had found a new tenant so quickly but a little surprised as well. She couldn't help but wonder if news of the hidden gold or grisly deaths might have caught the interest of some with unsavory motives for taking a room. One could never tell underlying intentions from outward appearances. The most elegant gentleman could harbor a heart as hard and cold as a lump of coal. The most gentle-faced woman could turn out to be capable of the most heinous crimes. As Inez well knew.

But more immediately, she had to plumb the depths of yet another devious soul: that of her ward.

Antonia's coat hung on the coat stand in the little entryway, answering the question as to the girl's whereabouts. Inez went up the staircase, treading silently, and entered the apartment without announcing herself. Antonia popped out of the kitchen looking guilty. Inez surmised she had been sneaking sugar cubes from the sugar bowl or perhaps had found and devoured the last *cornetti*. "How long have you been home?" Inez inquired.

"Oh, a while," Antonia said vaguely.

"Why didn't you come to the shop first, as I had asked you to?"

"I forgot. Besides, you always have lessons Monday afternoons, and I didn't want to disturb you. Is it time to leave for dinner? I'm hungry."

"Monday is also laundry day," said Inez.

"I put my dirty clothes in the bag this morning."

"Not all of them." Inez watched her ward closely.

Antonia frowned. "Did I forget a stocking or something?"

"You forgot your nightdresses."

She looked perplexed, then realization dawned. "Oh."

"Yes. Oh. I found them both." Inez crossed her arms. "So, how did your second nightgown end up as filthy as the first?"

Antonia hesitated. She wiggled her fingers, then jammed them into the pockets of her ink-stained school pinafore and fixed her gaze on Inez. "Charlotte and I, we, uh…" She faltered, then burst out, "Please don't tell Mrs. Krause. Charlotte will get in big trouble."

Those words did not bode well.

Inez braced herself.

She had hoped that spending time with Charlotte would increase Antonia's sense of responsibility. Instead, allowing the two girls time together only seemed to intensify a shared propensity for mischief. "Go on."

"Well, you see, Charlotte has these two kittens, Lucky and Eclipse. Or maybe they're grown-up cats. Or half-grown kittens. They're real cute, but they get into trouble sometimes, and they don't exactly listen when you call to them, like dogs do. But they're good hunters." She paused.

"Go on."

"Well, Mrs. Krause keeps them inside at night to chase down mice and crickets and spiders. Saturday night, I guess Mrs. Krause forgot to latch the back door shut, because Charlotte and me, we were playing with them after lights out, just a little, in Charlotte's room, and they ran out into the kitchen and out the door into the backyard. And Charlotte and I had to go outside to chase them and bring them back inside. They went under the porch, so our nightclothes got kind of dirty when we tried to catch them."

Inez's eyes narrowed. Antonia's stayed wide. "The inside of your second gown was filthy," said Inez. "How do you explain that?"

"I, uh, put it on inside out when we realized we had to go outside." She looked down at last and bit her lip. "I was hoping you wouldn't find out if the outside stayed clean."

Inez unfolded her arms. "That tells me right there you *knew* what you intended to do was wrong. Antonia! What were you two thinking? The cats spend all day outdoors. One night outside wouldn't hurt them. But you two aren't cats. You are young girls. It is *not* safe for you two to be out at night like that. Dear God, look at what happened there Saturday night. A man was murdered right on that spot!"

"But that happened later, after we were back in bed! We only were outside for a little, and we were fine! Nothing happened. We didn't see or hear anyone or anything. Well, the chickens made some noise, but that's all. We caught the cats by waving an old fish head at them and took them back inside and latched the door and went to bed. I'm sorry. Really, really sorry. I know we shouldn't've done it. Please don't tell Charlotte's ma." Antonia's hands finally escaped her pinafore pockets, and she clasped them together in a beseeching gesture. "Please!"

Inez wanted to order Antonia to leave off the melodrama, but she wasn't entirely certain that Antonia's desperation was faked. The girl seemed genuinely distressed and remorseful. But this was a transgression requiring more than a stern reprimand. Inez compressed her lips, deliberated, then said, "You are not going back to the Krauses until the murder and mayhem is resolved. If Charlotte needs help with her homework or you two want to spend time together, it will be here. And by here, I mean in my presence, where I can keep an eye on you both."

Aghast, Antonia said, "But…why?"

"Isn't it clear? I cannot trust you to make good decisions when you two are together. And I know how busy Mrs. Krause is. She cannot supervise you both while she is running the boardinghouse. And certainly not while she is asleep."

"But I promised to spend another night so I could help Charlotte with her arithmetic."

Inez shook her head. "You'll have to arrange to meet after school. Here."

Antonia looked crestfallen. That caused Inez to unbend a little, particularly when she realized she would probably have as much trouble supervising the two girls' activities as Moira did. "I will speak with Mrs. Nolan tonight. Perhaps you and Charlotte could meet there instead. Of course, Mrs. Krause must also agree to the arrangement."

Antonia looked away.

Inez thought this compromise was exceedingly generous. The fact that Antonia didn't embrace the prospect told Inez her instincts were correct: the two girls were "running wild" after hours at Moira's boardinghouse while all the adults were abed.

"Come," Inez said briskly, "dinner will be waiting, and I must find time to talk with Mrs. Nolan before we head back. When we return, you have schoolwork and reading. As for me, I have the usual Monday night card game downstairs and then Mr. de Bruijn will be by."

"Argh. Him again," muttered Antonia.

"Yes, him again." Inez stepped forward, set her fingers under Antonia's chin, and tipped up her ward's face so they were eye to eye. "As I told you before, he and I are working together. You should be grateful that he is involved because we will most likely find the person responsible for Mr. Harris's death sooner than the police, who have other crimes to solve. When that happens, we shall all sleep more soundly. Until then, keep this in mind: a murderer is on the loose. And we do not know who it is. We must both be on our guard."

Chapter Twenty-Nine

MONDAY, MARCH 13

Mrs. Nolan was more than willing to have Antonia and Charlotte come after school or on a weekend or even overnight. "It will add a bit of life to the house to have the girls around," she said. "And if it's a school night, I'll make sure they are both out the door on time and ready for the day." She pinched Antonia's cheek, adding, "They can help me make pies. I have my own special tricks for making the perfect crust!" Mrs. Nolan winked at Inez.

"Yes'm," muttered Antonia, giving the impression she looked forward to the "treat" of pie-baking about as much as getting a toothache.

"Thank you, Mrs. Nolan." Inez turned to Antonia. "So, there you go. You and Charlotte can make a special time of it and study here. I'll speak to Mrs. Krause about it."

It was dark when they started home after dinner, which had been a perfectly decent repast of clam chowder, biscuits, and, of course, pie for dessert. Antonia kept to her stubborn silence. This was fine by Inez, for she had much to ponder now that she was assured Antonia had a place away from the Krauses' "house of doom." A story she'd read long ago in one of her mother's *Godey's Lady's Book* magazines surfaced from some dark corner of her memory. *If we had found a cask of Amontillado and a hidden crypt behind the wall, we'd have a proper tale of terror, a la Edgar Allan Poe.* She almost asked Antonia whether she had read any of Poe's stories in her voracious book-devouring but decided against it. If Antonia were to take to Poe as she did to the *Treasure Island* tale written by the pseudonymous Captain George North, an obsession with the macabre would probably ensue.

"Well, if it ain't Mrs. Stannert." A voice pounced from behind her.

A shiver worthy of a Poe story ran through Inez. She spun around, shoving Antonia behind her. Inez's other hand was in her pocket, fingers resting on her pocket revolver. Its presence gave her courage to face the policeman whom she suspected of harboring a grudge against her.

A big man to begin with, MacKay loomed even larger now. His dark-blue uniform bled into the dusk, his helmet-like hat added inches to his height. Inez realized he'd picked the darkest point between two streetlamps. Any confrontation would be all shadows and gloom to any carriages or riders passing by in the street.

"Officer MacKay. What do you want?" She kept her voice firm and neutral, tamping down interior tremors so they wouldn't show in her tone.

"That's right. It's now Officer MacKay. Not Detective." The billy club in his fist thwapped softly against his trousered leg. "Of course, you knew about that even afore I did."

"I had nothing to do with what happened to you. I only heard of your…new position…when Mr. Buckley informed me earlier today."

"Who's Mr. Buckley?" asked Antonia, sliding out from behind Inez.

MacKay cocked his head and peered at Antonia. "That your girl?"

Inez sidestepped to shield her ward from his view. "What do you want?" she repeated.

His voice turned soft but no less menacing. "I've got a girl at home, too, did y'know that? Two girls, two boys. The pay increase I got when I made detective made them and Mrs. MacKay mighty happy. They ain't so happy now that I'm back on foot patrol, and at night. No siree."

"Is that why you stopped me? To tell me your domestic situation? If so, we shall be on our way." She began to move away, keeping a wary eye on him and pulling Antonia with her.

He followed along, just a few steps behind, swinging his club nonchalantly. "Why, I just wanted to *in-tro-duce* myself as the new night patrolman in your neighborhood."

"I don't live here," she snapped and immediately regretted sharing that snippet of information.

Even in the dark, she could see his teeth gleam as he smiled. "I know."

A chill wrapped around her shoulders, and she kept walking toward the pool of lamplight at the end of the block. "Well, Officer MacKay, you have your duties, and I must get home."

"As the copper who'll be keeping watch from dark to dawn, keeping the citizenry safe from harm and hooligans, I wanted to say you shouldn't be out this time of night. Not alone. Not with your girl. Could be dangerous."

"I'm not afraid." They were almost to the lamp. She increased her pace and tightened her grip on Antonia's hand and the revolver in her coat pocket.

"Mebbe you should be. Mebbe you should be real careful

when you get home, lock up tight, and check your windows. After all, I'm not the only one who knows you've got a fortune in gold locked behind an ordinary door. Anything could happen late at night when you're asleep."

Glad to step into the streetlamp's illumination at last, she turned and faced him, saying coldly, "No need to worry about us, Officer MacKay. I have dealt with trouble before."

She had never seen a nod that so strongly conveyed disbelief.

"That's good, that's good. Because sometimes folks get into trouble they can't handle and yell for the police." His massive shoulders moved in a shrug. "Sometimes help arrives too late."

"I shall keep your advice in mind, Officer MacKay." She kept her voice bland as milk. "Or did I misunderstand, and you meant it as a threat?"

He tucked his nightstick under one arm and looked up at the opaque sky. "Not much of a moon t'night. Might even rain. Watch sharp when you cross the street to Pine and Kearney. Hack drivers in a hurry don't always see folks in the roads."

He stepped off the sidewalk, crossed the street, turned the corner, and disappeared.

Antonia said, "Who was that?"

"That was a dangerous, poor excuse for a man," said Inez furiously. "One who is looking to blame me for his demotion, rather than admit it was his own doing that brought him down."

"How come he knows about the gold in your safe?"

She turned a hard eye on Antonia. "Do not speak about that to anyone or even say it out loud. Come along now. We should hurry home."

"Are you afraid of him?" Antonia sounded more curious than concerned.

Inez hesitated. "Not afraid. But not foolish. MacKay is part of the police force. If he is indeed on night patrol for our district, then it is best we remain circumspect and on guard." She looked at Antonia. "And keep our doors locked."

They made their way to Kearney without incident. Inez was heartened to see lights inside the store and a cluster of familiar figures gathered around Welles at the grand piano in their showroom. Upbeat music seeped through the window, along with muffled chatter.

When they reached the street-level entrance to their apartment, Inez finally let go of Antonia. Antonia flexed her fingers, and Inez realized she had kept a tight grip on her ward's hand. "I'll go upstairs with you," said Inez.

"Why? D'you think he's lurking up there in our kitchen? He'll starve to death if he is."

Inez ignored this dig at her nonexistent culinary skills. "We'll put lamps in the windows. Needless to say, don't open the door. If there is trouble, pound on the floor. I'll come right up."

"There won't be trouble. Besides, I've got schoolwork. I'll do it in the kitchen and watch out the window. If he tries to open the door, I'll open the sash and drop the kettle on his head."

"I wouldn't advise it," said Inez dryly. They went inside, and Inez checked every room, including the storage room in the rear. She tugged on the sturdy, seldom-used, and always-locked back door, which led to a steep outside staircase descending to the alley behind the building. She knew she was being overly cautious. MacKay wouldn't be so stupid as to break into their home. At least not that night. And if he knew the whereabouts of the gold, he probably knew it wasn't in the apartment but in the store. What he might not know was that it was secured in a safe. While not as "unbreakable" as Harris's door locks, it was secure, sturdy, and heavy enough to discourage all but the most determined gang of thieves.

After making sure Antonia was settled, Inez left, locking the apartment door at the top of the stairs, which she seldom did, and the entry door at the bottom of the stairs. Back out on the street, she sighed and looked up and down Kearney. Night traffic was thin but steady. The squeak of carriage wheels and the metallic clatter of shod hooves on cobblestones was a comfort. Nothing would happen tonight, she felt sure. As for tomorrow night and the night after...

"I'll deal with that when it comes," she said aloud and went to the store to gather her Monday night regulars in the back for an evening of cards and camaraderie. She hoped that Lady Luck might also smile and, through Haskell and de Bruijn, deliver information that shed more light on crimes past and present.

Chapter Thirty

Monday evening poker with the musicians wasn't as relaxing as Inez had hoped. Too many worries, concerns, and unanswered questions kept her from following the conversation that flowed around the table and distracted her from the game. At least the stakes were low. They only bet pennies and the occasional nickel or—if someone was feeling flush and lucky—a dime or two. As usual, the musicians played with a joviality combined with ruthlessness that put Inez in mind of the days when silver barons threw hundreds, even thousands, of dollars on the table on the turn of a card. It's all perspective, she thought. One man's plenty is another man's petty change.

Five of her "regulars" were present, along with the one she was really interested in hearing from that evening: newsman Roger Haskell. She had pulled him aside on the way to the table and inquired if she could talk to him after the evening broke up. His unkempt salt-and-pepper eyebrows popped up, creating a set of standing waves on his forehead.

"What about?" he asked.

"It would be about some very fine brandy and a chance for you to pontificate about San Francisco during the War for the Union."

He gave a short bark. "Now I know what kind of stories to tell. If you'd said the Second War for Independence or War between the States, I'd offer up a different set."

Knowing that Haskell was "primed and ready," Inez became increasingly impatient as the hours ticked by. Not that the gatherings ever lasted past midnight given that some players needed to be up early for work. But something about all the copper on the table—the plink of coins hitting, rolling, and winking—reminded her of the Confederate jacket buttons in the burlap bag tucked beneath the sideboard. Plus, she was getting a headache from Haskell's cigars, which had to be the foulest-smelling rolls of tobacco she had yet encountered.

Inez decided to force the issue so they would throw up their hands and depart. Usually, with mere pennies at stake, she took a laissez-faire attitude. But tonight was different, so she set aside the troublesome issues that bedeviled her and began playing in earnest. As the dealer, she had a tactical advantage, which she began to exploit ruthlessly. None of the others were experts at the game, being more in it for the company and the conversation. It didn't take long before the modest number of silver and copper coins in front of her started to multiply. There was some good-natured grumbling, but Haskell pointed out, "Our hostess seldom wins, so it looks like tonight is the lady's lucky night."

Percussionist Isaac Pérez tossed his losing hand down in disgust as Inez demurely raked in forty-two cents. He said, "I must leave before I join Mr. John Frazer in court, yes?"

"Who?" Inez stacked her new gains next to what she had already amassed.

Welles, who had wisely folded early in the round, explained,

"Frazer, a local dancing-master, petitioned for insolvency last week."

Pérez added, "He owes some of us money." Nods and frowns confirmed his comment.

Welles continued, "Turns out he owes more than a thousand dollars and his assets are, in the words of the *Alta California*, 'nominal.'"

She shook her head. "I missed that. I have not read the *Alta* in a while."

Haskell said, "Then you probably also missed reading about the spate of burglaries in the Mission."

"You should be careful, Señora Stannert," added Pérez. "They may target your fortune in coins next."

Inez froze and threw him a sharp glance. Before she could determine whether he was referring to the three dollars and change on the table or if he knew about the far more valuable currency secured in her safe, a tap at the back door had them all swiveling in their chairs.

"Come in!" called Inez.

De Bruijn entered and doffed his hat, which Inez noted was damp, as were the shoulders of his coat.

She said to the room at large, "This is Mr. de Bruijn."

Welles looked searchingly at Inez, who found herself blushing much to her irritation.

"Ah, the private investigator at the Palace Hotel," said Haskell.

A glance, quick as lightning, winged around the table.

"Well, it appears some of you, at least, know of him." She quickly introduced them. The players nodded their how-do-you-dos and started rustling with jackets and hats and scooping up their coins.

"Am I interrupting?" de Bruijn inquired. His gaze flicked to the table, the piles of small change, the discarded hands of cards.

"You picked a good time to knock," said Welles. "Mrs. Stannert was cleaning us out."

The musicians left in a rambunctious pack, lifting their hats with cheery see-you-around farewells. The musky, metallic scent of rain mixed with damp brick and dust swept in as they swept out. Inez suspected they were repairing to one of their favorite watering holes. Once there, they would dissect the evening, bemoan their bad luck, and talk about the things young men talked about when the liquor was cheap and the women were absent. Except for Welles, the consummate family man, who said, "I'll check the front of the store, make sure everything is locked up on my way out."

Haskell, brushing the cigar ash off the front of his waistcoat, was last to gather his money and rise, saying, "We can always chat another time, Mrs. Stannert."

She stopped him. "Actually, I would like Mr. de Bruijn to hear what you have to say as well. And I have plenty of brandy." She turned to de Bruijn. "Please, join us. I asked Mr. Haskell to share his wealth of information about the city during the war." She went to her office and extracted a bottle from her locked cabinet. By the time she returned, de Bruijn had hung up his rain-damp outerwear and was politely refusing a proffered cigar from Haskell.

"How do you two know each other?" Inez asked as she set down three brandy snifters.

Haskell said cheerfully, "I wouldn't be much of a newsman if I didn't at least have a nodding acquaintance with all the detectives in town, private and on the force."

With a sideways glance at de Bruijn, Inez said, "And the musicians? Some of them seemed to know you as well."

Haskell pointed the unlit cigar at de Bruijn. "Dancing-master Frazer, am I right?"

After a pause, de Bruijn nodded.

Inez frowned, "You mean that fellow Pérez mentioned?"

Haskell nodded. "The very one. Some of the boys are hot under the collar about Frazer's legal maneuver. They aren't the only ones. Heard tell one of Frazer's suppliers doesn't believe the claim of 'no assets,' so he hired an investigator who works out of the Palace Hotel to find out if the dance master'd tucked some away." He looked at de Bruijn. "Am I close?"

De Bruijn smiled.

"Well, if there is anything to be found, I am certain Mr. de Bruijn will find it," said Inez.

With his cigar, Haskell drew a line from Inez to de Bruijn. "What's your connection?"

Inez poured a measure of brandy into each snifter, considering her response. She was saved from prevaricating when Haskell exclaimed, "Naglee brandy? Local brand and excellent choice, Mrs. Stannert. It's won a number of awards." He lifted his glass. "Henry Naglee was a Union general in the war. Is that what this meeting is about?"

Inez sat. "Fascinating. But no, not quite. I am more interested in what San Francisco was like overall during that time. Here on the edge of the Pacific, so far from the main battles, I cannot help but think feelings did not run as high as they did in the East." She touched her glass to Haskell's and then de Bruijn's.

Haskell said, "There you'd be wrong, Mrs. Stannert." He turned to de Bruijn. "Our hostess admits to siding with the Union, if not in so many words. Do you, sir, lean one way or the other?"

"I am ignorant of all but the most general outline of the hostilities," said de Bruijn.

Inez was surprised to hear him say that. She could not recall when she had last heard de Bruijn profess ignorance of anything in such a straightforward manner.

"Since I am going to be telling old war stories, I suppose I'll get comfortable." He proceeded to savor the brandy and light a fresh cigar.

Inez held her breath as the obnoxious smoke wafted her way.

Haskell began, "San Francisco was much like elsewhere in the States. Sentiments ran high on both sides. Families fractured. Friends became enemies. Boys left to fight and didn't return or returned broken. Mothers, daughters, wives, sisters wore black." His face grew grim.

"A few incidents come to mind," he said, "as I was in the news business even back then. The big July Fourth pro-Union gathering in '61. Rallies that were held regularly at Montgomery, Post, and Market as well as at Union Square—named so for a reason. And there was a riot after Lincoln's assassination, when a mob fell on a handful of local secesh newspapers, including the *Occidental Monitor* and *The Democratic Press.*" He turned to de Bruijn. "Secesh is short for secessionist. Pro-Confederate."

De Bruijn nodded.

Haskell continued, "The rioters ransacked the offices, threw the printing presses and typesetting equipment into the streets. The de Youngs scooped it up afterward and used it to publish their *Daily Dramatic Chronicle*, as their paper was then called. At least, that's the story. Once the bricks and pistols came out, I cleared out of there. I didn't see the sense of covering a riot up close."

Inez leaned forward. "So, there were Confederates here?"

"Absolutely. They were in the minority, though. Sympathizers, and even those who expressed occasional displeasure with Lincoln or the policies of the Union, were regularly arrested and their civil liberties suppressed. D'you know Lincoln suspended the writ of habeas corpus in '63? Made it easy to accuse folks of spying for the Confederacy and have them tossed in the calaboose. I suspect more than a few innocents were charged with disloyalty and treason. All it took was someone deciding he didn't like the way you looked at him and a yell of 'Johnny Reb!' or 'Spy!' and…boom!" He gestured with his snifter, and the brandy sloshed dangerously. "Off you go to Alcatraz."

Alcatraz! Inez froze, her glass at her lips, thinking of the dead locksmith, his trips to Alcatraz, and the packets he delivered for Captain Taylor. Packets that he passed to a prisoner who was a Confederate sympathizer and charged with treason.

"I thought Alcatraz Island was a military prison," said de Bruijn.

"For the most part, that's true." Haskell paused to roll his cigar ash into the crystal ashtray at his elbow. "But Fort Alcatraz took all comers during the war, military and civilian alike."

Inez added a generous portion of brandy to his almost-empty glass. She offered the bottle to de Bruijn, who declined. To Inez's eye, it appeared he had sipped but little. Hoping to keep Haskell talking, she said, "Alcatraz Island appears to be in an excellent position to protect the city and its harbors. I imagine San Francisco being an important port town, there was concern that the enemy might attack from the sea?"

"Oh, sure. The fort and the military in general were on guard against that, though." He chuckled. "The commander of Alcatraz almost caused an international incident when he fired a cannon shot across the bow of a British warship. The story goes that the ship's flag was not visible as it entered the bay, and he wasn't taking any chances. To make things worse, the vessel was the flagship of the commander in chief of the British Pacific Squadron. The ship's admiral was not pleased, to say the least." Haskell smiled and exhaled. A cloud of noxious smoke encircled his head. "But you're right, Mrs. Stannert. There were concerns about possible Confederate raids in the

Pacific. California-minted gold was shipped regularly from San Francisco to support the Union effort."

A shock that was almost electric zipped through Inez at the words *California-minted gold*. She was afraid to look at de Bruijn, lest she give away her excitement. She refilled her empty glass so Haskell wouldn't feel he was drinking alone and commented, "That must have been quite the journey."

He nodded. "The ships traveled down the coast to Central America. The gold was loaded onto railroad cars, taken across the Isthmus of Panama, picked up by steamers, and carried to Union ports. Those ships were tempting targets for Confederate privateers."

A tingle raced across her scalp. "Privateers? Here?"

He nodded. "The *J. M. Chapman* plot might be the best known in these parts. Heard of it?"

"*Chapman?* No." She glanced at de Bruijn. He shook his head.

"Well, let's see if I can give it to you in condensed form. It involves a Confederate secret society called the Knights of the Golden Circle. The local branch had designs on the Presidio, the mint—"

Inez almost choked on her brandy.

"—the Custom House, and a handful of other targets. Some members, including a couple of prominent San Franciscans, decided to take to the high seas and target the treasure ships out of San Francisco. They bought a schooner, the *J. M. Chapman*, and secretly outfitted it with cannons, guns, ammunition, and even uniforms. They were very serious about it. In fact, they even had letters of marque from Jefferson Davis that essentially permitted them to commit piracy in the name of the Confederate States of America."

Inez could hardly breathe. "Were they caught?"

"One of the crew let something slip at a local watering hole,

and the authorities were alerted. No sooner did the conspirators lift anchor and set sail, than they were stopped and boarded
by the crew of the *USS Cyane* along with revenue officers and
local police. The whole lot was clapped in irons and delivered to
Alcatraz. Solitary confinement. Thus ends this tale of thwarted
piracy on the Pacific."

"What happened to the conspirators?" asked de Bruijn.

Haskell scratched his neck. "Tried and found guilty of treason. I can't recall the sentence, but I do know that once Lincoln
issued his amnesty proclamation toward the end of '63, politi-
cal prisoners were granted full pardons as long as they took and
kept the oath of allegiance."

"So, this occurred in '63?" Inez asked.

Haskell nodded. "In the spring."

Inez topped off her glass. "Did they catch everyone involved?"

Haskell picked up his cigar, which had gone out during his sto-
rytelling, shook his head ruefully, and set it back in the ashtray.
"I guess we have to assume so. If one of their number had stayed
behind, you'd think someone would've said something about it."

Or maybe not.

"So they were all released?" Inez asked. "None still remain in
Alcatraz?"

"It's been almost twenty years. If one of them is still there, it
would be unusual." Haskell pulled out his pocket watch, examined the time, and stood with a sigh. "Thank you for the brandy,
Mrs. Stannert, and thank you both for listening to me reminisce.
I didn't realize I remembered so much. Time marches on, and
my memory gets left behind, trying to catch up."

Inez knew that he was being modest about his prodigious
memory for facts and events. Which was one of the reasons
she'd decided to come to him in the first place with her questions. And, she had one more.

"Didn't you mention once that you have a relative working at the mint?" she asked.

He tucked his pocket watch away. "Might have. My brother-in-law works there."

"Could you ask him a question for me?"

Haskell looked at her sharply. Suddenly, he didn't appear as if he'd just consumed three glasses of brandy. "Maybe. What's your question?"

"I'm curious if he knows of the Taylor family. Jack Taylor was chief clerk at the San Francisco Mint until he went east, ostensibly to join the war effort. I'm wondering if a large sum of double eagles minted in '63 might have gone missing at the same time."

"That's very specific. And before his time. But, stories get passed around like coins and take a long time to go out of circulation, so I'll ask."

"Oh, and Bertram Taylor, nephew of the aforesaid chief clerk, is employed at the mint," she said, adding belatedly, "I suppose that could come into play."

"Uh-huh." Haskell went to get his hat off the peg by the back door. "I have a standing invitation to dinner on Friday nights at my sister's. I'll ask then." He turned, hat in hand, and glanced from Inez to de Bruijn. "So, are you going to tell me what this is about?"

Inez clamped her mouth shut. De Bruijn just raised his eyebrows.

Haskell continued, "Does it have anything to do with the cadaver and coins that recently came to light in the old Taylor house?"

"How do you know about that?" burst out Inez.

He grinned. "It's my business to know. I'm a newsman, remember?"

She kept her expression neutral. "I'm not saying another

word, one way or the other. However, once certain issues are resolved, I promise we shall revisit the brandy, and I'll explain."

He nodded. "Gold without an owner and a corpse without a name at a house you now own. And here at your table sits a private investigator, who specializes in 'finding what's lost.' It'll be interesting to hear your story when you're ready to tell it." He clapped his hat on his head.

"A last question if I may," said de Bruijn.

Haskell turned. "Ask away."

"Which side of the war were you on, Mr. Haskell?"

Haskell's grin grew wider. "Mrs. Stannert can answer that one."

They both looked at her. She thought back on the conversation. How carefully he'd avoided vilifying one side or the other. If one side or the other was going to be magnanimous, it was the winners. "Union?" she guessed.

"Good guess, Mrs. Stannert." He gripped the doorknob to go. "But I have a more general philosophy these days. Look at the masthead of my paper. I'm on the side of the common working-man, of course." He winked and let himself out the back door.

Chapter Thirty-One

Inez stared at the closed door after Roger Haskell left and then at de Bruijn. All she could think of to say was "Well."

"I will have to keep Mr. Haskell in mind for the future," said de Bruijn, picking up his brandy. "He seems well informed."

Inez returned to her own brandy. "Roger Haskell has been a great help to me in the past. As he said, he is a true believer in the workingman and works ceaselessly for their cause and their right to unionize." She set her glass down without drinking, feeling that she had had enough for the night. Perhaps even a tad too much. "So, let's talk about today. How did you fare?"

"I was able to complete two tasks related to this case," he said. "Earlier this evening, I joined Mrs. Krause and her boarders for dinner. It gave me a chance to talk with them informally during and after the meal. I was curious if there were any other observations Saturday night that might not have been mentioned to Detective Lynch. I did not want to let more time go by before questioning them. Most people do not have Mr. Haskell's impressive memory."

"Haskell would say that such a mind is a must for any newsman worth his salt. But go on. Did you learn anything new?"

"There is talk of ghosts walking the halls late at night and sounds emanating through the walls of the place next door. Particularly last Saturday night."

She frowned. "Someone was inside the vacant house on Saturday night? It must have been Joe Harris's killer. And I'd warrant that whoever that was now has the keys. Unless they are sneaking in the windows."

"I checked the windows," said de Bruijn. "Those on the first floor are all intact and shut tight. The upper story windows are not broken. To reach them, one would need a ladder."

"And I doubt anyone would set up a ladder to gain access. Too obvious."

"I agree. Some of the boarders mentioned hearing footsteps and sounds on other nights as well. According to Mrs. Krause, Mr. Harris occasionally patrolled the interior of the house, in addition to checking the integrity of the outside. Although doing so at night seems odd to me. I plan to visit his son and ask some questions."

Inez jumped in. "I met with Paulie Harris today. Duplicate house keys *do* exist. Unfortunately, they are locked up in the shop's safe, and he does not have the combination. He said he would get someone to crack it." Inez swirled the liquid in her goblet, restless. "Did you meet the newest boarder? A Mr. Morton?"

De Bruijn shook his head. "Not yet. Mrs. Krause said he does not expect to be at meals very often. She thinks he has a job that keeps him working late hours."

"Or perhaps he takes his meals elsewhere. Will you speak to him?"

"I am more interested in questioning boarders who left recently, including Miss Ashby."

"She gave notice in a hurry the morning Mr. Harris died. Perhaps she heard something more definitive than ghostly footsteps in hidden hallways.'"

"I would also like to talk to the man you bought the house from. Bertram Taylor."

"Ah. Bertram Taylor." She took a deep breath and felt her stays tighten on her chest. "He works at the mint, following in his uncle's footsteps, it seems. I went there today and spoke to him. It did not go well. I advise you to tread carefully when speaking of his uncle." She related her conversation, finishing with, "I hope to speak with him again tomorrow. Perhaps he'll be more receptive after he has had time to cool down. I also met a Mr. Russo, a guard who worked at the mint at the same time as Bertram's uncle. He promised to speak to me after work tomorrow."

De Bruijn nodded. "I did have an interesting conversation with the woman who lives in the house across the alley."

"Yes?"

"She is a young matron, the wife of a physician, and walks the floors all hours with a colicky infant. She claims she has seen lights flickering inside the house."

Half-joking, Inez asked, "More ghosts?"

"She is not aware of the history of the building and thought its owners 'spent time away.' Recently, she has started seeing dim lights on the third floor."

"Third floor?" Inez's mind raced back to when she and Moira had toured the house before making an offer to buy. Harris had accompanied them, dogging their very steps. Inez closed her eyes, the better to recall the layout of the third floor. It had one large room facing the street, with a big window for light. She remembered thinking it might have been a sewing or reading room. And two rooms in the back, small and dark.

She opened her eyes. "The third floor has no windows on the back side of the house."

"Are you certain?"

"Absolutely. I recall there were two rooms in the rear and thinking how small and dingy they were. They put me in mind of servants' quarters. No windows in either room."

He knit his brows. "Odd."

"Perhaps she confused the second and third floors."

"Perhaps. I will take another look at the back of the building tomorrow or the next day. Regardless, lights inside are suspicious enough. I left my card with her. The household has a telephone, so I told her to call me should she spot any more lights."

Despite her intentions not to drink more brandy, Inez discovered she had somehow drained her glass yet again. She cradled the empty snifter in her hands, and her thoughts drifted. Since she was sitting across from de Bruijn and staring at him, her thoughts began to veer in his direction. He was looking away to one side, pondering something. Free to gaze at him without being noticed, she couldn't help but think he had a handsome profile. With his dark hair, dark eyes, neatly trimmed beard, and vaguely militaristic mustache, he appeared very European and rather aristocratic.

At that moment, he looked rather more intense than usual, which appealed to her. It reminded her of the time or two she had glimpsed another side of him, sensed a certain fire lurking beneath his deliberate exterior. Now, with that slight frown between his brows and a certain acuteness of expression, he was very tantalizing. She wondered what he would do if she were to rise from the chair—he would do the same, of course, being a gentleman of manners and convention and not expecting anything out of the ordinary from her—approach him, take hold of his silk tie right below the precise Windsor knot, pull his face toward hers, and kiss him.

"Anything else you wish to tell me?"

She blinked at his voice and pushed aside her vaguely erotic reverie. "Pardon, I do believe the long day and the brandy have fogged my thinking." Clarity returned, and with it the memory of her interaction with MacKay. "Oh, yes. Coming back from Mrs. Nolan's this evening, Antonia and I ran into Officer MacKay. It was a very unpleasant encounter." She related what happened.

His expression darkened. "He threatened you both."

"He probably wanted to scare me. I'm not convinced he will actually do anything."

"I am not convinced he won't." De Bruijn gave her a deep searching look that secretly thrilled her to her core. "The Palace Hotel has any number of rooms available. I could speak to the manager about providing you with a set of rooms not far from my own."

Now, that raised some interesting possibilities. However...

"I don't think it's necessary at this time," said Inez. "We are keeping the doors locked. And I have this." She withdrew her revolver from her pocket and set it on the table next to the brandy bottle. She could see he was not convinced. Thinking to lighten things a bit, she added, "Antonia has vowed if she sees him at the door outside, she'll drop a kettle on his head."

"It's not safe," said de Bruijn bluntly.

The flat pronouncement turned her half-formed ardor into irritation. "What is *safe* about any of this? Someone killed Mr. Harris and took his keys. Someone killed a man decades ago, walled him up, and left him to rot. Someone is skulking around that old house. Why? Why any of this?" She leaned forward. "The day we answer the questions and identify the murderers, we may feel safe at last. On the day following, one of us could be killed by a runaway hack." She stood, and just as in her fantasy, he did the same. Only now, she didn't have the impulse to drag on his tie and kiss him but rather to strangle him a bit with that wrap of silk, just to remind him who she was.

"Perhaps tomorrow we will know more," she said.

"Perhaps." His gaze swept over her, foot to face. She reddened a bit, wondering if he, somehow, guessed at her earlier amatory musings. He continued, "Should any harm come to you or to Antonia, I would not wait for the law to find and pass judgment."

Normally, this concern on her behalf from someone she viewed as desirable would have pleased her. And she would have even approved of the hint of vigilantism. A man in pursuit of justice was, after all, a man after her own heart. But she was suddenly tired of the assumption that she needed others to fight her battles. "I can take care of myself and Antonia. I am quite capable of keeping us both from danger."

"That's not been my observation."

Left unspoken was mention of the times when she or the girl, and even she *and* the girl, had ended up in one or another tight spot all due to their purposeful entanglements in nefarious doings. "Neither Antonia nor I have suffered loss of limb or life," she said coolly. "If present events take a turn, I shall ask Mrs. Nolan to put us up. She would be glad to do so in a pinch."

"The hotel—"

"Thank you for your offer and your concern," she repeated. "But we shall be fine." The thought crossed her mind that she could guarantee to watch her own step, but there was no way to watch Antonia day and night. She glanced at the ceiling, wondering what her ward was up to, and said, "It's late. We should call it a night. Much to do on the morrow for us both. The sooner we put everything to rest, the sooner we put it all behind us." She gathered her revolver, her coat, and a lamp from the sideboard. When she turned to let him out the back door, he already had his coat on and hat and walking stick in hand.

He said, "I'll walk you to your apartment door."

Inez set her mouth in a stubborn line, preparing to refuse, then realized his mouth was set in a similar fashion. Impasse. She laughed a little, realizing the futility of arguing over such a trifle. *I must pick my battles with him carefully.* "Very well, Mr. de Bruijn, as you wish."

Chapter Thirty-Two

Antonia sat on the floor in the hallway of the apartment. Her back was against the door to the storage room, which was as close to the rear of the building as she could easily get. A gabble of muffled voices floated up from the music store's back room where Mrs. S was running her poker game. Antonia wished she could be there, just to watch, of course, not to play. Although she would've liked to play. But Mrs. S refused to let her even sit in the corner.

Every time Antonia asked, Mrs. S said, "It wouldn't be seemly." Sometimes she'd add, "It's a time when I can relax with other adults and discuss the goings-on in the city."

Antonia bet that if she were there she could pick up a thing or two about cheating at cards. That was probably another reason Mrs. S didn't want her hanging around. So, she kept asking, figuring someday Mrs. S would finally say yes. But she kept saying no, and it made Antonia grumpy. It seemed like whenever the grown-ups had something fun going on—cards, drinking, gabbing on about interesting things—she was shooed out of the room.

Besides, she was still smarting after Mrs. S gave her that dressing-down earlier and said she couldn't go back to Charlotte's house. How were she and Charlotte going to finish searching the Treasure House?

She'd figure out something.

And anyway, she had her own plans tonight, so being banned from the Monday night poker game didn't bother her as much as usual. Antonia did wish she could hear what they were saying. To do that, she'd have to pick the storage room lock, which was easy enough. She'd done it before. Tonight, though, there was a different lock she wanted to jimmy.

Antonia sat cross-legged, her wrinkled and stained pinafore forming a sort of hammock in her lap. The wooden box she'd grabbed from the table in the Treasure House's secret room lay on the fabric. Scattered in the same swoop of cloth were one of Mrs. S's hatpins and several hairpins. Antonia picked up the box and shook it.

It rattled.

Then she brought it close, eyeing the lock. It didn't look as if it would be hard to open. Antonia settled the box back on her lap, front facing up, the gold oval lock with its vertical keyhole reminding her of a cat's eye. She chose two hairpins and pulled them open, then she inserted a thin end of one into the lock and pulled up, bending it into a small hook. The other hairpin she bent into an L shape. Then, she went to work.

After a careful application of pressure and some probing and jiggling, Antonia was rewarded with a small click. She twisted, and the box lid sprang open a fraction of an inch. Pleased, she set her tools aside and, holding her breath, opened the box.

She wasn't sure what she expected to find. Diamonds? Rubies? More gold? Hopefully something valuable.

At any rate, she was disappointed to see the box only held a stack of photographs. They were mostly images of a large blocky building on a cliff over water, docks, roads, rows of cannons, stacks of cannon balls, and even a lighthouse. Antonia frowned, thinking the photos might've been taken on an island, since most showed water all around in the different views.

Whatever the place was, it sure wasn't a pirate hideout. There was even one photograph of a man wearing what she was pretty sure was a uniform. He stood gazing out to sea, one arm resting on a huge cannon that was way bigger than he was. It was pointing over a tall brick wall onto the open water. She could just make out a boat or two in the distance.

What was all this?

Then she remembered. Mick Lynch had said the "CSA" on her cipher disk stood for "Confederate States of America" and was from the war. And the paper Mrs. S had that she'd snuck a peek at was a commission for a privateer for the Confederacy. So maybe the privateer who had hidden the disk and the photos away was also a spy! Maybe the photographs with all their cannons and the fort-like building had something to do with the war!

Antonia went through the images again, fascinated by the views of "ancient history" and trying to puzzle out the location. It would've been more exciting if the box had jewels or treasure, but the photographs were kind of interesting and definitely mysterious. And at least the box hadn't held a bunch of sappy love letters. All of a sudden, she realized the voices coming through the floorboards had quieted. Listening carefully, she heard the murmur of Mrs. S talking to one other person, a man. *Probably Worthless Rotten Brown.* That meant the poker game was over, and Mrs. S might head upstairs soon. And when she did, Antonia knew she'd better be in bed with lights out or she'd be in even more trouble. Of course, that would be nothing compared to what would happen if Mrs. S caught her sitting up here with the cipher disk and box of photos. *That* she'd have a hard time explaining!

She'd brought her "booty" with her to school that day, but now she needed a good hiding place in the apartment. It couldn't be in her room, because Mrs. S had been snooping around and might just keep snooping. She had to find someplace Mrs. S wouldn't go poking around. Not the bathroom. Not Mrs. S's room. No time to jimmy the lock and go into the storage room, because the voices downstairs were moving around. Then, she heard the faint sound of the back door opening and closing. She had to come up with a hiding place fast.

Inspiration came in a flash.

The kitchen!

Mrs. S never cooked, except to make coffee and toast. She'd never check for anything sneaky in there!

Antonia folded everything into the apron of her pinafore and held it closed with one hand. She grabbed the handlamp with the other, skittered on stockinged feet to the deserted kitchen, and looked around. Her gaze finally lit upon the tall corner cupboard. The upper, open shelves held cups and saucers, the sugar bowl and the coffee grinder, some bowls and plates of various sizes, a few cans of condensed milk, and a bread safe. Down low were cupboard doors that she'd never seen Mrs. S open. Antonia ran to the cupboard and dropped to her knees on the floor. She opened one cupboard door and stuck a hand in, hoping there weren't any creepy-crawlies living inside. A spider web brushed the back of her hand, and her fingertips touched and slid across a curved metal surface before bumping into a metal handle.

Trying not to make any noise, she dragged out what looked like an old tarnished soup pot. And it even had a lid! It was very dusty. Antonia doubted anyone had used it in years and years.

Maybe even since the war. Cheered, thinking it'd be a cold day in hell before Mrs. S ever wanted to make a pot of soup or stew, Antonia lifted the lid and put the wooden box of photographs and the brass cipher disk inside. Once the lid was back on, she slid the pot into the kitchen cabinet, shoving it back extra far so it wasn't visible.

She shut the cupboard door, tucked the pins into her pinafore pocket, and stood. Just then, Mrs. S's voice drifted up from downstairs. "Thank you for walking me to the apartment, but as you can see, it was completely unnecessary. No one lurking in the shadows or the alley."

"It pays to be careful, especially now, given recent events." And *that* was Mr. Worthless Rotten Brown.

"Yes, well, let's meet again in a day or two when we both have more information."

"Agreed. Good night, Mrs. Stannert."

"Good night, Mr. de Bruijn."

Antonia doused her lamp and was out of the kitchen like a shot in the dark. She raced to her room, set the lamp on the night table, and struggled desperately to get out of her pinafore—not easy since it buttoned up the back. One of the buttons popped off, and she heard a *tink* as it hit the floor and rolled. Free at last, she flung the dirty apron onto the chair. The creak of footsteps told her Mrs. S was climbing the stairs to the apartment. Antonia unfastened her dress just enough to squirm out of it, too, and tossed it on top of her pinafore.

The key scraped in the lock. She threw back the quilt and dove into bed in her underclothes. The apartment door sighed while she tugged her stockings off under the covers. She shoved them out of the bed and onto the floor before closing her eyes. The door to her room squeaked open. Antonia forced herself to breathe slowly. The floorboards groaned, warning her that Mrs. S was approaching. She willed her eyelids not to flutter as Mrs. S laid a gentle hand atop her head before pulling up the quilt to cover her shoulders.

Then, silence. Until…

"Antonia, I know you're awake. The glass chimney of your lamp is still hot."

Shoot!

Antonia squinted and tried to sound sleepy. "Whaaat?"

There was enough light coming through the window to see Mrs. S had moved away from the bed and was now standing by the chair with its mess of clothes. Antonia watched her pick up the dress and hang it on a peg before picking up the pinafore and holding it at arm's length.

"This one needs cleaning." Mrs. S sounded tired. "Wear your other pinafore tomorrow. Wash this one in the sink after school and hang it on the clothesline over the tub." She dropped the pinafore back on the chair and turned to Antonia.

Holding her breath, Antonia wondered what was coming next.

"Antonia," said Mrs. S, sounding severe but also like her heart wasn't really in it. "I know you love to read. I understand wanting to stay awake late at night, and I know you have a magazine under your pillow. But when you don't get enough sleep, it just makes it harder for you to get up in the morning and to stay alert in school."

"Yes'm," said Antonia meekly.

Mrs. S came over to the bed again. "Now, give me that penny weekly, please." Antonia reached beneath her pillow, reluctantly pulled out *Young Folks*, and handed it over. Mrs. S said, "I will keep this tonight and leave it on the kitchen table tomorrow. You can read it when you come home from school. After you wash your pinafore."

"Yes'm."

Antonia felt a featherlight touch as Mrs. S smoothed back her hair, then lay the back of her cool hand against Antonia's warm cheek. "Antonia, you may not believe this, but everything I do, I do for your own good. I understand you yearn for a life of adventure, and I know how difficult it is to follow convention and strictures. But that is the way it must be. Do you understand what I am saying? It is one thing to read *Treasure Island* and day-dream about pirates and treasure. It is another thing, entirely, to court danger in real life. Now, rest."

She left, leaving Antonia to burrow under her covers and wonder how much Mrs. S knew about her exploits and whether her "buried" treasures were as well-hidden as she thought.

Chapter Thirty-Three

Inez opened her eyes Tuesday morning feeling as if it had been a lifetime since the previous week. Was it truly only Thursday that she and Moira had signed documents for the accursed building? As she lay there, she became aware of the patter of rain on the roof above her head. Rain meant donning waterproofs, pulling out umbrellas and overshoes.

With a groan, Inez pulled herself out of bed and went to stoke the small kitchen stove to boil water for coffee. She rattled Antonia awake. The girl was, as she had predicted, more tired than usual and tried to burrow under the covers. "Up!" said Inez. "It's raining. You'll need extra time to get ready and to stop at Mrs. Nolan's for your lunch bucket."

There was much grumbling and dragging of feet, but, finally, Antonia was up. Inez gave her hair a quick brush at the kitchen table. Antonia's tangled curls caught in the hairbrush, so there was much in the way of yips as Inez yanked and pulled and finally fashioned a clumsy braid out of the chaotic tumble of dark hair.

The toast was partly burnt and the coffee was stronger than usual. Antonia wrinkled her nose and ate the center of the bread, leaving the charred crusts behind on the plate and her coffee-and-milk untouched. She grabbed her book bag, and she and Inez clattered down the stairs. It was on with the water-proof overcoat with the too-short sleeves and the galoshes, which would probably not fit for another season. Inez shoved an umbrella into Antonia's hands with the admonition to not lose it and waved goodbye.

Next, she had to prepare herself. After dressing for the uncertain weather, Inez went down to the office, retrieved two copies of her standard agreement for a loan, and removed five double eagles from the bag in the safe. She scribbled a note indicating she was taking one hundred dollars from "her share" of the total, signed it, and stuffed it into the canvas sack.

As Inez left the building, she realized the rain had let up. But there were puddles enough on her way to the locksmith shop that she was glad to have put on overshoes. When she arrived at the shop, Paulie greeted her at the door looking wan. Inez noticed that he wore a black armband and that there was now a black wreath on the door. They went back to the little sitting area. After they both signed the papers, Inez gave one copy to Paulie along with the five gold coins. The young locksmith thanked her and said, "Now I can obtain a headstone for Father. We are eternally grateful. When all of this is done, Mother would like to thank you herself."

Touched, Inez said, "Of course, if it is not an imposition."

"Not at all. It is just the two of us now, and she never leaves our rooms above the shop." He lowered his voice. "Given her frail condition, I saw no reason to tell her how Father died. I spoke to Detective Lynch, and he agreed. She is aware Captain Taylor died some time ago, and his son sold the house. So, I told her Father had gone one last time to view the house he had faithfully watched over for Captain Taylor all these many years, and his heart failed him. Knowing Father was loyal beyond reproach, she accepted this."

Inez nodded. "I understand."

They stood and walked toward the shop entrance. Paulie said, "She believes Father's obligation to the Taylors is now fulfilled, his tour of duty completed. It brings her peace to think so." He sighed. "Father never told her about his other task—the meetings with the prisoner at Alcatraz. Tomorrow, I shall discharge that final obligation." He turned a gray-eyed gaze to Inez. "I will meet you before six in the morning at the Washington Street Wharf."

"I shall be there."

"Be prepared for weather." Paulie gazed out the shop window. The rain had begun again. "It may be a wet crossing."

Inez bid adieu and splashed her way to the mint. By the time she got there, she had determined her overshoes were no longer entirely waterproof, at least along the seams that joined soles to uppers. At least her umbrella was doing its job. Inez hoped the weather would improve after she spoke with Bertram Taylor. She was determined to repeat her questions and, if nothing else, gauge his reactions.

However, she was to be disappointed.

Upon entering the building, Mr. Russo, in his post by the door, called her over. "Mr. Taylor is not in today," he told her.

"No?" She felt a trickle of disappointment join an errant raindrop on the nape of her neck.

"He became ill yesterday afternoon."

"After I left." *How convenient. And a little suspicious.*

He nodded.

Inez sighed. "Are you still willing to talk with me, at least?"

"My shift is over at four. The weather being what it is, I'll probably take a few minutes to light my pipe outside these doors, out of the rain, before I walk home."

Inez smiled. "And I take my afternoon constitutional at four, no matter what the weather."

"Our paths might cross," he said amiably.

Inez turned up her collar preparing to brave the elements again. "I think the odds are very good."

Once outside, she surrendered to convenience and hailed a passing hack, took a hasty meal at a small restaurant catering to women, then began her rounds of music lessons in the more fashionable parts of town, including incursions into the rarefied atmosphere of Russian Hill and Nob Hill. Normally, her afternoons in the over-gilded, overstuffed, breathless music rooms of the rich and powerful brought unwelcome memories of her New York childhood close to the surface. Today, however, such recollections were flooded out by the grim events at Moira's modest boardinghouse establishment. Of course, the violence laid bare there and in the more lowly parts of the city could also be found in the more moneyed environs of the wealthy. They just had the means to bury it more efficiently and keep it that way.

She'd noticed that certain musical pieces seemed to simultaneously rise in popularity among her young lady pupils who, she surmised, probably all ran in the same set. Lately, the tune *du jour* seemed to be *Rosen aus dem Süden by composer Johann Strauss the Younger.* By the end of the afternoon, she was heartily sick of hearing the waltz medley many times over, with variable haltings and the inevitable missed notes. "Keep practicing," she told each and every one of her pupils. "It's not as simple as it looks."

The final lesson of Inez's day concluded at three thirty, and she begged off what promised to be a prolonged conversation with the mother, who wanted to discuss adding lessons for the second daughter. Despite this, that, and the other, Inez managed to be back at the mint just a few minutes past four. She was relieved to see the stocky figure of Russo at the top of the stairs, sheltered by the portico, pipe in hand, mackintosh over his uniform. He must have seen her as well, for he started down the steps, swinging a tin lunch bucket, as she started up.

"Good afternoon, Mrs. Stannert. Quite the weather for a constitutional. Either makes one stronger or gives one the croup."

"I'm counting on the fresh and bracing air to deliver the former," she said. They descended the stairs, and she asked, "Which direction are you going?"

"North. To North Beach."

"That is a fair way to walk."

He drew on his pipe. "Sometimes I take the streetcar. But today, I feel the need to walk."

She debated how to steer the conversation to Jack Taylor's time at the mint and decided an indirect approach was best. "So did you join the mint before the war?"

"Oh, yes. In the late fifties. In the old building on Commercial."

"What was it like?"

"Those were heady times. Gold, and then silver, poured into the plant."

"I imagine that with all that precious metal some might have gone astray." She hoped he would rise to the bait.

He chuckled. "Oh, the metals poured in and the money poured out. Inevitably, some trickled this way and that and disappeared."

"Embezzlement?"

"Not uncommon. For instance, there was a janitor at the old mint who was an expert rat-catcher. It turned out he was sewing twenty-dollar gold pieces—double eagles—into the dead rats before throwing them in the trash. He then visited the trash heap after hours and retrieved what he'd hidden."

Rats. Inez shuddered. "So, someone caught him?"

Russo cocked an eyebrow at her.

"You?"

"I started at the mint as a janitor and counted myself lucky. My father, uncles, brothers—fishermen and fishmongers, all. When I was promoted to night watchman and finally became a guard on the day shift, you'd think from my family's reaction I'd been crowned king." He smiled. "I am loyal to the mint, and my loyalty was rewarded, which has only made it stronger. If I knew someone was stealing from the Granite Lady, I'd not turn a blind eye."

They were now at Market. The rain had ceased she was glad to see. Her shoes were increasingly damp, but at least she could close her umbrella. The gray skies seemed to be lightening as late afternoon toyed with the idea of becoming evening. Right then, the clouds lifted and the sun shot a beam underneath, gilding the wet streets and mud puddles with a glitter that hurt the eyes.

The smoke from Russo's pipe drifted past her on a light breeze. She inhaled, detecting a hint of vanilla. "So, there were other incidents?"

He nodded. "With so much passing through so many hands, there was always temptation. But there were also false accusations. The first chief assayer, a clever Hungarian, was accused when a fortune in gold went missing. He blamed it on faulty blowers. He was cleared of possible crimes when thousands of dollars in gold dust was 'mined' from soot coating nearby rooftops."

"But there must have been times when it all just… disappeared?"

"Shortly after I started, it would have been '56 or so, almost 150,000 dollars in gold vanished and was never recovered."

"I'm curious what might have been happening around the time Jack Taylor left. I understand he left suddenly to join the Union war effort." She held her breath.

"Ah, yes. That was in the spring of '63. He wasn't the only one to go fight, but, like you say, he left suddenly, which is why I recall the year and the season. I think relatives—his brother, perhaps?—told the mint superintendent, who told us. Quite a surprise."

"A surprise? Was Jack Taylor not a supporter of the Union?"

They had walked toward the bay, down Market, and had reached Montgomery. Russo extracted the pipe and tapped his bottom lip with the stem. "I don't recall him voicing strong opinions one way or the other. Of course, during the war, one would be a fool to talk against the North and an even bigger fool to support the South. Mr. Taylor was the mint's chief clerk. He wasn't a fool. I and others were mostly surprised he hadn't said anything about his plans and left so abruptly. And then, there was the missing gold." His voice turned troubled.

"Missing gold?"

His gait slowed. "I wondered, but before I said anything, they caught the culprit. I am glad I stayed silent, because I would not have wanted to accuse an innocent man and a patriot."

"What happened?"

"A quantity of double eagles were stolen about that time. A coiner was accused of the crime when he was arrested for being a Confederate conspirator. He was part of a group that had outfitted a ship with plans to capture gold and silver shipments leaving from San Francisco."

The shock of disparate narrative threads twining together nearly sent her stumbling off the curb. "Are you referring to the *J. M. Chapman* incident?"

He nodded. "You've heard of it. So you see, it makes sense that the coiner stole from the mint to help fill Confederate coffers with Union gold. So, I thought no more about it."

The canvas bag of gold coins and the walled-in corpse loomed in her mind's eye. Linked together through the years in darkness. "You thought no more about…what? Did you think Jack Taylor had something to do with the disappearance of the money?"

Russo cleared his throat and looked north, up Montgomery. "As I said, it was nothing. So I said nothing. I will tell you what I saw. At that time, I worked as a night watchman in the old mint. The last time I saw Mr. Taylor, it was very late at night, and he was coming out of his office. He was carrying a leather suitcase. I remember it was a very fine suitcase, with brass locks and leather straps. Also, the way he carried it, the way it pulled his shoulder down, it seemed heavy. He said good night to me and left."

Russo looked at Inez. "Understand, he was chief clerk. That is a high position, right below the mint superintendent. He and several other mint officers had the privilege of entering the building at any hour of the day or night. I had no right to question the actions of one of my superiors. If I did, it would have been my word against his. I could have lost my position. And when I found out later he went east to fight, well, it all made sense. He must have left directly from work, and his suitcase was packed for his journey."

"Did the coiner confess to the theft?"

"He maintained his innocence, and none could prove otherwise."

"Did they find the money?"

"They did not. At least, as far I know. It was a long time ago. Many other scandals have pushed old ones out of most memories." He smiled. "Except for my memory, that is."

"So, who was this coiner, the Confederate sympathizer?"

He shrugged. "I don't recall his name. I suppose once he got his just deserts and was sent away for treason, he was forgotten. He is probably rotting there still."

"And where would that be?"

"Where they put all those who wanted to destroy the Union. Alcatraz, of course."

Chapter Thirty-Four

Uneasy after her conversation with Russo, Inez was not in a good mood by the time she returned to the apartment. Her disposition did not improve upon finding Antonia's filthy pinafore still crumpled and dirty on the chair in the bedroom, and Antonia hunched over her *Young Folks* magazine at the kitchen table. The girl whipped the pages shut and at least had the decency to look guilty. "I'll do it after dinner. Promise."

"In that case, I'll take the magazine downstairs with me to the office. You can have it back tomorrow, assuming you've done your washing as I asked you to."

With a grumpy expression, Antonia handed her the penny weekly. Inez tucked it under her elbow. "So, how was school?" ·

"Fine."

No expositions about the boring classes or complaints about Miss Pierce, which were usually readily supplied and detailed. Sensing something other than lessons was amiss, Inez asked, "And how is your friend?"

"What friend?"

"The Lynch boy. Michael."

"Oh." Antonia's sour expression deepened. "We're not friends anymore."

"No? What happened?"

She looked away. "I lost my temper. Said some things I shouldn't've."

"Well, then you should apologize."

She shrugged. "I don't think he'll talk to me ever again."

That surprised Inez. She had pegged Michael as a steady sort with a well-developed streak of chivalry, no doubt encouraged by his law-enforcing father. Also, she suspected Michael was a little sweet on Antonia. Inez concluded the girl must have been extremely rude or crude to put him off.

"You won't know until you try," Inez said, thinking that making the attempt to apologize would be good for Antonia, no matter how well or poorly it was received. "And next time you feel your temper rise, count to ten before speaking."

"Do you do that?" Antonia countered.

Inez admitted to herself she did not. "We should leave for dinner soon," she said. "Mrs. Nolan does not keep meals waiting."

Walking to Mrs. Nolan's always increased the appetite. Inez deemed the pot roast, potatoes, and carrots filling and the custard pie the perfect finish to the day. She drank an extra cup of coffee to help her complete her tasks that night. No one bothered them on the way home, and Inez was glad there was no need to brandish her pocket revolver. Which raised a question: Could she take the revolver with her to Alcatraz on the morrow? Was carrying a weapon onto the prison grounds even allowed?

She accompanied Antonia into the apartment. After doing a hasty reconnaissance and finding nothing amiss, she said, "I have some accounting to do tonight before I retire. I'll be downstairs in the office. And tomorrow, I will be leaving extremely early. Before dawn."

Antonia came to the kitchen, dirty pinafore in hand. "Where are you going?"

"To Alcatraz Island."

"Why?"

"For this business that Mr. de Bruijn and I are addressing."

She glowered. "Is he going too?"

"Mr. de Bruijn? No. The locksmith's son has business over there, so I will be accompanying him. I believe someone on the island has information about the poor fellow in the wall and the money." Money that almost certainly belonged to the mint. That possibility rather pained her, but after what Russo had said, she had to accept it was a distinct possibility. Antonia looked ready to ask more questions, but Inez pointed to her pinafore, saying, "You have your chores this evening, and I have mine, so we should get busy. If you need me, pound on the floor, and I'll come up."

Inez went back downstairs, locking doors as she went, and let herself into the dark and empty store. Once in the back, she lit a lamp, added coal to the warming stove, and set about looking through the new receipts that had piled up. She accepted they were a sign that business was good but resented the time involved in balancing the accounts.

She also spared some thought on the morrow. Bringing a sample of the "found money" and even the Confederate commission could be useful bona fides. She suspected the person old Mr. Harris met with regularly on Captain Taylor's behalf was the coiner entangled with the *J. M. Chapman* scheme. She couldn't quite figure out how the money had made its way into the wall, but perhaps with some encouragement, in the form of gold, he might be induced to say.

She felt certain Bertram's uncle, Jack Taylor, was involved. She suspected he did not march off to join the Union but came to a sorry end much closer to home. Once she deciphered the shape of past events, a number of things would fall satisfyingly into place, including being able to tell Moira that the fellow "incarcerated" in the wall finally had a name.

As for taking her revolver with her to Alcatraz… Well, it wasn't as if anyone would threaten them on the island, which doubled as a military fort and a prison. There would be plenty of guns around, both large and small bore.

Done with her paperwork, she went to the safe and retrieved two double eagles, the commission, the key, and, after a moment's thought, the glass eye. What better proof that the corpse was Jack Taylor? She closed the repository, gave the combination a few extra spins, and, out of habit, set it to 13, Antonia's assumed age. After extinguishing the lamp, Inez walked through the store and, after locking the door behind her, returned to the apartment. First thing she did was peek into Antonia's room. Light from the window by the bed touched the tumble of dark hair spilling across her pillow. Inez listened and heard only the soft breathing that announced a deep sleep not easily feigned.

In her own bedroom, Inez lit a lamp and carried it to a trunk at the foot of her bed. The trunk wheezed as she opened it, exhaling a scent of cedar and long-enclosed space. She unearthed some of her ex-husband's clothing, starting with a pair of ordinary black trousers, a simple white shirt, and a worn checked waistcoat and jacket. It had been a while since she'd extracted any of these items, and an unexpected pang in the vicinity of her heart caused her to close her eyes and gather herself. Leadville, and all that had happened there, normally felt so far away. But opening this trunk brought it all roaring back.

She banished her personal ghosts and demons, ordering

them back to the depths, and dug into the trunk for a pair of men's boots and hose. Inez held the trousers up to her waist to check that they still fit. All the good food at Mrs. Nolan's and a more sedentary life meant she was no longer as slim as she'd once been. Even so, the trousers looked as if they would do. She exhumed a warm overcoat, for she would be on the water and the island, and who knew what the weather would be? A utilitarian hat with a wide brim completed her outfit. She'd have to braid her hair, tuck it under her collar, and stay in the background as much as possible. But that was fine. She was content to have Paulie Harris take the lead.

After tucking the glass eye, commission, gold coins, and key into various interior pockets, Inez headed to the washroom, thinking to prepare for bed. Antonia's pinafore, now clean or at least cleaner, dripped on the clothesline over the tub. The sight reminded her that the girl's magazine was still in its banished state downstairs in the office.

"Hell and blazes," she muttered. Get it now? Wait until tomorrow?

But tomorrow would start very early.

In fact, by the clock, tomorrow was already here.

Swearing under her breath, Inez grabbed her keys, hurried down the apartment stairs, threw on her coat, and hastened up the deserted street to the music store's entrance. She unlocked the door and entered. The bell clunked, announcing her arrival to the empty space. She closed the door behind her, took a step, and froze.

Something wasn't right.

An errant whisper-current of air brushed her forehead and cheek. The distant *thwack thwack* of wood knocking against wood sounded from the very back of the building.

She was not alone.

Her revolver was out of her coat pocket and in her hand before she took another step. Her first impulse, which she did not act upon, was to call out, "Who's there?"

Her second impulse, which she followed, was to move quickly and quietly through the interior shadows, guided by the knocking and the breeze that beckoned her to the very rear of the store. The opening to the back room yawned before her, blinking from black to dark gray. All of which confirmed her initial theory: The door into the alley was open and hanging free, swinging idly back and forth in the wind.

Keeping to one side of the opening, she held her breath and listened. Nothing. Just the door moving to and fro, and the faintest rustling of papers in the breeze. Nothing seemed to move, nothing breathed. She counted to twenty, then, finger on the trigger, pivoted into the open space, putting her back to the wall.

Before she could react, a shadow detached itself from the wall by the back door and rushed out into the alley.

"Stop!" she yelled and fired.

The gun kicked against her palm, and a bullet plowed into the doorframe, head height.

She dashed to the door, intending to give chase in the alley, only to have the solid wood door slammed in her face. Pain exploded in her forehead, stars shot across her sight.

She gasped out a word she would never utter in polite society, staggered back several paces, and tried to regain her breath. Rage overpowered pain and prudence, and she darted back to the door, tore it open, and with gun at the ready, looked up and down the alley.

Light from a nearby streetlamp on Pine glistened on the mud in the alley. She could see the deep imprints of large shoes, newly planted atop older tracks. Then, she looked down. Sure enough, mud tracked up the back stairs and—she turned to look inside—all around the back room.

"Bloody hell!" she muttered.

She touched her forehead and looked at her fingertips. No blood. But there would be a goose egg soon enough if she didn't apply ice or at least a cold rag. But that would have to wait. She moved back inside, lit a lamp, and locked the door. Had she forgotten to lock it upon leaving? Most likely. Preoccupation was no excuse for sloppiness or stupidity, she thought grimly. She had been so focused on keeping her apartment locked and Antonia safe, she had neglected to check the store's rear entrance.

At least the footprints yielded the path the intruder had taken, once inside. She used the lamp to track his path. He had walked from one side of the large room to the other, probably getting the "lay of the land," then had headed to her safe. Which, thankfully, she *had* locked. Shining a light on the dial, she saw it now pointed at 23. So, he'd tried the safe, then returned to the meeting area with the round table. The receipts were a mess now, much to her chagrin, but he had, oddly enough, stacked the account books on top as if to keep the papers from blowing away.

How considerate.

Most of the remaining footprints, and they were faint at this point, were by the sideboard. Had he poured himself a drink? The bottle of brandy was still there, as was the decanter. She lowered the lamp and shone it around on the floor, then stopped and crouched to look into the hollow space beneath the sideboard. She couldn't believe her eyes.

It was empty.

The rolled-up greatcoat with its cache of buttons and tattered cloth was gone.

Chapter Thirty-Five

She debated calling the police. After all, the store had a telephone. But she decided against it. Her throbbing head needed tending to, but that wasn't the primary reason. All she could claim was that someone opened the unlocked back door and absconded with a bundle of rags. *Oh, that will go over well.* The second reason she decided not to call was that the officer who would come at this hour would undoubtedly be MacKay, the night patrolman for her neighborhood. And who was to say, she argued with herself, that it wasn't he who walked in, took a bundle of "useless" rags, and walked around, leaving muddy footprints everywhere, all just to annoy and alarm her? And who was to say that MacKay might not have been the one to meet Harris, kill him, and take the keys with the intention of exploring the house later?

Still, Inez was not going to be a fool and fob the whole thing off.

Someone who had heard the gold was under her care could have been checking the locks after hours these past few nights and finally gotten lucky, thanks to her carelessness. Taking the rags might have been an afterthought. The intruder could even have been a vagrant who happened by and at the last moment snatched up the still-serviceable coat.

But best not to take any chances.

She gathered the lamp, Antonia's *Young Folks* magazine, some paper, and a pencil and returned to the apartment, locking, checking, and double-checking the doors behind her. In the apartment kitchen, Inez put the items on the table and went to the tiny icebox. Icepick in hand, she hacked off enough ice to wrap in a kitchen towel. Towel to aching forehead, she sat at the kitchen table, her lamp hissing faintly, pushed the magazine to one side, and pulled a sheet of paper before her.

She picked up the pencil and scribbled a quick note to Thomas Welles and John Hee, briefly explaining the mess in the store's back room and noting nothing of value was missing. Which was true, from their standpoint. Their concern would be for the music store, not Inez's side activities. The thought flitted through again that it might be best to set up a small office elsewhere to deal with her "other" business matters. Perhaps at the Palace Hotel. De Bruijn's face rose in her mind, and she wondered if she should call him about the break-in. After all, items pertaining to the investigation had disappeared. She decided to tell him when they next met. After all, the important items— the naval commission and the mysterious key—were in her possession, and the gold was in the safe. And she had another missive yet to write before retiring.

The next note, short and to the point, was for Mrs. Nolan:

I have business at Alcatraz Island today and may not return until late. If you would please keep Antonia with you after school today and overnight, ready her for school

*in the morning, and send her on her way, I would be very
grateful. Thank you!*

She signed it, folded it in half, and sighed. With Antonia
safely tucked away under Mrs. Nolan's sharp-eyed gaze, she
would be able to focus on the investigation without worrying
about the girl.

Inez set the wet towel in the kitchen sink and gently probed
the swollen, tender bruise. She was glad she'd be wearing a man's
hat for the trip to Alcatraz. With luck, she could pull it down far
enough to hide what was sure to be a black and blue lump of
generous proportions.

Once in her bedroom, Inez pulled out her seldom-used
alarm clock, wound it, set the alarm for quarter to five, and laid
it, ticking merrily away, next to her revolver on the nightstand.
She prepared herself for rest, extinguished the lamp, and, with
the *tick-tick-tick* of the small clock sounding in slow 4/4 time,
closed her eyes and tried to sleep through the throbbing just
below her hairline.

The hollow, high-pitched tin-can rattle of the alarm jerked
her into consciousness, and she shut it off quickly before it woke
Antonia. She was tempted to close her eyes for a little longer but
didn't dare slide back into sleep. As it was, the pain between her
brows compelled her to sit up. She fumbled for the oil lamp and,
once it was burning, hustled through her dressing. Shivering in
the cool air, she wrapped a broad linen strip about her chest,
flattening her breasts, thankful that she didn't have to put on
a corset as well. Once she was finished dressing, she slid the
revolver into the nightstand drawer, uneasy at leaving it behind.
She reassured herself that it was not far to the pier, the city was
already astir, and there would be many others around. She reset
the alarm clock for six fifteen and, with lamp and clock in hand,

went into Antonia's room. She put the clock on the table by Antonia's bed, along with the lamp, and whispered, "Antonia."

Antonia turned at her voice, opened her eyes, then bolted upright.

"It's me," Inez assured her, realizing the garb she was wearing probably heightened the girl's confusion and concern. "I am leaving for Alcatraz. The alarm clock is set for you to sleep another hour. There is a note on the kitchen table to give Mrs. Nolan when you pick up your lunch bucket on the way to school. It's very important that you give it to her. After classes, I want you to come directly home, gather your night things, and go to her house for dinner and the night. And be sure to lock all the doors when you leave the apartment."

She rubbed her eyes. "What's going on? And what happened to your head?"

"Someone broke into the office downstairs and slammed the door in my face when I chased them." She touched the bruise. "This is the result."

"Did they break into the safe and get the gold?"

"They didn't take anything valuable. But we must be careful."

"When will you be back?"

"Probably late. Which is why I want you to stay at Mrs. Nolan's tonight. And no arguing," she added firmly. "I must leave now. I am meeting Mr. Harris's son at the wharf to catch the steamer to the island."

"Alcatraz Island," Antonia said wistfully, flopping back onto her pillow. "You have all the fun. Chasing down robbers and murderers."

Inez forbore to mention that getting a door slammed on her face was not fun. "Do what I say, Antonia. Please." She gave Antonia's shoulder an encouraging squeeze, quenched the lamp, and retreated, remembering to pick up the note for Welles and

Hee before leaving the upstairs apartment. Once outside, she slid the note under the door of the music store. Glorying in the long strides that wearing pants allowed, she hurried down Pine Street toward the wharves.

Pine spilled onto Market, which ended at the cluster of wharves and slips for ferries and steamers with routes across the bay and up the Sacramento River. She veered north along the waterfront, past the slip for the steamer to Vallejo, and stopped at the Washington Street wharf, wondering how she would identify Paulie in the masses of people hurrying past. Almost entirely men, none spared her a glance. All seemed bent on destinations unknown, schedules kept private. The sky over the East Bay hills was lightening. The sun, not yet risen, cast promise on the underside of scattered clouds, as the seabirds screamed and wheeled above her head, mirroring the frenzy of the two-legged beings bound to the earth below.

"Mr. Stannert?"

Inez turned. Paulie stood at her elbow, toolbox in hand. Suddenly aware that she had arrived empty-handed, Inez said, "Mr. Harris. Good morning. I neglected to bring…" she gestured to the case and finished, "anything."

"No matter," said Paulie. "You can keep me company, hand me tools. My father prepared some locks we'll need to install. There may be other small projects to do. Replace a lost key or two, tighten a doorknob. Then, we will have our meeting. It could be a full day. We'll see."

"As long as we have a chance to speak to the man Captain Taylor kept in contact with through your father, it will be well."

Paulie nodded. "Let's board, then." As they joined the passengers heading into the small steamer, hardly bigger than a tugboat, he added, "The *General McPherson* stops at Alcatraz first." Inez looked around at the passengers, suddenly aware that most were wearing uniforms. "Is this a military transport?"

"The steamer is used by the military and civilians," Paulie assured her. "I picked up our passes when I got here. My father and I are," he hesitated, "or should I say *were*, among the many tradesmen and suppliers who travel regularly on the ship. Of course, those who live on the islands who are not military also come and go. The *McPherson* also carries supplies and tanks of drinking water. Angel and Alcatraz, being small islands, do not have sources of fresh water."

Paulie showed the passes to the officer at the wharf before they embarked. As they walked along the deck, he nodded to a few of the men gathered along the railing and greeted a few more. One in workingman's civilian garb clapped his hand on Paulie's arm, below the black mourning band, and said, "Sorry for your loss, laddie. He was a good man, your father."

Paulie murmured thanks and moved on.

"People already know of his death?" Inez inquired.

"It is a small community that travels regularly on the steamer. They all knew him." Paulie picked a place along the rail for them to stand and settled the case between his feet. "My father..." his voice cracked. He cleared his throat and continued, "My father loved to tell stories about the journey before the *McPherson*. It could be an all-day affair to go one way on a sailing vessel, depending on the route. He was never so happy as the day the steamer took over the route, allowing him to leave and return on the same day. He hated being away from hearth and home overnight but performed the task for Captain Taylor without complaint."

With a rumble and a loud blast of the horn, the steamer began to move. "I usually stay up top for the sunrise and then move inside," said Paulie.

Clutching the rail, Inez replied, "Certainly." What she didn't say was she had suddenly remembered how she was not overly fond of being on the water. Particularly *large* bodies of water as opposed to, say, lakes, rivers, and ponds. The steamer lurched, causing her stomach to lurch with it. It wasn't so much seasickness, she told herself, as a certain gastrointestinal discomfort about the many fathoms of water that lay beneath her and were now heaving all around in not so gentle waves.

"Good weather this morning," said Paulie, surveying the sky. "We may not be so lucky later on. We shall see."

The sun came up over the hills. After properly admiring the sunrise, Inez and Paulie headed inside and sat on one of the benches. "How long does it take to get to the island?" Inez asked.

"About twenty minutes," said Paulie. "The return trip takes longer. There are a few stops along the way."

"How much longer?"

"It's about an hour and a half total, in good weather."

They steamed along, the boat rocking this way and that. Not violently but enough for Inez to decide she would be careful what she ate before the return trip. Not that she had had time to eat breakfast or had remembered to pack any victuals. She rubbed her forehead, forgetting about the bruise, then winced. As she gingerly pulled her hat lower over her brow, she became aware of the silent engines and the other passengers preparing to disembark. Paulie stood and picked up the case. "We've arrived."

Inez's sigh of relief at stepping off the steamer was cut short by a stiff, cold breeze from the west that smacked the wharf and nearly whipped her hat from her head.

"This is the southeast end of the island," said Paulie. "The wind is most fierce on the other side."

Inez hoped they wouldn't be going there. She now noticed

that Paulie wore a thick, winter-style coat. Inez thought of some of her Colorado winterwear tucked into the wardrobe in her bedroom and wished she'd added an extra underlayer.

"This way," said Paulie. In truth, there was only one way forward: past a pair of heavy oak doors, which looked to be at least ten feet tall, and through an equally lofty sally port that burrowed through the center of a massive brick and stone building. As they entered the dark tunnel, it seemed as if they were being swallowed up by the island, an oppressive feeling that was probably deliberate, Inez thought. They joined a line to have their passes examined yet again. After a brief greeting and a wave forward from the inspecting officer, they exited. Paulie pointed toward the road before them, filled with wagons and patient mules and drivers waiting for passengers and supplies. "We go up."

Inez's gaze followed the switchback thoroughfare, cutting along a wall of rock cliffs, leading to the top of the island. Buildings dotted the road—blocky fortress-like shapes, slapped-together timber sheds, and perched halfway up, a few prim residences with a view of the bay. At the very top sat a square, squat brick building, looming over all.

As they began their walk, Paulie said, "My father said that, during the war, prisoners were housed in the basement of the guardhouse we just passed through. This," he nodded at a frame-and-brick building, looking a little worse for wear, "is the prison."

Inez raised her eyebrows. "The prison? It doesn't look particularly secure."

Paulie tossed her a brief smile. "If someone escapes, he has nowhere to hide on the 'Rock.' It is an island, bristling with military men and fortifications. If he tries to swim across the bay, he will drown. The waters are bitterly cold, and the currents are unforgiving." He sobered. "The man you want to talk with is in the prison, so that will be our last stop today."

"A…word about that," puffed Inez. She was having trouble keeping up with Paulie, who managed to talk, walk the steep road, and carry a who-knows-how-heavy toolbox. "I know you plan to tell him your father has died. After you do so, please do not say or promise anything more. I suggest you say a 'confederate' is with you who will take over the discussion. And don't name me. Let's keep him on his toes and guessing."

Paulie nodded. "As you wish." They were now passing the neat little houses that looked like they belonged on an up-and-coming avenue in the city, not on a military prison island. As if guessing Inez's thoughts, Paulie said, "These are new living quarters for officers."

"Where…are…we…going?" Inez was glad she wasn't attacking the inclined road in a corset and long skirts. She was also beginning to be glad she hadn't added an extra underlayer of clothing.

"To the top. The Citadel."

Inez stifled a groan.

They continued walking, with Paulie providing a running commentary on Rodman cannons, batteries, casements, and magazines in traverses. "Alcatraz also has a blacksmith shop," said Paulie. "Father declared it and the two forges in very poor shape."

They passed a group of men toiling with picks and shovels on a small rockfall by the side of the road. The only similarity in their clothing was the letter "*P*" stitched or painted on their jackets and hats. "Prisoners?" Inez inquired.

Paulie nodded. "You find convicts laboring all over the island. Painting metalwork, scraping moss off the walls, quarrying rocks. Even tending vegetable gardens, although the island is too rocky to grow much greenery."

They were near the top. The three-story building Inez had glimpsed from below was even more impressive up close. Beyond it…

"A lighthouse!" Inez added hastily, "Of course."

"Of course." Paulie paused. "I should let the lighthouse keeper's family know of Father's passing as well. He did some ironwork for them, other small projects." He turned to Inez. "We've reached the Citadel. The past year or so, it was converted to officers' quarters. You can wait here. I won't be long."

Inez sank onto a stone bench. The breeze, which had taken her breath away below, was now welcome. She looked out, marveling at the view. The city spread before her, a dreamy vista, promising new wealth and new possibilities for the many who came to start a new life. Yet in the shadows lurked all the usual vices of mankind: envy, avarice, gluttony, lust, sloth, wrath, and pride. Which one would play the biggest part in the deaths of Jack Taylor and Joe Harris? Inez thought if she had to place a bet, she'd put her money on avarice, specifically the desire for more, more, more. In this case, more gold. She thought the missing money was probably the key that would unlock the truth.

Paulie emerged a bit later settling his hat back on his head. He sat beside Inez and said, "Well, that is finished."

"Finished? So they gave you a thank-you-very-much-but-we-are-done sending off?"

Paulie turned to Inez, gray eyes shining. "They would like me to continue in Father's stead. Once a month, to come in and work for a day."

"Is that what you hoped for?"

Paulie smiled. "I could not ask for a better outcome. And I now have a number of small projects which should take us through the rest of the day nicely, until our visit with the prisoner." He looked into his toolbox. "Are you hungry?"

"Well…" Inez's appetite had vanished on the steamer but had returned with the walk.

"I brought enough to share. We should eat now. I doubt we'll have time until we return to the city." Paulie pulled out paper bundles wrapped with string, which turned out to hold half a loaf of sourdough, hefty slices of salami, and a hunk of milk-white cheese. He handed Inez a knife, keeping another for himself. "If you would slice the bread, I'll take care of the Jack cheese." To Inez, the simple meal rivaled Mrs. Nolan's best. After they finished, it began raining, and Paulie said briskly, "To work! I must earn the next loaf of bread."

True to his word, Paulie had Inez help him. Inez, still feeling slightly fuzzy from the head blow, had all she could do to keep straight the various tools and items. Keys—blank and already cut—doorknobs from plain to elaborate, locks, hinges, screws, nails, and hammers, those she knew or could identify. But, lock cases? mortise latches? escutcheons? Her head, already aching, now swam. Escutcheon, Paulie explained, was the proper term for the plates on either side of the door. "One for the knob, one for the keyhole," he added.

When he started to explain the intricacies of a latch lock, Inez stopped him. "I understand your enthusiasm and applaud your passion for your trade, but I am not intending to apprentice." She smiled to remove any sting.

It was nearly three o'clock, with the steamer scheduled to arrive at four, by the time they'd worked their way down the hill again, project by project, to the prison. Inez was glad she had spoken to Paulie about the interrogation of the prisoner beforehand. There was little time to delve into it now. "Have you any tasks in the prison?" Inez asked.

"Just the meeting with The Spider." Paulie gazed at the building, face troubled. "By the way, his last name is Abel. The officer in charge told me when I obtained permission for our visit."

Inez said, "Shall I come in with you?"

Paulie shook his head. "Best you wait here. When I'm done, I'll come out, and you can go in." He approached the guard standing under the overhang by the entrance. They spoke. The guard opened the sturdy wood door. Paulie turned, gave Inez an encouraging nod, and went in.

Hearing the crunch of footsteps overhead, Inez glanced up and spotted an armed sentry walking along the roof of the flat-topped prison. The wind gusted and lifted her hat from her head. Inez grabbed it before it could sail away, then pulled it carefully down over the bruise. Catching the guard watching her, she wondered if her hair, still under her collar, had somehow given her away, until the man said, "Rough night last night?"

She frowned, uncertain. He pointed to his own forehead.

Comprehension dawned. She lifted her shoulders and lowered her voice. "Had too much beer and walked into a door. Was lucky not to black my eye."

He nodded sagely. "Doors can be ferocious."

They exchanged a quick grin, and Inez relaxed. She decided to venture a question. "D'you know the prisoner Abel?"

He rubbed his jaw. "You mean The Spider? A-yeh. Most of us here do. He sure gets the visitors. Never quite figured out why. Couple of new faces these past days, including yours." He looked at her, clearly expecting a response.

Before Inez could weasel up an answer, the door opened and Paulie came out. A guard inside the building pulled the door shut.

Paulie jerked his head a little, indicating they should move away from the entrance. They walked out of hearing. "How did it go?" Inez asked.

Paulie's features were pale, brow pinched. "I told him about Father's death. I hardly got the words out, and he started asking strange questions. Ones I couldn't answer. 'Did that young whelp send you? Where's my money? Are you trying to threaten me?' And something about chocolate. I told him a man—didn't mention your name—would be in directly to talk with him." He bit his lip. "I hope that was the right thing to say."

"It's good," Inez said. She glanced at the guard outside, who was watching them. "Just a warning, the guard there is curious. He may ask questions."

Paulie patted a jacket pocket. "I've got tobacco and papers. We'll shoot the breeze until you are through. Remember, we have to be at the dock in about three-quarters of an hour."

Inez nodded. They returned to the entrance, and the guard said heartily, "Next!" He knocked on the door. It swung open, and Inez stepped in. The door shut behind her, and she blinked in the dim interior. A collection of men in uniform, lounging nearby, stopped talking and eyed her. The sentry at the door turned to them announcing, "Another to see The Spider."

"I'll take 'im." One of the men jerked his head. "This way."

They walked down a short hallway, brick giving way to wood. Inez realized that here was where the prisoners were housed, in this wood building. They turned and began walking past cells blockaded by heavy wooden doors. Skylights offered some illumination to the corridor, and Inez wondered if the cells behind the massive doors had windows for light. One door hung partly open, and Inez glimpsed a tiny dim space with a small window high on the back wall. The cell held a bed, a bucket, and little more. The shufflings, murmurs, and voices of men seemed to spiral through the tall space. She glanced up. "How many stories is this?"

"This cellblock's got three levels." Her guide glanced at her. "So, here to see The Spider, eh? He's a popular man."

"Will I be able to speak with him privately?"

"As privately as anywhere around here," he said. "I've got to stay in the hallway, and you've got to sit on the chair where I can see you. But others've done just fine."

"Chair?" And then she saw it, down at the end, a lone chair placed in the hallway. The echo of their steps faded the closer they got to the chair. Just short of the end of the corridor, the guard held up a hand, indicating she should stop. He walked to the cell opposite the chair and said, "One more visitor for you."

Inez stepped forward and was surprised to see that this cell had metal bars instead of a wood door. Thin fingers, the color of bones, emerged and wrapped around the bars. "At least I'll be done before supper. I wouldn't want to miss supper." The voice was halfway between a hiss and a whine.

The guard glanced at Inez. "No more than half an hour. You've got a steamer to catch, and The Spider doesn't like to miss a meal." With that, he backtracked several cells past Inez, leaned against the wall, pulled out a pre-rolled cigarette, and struck a match on the sole of his boot. Behind one of the solid doors, someone yelled, "Did ya just light up out there? You're gonna burn us all down in this rat-trap!" The soldier ignored the shout.

Inez moved toward those white hands wrapped around the bars, and the cell's resident came into view. The face peering at her was round, white, adorned with a sparse white beard on the chin, matched by a greased-down shock of white hair on the pate. The mouth parted in a slash of a smile, displaying brown and rotted teeth.

The voice purred, "Good! Good! Finally, the man who knows the dance and the tune." His pale eyes gleamed avidly. "So, did you bring my chocolate?"

Chapter Thirty-Six

WEDNESDAY, MARCH 15

Trying to control her initial revulsion, Inez tore her gaze away from The Spider's luminously pale face. She noticed that his stick-thin figure was clothed not in garb with a "*P*" emblazoned on it but wrapped in a dressing gown of maroon, with feet shod in matching slippers. Beneath the wrap, he wore standard black trousers and a waistcoat.

"Well?" he demanded.

Inez steeled herself to step forward boldly and calmly take the chair. She delayed her response, taking a moment to survey the interior of The Spider's abode. Compared to what she had glimpsed in the hallway, The Spider's cell was as different as day is to night. To begin with, it was easily twice as large. An easy chair, upholstered in worn maroon velvet, occupied one corner. The bed had a luxurious coverlet of the same color and a thick wool blanket folded neatly at the foot. A desk topped with a glassed-in bookcase sat opposite the bed. An oil lamp perched on a tiny table with graceful legs. A stack of paper, a pen, and a bottle of ink waited for the writer to return. Several books shared space with a potted plant, which was alive and apparently thriving in the light shed by not just one but two barred windows overlooking the bay. There was even a Turkish rug on the rough planked wood floor.

Inez finally replied with a neutral, vague statement that she hoped would elicit more information. "You were expecting me."

"No. That is, I thought perhaps. Perhaps. And when the locksmith's son showed up, I was so certain. I thought, like father like son. So perfect. So parallel. Bookends. Two-by-two. Continue the cycle. Yes. Yes. The music of the spheres. *Musica Universalis.* All in harmony." His fingers fluttered on the bars.

Like father. Like son. Her mind raced. Of course, she reasoned, he meant the Harrises, father and son. But he suggested others. Two-by-two. Bookends. Then, the light went on, bright as the sun. The Taylors: The captain and Bertram, father and son. The dampness of the prison, the wind purling through the windows, none of it could be any colder than the certainty that gripped her. *Bertram. He's been here.*

As if in confirmation, The Spider continued, sing-song. "Young Taylor said he would return or send someone. So, when I heard young Harris was coming, I thought: how perfect! And how admirable, to be so quick about it!"

Like a snake slithering in the weeds, the faint lilt of the South wound through his words and sentences. This was a music she could play by ear, if needs must. *And needs must when the devil drives.* Inez echoed The Spider's cadence as easily as she unfurled the opening chords of a familiar waltz on the piano. "You already knew of old Harris's death?"

He drew back a little. "Old news, old news, stinking of fish. Young Taylor told me yesterday. Then young Harris told me again just now." He rolled his eyes. "I thought young Harris might be the man. But when I asked questions, he knew nothing. Like his father.

No, not quite like his father. For old Harris knew just enough to hate me, yet he still did Captain Taylor's bidding." A wheezy chuckle. "Puppets, all of them. All except for me. I held the strings that made the great, honorable Captain Taylor dance! Me! The honorable captain and his locksmith lackey hated me for that."

He jerked forward, cheeks pressing against the bars. Inez forced herself to sit still, to not pull back from the fetid breath as he whispered, "When young Harris said a 'confederate' was here to speak to me, I knew. You're one of *us*. More than the money, more than the chocolate—well, maybe not more than chocolate—I've longed for a fellow *confederate* to talk to. Did you bring the chocolate?"

"I did not. Chocolate was not mentioned. And, sir, just so we are clear, I am not a puppet dancing on anyone's strings. You see, I am the man with the money." Inez pulled out one of the gold coins and held it up for inspection.

The Spider's pale eyes widened. "Is it, is it…"

Inez nodded. "The coins from the mint."

"Had to be," he breathed. "So clean. So bright. Never in circulation. Virgin, untouched." One hand emerged through the bars, fingers stretching.

Inez moved the coin just out of reach. "As the one with the money, I'm thinking this might be too high a price for what you offer."

"Too high!" He sputtered, drew back, affronted. "It takes a certain income to keep me in the manner to which I am accustomed." He gestured to the well-appointed cell. "Captain Taylor's connections kept me out of the work gangs. No breaking rocks for me! I need my creature comforts. And my chocolate. I have kept my part of the bargain all these years. I am trustworthy." The last word had a whine to it. "*Worthy* of your *trust*. Worthy of that coin and more, for my acquiescence."

"That may be. I don't know the full story." Inez cocked her

head. "I am willing to be persuaded to a different opinion." She palmed the coin, removing it from his sight. "We haven't much time, so I suggest you not shilly-shally but tell it straight."

The Spider sighed, "A moment." He shambled to the desk and dragged the desk chair to the bars.

The guard was over like lightning. "What's all this?"

The prisoner held up a hand. "We are just talking. Just talking. Passing time until dinner."

The soldier gave Inez a sharp glance. "No funny business. He gets his privileges, but I'll not get a reprimand on his account."

"Dear Private, privacy, please, while we discuss private matters," said The Spider.

The soldier rolled his eyes but returned to his post midway down the corridor.

The Spider adjusted his gaunt limbs to sit as close to Inez as possible, velvet-covered kneecaps protruding between the bars. "You know of the *Chapman*."

"In general shape, yes," said Inez impatiently. She could feel the minutes ticking away and was afraid she would not get the information she needed before having to leave. "But you and Jack Taylor. Your part."

He clapped his hands. "To the money! To the money! Let's not talk of states' rights, the glorious South, et cetera et cetera. Yes, I see. They sent the right man to me. Excellent. Excellent. But allow me to set the stage." He wiggled his bony fingers—a pianist preparing to perform. "Now, the *Chapman*. First, we have a true son of the South, Asbury Harpending, who was the lynchpin for the entire operation. He procured a letter of marque from Jefferson Davis authorizing him to prey upon the commerce of the United States and to burn, bond, or take any vessels of its citizens. The plan was to procure a schooner, sail it from San Francisco to Guadalupe, and outfit it for privateering.

Next, we have Ridgeley Greathouse, the capitalist who purchased the schooner *J. M. Chapman* and furnished the money
for buying arms, ammunitions, stores, crew." He paused.

"Annnnd?" prompted Inez.

"I worked at the mint—"

"As a coiner?"

He looked insulted. "I was no journeyman on the milling
machines or coin presses! I was a supervisor! In charge of the
adjusters."

Inez frowned. "Adjusters?"

He waved an impatient hand, digits crawling through the air.
"Women who weighed the coin blanks and filed down those
that weighed too much. Very precise work, requiring nimble
fingers, a light touch." He leered.

Inez tamped down her repugnance. "So, you had access to
the coins afterward? Once they were stamped and finished?"

"I acquired access, yes." His pale tongue darted out, and he
licked his lips. "To explain how I cleverly, oh so cleverly, and
patiently arranged for the coins to fall within my grasp and then
hid them such that none could stumble across them unawares
would take more coin than you showed me today."

"Another time then," said Inez gruffly. "And Jack Taylor?"

"As chief clerk, he had access to the mint. Day, night, any
time he wanted. He came and went freely. Easy enough for *him*."
A shadow darkened his features. "I took all the chances. He got
all the glory. Promise of a commission, promise of a vessel of
his own from those we planned to capture. Our first target was
to be a Pacific Mail steamship carrying California gold, bound
from San Francisco to Panama. And others would follow. Just
think—capture a Pacific Mail steamship, turn it into a privateer,
and use it against its sister ships! How clever we all were! There
were so many plans! The money from the mint would further

these efforts and the cause." He sneered a little. "*The Cause.* I apologize if you are a true believer."

"Do I strike you as such?" Inez asked.

"No, no. You strike me as an eminently sensible man. Someone like myself. I believe in the power of gold, as you do. Now, Jack Taylor was a true believer! He was quiet, never talked in public about it. So none guessed. Not at the mint. Not at the taverns he frequented. The quiet ones, they are the ones to watch out for. Not those that huff and puff snorting about states' rights. *Bah!* Such a delusion! It was always about the money in the end, you see. Slavery. Free labor! More money to be made!"

Inez shifted, impatient.

"We shall talk more about that another time," hastened The Spider. "The plan was for Jack Taylor to join us in Guadalupe, Mexico, with the gold, which would be used to hire more men and finish outfitting the schooner." Eyelids closed over the staring eyes. "But that drunken lout William Law got loose-lipped and sloppy. Word of our plans made its way to the authorities. We were captured, nineteen years ago, to the day. To this very day! March 15, 1863. We were caught and Jack Taylor was not. We assumed he slipped the net, went to Southern California, where many of similar mind would help him move the money east."

He stopped and looked at Inez. "I thought that the most likely story. I thought Captain Taylor sealed my lips with gold to keep the Taylor family's honor intact. The agreement was I was not ever to mention the name of Taylor in connection to the *Chapman* incident or the gold. For that small promise, he made payment every month. For all these years!"

Inez opened, then shut her mouth, debating how much to reveal. Finally, she said, "Jack Taylor never made it south or to Mexico or anywhere else. He and the gold were buried within the four walls of his home."

"Have you proof of what you say? The coin, it could be one he left behind."

She glanced at the guard, who, leaning against the wall with arms crossed and head bowed, appeared to be napping standing up. She opened her jacket and pulled out the glass eyeball from an inner pocket.

The Spider's pale eyes widened. He wheezed, "So, it's true! He's dead!"

She returned the orb to her pocket. "Been dead a long time. And the money was buried with him. Along with this." She extracted the commission and unfolded it enough for him to read the top section.

He rapidly scanned the lines, sat back, and shook his head, which reminded Inez of a billiards cue ball. "Young Taylor told me about the corpse and the money. I didn't know whether to believe him. Jack Taylor, walled up in his own house. A house of many secrets." He sat up straight. "Did you find the hidden room where the meetings took place?"

Inez's breath stopped. Hidden room. Lights on the third floor. Rooms with no windows. "On the third floor?"

"Ah! So perhaps you've seen it, in all its Confederacy-draped glory. The room where they planned and plotted. I was only there once, and they forced me to wear a blindfold when I entered the house. They let me know I was not considered one of them. I was there only by leave of Jack Taylor." He leaned forward, nose pressing against the iron. "But I counted the flights of stairs. Three floors up. Yes, I recall."

"And you never told Joe Harris? Or Captain Taylor?"

He sat back in the chair and wiggled a little. "Why should I? They didn't pay me for information. Only for silence."

Inez frowned. "But if you knew of the part Jack Taylor played and the money from the mint, why didn't you or the others talk of it when captured?"

"Oh, all hoped that Taylor escaped with the coin, of course. And the others, Greathouse and the like, knew they would eventually be released. They had connections. Not like me or the crew." He shivered. "When they brought us here, the conditions were dreadful. A trapdoor in the guardhouse. Down, down an iron ladder. Into a dungeon. Cold. Damp. Straw pallets on the floor. No running water. No amenities. We were interrogated most cruelly. There was a trial. Everyone convicted of treason, of course, of course. The others swore allegiance to the Union and were released. As for me, Captain Taylor made certain I'd never leave. But as you can see," he spread his arms wide, signaling his quarters, "I have made myself a home here. The food is good. I do no manual labor. They have a library, which I frequent. The other prisoners leave me alone, assuming I have some glorious hold over the powers that be. Which is why they call me The Spider." That horrible grin again. "They think my web reaches far and wide. When truly, I have no idea what would happen if the Taylors, or you as their representative, do not continue to drop tidbits onto my web for my consumption. I have told you much."

"Ah, but I have one more thing to show you." Inez fished out the key. "Have you any idea what this goes to?"

"It has been a long time."

"It was well hidden. With the commission. Better hidden than the gold."

His eyes shuttled from side to side. He smiled. "A box? A small box of the size to hold photographs?"

She waggled the key. "You tell me."

"Why should I? Maybe next time."

"Now!" Inez snapped, thinking there would not be a next time for her. Glancing at the yawning sentry, she set the single gold coin on her trousered knee then pulled a second from her pocket and set it beside the first. "Tell me now, you get them both. Refuse, you get nothing."

"You are not an honorable man! Here, I gave you my story, and you threaten to renege!"

"Tell me. Now."

The Spider drew a breath and rattled off quickly, "I heard talk of photographs taken of this island, this very island, showing all the fortifications, the artillery, the batteries, everything! What a coup to bring to Jefferson Davis and his ilk! If I were to guess, I would guess that key goes to a nicely crafted, beautifully inlaid box, no larger than the images it might hold."

"It sounds to me as if you have seen such a box." She waggled the key.

"I may have. I may have. Or it may have been a dream. So long ago, you know. And now, I must ask *you* a question."

"Yes?" Time was short. Inez hoped his question and her answer would be short as well.

"The old locksmith, is he truly dead?"

"Oh, he is very dead."

The Spider looked doubtful. "Are you certain? I do not trust young Taylor nor young Harris. It could be a trick. A trap. Taylor told me the locksmith's head was split with an axe." The tongue made another sweep across the lips. "It must have been a truly grisly sight. Did you see the remains? Can you verify?"

Inez ignored his question. "So, let me see if I have this straight. Jack Taylor was an embezzler and a staunch, secret friend of the South. His brother, Captain Taylor, believed in and fought for the North. The captain paid you all these years to keep quiet, while letting on to Bertram and the world that Jack Taylor had run off to fight for the Union. The captain eventually told Bertram that Jack had been killed in battle." She looked at The Spider. "Captain Taylor spun the whole story. So, he knew.

More than knew. He was the instrument of fate. Captain Taylor killed his own brother."

"How very clever of him!" The Spider slid his hand through the bars. "My payment?"

She took up the two coins, then paused. "Did you tell Bertram Taylor of this? Of the hidden room, his father's payments to you, the stolen mint money, and so on?"

"Of course I did. After all, he *does* want to continue to keep it quiet." He shivered a little, scrawny limbs jerking this way and that. Wiggled his fingers. Inez dropped the coins into his palm. He continued, "I was glad to have this iron barrier between us. It was a story he did not want to hear. I think he itched to lay his hands around my neck and silence me. He kept saying, 'John Morton Taylor is a good man! A good man!'"

"Wait. John who?"

"John. Morton. Taylor." He spoke as if she were slow-witted. "His uncle's given name."

"Morton." Inez sank into her chair, thinking of Moira's hasty note about her newest boarder, Mr. Morton. *Oh, Lord. It cannot be.* She straightened up. "And you told Bertram Taylor about the hidden room on the third floor, what was inside."

"Of course. And about the treasure." He looked sly.

She frowned. "*I* have the treasure."

Lips parted into a decayed smile. "Ah. But do you have it all?"

"All one hundred double-eagles."

He giggled as if at a rare joke. "Well. You *haven't* got it all. Jack Taylor walked out of the mint with twice that amount."

Her mouth fell open. "*Twice* the amount?"

"Two hundred double eagles, minted from the purest California gold, flew into two bags." His face loomed even closer, the face of a mad man-in-the-moon. "So, I'll ask you what I asked young Taylor: Where is the rest of it?"

Chapter Thirty-Seven

The rest of it? Inez's mind whirled. Another hundred double eagles? But where? Still in the wall? Elsewhere in the house? Spent and gone?

The guard was at Inez's elbow. "The steamer's leaving soon. You don't want to miss it."

"Oh, but if you stay, you can have dinner with us!" said The Spider. "The food here is lovely. But there is no chocolate."

"Another minute," Inez said to the soldier. He moved a short distance away. Inez rose, calculating. How long to get back to San Francisco? How quickly could she get to Moira's and ascertain if what she feared was true? That Moira's new boarder, who so conveniently showed up to take the room almost before she posted the sign, the "very polite Mr. Morton" was none other than Bertram Taylor.

She grabbed the iron staves. One was still warm from The Spider's touch. She wanted to pull her hands away and rub them on her trousers. "Bertram said the locksmith was murdered with an axe?"

The Spider had gone to the desk, unlocked the glass cabinet. He put the gold into a shallow vase, the coins clinking sharply against the porcelain. "He did." He locked the cabinet and glided back to the front of the cell.

The guard said sharply, "Stand away from the bars."

Inez retreated, saying, "I must go."

As she started to walk away with the guard at her side, The Spider said, "I look forward to our next visit. I'll expect you next month, same day. It's sooooo nice to have someone to talk to. A kindred spirit. Someone who understands. The stories I can tell you! The Centennial? Six years ago, while the island guns tried for Lime Point and the august visitors watched from the Citadel rooftop, we prisoners broke into the commanding officer's reception room and raided the brandy, whiskey, rum, and all the rest of the aqua vitae. And if you want to know the details about the *incident* we discussed, perhaps I will tell you more. Next time." A wheezy cackle chased her, his promise of "more" a last cast of spider silk reaching out to snare her return.

Inez was nearly at the end of the corridor when he shouted, "Next time, bring the chocolate. When the wind is right, the smell from the city is transported through the windows. Pure torture, I tell you!"

When they were inside the guardroom, her escort said, "Word to the wise, if you plan to visit The Spider again. He's being transferred to San Quentin on Friday. Orders from the top."

"What?" Inez was still trying to digest all that she had heard. "He didn't mention that."

One of the other soldiers stood up, adjusted his belt. "We were told not to say anything to him. He's gonna scream and holler as it is. Commander wants to spirit him out at the last possible minute. Less fuss. Less trouble. And The Spider likes making a hell of a lot of trouble for the other inmates and for us. He'll get no special favors at San Quentin. He'll get what he's got coming to him there, he surely will."

A murmur of assent circled the room. The soldier looked around at his companions. "Remember, I drew high card for The Spider's desk. It's mine, even if I'm off shift when he's moved."

Inez's escort opened the outer door for her, saying to his comrade, "It's yours only if the sergeant doesn't pull rank and claim it for his missus."

She exited, and the door swung shut behind her. Paulie and the outside sentry stood nearby, smoking. "Good," said Paulie. "I was wondering if they decided to keep you inside."

The sentry added, "You fellas better hurry if you want to get home tonight."

"What time is it?" asked Inez.

Paulie extinguished his cigarette and picked up the toolbox. "Nearly quarter after five. We've got about five minutes."

As they ran toward the wharf, rain began to fall. A few large splots darkened the dirt. A sudden gust followed. The desultory raindrops turned into a slanted downpour.

"Jesus!" Inez clamped her hat down with one hand. A throb of protest shot from the tender bruise on her forehead to the rest of her face.

They showed their passes and rushed on board the *McPherson*, joining the others inside the cabin.

Paulie set the toolbox between his feet and asked, "Did you get what you came for?"

"And more," Inez said grimly. "He was very loquacious." She didn't want to say his name out loud. Who knew how far his web stretched or who might be listening?

"What do I say when I'm here next time?" Paulie sounded troubled. "I suppose I'll have to see him. He will expect it."

"We can talk in detail when we are alone. But you needn't concern yourself about him on your next visit or any future visits. He won't be on the island much longer."

Paulie raised his eyebrows. "No?"

"His time of privilege is over." She lowered her voice. Paulie leaned in closer. "After Captain Taylor died, I suppose those in charge decided whatever obligations or courtesies they had extended these many years were ended. The fellow in question is heading to San Quentin, where he will have more to worry about than chocolate." Inez glanced at the gloom outside. She was pretty sure she spotted whitecapped waves on the bay. "Will we be able to get back in this?"

"The *General McPherson* has weathered worse than a spring squall. But we'll probably dock late." Paulie glanced at her. "Got a train to catch?"

Not a train, but a murderer.

"Has Bertram Taylor tried to reach you?" asked Inez.

Paulie shook his head.

The steamship lurched and ground underway, jostling those standing inside. Inez braced herself against a window frame. "If he does, be careful. If you must speak with him, I'd suggest you meet in a public place. With many people around."

Paulie frowned. "I've never even met the man. Is there something I should know?"

Inez looked out the window. The ship rocked side to side, with an occasional nosedive forward. Waves washed over the empty deck and smacked into the panes. She looked away, stomach churning in time to the engines' rumble. "He may have killed your father."

Paulie drew back, aghast.

"I could be wrong," Inez added hastily. "I am thinking your father may have met Bertram that night behind the house intending to… I am not certain what he intended, to be truthful. I am guessing here. Give Bertram the keys, so as to let him take a last look around inside the house? Tell him about Alcatraz and The Spider and insist that, as a Taylor, Bertram had a duty to continue the payments? Tell him, if he didn't yet know, that the corpse in the wall was most likely his uncle?"

Paulie looked confused. "The police have identified the remains?"

Inez shook her head. "Not yet. But certain evidence points that way." She didn't want to go into the glass eye and the Confederate commission. Not here. Not now. She continued, "Whatever your father's intentions, I think he may have disclosed information about the Taylor family that threw Bertram into a murderous rage."

"My God," Paulie whispered, clutching his chest as if to hold his heart in place. "What could Father have said about the Taylors to induce such a reaction? He worshipped the captain. He'd never…"

Inez looked around the cabin. "I'll explain more later." There was another possibility she considered but didn't voice. Perhaps Paulie's father had learned about another treasure equal to the first, still hidden, and told Bertram. And Bertram killed him, meaning to keep the secret to himself. With the keys to the house, he could search at his leisure.

At least, until Paulie freed the duplicate keys in the locksmith's safe.

Inez stiffened as the boat lurched again, shocked by the realization that she had mentioned the existence of duplicate keys to Bertram at the mint. So, Bertram now had two reasons to lure Paulie into a private meeting from which Paulie might not return: To delay the delivery of the duplicate keys and—if he believed the old locksmith had shared certain information with his only child—to silence Paulie.

There was also peril in another direction. If it truly were Bertram who had taken up residence in Moira's boardinghouse under the name of "Morton," then Moira needed to be warned. And soon.

They steamed to Angel Island, where more people—again, almost entirely men—piled into the cabin, out of the rain. The ship rumbled to life, an ear-splitting metallic shriek sounded underneath their feet, then silence.

Groans and grumbles rose from the cabin. "Och, not again!" shouted a frustrated voice.

Someone else hollered, "Drag this tin bucket to drydock and fix 'er right for a change!"

Paulie sighed. "We will definitely not get back to the city on schedule."

"So, what do we do?" Inez asked.

"We wait."

They waited four hours.

Inez decided this must not be an uncommon occurrence, for most of the passengers seemed to take it in stride, pulling out pints, pipes, and cigars as well as books and newspapers. Some even dove into their lunch pails to devour leftovers from their midday meals.

Time ticked on.

It rained relentlessly. Banging and thumping below deck vibrated through the soles of their shoes. Tobacco smoke filled the enclosed cabin to the choking point. Inez fretted silently. She wasn't about to jump overboard and swim, so there was nothing to do but resign herself and pray for patience.

Passengers turned to each other to converse and gossip. Inez learnt a great deal about the design and fabrication of stained-glass windows from a bearded glazier named Greer. She deflected his questions about locksmithing to Paulie. Paulie, perhaps in desperation, also offered up a few facts about Angel Island, invisible in the dark. Inez nodded numbly, paying intermittent attention. Angel Island was like a small city, with homes for officers and families, a bakery, blacksmith, laundry, shoemaker. And much of the rock for the Alcatraz forts was quarried from Angel Island. And—"The chapel is also a schoolhouse!" interjected the glazier.

Finally, the engines knocked and thundered to life. Everyone in the cabin cheered. Inez pulled out her pocket watch. "How long will it take to reach the city wharf?"

The glazier answered cheerfully. He was, Inez had come to learn, a perennially cheerful man. "Only an hour. Unless we run into more trouble." He nudged Inez with his elbow. "*Run into* trouble. Ha! Let's hope not!"

That meant they would arrive close to eleven at night. Inez's bruise had given birth to a headache, which now joined her stomach in clenching and releasing in time to the ship's rolls. She gave silent thanks she'd had the foresight to send Antonia to Mrs. Nolan's for the night. At least she could set that worry aside.

When they reached San Francisco's Washington wharf and disembarked, an exhausted Inez bid Paulie good night. "I shall come see you again soon," Inez promised. "Tomorrow, if you are in the shop. Midmorning? We can talk privately. Perhaps I'll know more by then. But please, heed my words. For if Bertram Taylor thinks your father confided certain close-held secrets…"

Paulie touched his hat in acknowledgment and farewell. "I understand. Take care, '*Mr.*' Stannert. Until tomorrow."

They parted, Paulie heading south to Market, Inez heading west to O'Farrell. The rain had stopped, the air was fresh, although the sky remained opaque and starless. As she walked, Inez worried the Taylor family puzzle like a dog with a bone.

If Captain Taylor murdered his brother—and who else would have motive and opportunity back then?—why didn't he take the money? And why did he seal it up? Too, the corpse would have begun stinking very quickly.

If Jack Taylor, that is, John Morton Taylor, had been killed in mid-March, summer would have been approaching. The two attached residences would have reeked. No one would have been able to live in either place. Surely Harris would have realized something was very wrong. Was he so loyal to the captain that he ignored it? Or maybe the captain had confided in him, at least enough to alleviate the locksmith's suspicions.

Inez wondered how far Captain Taylor's influence and connections had reached. He had apparently been able to convince Alcatraz superiors to hold a civilian for nearly two decades. She had to admit, there was much she didn't know about Captain Taylor and most likely never would.

But as for Bertram, she was determined to rip off his mask and view what lay beneath.

Who else could be hiding secrets? Who else could have motive for murder?

Her pace slowed as it hit her. The two Edward brothers, particularly Master Edward. But, no, that didn't explain Bertram's sudden appearance at Alcatraz. Perhaps the old locksmith had urged Bertram to go negotiate with The Spider.

The axe, murmured the little inner voice, the voice she had learned, at her peril, to never ignore. *How did Bertram know about the axe?*

Now Inez realized what bothered her. It all had to do with timing, who knew what when.

Late Saturday night, Harris had been killed with an axe. On Monday, she had met with Bertram at the mint, and he was already aware of the murder and the means. When Inez asked how he knew, Bertram said his lawyer, Sherman Upton, had told him. Yet earlier that very morning, Inez's own lawyer, Buckley, had mentioned in passing that Upton had left town late Friday, before the locksmith was killed, and wasn't due back for a week. If true, Upton could not have known about the locksmith's death, much less told Bertram. Either Buckley or Bertram had lied. Only one of them had a reason to do so. That being the case, how else could Bertram Taylor have known about the murder, much less the axe, unless he had been there with the murder weapon in his hands? Her stride lengthened.

Out of breath, Inez reached O'Farrell and decided to go up the alley first. It was dark, but all it would take is a break in the clouds and a bit of moonlight for her to inspect the rear of the locked, unoccupied building for a third-floor window. Shoes crunching on gravel, she hastened up the narrow side street until she faced the back of the two houses with their common wall.

A couple of second-floor windows at Moira's boardinghouse leaked dim light through window shades. The back of the unoccupied house was dark and blank. Or—she squinted—maybe not. Was it simply her eyes, tired from the long day out in the wind and on the island? Or the knock on the head affecting her sight?

There was a light.

Flickering up high under the eaves. Out a third-floor window she would have sworn didn't exist.

Dammit. I will break into that house this time, if I must.

She ran to the front of Moira's boardinghouse and yanked on the door. Locked.

Of course.

She didn't want to ring the bell and wake the boarders. Suppose, after all this, it was actually Master Edward and not

Bertram? Then she remembered: Dinner at Moira's, just a handful of nights ago. The two Edward brothers across the table. Moira asking, "Who didn't put the extra key back under the flowerpot?" Master Edward looking abashed.

Inez scanned the front porch. Ceramic pots of pink flowers sat to either side of the door. Moira was left-handed. Inez tipped up the pot on the left and was rewarded with the glimmer of a key. She set key to lock and cheered silently when it fit and turned without complaint. Inside, an oil lamp, turned low in the entryway, yielded a small but steady light. Inez recalled that Moira's room was toward the back of the house but before Charlotte's and the kitchen. She stopped outside the room she thought was Moira's and bent her head to listen. A gentle snore seeped out around the hinges.

She tapped on the door, whispering, "Moira! Moira! Wake up! It's me, Inez!"

The snoring stopped. There was a squeak of springs. A weak light sneaked through the crack between door and frame, growing brighter. The door opened. Moira stood there swathed in a long ivory flannel and lace wrapper, her hair in a long braid, with a stub of candle flickering in a candleholder.

"Inez?" She sounded half asleep, bewildered. "How did you get in? What are you doing here, in those clothes? Is something wrong? Are you here to take Antonia home?"

Chapter Thirty-Eight

After Mrs. S left for Alcatraz, Antonia fell back asleep until the rackety alarm clock went off. However, she didn't get up right away like she was supposed to. Instead, she lolled in bed, imagining what it'd be like to be a pirate queen with her very own ship, maybe one like the *Hispaniola* in *Treasure Island*. She'd boss everyone around and tell them what to do. Make them walk the plank if they didn't listen to her. Thus, rebellion was already on her mind before she dressed, grabbed her book bag, and snatched up Mrs. S's note to Mrs. Nolan.

Of course, Antonia had to take a peek at it. And when she realized Mrs. Nolan's name wasn't on it, well, that started her thinking. Mrs. S wasn't going to be back until late that night. They wouldn't even see each other until the next day.

As she trotted to Mrs. Nolan's to pick up her lunch bucket for school and deliver the note, her plan started to take form.

What if she, Antonia, were to go to the Krauses' boarding-house and give the note to Charlotte's ma instead? She could eat dinner there, spend the night, and she and Charlotte could do another exploration of Treasure House!

Antonia turned this seditious plot over and over, looking for a flaw.

Of course, Mrs. S might change her mind and decide to come get Antonia and bring her home. But someone had broken into the store, probably trying to get the gold. And, it was a school night. So Mrs. S wouldn't want to interrupt Antonia's sleep by showing up late and waking her just to bring her back to a *possibly dangerous situation.*

And, if she were caught, Antonia could just say she'd not been all awake when Mrs. S woke her in the dark that morning. Antonia'd say she thought Mrs. S said to give the note to Mrs. Krause. After all, there wasn't a name on the note to say for sure who to give it to, and Mrs. S wasn't around to ask.

So, Antonia didn't give Mrs. Nolan the note. And she didn't say anything more than "Morning!" when she dashed in and grabbed her lunch bucket from Mrs. Nolan's kitchen table. Mrs. Nolan made it easy by shoving an umbrella in Antonia's free hand and shooing her toward the door, saying, "And a good morning to you! It looks like rain today. You'd better hurry along, or you'll be late for school as sure as eggs are eggs."

She didn't have time to think about it anymore until the noon hour. Since it had started raining, the entire school was kept inside but allowed to sit in the hallways. So she sat on the cold floor with her back against a wall, unwrapped her cheese and pickle sandwich, and reviewed her plan.

She was feeling pretty pleased with her cleverness when she heard a "Hey."

Antonia looked up as Michael Lynch slid down the wall to sit beside her. He grinned at her. She noticed how he had to keep his knees bent up so as not to trip anyone walking by and how his trousers must've been let down recently. She could see the faded line where the hem had been before. She wondered if the pants once belonged to his da or maybe one of his older brothers or many uncles.

"Hey, yourself, Copper Mick." Antonia looked down at her sandwich and took a big bite. Then, prodded by guilt, she said with her mouth full, "Sorry I yelled at you the other day. When Charlotte and I were at the, uh…" She didn't even want to say the forbidden word "waterfront" as if Mrs. S would somehow hear her confession all the way from Alcatraz.

"That's okay," said Mick. He was turning an apple over and over in his freckled hands. "About that cipher disk—"

She stopped chewing. "Yeah?"

"I asked Grand-da about it. He showed me his. It looked just like yours." He glanced at her. "But he wouldn't let me bring it to school. Said it was valuable."

"Huh." She hadn't considered the value of the item. It was just something hidden, secret. Part of the "treasure" from the house.

"But he said I could use it to write notes in code. He said it's based on the Vigenère cipher." His brow wrinkled, and he said slowly, "A polyalphabetic substitution."

"Gah!" Antonia rolled her eyes skyward. "What does that even mean? Did he tell you what key they used in the war?"

"He remembered a couple of phrases. 'Complete Victory' was one. 'Come Retribution' was the other. There were more. Those were the only ones he could remember."

Antonia frowned, disappointed. She thought of the coded letters in the Treasure House's secret room. It sounded like breaking the code wasn't going to be easy.

"Grand-da said we could just make up our own keyword," Mick said. "Or substitute letters, like we talked about."

"Yeah, but it won't be what they used during the war," muttered Antonia.

He shrugged. "So? Listen, if you want, maybe sometime, if it's okay with your aunt, you can come visit after school, and you can ask Grand-da about it. He'll talk your ear off about the war. He's got lots of stories and would probably like to tell them to someone who hasn't heard them a million times." He held out his apple. "Want some?"

Cheered that Mick wasn't mad after all, Antonia took the apple and chomped down, thinking about his invitation. If she visited, maybe Mick's grand-da could show her more about the cipher.

Mick cleared his throat and said, too casual-like, "Where'd you get that disk anyway? Since they're so rare and all."

She squinted at him, suddenly wary. "Why?"

He stretched his neck, like the collar of his blue flannel shirt was too tight. "Well, my da asked me to ask you."

"Why?" Her wariness increased.

"Uh, well, he's working this case. You know the one, 'cause he talked to you after you found the guy, um, killed in the backyard of that old house your aunt bought. And he told me you and your aunt were there the night an old corpse from the war was found inside. And now, there's this disk." He waved his hands around aimlessly, then gripped his kneecaps. "So, uh, he just wondered if you might've found the disk then. Maybe pinched it when no one was looking."

Pinched it? Antonia bristled. How could it be considered stealing when all she did was take the disk from the secret room upstairs to her and Mrs. S's apartment? Mrs. S owned both places, right? So—

"I didn't *pinch* it," snapped Antonia. She thrust the apple back at Mick. "Here. It's all mushy anyway."

He turned red. "Antonia, I didn't mean—"

She flared. "You don't have to be your da's snitch, Mick. If he wants to know where I got it, maybe he should just ask me his-self." She stopped, mouth open. She couldn't believe she'd just said that. The last thing she wanted was for Mick's da, Detective Lynch, to come question her about the cipher disk. Because Mrs. S would probably be there listening, and, uh-oh, Mrs. S would start asking questions too, and, oh boy, she'd end up in hot water for sure.

Antonia backtracked. "Listen. Maybe I could come over and visit sometime. And I'll bring the disk and talk to your da about it and listen to your grand-da's stories, and you and me could do our own codes. How does that sound?"

Mick blinked twice as if bewildered by Antonia's attitudinal whiplash. "Uh. Sure. That sounds great. When?"

Stall. Stall. "Not this week. Maybe next week?"

A teacher came out of a nearby classroom and started walking the hall, ringing a handbell. "Back to your rooms, students. Lunch hour is over."

Antonia popped up, never so relieved to go back to Persnickety Pierce's classroom as right then. "We'll talk about it later, okay?" Without waiting for a reply, she dashed off.

After school, she hurried straight back to the apartment. She didn't want to give Mick or Charlotte a chance to corner her. Or, worse, both of them at once. Things were getting complicated as she tried to keep straight what she'd said to one or the other and who knew what. She packed her nightwear, two pairs of socks, and a clean set of underthings and stockings in her valise. From the kitchen cupboard, she gathered the cipher disk and the fancy box of mysterious photos, packing them beneath the clothes. She settled her book bag over a shoulder, grabbed the valise, and at the last minute remembered to take the umbrella Mrs. Nolan had lent her. Antonia left the apartment, locking all the doors behind her, just as Mrs. S had told her to do.

She arrived at Charlotte's house well before dinner and knocked, just like a proper guest, not barging in like she lived there. Mrs. Krause answered the door and looked surprised. "Why, Antonia, hello!"

Antonia thrust the folded note at her. "Here's a note from my aunt. She's at Alcatraz."

"Alcatraz?" Mrs. Krause sounded horrified and curious at the same time. "Whatever for?"

"Dunno," lied Antonia. "But it happened real sudden," she added.

As Mrs. Krause opened the note, Charlotte peered around her mother. "Antonia!" she sang. She bolted out and gave Antonia a big squeezy hug and bounced back. "What are you doing here? Are you going to have dinner with us?" She looked at the valise and gave it a little kick. "Are you going to spend the night?"

"If your ma says it's all right," said Antonia, trying to sound polite and piteous all at once.

Mrs. Krause was staring at the note, frowning a little. Right then, it started to rain again. Mrs. Krause looked at Antonia and said, "Well, of course you can stay. Come in."

Antonia and Charlotte beamed at each other. Antonia stepped inside with her things, and the rain started coming down hard. Mrs. Krause closed the door, saying, "Charlotte, take Antonia's valise to your room." She shook her head. "This is quite mysterious. Your aunt's note is very cryptic. But I suppose she will explain more when I next see her."

Uh-oh. That was something Antonia hadn't considered in her plan. She decided she would have to fall back on the "half-asleep" story when Mrs. S took her to task. To bolster her case for later, Antonia said, "She left really early this morning, before dawn. She woke me up and told me she wrote this note, but I don't remember what else she said. Except that she was going to Alcatraz and would get back late."

Mrs. Krause nodded, like she wasn't listening or didn't quite believe her. "You and Charlotte have about an hour before dinner. Perhaps you two can start on your schoolwork."

"Yes'm." Antonia and Charlotte skittered off to the small bedroom. Charlotte danced in circles, twirling the valise. "An-ton-i-a! An-ton-i-a! We can go adventuring tonight!"

Antonia shushed her. "Not so loud! We have to be properly sneaky about this." She took the valise from Charlotte, opened it, and retrieved the cipher disk and the fancy wood box, asking, "D'you have the map still?"

Charlotte nodded.

"Let's work on it before dinner," Antonia said. "We can mark where we want to look next. Recite your times tables loud so if your ma is listening, she'll think we're practicing your numbers." Antonia waggled the wood box. "I opened this. Wait 'til I show you what's inside."

They had a grand time looking over the "loot," including the gold coin they had found on the stairs, and marking up the map while Charlotte worked on her twelve-times. "Twelve times eleven is one hundred thirty-two," chanted Charlotte, while examining the photographs with wide eyes. Then, in a whisper, "This must be of the pirate hideout! They have cannons and all kinds of guns!" Then louder, "Twelve times twelve is one hundred forty-four!"

She had her thirteen-times memorized by the time they sat down for dinner. Antonia saw a stranger sitting by Mrs. Krause. "Who's that?" she whispered to Charlotte.

Charlotte whispered back, "That's Mr. Morton. He's brand new. Ma says he's a very polite, proper gentleman." She pushed the tip of her nose up. "I think he's snobby. This is the first time he's been here for dinner. I think Ma wants to impress him."

Antonia looked down at her plate. Lamb chops and roast

beef, potatoes and beans, and artichokes. Plus homemade applesauce and a lemon cake promised for dessert. She was inclined to agree with Charlotte that her ma had cooked to impress.

"So where is your aunt tonight?" Master Edward asked Antonia.

Mrs. Krause answered from the head of the table, "Mrs. Stannert has gone to Alcatraz for the day, so Antonia is staying with us tonight."

Antonia gulped a little. Master Edward's eyebrows wiggled up and down. "Alcatraz Island is a military post. What could your aunt be doing there? Of course, there is a lighthouse. Perhaps that is her destination."

Remembering Mrs. S all dressed in men's clothes, Antonia didn't think so but just mumbled and shrugged. She glanced at Mrs. Krause, feeling betrayed by the public announcement of Mrs. S's whereabouts. Antonia caught the new boarder, Mr. Morton, staring at her with the oddest expression.

He turned to Mrs. Krause and said politely, "This young lady is Mrs. Stannert's niece?"

Charlotte's ma nodded. "As I explained, Mrs. Stannert and I are in partnership." She pointed with the carving knife at the nearby wall. "The adjoining house. As I explained."

"Oh. Oh, yes." After another glance at Antonia, he bent his head over the potatoes.

To Antonia, it seemed to take forever for dinner to be done, the boarders to go to their rooms, Charlotte's ma to finish evening chores and come in to say good night to Charlotte and her. "Say your prayers, girls, if you haven't, and sleep well," she instructed. "You will both need to rise early for school." She kissed Charlotte, tucked the covers around them both, turned down the nightlamp, and glided out of the bedroom.

Time ticked by. Eventually delicate snores floated through

the wall. The girls jumped out of bed. "Hurry!" Antonia whispered. She felt on edge as if something in the night was watching them, tail thrashing, getting ready to pounce. That reminded her: "Charlotte, where're the cats?"

"Outside," Charlotte whispered back. "The new boarder complained to Ma. He doesn't like them, especially wandering around at night." She sounded insulted.

They donned thick socks, and Charlotte pulled a men's workshirt destined for the week's laundry over her nightgown while Antonia put on her dark wool coat over her nightdress. "You're going to wear that?" asked Charlotte.

Antonia nodded. She didn't want to put on some old man's stinky shirt and figured any additional dust on the coat could be easily explained. Mrs. S always complained that Antonia's coat and clothes looked as if she'd rolled around in the dirt on the playground at school. At the last minute, Antonia slipped the cipher disk into her coat pocket. Maybe it'd bring them luck, and they'd find the key phrase up in the desk with all those papers. Charlotte picked up the nightlamp, and they snuck out of the bedroom, hurrying to the kitchen pantry.

Antonia removed the boards hiding their entry hole. Charlotte kept watch by the pantry door in case someone, like the new boarder, decided to wander in and help himself to the leftover cake.

"D'you have the map?" Antonia muttered to Charlotte.

"Oops! I'll be right back!" Charlotte disappeared, taking the nightlamp with her.

"Dang it!" grumbled Antonia in the dark, setting the last board aside. Just then, something soft brushed past her ankles with a feline trill. Antonia jumped and saw the ghost of a tail whip into the opening in the wall. "Shit!" she whisper-screamed.

The lamplight wavered into the pantry and Charlotte gasped. "Lucky! What're you doing here?"

Antonia spun around to see Charlotte scoop up the black-and-white cat with one arm. "Charlotte! Eclipse got into the wall! I've got to go get her! Give me the light! You go back to your room with Lucky. I'll bring down Eclipse when I catch her, and we can put them both outside. Now go!"

Antonia ripped the lamp from Charlotte's hand and without waiting for a response, dashed into the enclosed wall space. She shone the light around. A small sound drew her eyes upward. The multicolored cat sat on the little landing at the top of the first flight, washing her face with one paw. Antonia started climbing the stairs. "Here, kitty, kitty! Puss, puss!"

Eclipse froze, paw raised, and watched Antonia approach, head cocked as if listening. Antonia put an extra dose of pleading in her whisper. "C'mere, Eclipse. Nice kitty!" Eclipse wasn't about to be conned with sweet-talk. She stayed put until Antonia was just about to grab her, then sprinted up the second set of stairs to the top floor. "Shit shit shit!" panted Antonia. She abandoned the slow approach and raced up after the cat, holding her nightgown high so she wouldn't trip on the steep risers. "Dammit, Eclipse! Stop!"

Of course she didn't stop.

And of course the door to the secret room was open a little, just as Antonia and Charlotte had left it. And of course Eclipse dashed through the crack and into the room. "Oh no," gasped Antonia, trying to remember if the secret panel that led into the rest of the house was *also* open. "Please, please, no, no."

Inside the secret room, Antonia stopped. Finally, a bit of luck. The panel was shut.

Eclipse was strolling around this new space, investigating the legs of the table and chairs. Antonia closed the door behind her so Eclipse couldn't escape, then went over to the desk, trying to get close without spooking the cat. Spotting one of the coded letters, Antonia grabbed it, then crinkled the paper to get the cat's attention. Eclipse sat down under the table and watched her. Remembering how Eclipse had liked to climb into her lap in the bedroom, Antonia set the lamp on the floor by the desk, plopped down cross-legged, stuffed the letter into her coat pocket for later, and patted her lap.

Sure enough, Eclipse moseyed over, set one paw, then another, and finally all four into the well of cloth stretched across Antonia's legs, padded a little, purred, and settled, tail swishing.

Antonia set two fingers between her ears, scratched gently, then froze.

She heard a sound, on the far side of the room.

Right where the panel door was.

Her breath catching in her throat, she twisted the lamp key and doused the lamp.

The panel rattled.

Antonia, holding the surprisingly complacent cat close to her chest, rose a little and eased into the hollow space beneath the desk, pulling the lamp in with her. Her coat snagged. She tried to free the fabric. It was caught on a slightly deformed floor plank—*a handle?*—under the well of the desk. With no time to explore, she yanked the material free.

The last thing she saw was the panel open and a brilliant light pour in. The last thing she heard, as she squeezed back against the kickboard of the desk, was a sob, followed by a curse in Chinese, and then, "Oh, my God. It's true. All true!"

Chapter Thirty-Nine

WEDNESDAY, MARCH 15

Inez and Moira stared at each other in bewilderment at the threshold of Moira's bedroom. Moira in her nightwrap, Inez in her ex-husband's garb.

Moira repeated, "How did you get in? What are you doing here, in those clothes?"

"I used the spare key under your flowerpot." Inez held up the key. "The clothes would take too long to explain right now. Did you say Antonia is here?"

"Of course she is," Moira rubbed her eyes. "Where else would she be? You sent her with that note, asking that we keep her for the night."

Anger flared, washing aside Inez's confusion. *Damn that girl!* "Is she with Charlotte? I need to see her now, please."

"She's in Charlotte's room. Asleep." Moira stepped out of her room with the candle, and the two women moved down the hall. "Unless we woke them up just now," Moira added sourly. "What is going on?"

"Your new boarder, Mr. Morton. Is he here?"

"Of course. He retired with the rest of the boarders, earlier tonight." They had reached Charlotte's room. Moira opened the door, saying softly, "Antonia? Your aunt is here."

The flickering light of Moira's candle revealed no Antonia. Just a wide-eyed Charlotte sitting on the floor holding a black-and-white cat on her lap, a single double eagle winking up from the rug, and photographs scattered around her. At a glance, the images looked like scenes from military installations. Alcatraz? Inez spotted more in a little open wooden box, inlaid with an intricate design. Exactly as The Spider had described.

Charlotte gaped up at them.

"Where's Antonia?" Inez demanded. "And where did you get that coin?"

Moira stepped into the room, stationing herself protectively between Charlotte and Inez.

Inez closed her eyes and tried to rein herself in. She realized she had never used that tone of voice with a child before, only on malefactors and dangerous scoundrels. Inez opened her eyes and tried again, more gently, "Charlotte, it is important that you tell us."

Charlotte looked at her mother. "Sorry, Ma," she said in a small voice. "Antonia went to rescue Eclipse. She got into…" She pointed to the wall behind her.

At the locked house next door.

Moira looked down at her daughter. "What? How did she get in?"

"Through the hole," said Charlotte in a whisper. "That's where we found the gold. It must've dropped out of the bag."

Inez stepped into the room. The girl cowered a little. "Show us."

Charlotte released the cat, which dashed under the bed. She stood and led the two women out of the bedroom and into the kitchen and pointed at the pantry. "There."

Moira raised her candle.

Inez saw several vertical planks had been removed from the pantry back wall. Her anger and worry were now tinged with admiration. *Too clever by half!* She turned to Charlotte. "What is inside?" She wasn't going to venture blind into that dark space.

In a soft voice, Charlotte said, "Stairs." She pointed toward the rear of the house.

"Where do the stairs go?" Inez thought she knew but wanted to hear the girl say it.

"The hidden room. On the top floor."

Inez nodded grimly. *The light in the window.* She crouched eye-level with Charlotte, who shrank back. "Did Antonia take a light? And is there light enough to see, going up the stairs, without a candle or lamp?" She tried to project calm.

Moira took Charlotte's hand, gave it a squeeze. "Answer Mrs. Stannert's questions, Charlotte."

"Antonia took the nightlamp. And there's a little window, halfway up."

Inez stuck her head cautiously through the hole. She could just detect a steep staircase, not far away, and a dim square of light at what must be a landing. So, she could navigate the stairs in the dark. Antonia would be in the room at the top, with a lamp. *Or maybe someone else is up there with her,* murmured that little voice. *You don't know for certain who was holding the light you saw flickering in the window.*

Inez fervently wished she had her revolver. She turned to Moira. "I need something sharp. A butcher knife, whatever's handy. Send Charlotte to wake the two Edwards. Ask them to check Morton's room, see if he is there." If he was, then perhaps this was simply a matter of Antonia chasing down a cat and the girls being where they should never, ever have been.

But Inez didn't think so.

She laid odds that they would find Morton's room empty, that Morton was Bertram, and that Bertram was even now inside the house, having gained entry with keys he'd taken off Joe Harris after he'd split the locksmith's skull with Moira's axe. *I hope Bertram doesn't know how to access this hidden room. If he should find Antonia before I do...*

She said quickly, "If Morton is not in his room, one of the Edwards should get the police while the other Edward stays with you here, in the kitchen. Send another boarder, someone quick on his feet, to the Palace Hotel for Mr. de Bruijn. And you should have a weapon handy, a knife, just in case." She didn't want to think any more about it. Now it was time to act.

The hole in the pantry was wide enough for a slight girl to wiggle through but not an adult. Inez grabbed the nearest intact plank, set her feet, and ripped the board free. The entrance was now large enough for a woman—at least one dressed in non-confining menswear—if she didn't mind ducking and squeezing and perhaps getting a few splinters along the way. Inez tossed the plank and her hat to the pantry floor.

Moira returned with a meat fork that smelled faintly of bacon. "What is this about Mr. Morton? What is going on?"

Inez took the fork, saying, "I think your Mr. Morton may be a murderer, and he may be in the house next door."

Moira gasped. "What makes you say that? He's such a polite, nice young man!"

Inez, wiggling through the hole, didn't answer. Glad she wasn't corseted, she exhaled and scraped through, emerging into the dark, dusty space between the two houses. She advanced toward the staircase, the long, sharp-pronged meat fork by her side in case Antonia barreled down the stairs in the dark. She certainly didn't want to gore the girl.

The steep stairs were treacherous to climb, and Inez was glad for the splintery rail. She reached a tiny landing and looked back down. Moira's candle sent a weak, flickering light through the gap in the pantry. There must be a ground-level secret entrance somewhere, since the original users didn't come in through a hole in the pantry. *Even if Bertram should try to escape by some other secret entrance, he cannot. He'll be trapped in the wall. Like a rat.*

Suddenly, she heard a terrible crashing above. She set a palm against the inner wall of the locked house. The wood frame shivered as if the very house was under assault. Inez swallowed hard, heart pounding. Gripping her "weapon" tighter, she advanced up the second flight of stairs, stepping quietly. But with all the racket, she needn't have bothered. She could now hear a voice, gabbling in what sounded like Chinese. The voice switched to English, with a sob. "All lies! They all lied to me!" Then another crash.

Approaching the end of the second flight, Inez spotted a door with a ring-shaped handle barely visible in the suffocatingly dim space. She pulled herself up the last steps, grabbed the ring with one hand, and listened to what sounded like rampant destruction on the other side of the door. Inez reminded herself that Bertram would not be expecting anyone to burst in, otherwise he wouldn't raise such a din. And he certainly wouldn't be expecting a strange man, yelling in a woman's voice, to leap out of the wall! Did he have Antonia with him? An audience to the annihilation?

"Tell me what you know!" His voice rose, frantic. "Give up your secrets, damn it!"

He's talking to her! She's in there!

Inez yanked the door open, shouted "Stop!" and charged in. She immediately ran into a tangle of cloth hanging down over the opening. The rough, heavy material thwacked her in the face, blocking her view. Pain flashed from the tender bruise on her forehead. Momentum lost, she shoved the fabric away in time to see Bertram whirl around. A candle on the floor illuminated the scene with a ghastly flicker. In the yellow glow, she caught a hellish glimpse of stark, hollow eyes, hair plastered to his skull, sweat streaking his face. Or were those tears?

He held a small axe in one hand. In the other, a framed photographic portrait of a round-faced man with old-fashioned muttonchops and gentle eyes, one eye slightly askew. In a split second, Inez realized two more things. He was closer than she expected. And Antonia was nowhere in sight.

Relief at not finding Antonia cowering under his axe slowed her reaction. Before she could retreat or attack, he was at her, the sharp edge of the axe at her throat. "Drop that," he said in an almost normal tone.

She opened her hand. The meat fork clanged to the floor. He maneuvered around her, the axe sliding along the skin on her neck, until he was at her back. The axe prodded her between the shoulder blades. "Inside."

She stepped farther into the room. The remains of a polished wood table, pieces of wood intermixed with a scatter of papers and maps on the floor were spread before her, like the set piece from a play. From behind he said, "Who are you?" Then, "It doesn't matter. None here but ghosts of liars and traitors!"

The pressure of the axe disappeared. The crack of glass followed. She turned to see the portrait glass shattered on the floor. He set a heel on the paper image, ground it with his shoe. He looked up at her, fierce expression returning. "Back up. More."

Inez retreated, glass and bits of wood crunching underfoot. The police will be here soon, she told herself. Maybe even de Bruijn. *I just need to keep him here, at bay, and keep clear of the axe.* She could now see the blade was stained. Shuddering, she glanced around, hating to take her eyes off him but needing to know if Antonia was there.

He said, "You!" Her attention jerked back to him. He pointed to the opening she came through. "Where does that go? The truth! No lies! I'm sick of lies!"

She found her voice. "To the pantry in the boardinghouse."

He laughed bitterly. "So, I didn't have to kill Harris to get the keys? But, no, he had to die! Because he lied. About my uncle. About the captain."

For a moment, she floundered in the fog, then it cleared. "The captain! Your father?"

"No father to me!" spat Bertram. "And he never saw me as his son. I was never man enough for him. Never worthy of the Taylor name. Not a man of the sea. It was always 'Take your punishment like a man! There's more where that came from! I'll beat the truth out of you! Spare the rod and…' He never spared the rod. Not once. And he was a liar! And a murderer!"

"He killed your uncle," said Inez.

Bertram stared. "Who *are* you?" Holding the axe up, he cautiously moved closer, his gaze, wild and desperate, roving over her features. "Mrs. Stannert?" He laughed incredulously. "Of course! You went to Alcatraz. So you know as much as I do." He backed up again, keeping his distance.

"You broke into my office, didn't you?" said Inez. "You tried to open my safe, take the gold."

He blinked, off-balance, confused.

If only he were closer, I might be able to disarm him.

Then his face cleared and he choked out a laugh. "The gold? What would I want with gold? I have the money from the sale of this, my uncle's home. Christ, I *work* in a manufactory of gold! I wanted the clothes. The proof of my uncle's hidden life. The life he never shared with me, although he professed to love me as the son he never had and gave me asylum from the captain. I didn't break in. You left the door unlocked. I thought the clothes would be in the safe. But, no. To you, they were only rags that you rolled up, tossed aside on the floor for the trash. So, I got what I came for. And I burned them. They are gone. But there is still all this." He looked around the room.

Inez followed his gaze, seeing what he was seeing. The huge desk. The destroyed table. A sideboard. More photos and maps on the walls. The Confederate flag that had hindered Inez's advance, hanging limply by one nail above the door to the staircase in the wall.

He continued, "All those years. All these secrets. All so the Taylor name would not be tarnished. Harris lied. That wretch in Alcatraz lied. My uncle was a *good* man. A *kind* man. That is how he should be remembered. Not by all this." He looked around the room. "Strange," he said bitterly. "I just realized, for the first time in my life, the captain and I agree. No one should know. All this needs to be destroyed."

She started moving toward him, trying to sound soothing, "Bertram, it's too late. Too many know. And it's all part of the past anyway. Give it up. Don't make things worse."

"Stay where you are!" he screamed. She froze, standing in a drift of wood fragments, ripped and crumpled maps, and shattered glass. She wondered if he intended to kill her. Maybe not, since he hadn't yet. She wondered if he might actually get angry enough to throw the axe at her.

Throw.

Her hand crept into her pocket, closed around the glass eyeball.

He picked up the candleholder and, watching her, backed toward the stairs in the wall. "Fire purifies. Fire destroys. I'll burn this house to the ground and all this—and you—with it."

He stood on the threshold leading to the staircase. The Confederate flag over the door dangled down by a single nail, a wick waiting for a flame. He raised the candle.

Inez threw the glass eyeball at him with every ounce of strength she had. It smashed into the doorframe by his head with a crack like a pistol shot, showering his face and eyes with glass splinters. With a cry, he staggered backward toward the stairs.

An unholy scream pierced the air behind Inez, and Inez's heart jumped into her throat. As she turned to see where it came from, a small dense shadow detached itself from the dark by the massive desk. Low to the ground, swift on four legs, tail outstretched, a small dark-furred cat streaked past Inez and careened between Bertram's ankles in a mad-dash bid for the stairs.

Off balance, Bertram staggered back again, trying to hold the candle aloft. Before Inez could yell a warning, the flame wavered, and Bertram, arms windmilling, gave a startled yelp and disappeared. A rolling series of thumps and clatters followed by a final thud told her she was too late. Bertram, balance and footing lost, had fallen down the steep stairs.

She raced, in the near dark, to the door. The candle lamp lay on its side, a few steps down, its flame tentatively lapping a wood riser. She shed her jacket and threw it over the hungry flicker, dousing the fire. That done, Inez rushed back into the room, yanking the offending flag off its nail. "Antonia!" Her voice echoed in the dark space. "Are you here?"

Not even a dozen steps into the room, a solid body careened into her, chest-high. Inez staggered and clutched Antonia's shoulders, fingers tangling in the snarl of hair. "Are you hurt?" Inez explored the girl's head, face, arms, by touch.

A small hand wrapped in a soft fabric patted Inez's face. "I'm okay, Mrs. S." Antonia said. "Well, Eclipse bit me good. That's when I screamed, and she got away. My hand was bleeding, so I wrapped it in my sock so's the blood wouldn't get on my nightdress. And I was hiding under the desk and couldn't see anything, but I heard *everything*. Mrs. S, you saved *everyone* from getting burned to a crisp! And wait'll you see what I found!" She pulled away from Inez and disappeared back into the dark.

Reassured that Antonia was alive and relatively unscathed, Inez finally became aware of a babble of voices echoing up the stairwell. Venturing out to the top of the stairs, she saw the landing below was bathed with reflected light. Inez stepped carefully down to the tiny platform, stopped, and looked down the final flight of stairs. Bright light streamed in from the gap in the pantry, casting Bertram's still, crumpled body into sharp relief at the very bottom of the stairs. The illumination dimmed momentarily as a man climbed through the opening. Someone handed him a lamp, he stepped around the body, headed toward the stairs.

The man lifted his face, and her heart gladdened when she saw it was de Bruijn. A little late. But better late than never. Another figure eased through the gap with a lamp, and Detective Lynch crouched by the body.

De Bruijn reached her. He was hatless and tieless and, for the first time that she could remember, the perennially debonair private detective's collar was not properly attached to his shirt. "Mrs. Stannert," he panted. She wondered if he had run all the way from the Palace Hotel to the boardinghouse, for he seemed uncommonly out of breath. "Are you all right? Are you hurt?" He gripped her shoulder with his free hand, searched her face, her forehead. "You *are* injured! What did he do to you?" His dark eyes filled with deep concern.

For a moment, just a moment, she thought he might pull

her in and kiss her. And for a moment, just a moment, she was very, very tempted to throw her arms around him right then and there on the narrow landing, in front of God and Detective Lynch, and do the same. Except she *was* afraid they might both tumble down the stairs, perhaps breaking their necks in the process, and maybe even succeed where Bertram failed in setting the place afire with a dropped lamp.

Charlotte squealed, her voice carrying from somewhere below, most likely the kitchen. "Eclipse! Kitty kitty! She's back!"

Her happy chatter was drowned out by Antonia's voice above them. "Mrs. S! Mr. de Bruijn! Look what I found!"

They looked up. Antonia stood by the open door wearing her begrimed school coat over her nightdress and holding a bulging bag marked "U.S. MINT CENTS." One of her hands was wrapped in a dirty sock. She beamed, cobwebs caught in her messy curls. "I found the hidden pirate treasure!"

Chapter Forty

"Are you certain you want to do this?" murmured Inez as she threaded her hand through the crook of de Bruijn's arm.

He nodded. "Never more so."

They stood inside the entrance to the Library Room on the second floor of the Mechanics' Institute on Post Street watching Antonia. She wandered along a nearby wall of books as one of the staff trailed after her. From floor to ceiling, full shelves lined the enormous room. "You have so many books." Antonia sounded awed.

The staff member, an earnest young man with an impressive beard, said loud enough for Inez to hear, "That we do, Miss Gizzi. Over thirty-three thousand volumes."

"Right here?" Antonia tipped her head to view the topmost shelves, which could only be reached by a staircase that led to a railed gallery circling the room.

"Yes, miss. You can help yourself to any book you see and read it here." He gestured to the long wooden tables with their accompanying chairs and the upholstered settees stationed back-to-back throughout the open space. "If you are looking for a specific book or author, you can ask for help from one of the staff. Since Mr. de Bruijn has paid the initiation fees and annual memberships for you and your aunt, why, you can both come and go as you please, between the hours of nine in the morning and ten at night."

"Can I visit by myself? After school?" Antonia asked.

"If your aunt and Mr. de Bruijn will vouch for your behavior, it could probably be arranged." The bearded fellow threw an anxious look at the two of them. De Bruijn looked at Inez, awaiting her response. Inez hesitated, then nodded. De Bruijn glanced at the staff member, who, reassured, continued, "We have a Ladies Parlor as well."

"I hope we do not have occasion to regret this," murmured Inez.

"I imagine all will be well," said de Bruijn. "Antonia appears to respect books and the written word."

The bearded staffer added, "Anyone can be a member. Gentlemen, ladies, children, regardless of creed or color. Most of our members, but not all, are 'mechanics,' that is, they are engaged in trades or activities wherein they work with their hands, such as artists, scientists, writers, and architects. For instance, we have several ladies from the Women's Co-operative Printing Union who are members."

Antonia glanced at Inez, then asked him, "D'you have musicians?"

"Indeed we do."

"And private investigators?"

The fellow didn't even blink. "No doubt a few. As well as business owners, government employees, and even lawyers. We also have tables where members can play chess and checkers. Boards provided, of course."

Antonia turned to Inez. "Mrs. S, do you play chess?"

"Poorly," said Inez.

The girl looked at de Bruijn.

De Bruijn said, "If you wish to learn, I'd be honored to teach you, if time and Mrs. Stannert allow."

Inez, marking the anticipation in Antonia's answering grin, said to de Bruijn, "How kind of you to offer." Tipping her head toward him, she murmured, "I advise you to brush up on your games and gambits. Once she has the basic moves, you will be facing a determined adversary."

Antonia had wandered over to the periodical display shelves in the center of the room. "D'you have *Young Folks* here?"

"Indeed we do."

"D'you have the January seventh issue?"

The institute employee joined her at the display. They walked around to the far side of the shelves, conferring. He finally pulled out a slim periodical and handed it to Antonia.

Antonia returned to Inez, eyes shining behind her tinted spectacles. "Mrs. S, he said I could read this right now. Can I stay a while?"

"As long as you mind the rules," said Inez. "And you must be back at the store by four thirty so we have time to walk to Mrs. Nolan's for dinner. No later."

She nodded vigorously. "Yes, ma'am. Thank you, ma'am." Inez held her breath, waiting. Without prompting, Antonia turned to de Bruijn. "And thank you, Mr. de Bruijn, for the membership." Inez exhaled, satisfied. Perfect. What's more, Antonia had pronounced his name correctly and had not inadvertently thrown in *Worthless Rotten* out of habit.

But then Antonia demanded, "Why'd you do it?"

Inez winced. Almost perfect.

De Bruijn didn't seem to mind the blunt interrogation. He

said, "I wanted to thank you and Mrs. Stannert for helping me solve what turned out to be a very complicated case. And as you are a resourceful, intelligent young woman, it seemed to me that the gift of knowledge would be more to your taste than, say, ribbons and bows."

Antonia wrinkled her nose. "Oh, this is *much* better." She gave the private detective and Inez the once-over, lingering on their arm-in-arm stance. "You can go now. I'm fine."

"I will keep an eye on her," the institute employee assured them.

Inez stepped forward and straightened Antonia's coat collar. She bent down and whispered in her ear, "Best behavior. No sliding down the bannisters."

"Don't worry. I'll be busy with this." She flapped the penny weekly at Inez.

As they left the building, de Bruijn asked, "Shall I walk you back to the music store?"

Since she had captured his arm again, it was a reasonable query. Inez said, "That would be lovely. It would give us a chance to talk."

"Very well. I am at your service, then." A spring-like gust nudged them toward Kearney. They set off in that direction, taking their time.

Inez began, "First, I must say, Mr. de Bruijn, that was truly most kind and generous of you to purchase memberships for Antonia and me to the Institute. Thank you. At this point, having Antonia fall into *Young Folks* and *Treasure Island* or chess would be a blessing." Inez glanced at him. "She didn't want to give up those photos. The ones that she found in that room. She was quite convinced they had something to do with pirates."

"You identified the location?"

"I recognized some of the buildings from my jaunt to

Alcatraz. I showed them to Paulie, who concurred and advised us to take them to the office of the Army Corps of Engineers, which happens to be a scant two blocks away from the music store. Paulie said to ask for Lieutenant-Colonel Mendell, who oversees engineering activities on Alcatraz Island. So I marched Antonia there with her box of treasures. She was most unhappy, claiming 'finders keepers.'"

"I can see her point," said de Bruijn.

She waggled a finger at him. "Now, now, Sir Finder-of-the-Lost, do not take her side against me, please. Anyhow, they turned out to be part of a set created during the war at the behest of the post commander. The commander apparently intended them to be documentation of the ongoing work to fortify the island. However, when he presented them to the War Department, there was quite a to-do. The department feared that if the images fell into the wrong hands, they would be invaluable to the enemy. The photographers were accused of being spies against the Union, the negatives seized, and the pictures destroyed. However, the photographers had made copies, resulting in a scramble to retrieve them all. Clearly, one set made its way to John Morton Taylor but went no further than the hidden room where Antonia discovered it. The lieutenant-colonel was so pleased at Antonia's 'honesty' in returning them that he offered to arrange for a tour of the island this summer. Antonia asked if she could bring a friend. You can probably guess who."

"Charlotte."

"*Exactement.* This was before, well, before we learned of Moira's decree."

"What decree? Clearly a lot has happened in the week I was gone."

They had only two blocks to go, so Inez slowed her pace and speeded her narrative. "Yes, I have no doubt that your disappearance was due to some case or other. I took no offense, of course, but as you say, a lot has happened. Once Moira learned the full extent of the two girls' escapades, she forbade Charlotte to see Antonia again. To be honest, on hearing what transpired behind my back, I was tempted to mete out punishment as well. But I could not. Antonia being denied Charlotte's company was punishment enough." Inez shook her head. "Poor girl. I thought her heart would break. She actually *wept*, claiming over and over that she now had no friends at all. 'A friendless orphan' was how she described herself."

"No friends? What about Detective Lynch's boy?"

"Ah, Michael. They were at outs for a while. I think she felt betrayed when he told his father about that cipher disk. They have reconciled and are busy trying to decipher a coded letter Antonia found in that room." Inez tightened her mouth. "I cannot believe Antonia and Charlotte were creeping around that cursed place those nights they were together. I was entirely too trusting."

"She *is* very clever," said de Bruijn. Inez narrowed her eyes at him. "I am simply agreeing with what you have said in the past," he pointed out. "What does all this mean for you and Mrs. Krause?"

"It is now strictly business by the book between us. No friendly tête-à-têtes or dinners at the boardinghouse. Moira will repay me over time, per our contract. That is all fine by me. Not every business associate becomes a friend." She gave his arm a squeeze.

"And the Taylors? Their final disposition?"

She looked away, not wanting to meet his gaze. "You know as I do that Bertram broke his neck in the fall down those stairs. I feel partly responsible for his death. But I had to stop him from setting fire to the place, and I had limited options. I had no weapon to subdue him, and he wouldn't listen to me. In his pain and distress, he was past listening. I don't believe Bertram was evil. I have known evil in my life, and Bertram was not that."

"Perhaps not, but he was a murderer. He did kill Harris."

Inez sighed. "No denying that. One can do evil and yet not *be* evil."

"With Bertram Taylor gone, we'll never know the story in its entirety," said de Bruijn. "But you were correct about the cases intersecting—the corpse and gold in the wall and Harris's death behind the house."

"Well, they had to. The house was the key, so to speak. The nexus for murder and lies. After seeing what the girls found, and talking to Paulie, and thinking about it all—truly, I've thought of little else this past week—I believe I have the general shape of things." She slowed her pace again. He obliged. They now strolled at a speed usually employed by lovers who, although they must part, hope that by lingering they might stop time itself.

"And that shape would be?"

Inez took a breath. "We know Captain Taylor killed his brother, John Morton Taylor, for his treasonous and criminal acts, for almost destroying the family's good name. To hide his murderous deed and his brother's sins, the captain buried the body and the money in the wall. The captain moved his family to Monterey until war's end. They then settled in China, where Bertram picked up his facility with the language. By Bertram's own words and others' accounts, Captain Taylor treated Bertram harshly, even cruelly. Master Edward's remarks back that up. He sailed with the captain as his master-at-arms. Edward enforced the law onboard and punished wrongdoers, a job at which he excelled. To remember and remark on Captain Taylor's treatment of the son means it must have been brutal indeed."

"Yet, Bertram stayed with his father to the end it seems," said de Bruijn.

She sighed. "I have seen such situations before, as have you. We wonder why the victim does not flee or rise up against the one who delivers the pain. I think it is complicated and not for us to condemn those who suffer for not doing *something*. It appears that the captain and Bertram returned to the States shortly before the captain passed. Once he was dead and buried, Bertram had the chance to seize life at last and forge a future of his own making, one that would atone for the severe nature of his early years. It's not surprising he would yearn to follow in his uncle's footsteps, a man he admired and loved. So, Bertram got a job at the mint, where his uncle had worked decades before, and set to burnishing the Taylor name in his own fashion."

"And he decided to sell his uncle's house to Mrs. Krause, who was eager to buy."

Inez nodded. "I can understand why. His father had decreed the house never be sold. But once the captain was gone, why not? Bertram liked living in Oakland on the edge of a vibrant Chinatown. He had employment that engaged him. He did not, apparently, want to *live* in the house. So why not sell it, take the money, and be done with the past? And so it went. He was clearly as surprised upon hearing what fell out of the wall as we were upon seeing it."

"So he did not suspect the corpse was his uncle?"

"I think not. At least, at first. He'd been told all his life that his beloved Uncle Jack died a hero, far from home, fighting for the Union. So, it was not until Bertram talked to the elder Harris that he received a double shock: Not only had his father lied to him but Uncle Jack, his idol, had feet of clay. Uncle Jack, that is, John Morton Taylor, was not a war hero but a traitor and an embezzler to boot. I think Bertram killed Harris on impulse, with no forethought. Moira's axe was at hand, and I imagine Harris didn't expect any violence from Captain Taylor's son."

"So the murder was a matter of killing the messenger?"

"Possibly, but I also think Bertram sought to kill the truth and bury it, just as his uncle had been buried in the wall. But this truth wouldn't be sealed away. After Harris told him about his uncle's part in the *Chapman* incident, Bertram had to talk to the Alcatraz prisoner himself. Once the whole awful truth was laid out before him... Well, I can understand his desire to set that house afire and burn it to the ground. I am just saddened two additional lives fell in this tale—old Harris and young Taylor. There was no reason for it."

"You expected a reason?"

"I had thought it would be one of the usual deadly sins. Avarice, for the gold, seemed most likely. It turns out the gold had nothing to do with it. I suspect that, in many ways, Bertram was a good man. He just never had a chance to become what he could have been. He was like a plant that never received proper care and so pined away unable to find the sun and flourish."

They had reached the music store. De Bruijn said, "I hope you do not feel guilty for how this all turned out. The wheels had been set in motion long ago from what you say. And you did succeed in what you set out to do. You recovered the name and identity of the long-dead John Morton Taylor."

"Ah, yes, another aspect of this case that gave Moira pause." Inez released de Bruijn at last and wrapped her arms around herself against the chill. The wind had picked up, tugging at the hems of her long skirts and coat. "She wanted to give the fellow a name and a proper burial. But then it turned out he was a traitor and a criminal and, what's more, we had a second soul with no family who needed a final resting place." Inez gave a little half smile and shrug. "A simple burial, a simple headstone for both uncle and nephew. They now lie together." She gave herself a little shake. "That is the end of my tale."

"Not quite." He leaned one shoulder against the building, facing her. "What about the gold? Have you decided what to do with it?"

She sighed. "It's a conundrum. Moira wants none of it. Tainted, she says. She insisted Charlotte return a double eagle the girls found lying on the stairs. And now, Antonia having found the rest of the missing money…"

"Would you return it to the mint, then?"

"I have considered doing so. It is all there, minus eighty dollars. I originally took one hundred dollars to make a business loan, which I quickly replaced. So, forty dollars for the Taylors' burials and headstones. Forty for," she cleared her throat, "certain 'unavoidable expenses' incurred at Alcatraz. But on the other hand, possession is nine-tenths of the law."

"There is that final tenth."

"The final tenth, yes." She took a station by the wall, next to him, eyes trained on the buildings across the street. "Honestly, I would give it all up in a heartbeat if it meant the girls could be together again. But given how Moira is, well, perhaps it's for the best. The girls will find their own way back together if they are determined enough. Their schools are not far apart, and Moira can't watch Charlotte every minute."

He raised his eyebrows. "Mrs. Stannert, are you advocating active disobedience?"

"A little rebellion is good for the spirit."

"I see. Rebellion is allowed as long as you approve of it."

She flipped her hand, which then found its way to carelessly rest against his sleeve. "That goes without saying."

"But is it truly rebellion then?"

"Oh, don't try to argue with me out here. This is a

philosophical debate that requires comfortable chairs, a nice fire in the fireplace, and glasses of cognac. Not here, where the wind is blowing straight from the Golden Gate, and we could be arrested for loitering."

Her grip tightened on his folded arms. "Do you know what Moira said to me about Antonia after she finally obtained the house keys, all the burial arrangements were finalized, and she announced Charlotte, would not be allowed to see Antonia again?" Darkness edged her voice. "She said she feared Antonia encouraged Charlotte's sinful side. As if the girls didn't encourage each other! If I had not been so agreeable and just forced a door or window of that accursed house, a lot of this wouldn't have happened."

"You cannot take all of this on yourself," de Bruijn said again.

"And you never do? When cases go awry?"

"My cases never go awry."

She rolled her eyes and faced him. "Well, before I change my mind, I would like to ask you if you might dine with Antonia and me at Mrs. Nolan's tonight. Mrs. Nolan has made it clear, more than once, that her door is always open and a chair available should you wish to sit at her supper table. If you say yes, the boarders will be pleased, as will Mrs. Nolan."

"And you? If I say yes, will you be pleased as well? Or is this invitation a way of thanking me for arriving too late to save the day at the Taylor house but in time to help sweep up the damage and deal with Detective Lynch?" He was smiling at her. The warmth in his voice and his deep brown eyes sent an answering heat spiraling through her.

She returned his smile. "I'm inviting you and hoping you will say yes. That should be answer enough."

"Very well, I accept. And now, I have an invitation for you." He paused. A man who was never at a loss for the right word, he now seemed to be searching for one. "Dinner. Just the two of us. Perhaps afterward we could continue our philosophical discussion or enjoy that game of chess and the fireside cognac you mentioned."

Inez hesitated. So far, their interactions had been mostly collegial investigations, interspersed with verbal sparring and, at least on her part, the occasional come-hither aside and libidinous urge. Was this an offer best accepted or gracefully declined? He left the door open for her to do either without causing harm to their current businesslike arrangement.

She thought of her latest letter to Reverend Sands, the man she most regarded as a kindred spirit. That letter had returned the past week, unopened, marked "no longer at this address." She knew what that most likely meant. He had moved on to a new ministry. If things proceeded as they had over the time they had been apart, she would eventually get a letter from him letting her know where he was, where she could write to him.

But...

What if this time he didn't write?

What if she waited and waited and a letter never came?

"Mrs. Stannert?" De Bruijn's voice, warm, gentle, broke her reverie, and her indecision dissolved.

She looked at him. "I would very much enjoy a leisurely dinner with you, Mr. de Bruijn. Let us pick an evening, and I shall be sure Antonia is safely ensconced at Mrs. Nolan's. That way we shall have fewer...distractions. As for that game of chess," she tipped her head, "have you a chessboard at the Palace Hotel?"

He covered her gloved hand with his own. "I promise to have one waiting for us." The tone behind the words promised more than that.

They parted. Inez watched him walk away, down Kearny. He easily blended into the late afternoon crowd of businessmen heading hither and thither, dressed in the no-nonsense all-black of those who ran the city's powerhouse of enterprise and investment. Yet she picked him out from the others without difficulty.

The breeze pushed insistently at her back. She turned to face it, lifting her head to feel it breathe on her throat, a cool pulsating whisper. She stood miles from the ocean, yet scented the sea. Longing, buried deep inside her, rose and opened. The visit to the Institute, the walk with de Bruijn, their conversation, his invitation, all left her with a feeling she had not experienced in a long while.

Hope.

The widening of horizons.

The casting off of anchors and setting sail into freedom, into the unknown, searching out new worlds. Who could say where the wind would take her, whether she would pause and linger along the way, reverse course and return home, or simply keep moving forward? Would the journey be short or long? It didn't matter. She was ready and ached to begin.

Inez gave herself a shake, turned, and entered her music shop. The sullen bell clunked above the door, as it always did, a temperamental little annoyance, which now didn't annoy her at all. The store's manager, Thomas Welles, met her with his perpetual frown, which really didn't mean anything other than he was preoccupied.

Without preamble, he said, "Good! You're back. Two men stopped by to talk to you. Didn't leave a message but said they'd return. Didn't seem the type to be in the market for anything music related. Maybe some of the Oriental artwork."

"And they wanted to talk to me? Well, I'll probably just send them to Mr. Hee, who is, after all, the expert. I'll be in the office." She sailed into the back room and, with a happy sigh, sat at the round mahogany table with the latest stack of invoices.

She had barely opened the accounts ledger when there was a knock at the partially open door. She lifted her head, startled. Two gentlemen stood on the threshold. Very serious sorts of gentlemen. Not the kind who were looking to buy a piano or to engage a music teacher for their daughters. Inez studied them, trying to divine their intent. "May I help you?"

"Mrs. Stannert?" said the slightly taller one.

"Yes?"

He and his companion reached into their waistcoat pockets. Inez tensed. They pulled out badges, and the taller one said, "Treasury agents. We understand you have something of ours."

Inez stared at them in disbelief, then threw back her head and laughed. She finally said, "And here we have it. The final tenth."

The two agents looked a trifle bewildered. The taller one said, "We can offer a reward. 'We' being the United States Department of Treasury."

"Please, come in." Inez rose from the table. "How much of a reward, if I may ask?"

"We are authorized to offer up to two percent of the total. So for two hundred double eagles or four thousand dollars, that would be—"

"Eighty dollars." Inez was tempted to laugh again but composed herself and moved toward the safe, saying, " Yes, gentlemen, I do indeed have what you are looking for. And you and the United States Treasury are welcome to it, with my blessing."

AUTHOR'S NOTE

Warning: This note contains spoilers. If that's a concern for you, you may want to stop reading and return later.

The initial spark for this story came in 2016, the result of a *San Francisco Chronicle* article, "Little Girl, Rose Still in Hand, Found in Coffin Beneath SF Home." The article reported on the discovery of the 145-year-old glass-and-bronze casket in an area that was the city's Odd Fellows Cemetery from 1860 to 1890. The house's owner was told by the medical examiner's office that since the body was found on private property now belonging to her, she had to deal with the coffin and the remains. At the time, the identity of the perfectly preserved little girl who died a century-and-a-half ago was unknown.

This strange event and the mystery at its core rattled around in the back of my mind until late 2019, when it morphed into the opening scene, in which Inez finds a body not in the floor of a house but in a wall. From there, a whole host of questions arose. Who was the deceased? When did he die? Why? And why the heck is he in the wall to begin with? On a whim (and because my character Antonia Gizzi had developed a fixation on *Treasure Island* way back in the first book of the San Francisco

cycle of my Silver Rush series, *A Dying Note*) I gave my skele-
tonized Civil War–era corpse a glass eye and a bag of gold. Little
did I know where all that would lead me!

Researching San Francisco's Civil War history and its naval
endeavors introduced me to the *J. M. Chapman* incident and
Alcatraz Island's role in imprisoning civilian secessionists and
those suspected of siding with the South. I had already posited
and deployed a "what if" scenario in which a fortune in twenty-
dollar gold coins was stolen from the San Francisco Mint during
the war, when I happened to stumble across a series of *San
Francisco Call* articles regarding the disappearance of thirty thousand dollars in double eagles from the mint in summer 1901. By
fall 1901, the chief clerk was in very hot water and on trial for
theft. I gleefully borrowed some of the details from the trial of
real-life San Francisco chief clerk Walter Dimmick and trans-
posed them onto fictional chief clerk John (aka Jack) Morton
Taylor. If you'd like to read more about the real-life events, go
to https://cdnc.ucr.edu/, pull up the *San Francisco Call* for the
year 1901, and search "Dimmick" for articles beginning July 4.
It's quite a saga.

Other San Francisco facts I wove into fiction include dancing-
master John Frazer's insolvency petition (notice appears in March
10, 1882, *Daily Alta California*), the 1882 product placement of
Hills Bros. Coffee and Naglee Brandy, the cohabitation of the
city coroner's office with a prominent undertaking firm, the sailing schedule of the steamer *General McPherson*, and the location
of the buildings on Alcatraz Island. I did bend fact here and there.
For instance, the photos taken of Alcatraz Island during the Civil
War that Antonia discovers in the little box are real, as is their
general story. However, they were actually taken in early 1864, so
I did fudge the time frame. And the cell doors for Alcatraz Island's
Lower Prison were solid wood until the 1890s, so I decided that

the fictional Spider with his fictional special privileges would have bars on his door. (Note: Alcatraz was an entirely military prison at this point as well.) I also found nifty bits online such as images and descriptions of a "Jefferson Davis Signed Naval Commission" and a "Confederate Cipher Disk." These and more I pinned onto my Pinterest boards for this book. If you are interested, go have a look at pinterest.com/annparkerauthor.

As for the people in these pages, most are fictional. No famous faces, no glimpses of the nineteenth-century glitterati. Instead, we have boardinghouse keepers, locksmiths, office clerks, and retired seafarers. Moira Krause and Mrs. Nolan are typical businesswomen for their time, according to Mary Lou Locke's thesis on urban working women in the Far West of the late nineteenth century. Locke notes, "Well over a third of all the working women in San Francisco, Portland, and Los Angeles in 1880 either ran a small business like a boardinghouse or worked in the needle trades." Locksmith Paulie Harris is pure fiction, but you don't need to look far in history to find counterparts, such as California's "Stagecoach Charley" (aka Charley Parkhurst aka Charlotte Parkhurst aka One Eyed Charley), a renowned stagecoach driver.

Some of my references, both online and paper, you might enjoy perusing include:

CALIFORNIA, SAN FRANCISCO, AND THE CIVIL WAR:

California and the Civil War, by Richard Hurley (2017)
"The Attitude of California to the Civil War," by Imogene
    Spaulding, in *Annual Publication of the Historical Society of
    Southern California, 1912–1913*, http://www.jstor.com
    /stable/41168901

"The Confederate Minority in California," by Benjamin
   Franklin Gilbert, in *California Historical Society Quarterly*,
   June 1941, http://www.jstor.com/stable/25160938
California's Role in the Civil War, National Park Service website,
   https://www.nps.gov/goga/learn/historyculture/california
   -in-civil-war.htm (A good jumping off point with links to
   pages about Civil War history at Alcatraz, Fort Mason, etc.)
"Search and Destroy," by John A. Martini, in *American Heritage*,
   November 1992. (About "those photos" taken of Alcatraz
   fortifications during the Civil War.) https://www
   .americanheritage.com/search-and-destroy
The following link will take you to the case of *United States
   v. Ridgeley Greathouse*, et al., (1863), 26 F. Cas. 18, which
   is prefaced by a variety of notations and followed by the
   actual opinion in this matter by the Federal Circuit Court
   Judges of the 9th District, located in the Northern District
   of California. (aka the *J. M. Chapman* incident) https://
   law.resource.org/pub/us/case/reporter/F
   .Cas/0026.f.cas/0026.f.cas.0018.2.pdf

ALCATRAZ ISLAND:

Alcatraz at War, by John A. Martini (2002)
A History of Alcatraz Island, 1853–2008, by Gregory L.
   Wellman (2008)
Alcatraz History—https://www.alcatrazhistory.com/rock
   /rock.htm
The Post on Alcatraces—https://www.nps.gov/alca/learn
   /historyculture/the-post-on-alcatraces.htm
*The Rock: A History of Alcatraz Island, 1847–1972: Historic
   Resource Study, Golden Gate National Recreation Area,
   California,* by Erwin N. Thompson

Cultural Landscapes Inventory, Alcatraz Island—http://
npshistory.com/publications/alca/cli.pdf

SAN FRANCISCO MINT:

The Old U.S. Mint at 5th and Mission—https://www.foundsf
.org/index.php?title=The_Old_U.S._Mint_at_5th_and
_Mission
San Francisco U.S. Coin Mint—https://www.usacoinbook
.com/encyclopedia/coin-mints/san-francisco/
*A Mighty Fortress: The Stories Behind the 2nd San Francisco
Mint,* by Rich Kelly and Nancy Oliver (2004)

SAN FRANCISCO—PEOPLE, PLACES:

*Capital Intentions: Female Proprietors in San Francisco, 1850–
1920,* by Edith Sparks (2006)
*'Like a Machine or an Animal': Working Women of the Late
Nineteenth-Century Urban Far West, in San Francisco,
Portland, and Los Angeles,* by Mary Lou Locke (1982)
The Tenderloin District of San Francisco Through Time, by Peter
M. Field (2018)
*Strangers' Guide to San Francisco and Vicinity: A complete and
Reliable Book of Reference for Tourists and Other Strangers
Visiting the Metropolis of the Pacific, with a Map Showing
the Distances to Different Points,* by William C. Disturnell
(1883)

IMAGES AND MAPS:

OpenSFHistory—https://opensfhistory.org/index.php

David Rumsey Map Collection—https://davidrumsey
    .reprintmint.com/
OldSF.org—http://www.oldsf.org/#

A final personal note in a minor key: this book is my "pandemic year novel." Unable to conduct my usual boots-on-the-ground research, I relied on information gleaned from previous endeavors, the internet, and books, while sheltering in place. It was quite the mental trick to create and hang on to my fictional universe while the world swirled in chaos outside my little "bubble." If certain scenes (in the icebox and the walls) seem a bit claustrophobic, chalk it up to me channeling my panic and my general feeling of being boxed in by four walls. My fervent wish is that by the time you are reading this, we are all—like Inez in the final chapter—able to take a deep breath and look forward, with hope.

ACKNOWLEDGMENTS

Thanks to all who lent a hand in bringing this book out into the light: critique partners and beta readers Camille Minichino, Carole Price, Janet Finsilver, Mary-Lynne Pierce Bernald, Nannette Rundle Carroll, Penny Warner, Staci McLaughlin, Sue Stephenson, Susan Miller Silva, Colleen Casey (who also helped keep my lawyers "lawyerly" and shared my boundless enthusiasm for San Francisco historical minutiae), Joel Parker (who helped with maps), and Devyn McConachie (who came to the rescue at the eleventh hour to catch discrepancies and offer insightful suggestions on my draft). Laurie Pinnell for "fictional use" of her two lovely cats, Eclipse and Lucky. National Park Service rangers and researchers at Alcatraz Island and the San Francisco Maritime National Historical Park, and San Francisco Mechanics Institute's Taryn Edwards, for their expertise and help.

I'm very grateful for the guidance and encouragement of my agent, Anne Hawkins of John Hawkins and Associates, and for the support and assistance of Poisoned Pen Press and the Sourcebooks staff. Last, but never least, to my family—Bill, Ian, Devyn, and the wider McConachie and Parker clans—my love and appreciation, always.

ABOUT THE AUTHOR

Ann Parker is a science writer by day and fiction writer by night. Her award-winning Silver Rush Mysteries series, published by Poisoned Pen Press, a Sourcebooks imprint, is set primarily in 1880s Leadville, Colorado, and more recently in San Francisco, California, the "Paris of the West." The series was named a Booksellers Favorite by the Mountains and Plains Independent Booksellers Association. *The Secret in the Wall* is the eighth and newest entry in the series.